THE
EVERLASTING
EARTH

The Everlasting Earth.
Copyright © 2022 by L. A. Cummings.
All rights reserved.

This is a work of fiction. All names, characters, places, objects and events are either products of the author's imagination, or are used fictitiously. Any resemblance to actual persons, living or dead, places, objects or events is entirely coincidental.

Book cover design by ebooklaunch.com.

Print ISBN: 979-8-9856153-3-3
ebook ISBN: 979-8-9856153-0-2

THE EVERLASTING EARTH

a novel

L. A. CUMMINGS

CHAPTER 1
THE OCEAN

The storm that surrounded Lwo was constant, as it had been when the land was first named. Some three hundred years prior, after uncontrolled water and fire and shaking had all but eradicated the old civilizations, the Lords, pulling from the remnants of destruction, had managed to gather thousands together. Those that had migrated to the northern tundra–where valleys, and mounts, and glaciers, and great rocks had somehow shifted to form the beginnings of a new landscape–found hope, but little else. The first Lwoans had spent a century building and cultivating, gathering all of the resources they could find from an ocean overrun with discard to acclimate to the new environment, to its creatures, its plantlife, and its crisp, wild air. And for another hundred years Lwoans progressed, and grew, albeit modestly, in number. But the force of the storm also grew.

For over a generation the erratic, encircling winds, which flew over the ocean, and rolled over the mountains, pushing to the land's farthest points, had increased so much in speed that all but a few civilians had been forced into Lwo's growing city. There, shielded by the towering buildings that had been erected around the city's perimeter, and by the failsafe of electromagnetic energy, they could be safe and secure. They would not have to wear helmets or dense bodysuits or armor, or tread earth in heavy boots to keep from being sucked into the sky, where so many leaves and grass and dry debris violently littered the intermittent view to the sun. No. These outfittings were the trappings of the watchers, those who from the land's very founding had been tasked with keeping safe the sky, and the ground, and the mountains, and eventually the city.

Watchers were accustomed to their burdens, and often, when not dreading an increased threat from the storm, were proud to bear them. From the beginning, in each generation, scores of men and women had trained, from their earliest days of adulthood, to navigate the wildness of nature. In Lwo's early years, when the first watchers had trekked to uncharted places and first learned to navigate the unforgiving, unpredictable winds, many had died. But many had also lived. And so many more civilians had lived that watching came to be seen as the greatest calling, as military service had been in the old nations. And Fits, now more than ten years in as the commander of the Watchers of the Mountains, felt the weight of this calling, especially on days such as this.

The ocean seemed especially wild. Its waves were cresting higher, and beating upon the shore much more than they had on his last salvage survey the week before. He continued to scan through the windshield of his hovering gull, looking for a sign of the Southern Hammer out in the distance, but still seeing nothing. It was not behind schedule, but he felt a strong desire for the ship to dock early. The station at the Southern Range was a mile behind him, too far to just run if the gull were somehow knocked out of its relatively stable position and he had to jump out. As he glanced down through the clear floor panels beneath his seat, he saw the fin on the underbody, unmoved as periodic blasts of water and rock fanned around it.

He leaned his head back, and tilted his helmet upward off of his shoulders, feeling its weight as it settled in the rounded groove of the headrest. He took a deep breath of the cabin's air, and with his eyes unaided by the helmet's front panel, got another look at the ocean. Still nothing. Still no sign of the great, black ship. He shook his head, and looked down, past the control handle, to the center control panel. There was a readout of the gull's near-zero acceleration, and its minimal elevation, and its relative position to the coast and the mountains behind it. In the top of the display, in a short line, the readout of wind speed–steady near one hundred twenty-five miles per hour–blinked in red text. A rock suddenly bounced off the windshield, ringing Fits's ears. He reached back, pulled his helmet up and back down, secured it into the rounded cradle surrounding his neck, and gripped the handle. A moment later, the helmet's display of yellow text indicated his status inside the cabin, idle and unexposed to any winds.

The ocean's infinite, foamy crests continued to jump along in their unstable, familiar way, and in barrages, continued to rush in and hit the beach with forces that cast hard sand and tiny stones thirty yards back to where the gull sat idling over the ground. Finally, looking far out, and after whispering a command to magnify the view through the windshield, Fits saw the Southern Hammer, a dark, floating machine two miles off the coast, swaying in wild waves that rose up almost high enough to obscure it. It was a massive body of metal, formed by two buoys and a connecting deck. It was a wonder the salvage ships could navigate the ocean as they did, even with their heavy, plunging underfins.

Fits tapped a button on the control panel to his right, and a set of free-roaming, encircled crosshairs blinked into the windshield. They followed his eyes, and focused on the ship. Its size, distance and speed popped into view below the crosshairs, followed by the more important measures of gravity and wind speed.

"Contact," Fits spoke softly. He heard his voice project out from his helmet, and then heard the gull's system chirp in acknowledgement. "Salvage ship Southern Hammer." Another chirp and a short beep followed. A click indicated the open line.

"Commander Fits," a loud, grizzly voice answered. "This is the Captain. How can I help you, Sir?"

Fits could hear the commotion of loud voices and sea noise in the background. "It's been two hours, Captain," he answered. "My craft's engines are getting tired, along with me. How close are you to getting that haul you were tracking?"

"Well, it's perfect timing, Sir. We're closing the nets for the last time now. Should be to shore shortly."

"I'll be waiting at your anchor spot. Fits out."

Fits felt his breath slowing, and in the bottom of his helmet's display, saw his heart rate decrease two beats. His nose turned up at the unnecessary, automated readout, as he took hold of the control handle with both hands, moved his right foot to the wide pedal below it, and gently pressed down.

The gull bounced up ten feet, and he guided her out to the tall, heavy boulder at the edge of the shore. He could almost feel the winds as they whipped around the craft's body, and rumbled through the wind engines beneath the floorboard. Normally the carved stone vanes in the engines made little noise, even outside the mountains where the winds were their harshest. But today the storm required them to work much harder. It reminded Fits to check the status of his own wind-tech. With a quiet command, his helmet brought up a basic outline of the human form, and marked each piece of his tech–one at his back, one at the side of each shin, one on each side of his waist, one at each of his shoulders, and one encircling each of his forearms. Each piece had a green status, and no speed or outside forces. Fits dismissed the information from his view as he reached the anchor point.

He guided the gull's nose slightly past the front of the fifteen-foot boulder, and saw that the metal-rimmed hole inside of it was unobstructed. Looking back through the windshield, he saw that the ship was now less than one hundred yards from the shoreline. It moved in another fifty yards, and stopped. Fits moved the gull slightly to the left, and waited. A moment later, the control panel sounded a low warning tone, and he watched as the ship's cannon flickered, and a shining, metal spear shot out. It flew perfectly through the hole in the boulder, and its phalanges splayed out as it was yanked back against the stone. The sound of the sharp, heavy clank pushed even through the walls of the cabin. The boulder, and the others like it around the mainland's shores, had withstood generations of such use, and somehow had not yet broken. *If only every rock could take so much*, he thought.

The control panel sounded again, as the ship called to Fits. "Captain here, Sir," the man said. "Ready when you are."

"On my way," Fits answered.

He pressed down on the pedal again, and guided the gull up another thirty feet, further from the relative safety of the ground, and flew out over the water. Beneath him, water from the ocean surface splashed against the clear panels below. He checked the steadiness of the fin between them, and then looked out at the edge of the ship's deck. The hollow track for the fin's placement illuminated in the center panel. He held firmly to the handle as he followed the bright line, and gently eased his foot pressure, decreasing power to the engines as the gull descended toward the deck. To his right, the ship's port side buoy reached fifteen feet toward the sky, offering protection to the crew members who were outside its cabin. There were a handful of them, outfitted in bright, yellow suits that fit close to their bodies, and bearing harnesses that linked their metal safety lines to the supporting bars running along the yellow cabin wall. Their faces were obscured by helmets with tinted panels, but a few of them waved at him with gloved hands.

As the gull finally touched the deck, Fits looked down past his heavy boots and saw the dark, ridged surface. Sparkling beads of water flowed in every direction. Outside, a crash of water from above rolled over the gull's roof. He locked access to the craft's controls, stood from the pilot's seat, and walked to the port door. He tapped the small panel on the right, and watched as the cloudy, translucent door slid in, and then toward the gull's aft end. As he stepped forward, he felt the tech around his body activate.

As wind pushed through the engines on his boots and waist and arms and back, his helmet panel displayed the rapid fluctuations of speed, and relative distance to every nearby object. As he leapt out, and down to the deck, he felt his hard boot soles clank and grip, and felt the strongest streams of wind pulled through his back engine.

"Stabilize," he whispered.

His engines hummed as their vanes adjusted, and he crouched for a moment, touching the metal deck through his gloves, feeling the air rush all around him. He could feel the eyes of the crewmen on him. As the air settled at a lower speed through each piece of his tech, he stood, and waved at the few crew members, who were all moving toward the aft end of the ship. Behind the ship's cabin, he could see the outline of the two-yard high railings that surrounded the massive hauling area. Another crash of water passed over the roof of the gull, and hit his back. He stepped toward the closest of the five port doors to the cabin, the door that was also closest to the forward navigation end.

The door swung open before he could knock, and he ducked, and hopped through. His tech quieted, and the readouts in his helmet began to slow, as he stepped out of a square puddle, and up one level, to where the captain stood at the center of the room, waiting and smiling with his helmet in his hand. He was a large man, wide and nearly as tall as Fits was, but with a thicker, graying beard. Fits heard the door close behind him as he approached.

One crewman was sitting in a chair at the front end, his helmet resting on the floor beside him as he looked out through the wide window at the battered shoreline. A projection just before the window, glowing above a control board housing a row of blinking keys and four levers, revealed an electronic map of the coastline, along with a fluctuating readout of their anchor's tension. Fits tilted his helmet up and back, and took a deep breath. He could smell the raw, distinct scent of the ocean, and of exhausted men, but after hours of recycled air, it was somehow refreshing. He removed one glove, and rubbed his short beard on both sides.

"Commander Fits," the captain said with a grin, extending his hand.

Fits walked up to the man. "Captain," he said with a nod.

The man's yellow suit was dingy, and bore water spots all over. His eyes looked tired, but happy. He nodded back, and swung one arm out toward the rear of the cabin, where a station with a view to the aft end sat unattended.

Fits followed his lead, and walked. The rear station held two flat display screens at waist level, each of them angled up slightly toward the aft window. Through the window they could see that the cargo hatch had been fully opened. A container, a twenty foot cube formed by hardened netting in a frame of steel bars, was rising up between the hatch doors. There was a lone crewman stationed at each corner of the squared container, holding on to the surrounding railing, watching as the day's haul was brought up for examination. Their metal safety cables whipped back and forth with each wind gust, but they were steady in boots that looked even heavier than a watcher's.

When the container stopped moving it was only halfway up, but Fits could still see that it was full. There were all types of debris—metal bottles, ambiguous panels, sharp pieces, dull pieces, and even what he recognized as ancient electronics. A watcher's training meant holding on to what you had learned about the old, outside world, and being able to recognize it. Fits had seen more of the old world than any watcher, and more than any watcher would want to see. And each week, each haul seemed bigger than the last.

"Nice one today!" the captain said aloud. "Yes, Sir!" He pointed down to the screen in front of the watcher, and proudly raised a thumb before going to work on the control keys in front of his own.

"I suppose you could say that," Fits replied.

"Boy, it seems like it never stops for us. No, Sir. I doubt the

Roamer and the Maw are having this kind of luck on their ends. Their founders picked the wrong coasts." The captain let out a hefty, but short laugh. "What do you think, Sir?"

Fits sniffled once. "I long for the day when salvage ships are no longer needed."

There was no response, but Fits ignored the man's silence. Instead, he focused on his screen, as bright, green lines ran along a rendered image of the container, showing the shapes of every piece, large and small, that had been hauled in. Near the bottom of the image he saw a blinking, red light, indicating heat, heat that could be biological. Large fish, some dangerous and some dying, were not uncommon in salvage hauls. They often found their way with ocean waste to the doors at the bottom of the containers. Fits would normally have let it go, would have simply let the captain release a small amount of the haul to free the creature, but then there was another red signal.

"I see it, Sir," said the captain, before Fits could call it out. He hit a button beneath his screen, and radioed out to the crewmen on the deck. "Lower that container. We got a couple of fishies in the middle." Two of the crewmen waved back at him.

Fits watched both screens as the container went down, eventually getting its bottom half back into the waters below. It was shallow near the coast, but there was still enough water for the haul to loosen and begin to float. The screens showed the large and small pieces moving about, as the tide pushed through and around the container. But the red lights remained. Fits watched for another two minutes. The crew looked back at the cabin. The lights remained.

"Must wanna be eaten, these two," the captain said, and then let out a full-bellied laugh. Behind him, his helmsman laughed along.

"You know I can't allow you to take them inland," Fits said without looking at him.

"Yes, Sir. Just a joke."

"Right. Raise the container, Captain. All the way."

"All the way!?" the captain yelped. "The sorters aren't even here yet. You go digging before they come and I could lose half of what we pulled."

Fits leaned away from the screens, and turned, and stared into the man's eyes. "I've been doing this much longer than you have been a captain. Two signals in such proximity that will not descend means that two creatures are trapped. We have a balance to maintain with the ocean. Do you want to interfere with that balance?"

The captain lowered his head, and grumbled, and then shook his head. "No, Sir." He turned back to the station, and radioed out to the crew again. "Raise it up to deck level, set the posts, and prepare to open the gate." The crew stared back through the window, all of them hesitant, and confused in their very demeanors. There was a short click at the panel as one of them attempted to respond, but the captain interrupted. "Now, men! Watcher's orders!"

The crew swiftly went to work. Fits watched as the container began to rise again. A few tense minutes later, the sides of the cube were fully exposed. Each of the crewmen retrieved long, metal bars, and in pairs, set each one at an angle, with one end hooked to a corner post of the cube, and the other attached at a hole in the deck. When all four bars were set, they waved back to the cabin. Fits put his gloves back on, and made sure both were secure. He reached back, and pulled his helmet up and back down over his head, and made sure it secured around his neck. Then he turned to the captain, who quickly donned his own helmet and gloves, and then led the way to the nearest port side door.

The water and winds hit them both hard. As the captain secured a metal safety cable from his waist to one of the bars along the cabin wall, Fits felt the winds passing through all of his tech. He walked behind the captain, slowly at first, but then began moving in a steady stride, as each of his engines compensated for the various forces pushing through them.

As they approached the container, Fits could feel the eyes of the crewmen. Their agitation seemed to push even through their bulky headgear. He quickly ordered his system to discard the blinking heat signatures that identified each of them. They were not ordinary Lwoans, after all, who might need saving from the high forces of the winds over the ocean. And they were not a threat, not a handful of sailors against a commanding watcher. The only threat was to the creatures who had somehow become ensnared in the resources necessary for creating comfort on Lwo. The only threat was to the system of life, however chaotic it was, that still lurked beneath the ocean's surface.

Fits held a hand up to his helmet, and moved two fingers forward, toward the bottom of the container. The two life signs popped up into his display as red dots, just as they had on the screen in the cabin. They were directly in front of him and the captain, just at arms length behind the container wall. He set a hand on the captain's shoulder, and yelled through the loudness of the storm. "Open it!"

The captain motioned for two of the crewmen to open the front gate. The haul was so comptacted that as the metal section began to slide up, most of the items stayed in place, but the man almost wept as the gate finally stopped, and an array of plastics, and hard textiles and unknown devices either fell to the deck, or flew out and into the winds, and over the massive, metal buoys on both sides. The man was distraught and distracted. Fits disregarded him, and dove for the open gate. Short, heavy gusts of air flowed from the tech on his arms and legs and back and waist, keeping him steady without a single safety cable.

Fits kept one knee on the deck, and one foot near the gate, as he reached into the heavy rubble of the haul. The dense, smooth fabric of his suit kept what he knew were sharp objects from penetrating, and kept heavy objects from pressing for too long. Looking through his helmet panel at the darkness of the haul, he got a hold of something large. When he saw that it was white, and oblong, he grabbed it by an attached bar, and pulled with as much strength as he could. As it loosened, he stood, and fell back, crashing to the deck, his helmet and

13

tech bouncing hard off of the metal surface. The ambiguous container that he had pulled with him screeched, and slid to a stop near the rear wall of the cabin.

"Close it!" the captain yelled to his crew.

Fits shook his head, and took a deep breath of filtered air, and slowly, got up to his knees. He rubbed the spots that he already knew would be the next day's bruises, wiped dirt from his helmet panel, and looked down at what had been found. His display showed the same two red dots, there, in a long, white object made of two identical, oblong, concave sides. They were made of some kind of metal, attached by bolts, and there was the outline of a doorway on one side. Fits walked up and knelt down to the contraption. With his left hand he reached for a grip in the door. With his other, he readied the gauntlet on his right forearm, pressing two fingers into his palm. He felt the sides of the cannon extend around his forearm, and caught a glimpse of the hazy glow near his wrist. Over his shoulder, he sensed two of the crewmen backing away, and clinging to the railing around the container.

In a single motion the watcher grabbed the door grip, pulled, and leaned back. There was nothing. No movement. No sound. There was a murky, wet darkness inside. At his whispered command the narrow lens on the top of his helmet beamed on, and shone a bright light down through the doorway. There, he saw a human arm. Without another thought he lunged in, and felt the shoulders, and the ribs beneath them, and pulled. Even through his filter, the smell was pungent. He struggled against it, and something else unseen, a hook or a rough surface. A moment later, he yanked the man out onto the deck. He looked at him, and sat in shock. Behind him, the crew was in the same state. But the captain ran up, his boots clanking and shaking the deck, and knelt down next to the man.

"Get a mask!" the man yelled and motioned. "I'm sorry, Sir," he said loudly to Fits.

How? Fits thought to himself. *How did he get past us? How did he make it so far out?*

The man had breath, though it was faint. Fits examined him, gently running his gloved hands along the man's arms, and chest. His clothing was wet, and thin–a long, ripped shirt and pants, shabby looking boots–but he was mostly covered. His skin was a pale brown, the palest Fits had ever seen, as if he had been out to sea, with no sun for years. And the man's closed eyes were sunken, and weary.

A crewman knelt down next to the man, placed a fitting mask with a clear front panel over his face, and secured it behind his head. "We'll take him in," the crewman said loudly, and waved another over to help him.

In Fits's helmet there were still two life signs blinking. As two crewmen got hold of the unconscious man, he moved carefully back to the small, open door, and leaned his helmet over into the strange boat again. He could see now that it was indeed strong enough to have survived the waves and currents that must have taken it under. But its weaknesses–the shabby hinges, the small, cracked windows–had not

15

been shored up properly. The boat had flooded, though the water was still shallow. Fits looked from side to side, letting his helmet's light bounce off every surface. He heard the captain yelling something behind him, but could not make out any words. Then, he felt a tug on his right arm, just above the rear of the cannon. He quickly deactivated the weapon, and pulled the child up by his arms, out onto the deck. Then he lifted the boy up into his arms, and stood.

The boy was awake, but barely. Though the winds blowing about made him impossible to hear, he could see the child weakly mumbling something. His mouth seemed to be saying 'father' over and over, without any thought, as if he were dreaming. He held the child tightly to his chest, and moved with swift steps back toward the cabin, staying close to the wall as he made his way to the nearest door. Behind him, the rest of the crew and the captain followed.

Between the forward and aft stations in the cabin, on the starboard wall, there was a bed laid out, set down on the floor, with the man already lying on it. His mask had been removed, and he was breathing short breaths with two crewmen kneeling down at his sides. They were each about to remove their helmets.

"Put his mask back on!" Fits ordered them.

They looked back at him strangely.

"We don't know what they've been exposed to. Put his mask back on. And get me one for the boy."

Fits moved quickly, and laid the boy down next to the man. The child was barely moving now, and had stopped his utterances. He coughed up a splash of dark colored water, the same as what had been inside their boat. One of the crewmen handed Fits another mask, and he secured it, over the boy's face and behind his head. He looked to the father, to his reattached mask, and saw dark spittle on the inside. Then he stood, and took a step back, surveying the situation. He felt the captain walk up next to him.

"I'm sorry, Sir," the captain said. "I would never have guessed. I've only heard of people wanting to escape. But to make such an effort, and in this weather..." The man removed his helmet, and ran a hand worriedly through the thick hair on his head.

Fits, having run through the possibilities as the captain was speaking, was hesitant to respond. He knew more than the captain could. Every watcher had to know more. He whispered a command, opening a secure line to the station at the Southern Range. The sound of someone answering clicked into his left ear.

"Commander Fits, Sir," a young woman said. "This is Ensign Rial. Go ahead."

"I'll be bringing two people back for medical attention," he answered quietly. "Get our doctor ready in a secured room. Tell no others."

"Yes, Sir. I'll direct you once you're on approach."

"Very well. Fits out."

Fits lifted his helmet and pushed it back, and continued looking down at the unfamiliar father and son. Then he turned and faced the captain. "You and your crew did well today. This was an

17

unfortunate, and unexpected interruption." He extended his right hand.

The captain looked taken aback, and appeared hesitant to reach near the watcher's gauntlet, but he nodded, and did so. He wrapped his hand around Fits's metal-covered forearm, around the cooled surface of the weapon that was now retracted. Fits kept his grip firm as they shook.

"Yes, Sir, uh, Commander," the man answered humbly. "And, uh, what do you think happened? With these two, that is?"

"I don't know. We'll find out. But once I'm gone, you can go about your business. I'm sure the sorters are close by now."

"Yes, Sir." The captain said, and looked back down at the man and the child. "They're dressed oddly."

Fits followed his gaze, and looked at the two again. The whole crew's attention was on them now. The captain was right.

"Looks like they haven't eaten in a while either," said one of the crewmen. He reached for a box nearby, and tilted the lid up, and pulled out a small metal bottle and something wrapped in a waxy paper.

"No!" Fits shouted. He felt all of the eyes in the cabin turn toward him. He had spoken too quickly. He was processing too much information, and too fast, risking revealing what he suspected, what he was almost sure of. "Excuse me, crewmen. We just can't know what they've been exposed to, or for how long. Leave their treatment to us. Now, if one of you would, strap them to that bed, and help me get them into my gull."

18

The crewman who had offered the aid put both items back in the box, and pushed it aside, and stood and stepped away. Another crewman found the straps beneath the bed, and another helped him position the man and the boy on the soft surface, and then secured them in place. The man coughed loudly, spitting more dark water into the front of the mask. His eyes seemed to open, for an instant, before shutting again. Both he and the boy were nearly limp, only shaking slightly as the two crewmen raised the bed up on its mechanized supports. They looked to Fits, and at his direction, carefully turned the bed with its occupants toward him. Once again he lowered his helmet, and turned, and headed for the nearest door to the deck.

CHAPTER 2
THE CITY

There were too many civilian craft now, flying through the city's criss-crossing, concentrated streams of air. There were a dozen more than the same day of the previous year. The change was not discernible in the traffic of the busy first-level stream, nor in the two less-populated streams above, but Nico could see the number in a row of glowing text on the bottom of his helmet's visor. The values were reported daily from the city's headquarters, making any on-duty watcher fully aware, not only of the number of newly-registered craft, but to whom they belonged, and of what materials they were composed, and of the amount of tech outfitting their frames. The numbers had been steady for months, until that morning.

More craft in the city meant more work for its watchers. Most citizens were careful pilots, following the flows of air in their chosen lanes, not moving between the three levels at high speed, adhering to the signals at the quartets of air movers that designated each intersection. But with the growing population, with people moving into the city for shelter from the storm's ever-increasing winds, there were inevitable disruptions in traffic flow. One week prior, Nico and a patrolman had rushed to the scene of a collision. A craft had descended from level three to level two at such speed that a much larger craft had spun out of its trajectory. Each craft's tech had compensated. Each craft had suffered little damage. The pilot at fault, however, had not been pleased with Nico's decision to revoke his license for five days, and seize his brand-new craft for the same. But as far as Nico was concerned, any citizen's frustration toward a watcher meant the city was safer.

It was past midday. The sun had not been seen for what seemed like months, but Nico could still tell that it was there. Enough of its light still managed to push down through the dense, pillowy clouds above, reflecting off the metal and glass panels of the tallest buildings, which cast shadows into the multi-level pathways between them.

Nico was idling in the first stream, fifteen yards up, at the northeast corner of a residential building. Most of the city's buildings were designed only for living. This one was made of smooth, red and brown stone, and stood ten stories. To his left, behind the north-facing wall, was one of the building's walkways, covered in a typical clear, pliant barrier made up of dense panels of re-formed plastics from the ocean. On the other side of the windows he could see a few familiar people walking. One of them also recognized him, and waved, assuring him that he spent his time in the sector at this particular point much too often. Over his shoulder, in the same wall, there was a pair of secured access gates for craft to enter and exit.

He sat upright. The air from the stream ran steadily beneath his seat, passing through the two wind-tech engines upholding his jumper. He kept his boots steady on either side of the seat, along the running boards, and could almost feel the cold air beneath their heavy soles. He gently pressed his knees into the panels on either side of the seat, keeping hold of the steadying controls behind them. He kept his left hand on the curved handlebar, just above the front end of the body support, just behind the glowing control panel. The small screen, overshadowed by the swooping windshield, currently displayed values for the craft's unwavering acceleration, and its unmoving pitch.

Like all watcher craft of the city, the jumper's body was painted a shining white, with black-lined lavender lettering on each side to confirm its designation and its belonging to the watchers. For jumpers there was never any confusion. They were not allowed for civilians. They were too fast, and too agile, too easy to tumble from without body-attached tech. For watchers, however, they were perfect, especially for emergency response.

Along the jumper's underbody was a row of lights, forming an encircling rectangle, running even along the corners of the engines, which provided a status for other watchers and for any civilians passing by, on-foot or otherwise. Nico was maintaining an intermittent, radiating yellow, indicating that he was on-duty, and that the situation in the immediate vicinity was normal. Two blocks behind him, a carefully-placed light near the second stream was glowing blue, indicating stability in the city's surrounding electromagnetic shield. In his visor display, he could see the position of the other six watchers in the sector, patrolmen whose signals were also glowing yellow. One block ahead of him, and four stories below, he could see a crowd gathering, the one he had anticipated, in the city's park.

Two centuries before his time, as the people of Lwo had neared completion of the city's construction, the Lords had ordered that a central space, one they had already left open in the city's plans, be developed into a park. The people, they had said, whose numbers were already low, would need such a place in the midst of utilitarian buildings, which despite their potential to shine in and absorb sunlight, had been designed primarily to protect their occupants from the unpredictable wildness of Lwo's atmosphere. The people had then followed through, creating a shared space that emulated some of the earth's more flourishing past.

The park was a ninety-nine yard circle, full of rich, green grass, with multi-colored flowers from the forest providing a distinguishing round outline. Within the grass there were pathways made of varying types and colors of flattened stones, stones that the oldest Lwoans often said would have been polished and used inside some people's homes long before Lwo had been formed. Amongst all the intertwining paths, in the grassy spaces between them, were set larger stones that were hewn at the top to allow some form of seating for those who so desired. And near the southern end, along the circle's center line, was a platform. It was the most unnatural looking thing in the park, supported by cylindrically-cut rock, and topped with painted wood and metal. It was fifteen yards wide on each side, and ten yards wide on each end, allowing any speakers or performers plenty of room for expression, something the Lords had also known would be needed.

At each corner of the stage there were lights set on high posts, and at the base of each post there were short columns of large, open-ended, truncated cones, all carved from wood, and facing outward to carry any sound that came from the stage. Today there would be plenty of sound. There were five microphone stands, four chairs, and a percussion set, all carefully placed and spaced.

Nico continued to focus on the park, and whispered a command into his system to magnify. A rectangle of light formed in the center of his visor, providing a closer view, while still allowing a peripheral view of the traffic and the buildings nearby. The number of people in the park was slowly increasing, and they were all getting closer and closer to the stage.

"Count life signals," he said softly. The number came up just below the magnification. There were close to five thousand citizens in the park. For the time of day, it was one of the larger crowds to ever gather there at once. Holidays–the First Sun of Summer, the Day of Winter Moon, Founding Day–were the only other days when so many might have gathered.

From the east side of the stage a group began moving up the set of wooden steps, and were greeted by thousands of loud cheers and waving hands. There were three men, and two women. Nico magnified his view more. The air was always cool outside, and like many in the crowd, the men all wore long pants, heavy shoes, and knit hats. Their long shirts were full of colors. Two of them had beards. One looked almost too young to grow one. He sat down at the percussion set. The other two remained standing, one with a large horn, and the other with a heavy, shining guitar. One of the women wore a long skirt of black, and a long, white shirt. An orange scarf was wrapped around her neck and shoulders. She was carrying a plain, black and white keyboard, and set it up near the percussionist before sitting down behind it. The other woman would be the star of the day's show.

As always, Loren was the last to step onto the stage, and as she did, the crowd cheered even louder. She strutted, and spun in her flailing lavender skirt, revealing brightly colored leggings below. She waved to the crowd as she made her way to the microphone at the center of the stage. Her hair was short and dark, beneath a short, purple headdress. She wore tinted glasses that seemed to sparkle in the light. And her dark sleeves, cut out at the shoulders, ran all the way down past her wrists, and fanned out around her fingers. There was more than enough room for her in the center of the stage, with the percussionist and guitarist on one side, and the horn and keyboard players on the other. The bandmates, almost in unison, looked out at her, and as she turned and smiled, they smiled back.

The band began to play, evenly at first, all of them following the same rhythm. The pace of the drums increased just enough to notice, but not enough to overcome the guitar. Loren began only with a low hum, mimicking the horn and the keyboard as they played the same notes softly behind her. Then, she let out a low howl. She had yet to articulate a single word, but there was a depth of feeling in the single, low note she sang. The crowd quieted in front of her. Nico felt his shoulders shift, and looked around, glad to see no one on the walkway in the building, or looking up at him from below.

As Loren began one of her famed verses, and the guitar dropped in key and matched her chords, the crowd began to sing along. Many danced, steady and slowly along with Loren. Nico remained still, holding back, knowing any expression might be visible to any passers-by. Loren's lyrics still managed to stick. She always sang of love, sometimes for another, but mostly for the land, and its wonders, and all that was unseen. She was young. Many young citizens had not seen much of Lwo, simply for preservation.

Two short beeps in Nico's left ear interrupted his spectating, and the magnification in his visor immediately decreased. The view drifted away from the stage, briefly revealing a closer view of the park before settling back into an unaltered view of the surrounding area. The letters 'HQ' beamed into the center of his vision. Below them, and slightly smaller, was the caller's designation–four encircled, upright crosses, with a single line to their left.

"Answer," Nico said softly, and heard the click opening the line. He kept an eye on the distant crowd, and the traffic flowing around him. "Commander, Sir. This is Lieutenant Nico. Go ahead."

"I need you back at headquarters," said Shil, her voice as

strong as always. "We have a situation at the Southern Range. Meet me on the roof."

Nico felt his brow furrow as he pondered the request. When the city heard from the Watchers of the Mountains, it was almost always a status update, on winds moving in, or the tide rising. But it had rarely required a call for him, or any other city watcher, to leave a post.

"Lieutenant!" Shil called again, sternly. "Do you copy?"

"Yes, Commander, Sir," he answered, quickly, coming to his senses. "On my way. Nico out." The line closed, and he opened another to the other watchers in the sector. "This is Nico. I have to return to headquarters. It's busy here. I need one patrolman to rotate to my current position near the park."

A man answered. "Acknowledged, Lieutenant, Sir. This is Patrolman Kine. Moving to that position."

"Very good. Nico out."

Nico pulled his jumper forward, just past the edge of the building. He adjusted his status lights, and glanced down to see that they had turned purple, indicating that he was on assignment. Then he leaned down, set his chest on the body support, grabbed the sides of the handlebar, tugged it back, and turned right, pulling into traffic. As he merged between two other craft, he increased his speed to keep up, steadying at fifty miles per hour. The rushing sound coming from his engines deepened as they opened wider. He felt the air being pulled through the wind-tech on the back of his smooth, protective jacket. A blinking image in his visor showed his body stabilizing against the speeding jumper.

For a few blocks he stayed behind a large, red civilian craft. Ahead and to the left he saw the wide front end of a puller approaching in the southbound lane, its lights glowing yellow. In a split second he and the woman piloting the patrol craft saw each other and exchanged nods. Then Nico increased his speed, passing the civilian craft, and then passing a long, silvery public transport. As he approached an intersection, his lane had the right of way. The bright, blinking lights of the air mover were green, and he prepared to ascend.

With the press of a button on the handlebar he signaled to the mover, and saw its center panel incline slightly. He leaned upward, just a few inches, as the underside of the jumper hit the incline of concentrated air. He felt the bump, felt the jumper's engines bounce within the stream, and felt the air moving through his tech angle downward. To his right, another civilian craft was moving up to the second stream along with him. To his left, there was space. A long row with buildings on either side of the pathway led west, its paved street now seven stories below. At its end, beyond the buildings, the dark craggy peaks of the Western Range sat against a backdrop of light gray sky.

With the top of his helmet still barely above the windshield, Nico kept the nose of the jumper angled upward as he floated. A cold blast of air rushed over his body as he passed into the second windstream and steadied himself. The top floors of most of the buildings in the city's north side were now visible. They formed long, even rows ten stories up from the city's street level. Most of them had the same convex barriers through which people could be seen walking, and through which those walking could see the city's condition. They were topped by flat roofs made of grooved metal, and their pattern was only interrupted by the occasional fifteen-story building. They were all, however, dwarfed by the city's tallest building, its headquarters, a brilliant metal structure with few windows, which stood well over two hundred feet. The city watchers' station, now just two blocks north and two more west, took up the top eight floors.

Nico made a left turn into a westbound stream, and then a right into a northbound stream. The traffic in the stream above was thin. Very few citizens had regular business in the headquarters sector. As such, and with the strong concentration of watchers nearby, it was the most secure place in Lwo's most secure region. Nico angled his jumper again, and shot upward as he hit another intersection. As he entered the third stream, he slowed his speed.

As he approached the high-reaching building, he looked down to get his bearings. The twelfth floor was a block's width of straight walls made up of plain brown stone and rows of dark window reliefs. It was adorned with bright, copper-plated columns at each corner, providing a sense of gravity for any citizen who may approach, for business or otherwise. Each of the eleven levels below was the same, with the entire vertical array forming the city's hub for governing and operations.

The base of the watchers' station formed the thirteenth level. It was a wide circle, nearly a block's width itself, with concave walls that curved further in with each level of rise. The outer surface was made of a plain metal that looked sanded and smooth, and was painted white. And on each of the eight levels, facing either north and south, or east and west, there was a pair of entries for watchers' craft. Individual air streams flowed in and out of each entry, angling down as needed to reach the third stream.

Nico stopped and hovered at the south hangar entry to the station's third level, the building's fifteenth floor. He waited for a departing puller as it approached the entry. He nodded to the saluting pilot, watched as its long, white body curved out and sped off, and then slowly guided his jumper in.

The increase in temperature was always the first thing Nico noticed. Despite the barrier of the shield, and the stout, high-rise buildings along the city's perimeter, its highest levels were always cold. The streams, especially on days when the heavy, primary wind engines at the city's entries were hit with more storm force, were known to drop to freezing temperatures. Even the city watchers' insulated, form-fitting uniforms were only somewhat effective at keeping their wearers comfortable at high levels. But inside every building it was much different. The city's foundation was set upon a naturally-formed, dense section of earth. All of its buildings had been designed to trap and distribute the heat that rose up from below. And they were all effective. Headquarters was no different.

As Nico guided his jumper through the hangar, toward a spot near the center lift, five other watchers, all patrolmen, saluted, raising their clenched, gloved right hands to the sides of their helmets. He returned the gesture, and then set the jumper down between two low, heavy railings. He sat up, and closed its engines just enough to keep the craft idled within the less-dense air flows of the hangar. The slick tech on his boots stayed strong. The rest of his tech weakened to near deactivation, but stayed ready, as was necessary. A watcher getting accidentally caught in an unexpected gust, or sucked out into a raw stream, had to be able to maintain control and navigate to safety.

Nico's tech continued to hum as he descended from the jumper and walked heavily across the metal floor. He passed between two pullers and several jumpers, and entered the open lift. With no others following behind him, he closed the metal gate and pushed the button for the top level.

At the next level, Nico looked through the gate and saw four watchers, all with their helmets set aside, sitting at individual stations with four-foot wide screens, monitoring their assigned sectors for any occurrences, or any calls from citizens. At the next level up, light from the outside shone through the open, south-facing hangar entry, illuminating the bodies of three idling craft. The pattern continued up to the top level, where a square room held a wall of lockers on one side, a wall of gauntlets on the other, and on the far wall, sets of tables and chairs. The gate slid open, and Nico stepped out.

31

There were no others immediately visible. He turned left, and through a small window saw the east-facing hangar. Next to the window was the closed door to the hangar, and next to the door was a twelve-foot-high ladder. Nico looked up. He felt the cool air pushing down, along with the faint beams of low, natural light. He looked to the readouts in his visor to confirm the status of his tech, and made his way up.

The walled observation space on the station's roof was small—twenty feet long and fifteen feet wide—and was not as shielded as any of the rooms below. There were heavy, sliding doors on each end, with thin gaps at the tops and bottoms that allowed uncontrolled, unfocused wind—wind that passed just over the top of the electromagnetic shield—to blow in without causing any damage. As Nico stepped off the last rung and turned to his right, he saw the long window facing south, offering a view of more than half the city. Below it there was a long workstation, full of screens, with a set of durable buttons below each one. On the far west end there stood one patrolman, who turned and saluted.

"Where's the commander?" Nico asked, returning the gesture.

"On the deck, Lieutenant, Sir," the patrolman answered, pointing past him and to the east.

Nico walked over to the closed door, and looked out through its small window. Shil was standing there, just a few yards out, protected by two pullers angled toward each other, and looking off into the distance between them. The dense, white skirt that fell down to just above her knees blew briskly around her fitting pants. The ends of the dark hair that was cut just below her ears were visible beneath her helmet, fluttering in thick, straight lines around her neck. Her arms were crossed over her chest, and Nico could see the tenseness in her hands as she clenched her biceps, with her hands brushing against the edges of her gauntlets. The air blowing through her heavy boots, keeping her grounded, was so concentrated that it appeared almost solid, as did the air blowing through the engines of the two idling pullers she stood between.

Nico turned, and looked back at the watcher on the other end, needing to ask. "Do you know what this is about, patrolman?"

"No, Sir," the young man said, turning to face Nico. "I asked. She would not tell me."

"Very well."

Nico turned back, and pulled the door to the side, into the frame, and felt the wind blow around every part of his body. He stepped out, and closed the door behind him, felt it latch back into place near the handle, and then turned and walked toward his commander. As the air flowed through the tech on his boots, arms, waist, and back, he settled into a slow gate. His visor displayed the wind speed, and the stability of his tech, as he carefully made his way forward, and stopped one foot behind her. He opened a secure line, and spoke. "You called for me, Commander, Sir?"

Shil turned her head to the side, but did not look at Nico. He could still see that her mind was racing, that she was having trouble focusing. It was why she was standing, unguarded, on the roof. Between the wall and the two pullers, the winds did not hit as hard as they could, but having to concentrate on not being blown away, and on the vastness of the city, and on the sky above, helped her to think. At least, this was what she had always told him.

"I've heard from Commander Jaan," she finally answered, turning back to look east again. "Commander Fits recovered two people during his salvage survey this morning. They were pulled in with the haul of the Southern Hammer."

"Runners?" Nico asked. People trying to leave Lwo, to run back to an old world they had heard so much about, despite it being dead for centuries, was not unheard of. It was, however, rare for any Lwoan's mind to break enough to take such risk.

"No, not runners."

"Just bones, then? From the sea floor? That's nothing new, Sir."

"No. Not just bones. Flesh and blood, and breathing."

Nico shook his head in confusion. "I don't understand, Sir."

"Jaan thinks these people are from the outside."

Nico felt his heart thump into his chest. "Outside what, Sir?"

Shil finally turned around to face him. "Don't be obtuse, Lieutenant. This is serious."

Nico took a deep breath. "Sir, that can not be possible."

"You doubt the commander?"

"No, Sir, I...I just suspect that he's rushed to a conclusion."

Shil shook her head. "No, Lieutenant. There's been no rush. I heard Fits's call. It was coded, but clear. In all likelihood, they are from outside the storm."

Nico paused, and took another breath. "How is that possible?"

"It's good to remember your education, Lieutenant, but do not forget your training. We see more of Lwo than any civilian. You have seen more than most watchers. There is much that is possible. Look at our land." She waved her hand in the direction of the obscured southern horizon. "Compared to the world that was."

Nico nodded, still doubtful. He was starting to feel the thinner air of the higher altitude sting in his lungs. "Very well, Sir. So what do we do now?"

"First, understand something. This cannot be shared outside leadership."

"Yes, Sir."

"Any crewmen who saw these two thinks as you did, that they were runners. You know how rumors spread, so let that one stay if it does. Not even the councilors below are to know. Understood?"

"Yes, Sir."

"This is for ranking watchers only. Jaan has called for all commanders to meet in his village. These people, whoever they are, will be there. That means I'll have to leave you in command for at least a day."

"Understood, Sir. When do you leave?"

"Now."

Shil took two steps back, and looked into the window of the puller on her left, and raised her hand to signal. The shining, translucent door slid back, revealing the pilot in the front seat, who looked back and silently, solemnly saluted them both. How much he might be privy to, Nico could not guess, but an escort was always necessary when leaving the city. Nature was too wild to risk going unsupported.

The craft's underbody engines growled, as they bounced it up another foot. The lights on its sides came up. Shil hopped up onto the cabin floor. Nico walked up behind her. On the opposite side of the cabin he saw the row of seats, and two packed bags at its base. At the rear was the small, gated holding cell, empty. Shil sat in the middle of the long row, and looked out at Nico. She leaned forward, and motioned for him to do the same.

"Do you think you'll need a co-lieutenant?" she asked, her voice still coming through his helmet.

"No, Sir," he answered. "I can handle this on my own."

"Anything happens, you'll have to humble yourself and pick one. Understood?"

"Yes, Sir."

"Very good. I'll see you soon."

She saluted, and leaned back. Nico nodded, and saluted back, and stepped away as the door closed. The puller rose up another two yards. He felt the wind around him pick up, and moved toward the other puller, gripping the bar near the door handle as the departing craft's engines roared, and dense, stabilizing streams were expelled all around its base. The short, narrow wings on its roof were almost vibrating as it angled east, jumped forward five yards, and then, in an instant, became a glow in the distance. Nico watched it fly over rows of flat roofs, heading for the long, dark line of treetops in the forest. He stood there, staring, feeling the raw wind push through all of his tech, pondering how predictable his world had been, and for how many decades, just hours before.

CHAPTER 3
THE SKY AND THE GROUND

It was nearly nightfall when Maia finally saw the watchers from the city approaching. The lights of their craft radiated in brilliant purple as they flew from the west, a glimmer in the shadowy landscape. The ground behind them was distant and dark, with no sign of the sparse trees and paths. Two nearby factories, a thousand feet below, were small spots, billowing clouds of white steam that dispersed nearly instantaneously as they hit the winds. The exhaust was, unsurprisingly, becoming less frequent with each passing moment. Most Lwoans' days were nearing their end. Watchers were in the midst of the day's most important, even if unexpected, task.

Maia maintained her idle hover, watching as lines of powerful air were pulled in below the red panels of the bird's wide front end. The puller was approaching at high speed, a dangerous speed given the conditions. Traveling in low light was always risky, whatever the method. The atmosphere was already unpredictable, but the darker it got, the harder it was to see floating leaves and debris, to have a visual hint of the wind's immediate direction. All craft were designed to compensate, and watcher craft spit out data at the same time, but Maia liked to fly by instinct, embracing nature rather than having a computer system quantify it. Jaan taught all watchers of the sky to do so. Most did not. And with the approaching night, and with visitors to monitor, Maia knew she would also have to fully embrace her bird's system. The conference, Jaan had told her, had to take place right away. There was no time to wait for better circumstances.

As the shining, white puller reached her position, she tilted the control handle in her left hand, pushed the one in her right, and pressed down on the pedal below the center panel, turning about and pulling ahead, meeting their velocity before they could pass her. Her front and side engines blew loudly as they opened, and the vibration from their vanes tickled the floor beneath her boots. Looking off her starboard side, through the clear side window and beyond the short, vented panel and its constant stream of dense air, she could see the puller's pilot, an indistinguishable patrolman in a white helmet. She briefly raised her fist, and he did the same. Behind him, through the translucent side door, she could see light, and the presence of the other watcher with him. She tapped her right control panel and opened a line.

"City watcher craft," she called. "This is Lieutenant Maia."

"This is Patrolman Woll," the man answered, looking over at her. "Go ahead, Lieutenant, Sir."

"Good to see you, Patrolman. Can your commander hear me?"

"Yes, Lieutenant," Shil answered. "I hear you. I told the

commander that this wasn't necessary."

Hearing her voice, and seeing Shil walk up and lean over the pilot's shoulder, Maia could not help smiling. "Commander, Sir. It's been a long time. He thought we should give you a more proper welcome."

"We can find our way to your station just fine," Shil answered, her words short and succinct. "If you wanted to be a guide, you might have met us further out."

"I was on watch over the factories, Sir. It was more efficient to meet you there."

"Understood."

"Will you have your pilot follow me in? Commander's orders."

"Very well. Shil out."

The line closed. Maia looked to the pilot again, who motioned for her to pull ahead. She accelerated, and once the puller was out of her line of sight, she let out a sigh. There had been a coldness in Shil's voice that she had not anticipated. In the past year, since her promotion ceremony, Jaan's voice had changed toward her in the same way. But Shil was closer. Shil was family. She had never been less than kind. Real family–blood family–was rare enough on Lwo, and the two of them had always behaved as if it were, leaning on each other from the time they were young, even after Maia had first been appointed as a watcher, after Shil had already served for more than ten years.

Must have been the presence of a subordinate, she thought. *That, and the unexpected haul from the boat.* Maia, at Jaan's request, had not spoken to anyone else about the new man and the child that had been found. He had likely told the other commanders the same.

She kept her bird on a steady line, and as the tower came into view on the center panel's map, gently decreased her speed, dropping below two hundred miles per hour. She saw the puller's signal blinking behind hers, and saw its speed decreasing at the same rate.

The Sky Tower was ten miles straight ahead, a well-lit, floating structure situated a thousand feet over the center of the land. As she neared it, its form became more visible. Its seventy-yard-high trapezoidal walls were outfitted with strong lights at all corners, which illuminated each section of dense, metal panels. Its bottom half was all engines, an array of the four largest pieces of wind tech that had ever been constructed. On approach, now just three miles out and with her speed steadily decreasing, Maia could see the fierce, white streams pushing down beneath the station, keeping it steady above their village. Unseen, intermittent gusts from smaller engines kept it from spinning about with the whims of the storm.

The top half of the station was a brilliant shade of blue, with short windows running in two long lines across each wall. Light crept out through the windows, giving even more light to the station as Maia got closer, and eyed the short, rectangular passageway to the tower's hangar. Now just one mile out, she could finally make out the lines of the west-facing support engine's vents. She slowed down even more to allow her bird to glide, and ascended several yards to avoid the strongest points of the engine's vortex. Her center panel showed that the puller had done the same.

As the bird neared idling speed, she felt the familiar, gentle push from below, and guided the craft into the hangar. Light beamed in through her windshield, and the bird floated ahead another thirty yards. She set it down on a luminescent rectangle on the metal deck. The bird's engines quieted to a hum, as they continually expelled the minimal amount of air.

Two helmeted airmen, outfitted in blue body suits denoting their rank, approached each side of the bird. Maia felt the thud of the clamps as they attached to the underbody. As the airmen backed away, saluted, and moved over to Shil's craft, Maia hit the button to lower the rear ramp, and then touched the back of her head, making sure the ring formed by the ends of her braids was still in place. Then she reached further back, pulled her helmet up and forward, and then pulled it down over her head and into its cradle. She removed the belts from her shoulders, stood, and turned, and walked back to the lowering rear ramp. As she took careful steps down, she felt the outside air push gently through the tech on her legs and arms. As she reached the floor of the hangar she looked over to her left, and walked. Shil was exiting the side of the secured puller, and motioning to her pilot as its door closed.

Maia stopped, and saluted as Shil approached. Shil returned the gesture, and then extended her hand. Each of them grasped the other's forearm, longer than was necessary. Maia kept her sense of relief subdued. They turned and walked together, passing between rows of blue, short-winged craft, approaching a high-reaching, convex wall with a wide gate at the center. Maia walked up to one of the flights of stairs that flanked the gate, and waited, as Shil had gone toward it.

"Lieutenant," said Shil, stopping and turning in place. "The commander said we were meeting in the village. Has something changed?"

"No, Commander, Sir," said Maia. "But he has yet to descend himself. He wanted to meet with us first, after you arrived. Please, follow me."

Shil's chin raised in agitation, but she changed direction. Maia moved up the stairs, and listened, as Shil's boots clanged behind hers on the metal steps. Atop the mezzanine, at its center, was the open entryway. The shaft around it was solid, rising another two stories into the ceiling. They entered, and felt the lift's floor bounce gently, as Maia pressed the button for the observation level. The dense, translucent door slid closed in front of them, and they were catapulted upward.

A moment later the door opened. Shil exited the lift first, and Maia watched as her sister moved slowly around the space, as if taking it in for the first time. It was the smallest room in the tower, just forty feet on each side, with a large, single pane of thick glass forming each wall. From the outside, in daylight, the windows would have appeared only as dark rectangles in matching metal frames, but they could magnify for miles. They allowed watchers of the sky to see more of the land at once than any of the other three divisions. In front of each viewing wall were two high-backed chairs with grooves for retracted helmets. In front of each chair were two screens set above a row of controls.

There were watchers in each of the survey seats. Shil was taking slow steps, making her way around the entire room, quietly observing each airman as they saluted her silently and then returned back to their work. Finally, she came upon Jaan, sitting in the right-hand chair at the west-facing station. Maia walked up behind her, and retracted her helmet, and stood in place.

Jaan's hair was gray, but thick. His jawline was strong, and full of stubble. Though he was the oldest watcher in the ranks, he was as fit as any, even as muscular as a watcher of the ground, though he was not near any of them in stature. His dark red suit still fit him well. Maia watched as Shil looked at their commander, no doubt remembering what it was like to serve under him, remembering how frustrating she had often said it was all those years ago. She walked up to him, and removed her white helmet, holding it under her left arm.

"Commander Jaan, Sir?" Shil said.

Jaan stood slowly, turned, and looked into Shil's eyes as they saluted each other. "Commander Shil," he said, extending his hand. His strong, rumbling voice seemed to carry through the entire room. "I saw you approaching," he said, still holding her arm. "Welcome back."

Shil gently pulled her arm away, and stood firm. "Thank you, Sir."

"Airmen!" Jaan called out to the room. "Wait for us on the mezzanine level."

In unison, all seven of the airmen in the room yelled out "Yes, Sir!" and within a few seconds, they had all entered the lift. Maia stepped aside as Jaan moved to the center of the room, and watched as the lift door shut in front of the group of watchers. As they dropped out of sight, Jaan turned, walked up to the stations at the south-facing wall, and stood, looking. Shil walked up behind him. Maia followed suit, keeping some distance between herself and her superiors.

"Commander," Jaan said, turning and looking at Shil. "I thought we should talk in private before descending to the village. You are second, after all, and should anything happen to me unexpectedly, you'll have to see this through."

"Yes, Sir," said Shil.

Maia sensed her heart beating at the thought of more unknowns.

"I have yet to see this man and child," Jaan went on. "But I am assured that they are from the outside. That means more of humanity has survived than we thought, and for longer than *our* ancestors expected. How many more is the question. That means that when they arrive at the village, as soon as they're stabilized, we will have to interrogate."

"Interrogate, Sir?" Shil asked.

"Yes. Whatever they say, whatever they've seen, we will have to determine how much of a threat there may still be outside the storm, which now, it seems, is not impenetrable."

"Yes, Sir. Understood."

"Maia?" Jaan said, glancing over his shoulder. "I can feel your agitation. What do you have to add? Spit it out."

Maia made sure to soften her tone. "Commander, Sir. As far as we know, these could be innocents." She watched as Jaan turned all the way around, and faced her. She met his eyes, and continued. "And one of them is a child, a thing that is rare here."

"Your point, Lieutenant?"

"We should question them without suspicion. They may know things that could be helpful to us. They may know why the winds continue to grow and push in, why the storm changes as it does. They may know why the clouds no longer part as often as they used to. They could help us to survive another century, and another."

"Based on what Fits told me of their tiny boat, I doubt they are people of science."

"But they made it here, Sir. They survived out there, in what is still, as far as we know, a world of darkness and death. They must know something useful."

"Maybe. Maybe not. Either way, we'll be responsible for what they bring here, good or bad."

"Sir. If there was a threat out there, it would be better to have

46

them as allies than to have them as enemies. And right now, they're weak. If we help them recover, they may be grateful."

Jaan shook his head, and looked into both their eyes. "Do either of you recall how long it has been since other humans actually *arrived* here?"

Maia looked to Shil, who looked back at her. Their parents had told them, decades prior, when they had lived in a small home in the Middle Lands. Their teachers had told them the same.

"Two centuries, Sir," Shil answered.

"Right," said Jaan. "The land's population, its biology, was essentially complete after just one century. What do you think new additions will do?"

"In their current state? Nothing, Sir."

Jaan turned away, and faced the window to the south again. "We'll see."

"Perhaps this would be worth a trek over the ocean," said Maia.

Jaan continued staring out at the magnified view of the land. "Not yet, Lieutenant." He took a deep breath. "However, I will give you the child to look after. A gentler type will be helpful to a young boy in a new, strange place. I will deal with the father."

Maia nodded. "Yes, Sir."

Jaan walked out, between the two stations, and stood directly in front of the glass wall, searching. He had increased the magnification to the point that the Southern Range actually appeared as a line in the distance. In the shadows, the light of the watchers' station there was just a twinkle. Its green color indicated that all was normal, which it was. Except, of course, for the arrival of life from a dead world.

Jaan whispered a command, and the magnification decreased. Maia, following Shil, moved closer, and stood in front of the empty chairs. Now they could see just ten miles out from the tower. There was very little sun left over the clouds, very little light to indicate any movement, but in the distance, two steady, white beams emerged. Between them was a line of green light. The objects were getting closer and closer, approaching the location of the village. A signal rang out from the station behind Maia, and as she stepped back to look, she saw the blinking 'GW' on both its screens. Looking back, and getting a nod from Jaan, she answered the call, and stepped aside. He walked past her and faced the screen.

"This is Commander Jaan. Go ahead."

"Commander Jaan, Sir," the man answered. "This is Commander Brun. We are on approach to the village."

"Yes, we see you. We will meet you there."

"We will need the hospital, Sir. Immediately."

"As I expected you might. I will make sure the doctor is ready. Fifteen minutes?"

"Fifteen minutes, Sir."

"Very well. Jaan out."

Jaan motioned for them to follow him to the lift, and Maia

walked beside Shil. Jaan pushed the call button and the door opened. As it did, Maia heard him open a line to the hospital. As the door closed, and the lift descended, she heard him conversing with Doctor Kile, one of the few civilians that lived in their village. Once the lift stopped, and the door opened to the mezzanine, their conversation ended, and Jaan pulled his helmet up and on. Maia followed suit, and saw her sister take up her helmet and do the same. Then, a blinking symbol in her front panel revealed the line Jaan had opened between the three of them. They stepped out of the lift together.

"Kile will be ready shortly," he said. "I've already briefed her on what's happening, and its sensitivity."

Behind them, the seven airmen still assigned to the observation level entered the lift, and ascended again. The three of them quickly descended the steps to the hangar floor, and made their way to the round wall at its center. As the gate opened, and the door opened to the ground lift, they saw the outer and inner rings of seats, most of them occupied by airmen who were returning home after their watches had ended.

There were three empty seats right next to each other on the inner ring, facing out. The seats along the outer ring faced in. All of the airmen saluted, as Maia and the two commanders took the three inner seats. Maia returned the salutes and strapped in. Shil did the same, as did Jaan, who motioned for all in the room to be at ease.

Maia could sense the giant metal cable behind her. It ran from the connection at the tower's center of mass, all the way down to the platform on the ground, which was settled a quarter mile outside their village. The energy from the cable's slight vibrations pushed against the pipe that surrounded it, which held the lift's inner seats. Through her boots, beneath the shallow-grooved floor, she could almost feel the evenly-spaced wind-tech engines, working along with the locked supports to keep the lift in place.

The bell chimed. Simultaneous, muffled clangs signaled their disconnection from the hangar level. The engines became louder. There were no windows to see what was happening, just distant sounds to give assurance that the process was proceeding as it always had, with the heavy, enclosed disc dropping out of the sky, and the tech keeping it steady. A few moments later the lift began to slow, and then bounced, softly, and floated down to the ground platform. The sound of more metal connections indicated that it had been secured, and after another chime, the door opened. Outside the lift, a long, curving row of bright lights illuminated the enclosed, covered pathway to the village.

At Jaan's direction, all of the airmen exited first. Some of them glanced at the trio in the center of the lift, but were careful not to let their curiosity cause their eyes to linger. After they had moved ten yards out, and the last one curved around a bend and out of sight, Jaan stood, and Maia and Shil followed him out.

The roof over the pathway was made of windows of re-formed plastic. None of the arched panels were perfectly clear. Some of them were cloudy. Some of them had streaks of different colors. But they were all strong, thick enough to protect them from forces seen and unseen. The sounds of small rocks and twigs bouncing away, and the gusts that had carried them, were noticeable.

The floor beneath them was made of sanded pieces of stone, and wide enough for five to walk side by side. Maia was still a step behind Jaan, but Shil had moved up to his position as the pathway straightened and they approached the north entry. Up ahead, and through the roof, the wall of stone that surrounded the village was visible. It was crowned with lights spaced five yards apart, and it reached five stories at its peak. Maia saw her sister staring up at the wall, saw her demeanor shift so slightly that only she would have noticed, and then looked ahead as they entered the village.

Except for the light chatter among the airmen who had stepped through the doors ahead of them and were now dispersing, the village was quiet. The stone roads were not bustling, as would have been the case in the city Shil had left. Maia could see a pair of civilians, and a group of five off-duty watchers, all walking in the distance. The simple, brick buildings, and their grate-covered windows, cast a plain, protective presence over Maia and her superiors as they walked. There was little sound coming from anywhere–a distant conversation behind a first-floor window, a door shutting behind another. The only real noise was that of the constant wind above, which was diminished by the energetic shield that roofed the entire village. Jaan continued to lead the way toward the village center, moving around corners, and down short pathways.

"How many live here now?" Shil asked.

"We are still at one hundred and nine in our division," Jaan replied. "A few civilians, and a few family members make up the rest. And only a handful of medical staff. But we make do."

Maia ran her hand along the front wall of a diner, where she had once eaten with Shil, where through its lone window she could make out a familiar patron sitting at a table inside. Her own two-story home was not far, just a few dozen yards south and west. "It's still a requirement," she said, entering the conversation. "For them to reside with us."

"Yes, I know," Shil answered.

"We don't need anyone here to be distracted by too much comfort," said Jaan. "That's what the city is for."

After a long, straight section of road, they made one final right turn, and saw the village hospital. It was three stories high, as were most of the other buildings in the village. Its flat walls were made of a plain stone, but were painted a light shade of blue, making it stand out. The doors and windows were outlined in white. Inside, every floor was well lit, and moving figures and shadows indicated steady activity. As they approached the door, Maia heard the roar of several wind engines.

From the west, between two other buildings across from the hospital, a ground watcher's fox–wide, and black, and formed mostly by its wings–hovered up to the front of the hospital. Its waist-high helm was as dark as its wings, but glossed, and behind it stood the pilot, a massive man in a black suit, with distinctive, shining, coppered tech attached at the same seven points as all watchers in every division. Behind him another fox, with a pilot just as large, flew up and stopped. Together, they hovered in place.

From behind the two watchers of the ground, a gull approached. Except for the muted green color of its body, and the large fin on its belly, it was much like the puller Shil had arrived in. The noise from its engines decreased as it settled into an idling position.

The hospital door opened, and Kile, wearing a long, light blue coat, and a clear face mask, exited. She approached the two watchers of the ground, and looked up at them, and set her hands on her hips, waiting. Then Jaan approached.

The watcher who had first arrived hopped down from his fox, and Maia immediately noticed his shining ranking pin, with its four upright crosses and the underlining bar denoting the ground division. It was the commander, Brun. He approached the doctor slowly. The metal in the soles of his boots seemed to land heavily against the road. He raised the visor on his helmet, and looked down at the woman. Through her clear mask, her freckled cheeks appeared blushed. Her eyes were as black as the braided ponytail slung over her shoulder.

"Do you know?" Brun asked, his heavy voice distorted by the broad mask that still covered his face from the nose down.

Kile managed a nod.

"Are you sure?"

Jaan walked up beside Kile. "She knows, Commander," he said, and extended his hand. "I told her myself, hours ago. Welcome back to our village."

Brun quickly saluted, and gripped Jaan's arm on the inside of the gauntlet. His own gauntlet was too wide, and too smooth for Jaan to get a firm hold. "Thank you, Commander, Sir," he replied. Then he nodded back over his shoulder. "Our guests have arrived."

They all turned and watched, as Fits and one of his ensigns approached, carrying a long gurney between them. It was covered by a raised netting that created a hazy effect over the two people lying beneath it. The man's skin was clearly unhealthy–a pale shade of brown that Maia had never seen, not even in a dead Lwoan. The child did not look much better. They both appeared to be asleep. As Fits came up to the doctor, Brun took hold of the rear of the gurney from the ensign. Fits, holding tightly to the front end, acknowledged Jaan first, and then the others. His pilot returned to the gull.

"They've been coughing up black water since we found them," he said to the doctor. "I can't say exactly how bad it is. Our scans at the station didn't reveal much, other than their vitals, and their ages–fifty…" he hesitated. "And seven."

Kile nodded. "Very well," she said, and waved. "Bring them in. Follow me."

Maia trailed behind the four commanders, and looked to make sure no one else followed. The hospital door opened to a softly-lit triage space, which, to her surprise, was completely empty. They walked on, down the long, bright main hall, which smelled of dry medicines and bitter disinfectants. It was also void of any others. They passed a lift on the right, and two closed rooms on the left, before reaching a set of double doors at the end of the hall. After five more yards they reached the doors to a treatment room. Kile stood aside, and quietly motioned for Brun and Fits to carry the patients in. She asked Jaan to follow. She asked Maia, and Shil, to wait outside the room, where they could watch the treatment through the windows in the doors, and they could keep others at bay.

Kile was a civilian, but the hospital was hers, and Maia watched as the three men followed her directions. They took the man and the boy from the gurney, and set them on separate, metal beds that were full of tiny holes. They removed the dirty clothing from their frail bodies, carefully pulling and cutting the water-beaten fabric and tossing it into a marked bin. From the wall behind the patients they dislodged short, white preparation machines, and let them lower over the patient's torsos, where they stopped a few inches above each of them. Then extensions from the machines slid out, and settled over both sides of the beds.

Through the doors Maia could hear them all talking–about vitals and fluids, about purification, about activations–all while they moved between supply cabinets, and the patients' beds, and each other. All watchers were required to be well-versed in medical treatment. For as long as humans on Lwo could live, with some reaching one and a half centuries, their tendency toward carelessness still lingered. Watchers had to be prepared to deal with the effects of Lwoans' tendencies. Even so, to her, the three men in the room seemed more efficient and focused than usual, and in a space more delicate than what they were accustomed to.

Looking at the two patients, Maia could see that each of them, though not yet conscious, were breathing more steadily than they had been, through fresh, clear, oxygen-pumping breathing masks. But the approaching sense of relief soon faded. She looked closer, and saw more signs of emaciation in the child. His skin was dry, especially around his fingertips and feet. And there were dark circles around his eyes.

Suddenly, she felt Shil's hand on her shoulder, and looked at her, and saw the same concern in her eyes. She was reminded, briefly, by Shil's slightly higher stature more than anything, of once being as small as this strange boy. Then she was reminded of their own mother and father, whose parents had helped build Lwo's city, and who themselves had left it for a simpler life in their old village. They had chosen a harder path, and, Maia was sure, had failed to pass one hundred and twenty years because of it. She remembered seeing them in their last days, seeing the youth in their eyes, but knowing that their bodies had endured too much to last. The same sense of despair she had felt then, of possible doom at any moment, was creeping its way back in.

She looked to Shil again, who had removed her helmet, and was now looking back and forth to the hall behind them, clearly wary of any others seeing two watchers so concerned with patients, and with each other. For a moment their eyes met, then Maia looked back through the window, at the boy and his father.

"They'll live," Shil whispered, and slowly let her hand fall back to her side.

"I know," Maia answered. She slowly lifted and retracted her own helmet, and felt it settle near her back. "Then what? Do they look like they need interrogating?"

"No," said Shil. "They don't."

"They need rest. If they're going to remember anything at all, they'll need rest."

"They'll get it. From the looks of it, they'll have days of rest."

Maia squinted through the window. "Why aren't they attaching feeding tubes?"

"Because they're foreign. We can't assume how their bodies will react to what we take in here. Not yet. They have to be acclimated first."

"Right."

Maia thought back again, to a somewhat happier time, when she was early on in her education. Any creatures arriving from outside the storm, big or small or any species, would have had to survive in murky, filthy darkness, and would have had to become accustomed to it. But those lessons had never referred to humans. The world had failed, in a multitude of ways. Lwoans, as far as anyone knew or believed at the time, were the only humans left.

She continued to watch as the white machines began to move up and down the patients' bodies, gently spraying out a liquid that was clear, but did not move like ordinary water. It ran slowly over their pores, down to the cold, metal beds, and off into unseen places below. Then the machines reset, and started again, this time pushing out a light green mist. After the man and the child were cleaned, the machines raised back up, and withdrew their extensions, and the three commanders repositioned the devices back on the wall. Then they partially covered each of the patients in a white gown, and stepped away as the doctor approached.

Kile went to the man first, and leaned over, touching his head with gloved hands. Then, from a nearby tray, she took a scalpel, and found a spot between two of his ribs, and cut a small incision. From a small machine behind the tray, she took a long, clear tube, and guided its end into the narrow hole. Then, for a single minute, she waited. Seeing no adverse reaction, she moved over to the child, and repeated the process. The liquid that flowed out through the tubes was watery, and red in color, but nearly black. The drying blood around the incisions, however, did not seem dark enough.

CHAPTER 4
THE NEW OLD WORLD

He awoke slowly, his eyelids heavy, and suddenly became aware that he was conscious, and that he was breathing with ease, and that they were no longer in the makeshift boat they had built to carry them away. Then, once again, he was not sure that he was not dreaming, or worse.

A gentle hand ran a soft cloth over his brow, and around his mouth. It felt warm, and real. Around the rest of his body it felt cool, but not nearly as cold as it had been at sea. He could not see much. There was light, but it was blurred. There was a nagging, numb feeling in his right side. He raised his eyelids as much as he could, and saw what appeared to be a white ceiling, made up of large, glowing squares. Wherever he was, it was quiet, but he could sense someone other than the caregiver nearby. There was a warmth, pushing through the coolness, coming not only from the woman, whose long dark hair he could now make out on his right, but also from someone standing beyond the foot of the bed he was lying on. He started to move his hands, and then slid his elbows back, and lifted his head from the pillow, and tried to sit up.

"Careful," said the woman. "You've been out for quite a while."

He laid back down. The softness beneath his neck and shoulders almost caused him to drift back off. "What's a while?" he asked. His voice sounded off. It sounded familiar. There was a dryness in his throat, making it raspy, but not the way it would be from an illness. He felt soreness, but soreness from injury, somewhere deep in his neck.

"Since you arrived here," the woman answered. "Two days now."

He winced at the thought, and swallowed, and winced again. He took as deep a breath as he could manage, keeping his mouth closed. Cautiously, he spoke again. "And...where exactly is *here*?"

"You are on Lwo," a man said.

The heavy voice had come from directly in front of him, and above. The man he had sensed was there had made his way up to the bed. "Low?" he replied. "Never heard of it. Where's that?" Feeling strengthened as his senses slowly returned, he sat up to his elbows. His vision cleared enough to see that the woman was wearing a white coat, and had freckles on her light-colored cheeks. She stared back at him, her hand on his arm, trying to comfort his confusion. He rubbed at his ribs, and felt the thick bandage. The woman set her hand on top of his.

"We had to clean out your lungs," she said. "That will come off soon enough."

"My lungs?"

"Yes. You and the child's. You were both coughing up-"

"My son!" he shouted, and felt a sharp pain in his neck. A splatter of blood flew from his lips onto the bright gown he was covered in. He sat upright, his hands pushing down into the mattress, and eyed the man standing in front of him. He looked aged, perhaps sixty years old, but he was visibly strong. He wore a dark red suit, something resembling what soldiers in his parents' old books had worn, and was staring back down at him, with his apparently armored arms crossed against his broad chest. "Where's my son!?" he yelled, pushing through the pain in his throat. He wiped his mouth. The old soldier pointed to the left, and he looked over to see the boy, lying in a bed just like his, sleeping, and breathing easily. He tried to slide his legs out from his own bed.

"No, no!" said the woman, reaching and pulling him back in. "You need to be careful. He'll be fine."

She pushed his chest, forcing him back down to the bed. She was strong, for a younger woman. Strong, and taller than most women he had encountered. He felt too tired, and too relieved to push her off. Had he still been at sea, had their answers not been good enough, he would have. He looked over, and stared at the boy. He had been sure they would both die in that terrible boat they had assembled. He had been sure they would die, trying to brave the ocean, aiming for the north, where every kind person they had ever encountered had said never to go. But they had run out of options. And for their effort they

61

had found more dark water, and stinking, stinging rain, and floating clothes and shoes, with a rare leg bone or skull on a nearby plank every so often. Then they had entered rough waters, and been taken over. So he had closed the boat, sure it would be their tomb, and sang his son to sleep.

"Do you have a name?" asked the man in red.

He kept his eyes on his son. "I do. It's…" He paused, trying to recall, still struggling to believe he was alive, and conscious. "It's Robbins."

"Robbins, eh?" the man replied, his tone full of skepticism. "And your son?"

"Devon," Robbins answered.

"And where are you from?"

"The East Coast."

"The east coast of what land?"

Robbins looked back at the man, and saw him squinting back at him. "We only ever knew it as the East Coast. That's all anyone ever called it, before we left."

"And why did you leave?"

"What!?" What kind of question-" He coughed, loudly, and sat up again, and held his fist up to his mouth. There was slightly less blood this time. "Why do you think we left!? It was dead! Just like the rest of the world!"

"Okay then," the man said. "When did you leave?"

Robbins looked at his son again. "I don't know. Probably

thirty years ago. I've lost count now."

"And how did you leave?"

He took a deep breath, and swallowed, and faced his questioner again. "Who exactly are you? What's your name?" He looked at the woman. She may have been kind, but she could still be a threat. "Who are you people?"

"I am Commander Jaan, of the Watchers of the Sky, and Lead Watcher of Lwo, the Earth's last continent."

Looking at the man, Robbins felt a new type of shock run through him, followed by a searing anger in his chest. He felt his arms tense, and his fists clench. He felt his joints tighten, and hoped it was not visible, though he was sure it was. He stared back at Jaan. "You're a liar, then."

Jaan shook his head. "No, Robbins. It is true. And this," he said, motioning toward the woman. "This is Doctor Kile. She runs the hospital here in the sky watchers' village."

Robbins continued looking into the man's eyes, and considered his bypass of the accusation, and his lack of explanation. *The worst kind of liar*, he thought. *One that believes his own lies.* He turned to the woman. "What did you do to us?"

"We saved your lives," she said. She set a hand on his arm, and squeezed. "You're welcome."

Robbins eyed her carefully. "I suppose you did."

Her eyes shifted, toward Jaan and then back to him, and she went on. "Actually, you should thank Commander Fits," she said.

"When you get the chance. He'll be returning soon, I would think, to see that the two of you are well."

He almost laughed. "And who is Commander Fits?"

"Tall. Red beard. Green uniform. Sound familiar?"

He stared up at the bright ceiling. "There was a ship," he said aloud, remembering something faint.

"There was indeed," Jaan said. "What else can you remember?"

"Too much," said Robbins, shaking his head. "Everything."

"Will you tell me about the place you left? The east coast?"

Robbins looked down, and thought about where he had grown up. There was so much darkness after he left, so much death and struggle, that his early years were still, at best, murky. "Life was okay for a little while," he said. "But we always knew everything was ending, that the land was sinking and there was no more inland to go to. My parents had told me from the time I was small, even smaller than my own son. They seemed old, and tired, but they managed to make it until I had grown up. Then food stopped growing. Most of the animals died out, and the ones left flying above became vicious. So I left. I got on a big boat with a few others at a port." He paused, recalling the last days he had spent on land. "I swear, I saw it sinking as we pulled out."

"The others," Jaan said. "The ones you left with. Did they survive?"

Robbins shook his head. "No."

"Then how did you last so long?"

Robbins looked up at the man, still doubtful, still angry. "How else? By moving. We moved from boat to boat, every few months or so. Sometimes we ended up on a boat we had already been on years before. That's how it's been all these years. Barely surviving. But you know that, don't you? I mean, this is the nicest boat I've been on, but it's still a boat."

"No, Robbins. You are on land."

"Ah. Right."

Jaan stared back at him, peering. "What about your son? How has he managed?"

He stared back at Jaan. "With me protecting him."

Jaan paused for a moment. "And his mother? Where-"

Robbins heard nothing else. He attacked fast, jumping to his knees and lunging in one motion. He planted his left foot before his first swing, and winced as his fist hit whatever metal was wrapped around the soldier's left arm. With the next swing, his other arm was knocked away from the man's chest plate with a sting. He felt it down to the bone. Then, he felt the soldier's heavy, hard palms slam into his chest, and he was knocked up and back. The clearness that had gradually come back to his throat disappeared, as his body tensed and he crashed back to the bed. A moment later, he felt the doctor's body weight as she leaned onto him, pressing one hand into his chest. Then he felt a sharp stab in his thigh. He tried to cry out, but there was barely a hiss. As his body shook, and the woman held him in place, he felt a rush of soothing warmth. Then, as his eyes shut, he felt nothing.

When Robbins awoke again he could barely move, though somehow his muscles felt stronger. He remembered being knocked back, and stung in his leg. Then, he remembered what had led to it, the things the soldier had told him, and asked of him. The brief thought of his wife's death jumped into his mind again, followed by the memories of their darkest days. As he tried to sit up, he felt the restraint, and looked down to see a large, white belt. It matched the sheets, and ran up from under the bed and was fastened around his chest.

He laid his head back down, and looked to his left. The doctor was there, sitting at the side of the bed where his son was still resting peacefully. He looked past the boy's bed, to the short window, where a gray light was coming in through thick lines of grating. He had seen sunbeams before. This light seemed artificial. Outside the window was what appeared to be a building, with brown, brick walls, and windows covered by the same metal mesh.

He looked away, and up at the ceiling. He felt himself breathing, slowly and steadily, easier than he ever had. The air at sea was unpredictable, and the recycled air inside old ships was often tainted, with the scents of oils and lubricants from unrepaired systems, or rankness from unburied bodies, or undumped waste. He shook his head, and breathed another easy breath. He noticed that his throat felt better, and opened his mouth to speak. "Where are we?" he asked. He turned his head toward the doctor. "Where are we exactly?"

A man answered. "Lwo is not far from the Earth's northern-most point."

He turned his head toward the foot of his bed, and saw the soldier again, near a wall, standing up from a chair a few yards away. He looked Jaan square in the eyes. "I had always heard there was only danger in the north. So where is it?"

"You passed through it. We're surrounded by it. Our sea is wild. Our winds are unending. Every danger of nature surrounds us."

"Maybe that's what they meant."

"*They?*"

Thinking about his encounters, over years of travel and travails, having only ever met a handful of good and honest people, Robbins suddenly felt a wave of fatigue. He struggled to speak again. And he remembered, again, the sting that had come from Jaan's hands. "A few people we met over the years had said that the north was in the worst condition. No one had ever ventured there and showed up again. We came to believe it was deadlier than any of the dead swamps or barren seas, so we stayed away, until there was nowhere else to try."

"You and your son are the first to reach us in generations. I'm afraid any friends you had that came our way did not make it."

"We didn't have any friends."

"Very well. Perhaps, Robbins, you could tell me how you found us?"

Robbins shook his head. "We didn't...We..." He struggled, and looked away, thinking again of the metal contraption they had

67

built, of the tear-filled wails that had come from his son as they had descended from the last rusted old ship. They had seen others descend before them, and not long after seen them swallowed up by things unseen in the water. "We were just lucky," he said finally. "I pointed us north, and turned the old motor on. We kept watch for some days. I can't remember how many. But eventually the water was too strong, and we were too tired. We just had to sleep. We'd barely been eating or drinking before we left, and hadn't brought much with us."

Jaan stepped away, and Robbins watched him walk past Devon's bed, and over to the window. He looked out at the buildings. "I have to say you're brave to have done so. It would seem I was too quick to question you the way I did."

Robbins offered no response to the near-apology. He took another look at his son, and at the care of the doctor looking over him, and the strength of the old soldier standing near him. Another rush of fatigue flowed from his head to his toes. Before his heavy eyelids shut again, he felt the doctor coming and sitting at his own bedside.

The next time Robbins awoke he had been moved. He was lying closer to the window, where his son had been. He sat up quickly, and realized the restraining belt was gone. And he felt even stronger, and felt no hunger. His lungs felt full, and he took in one big breath and exhaled. He touched his throat, and then his chest. There was no discomfort. He turned to the right, and there, sitting in a chair on the far wall, looking back at him, was a woman in red. Her eyes widened as they met his.

68

"Robbins, is it?" she said with a smile.

She looked young. Rows of thin braids flowed from the front of her head to the back, where they formed a partly visible ring. Her clothing was not unlike Jaan's, though the red was not as deep. A shining pin near her left shoulder bore what appeared to be three circled symbols with a line above them. He looked at her face again. It was much kinder than Jaan's had been.

"Yes," Robbins finally answered. "That's my name."

He reached to pull back the covers that had been over him, but found none there. Instead he found that he was fully clothed, in thick gray pants, and a matching shirt, and dark boots that felt heavier, and fresher, than any he had ever worn. He swung them out, and felt the soles almost pull him down to the floor as they hit. The thudding sound startled the figure next to the woman, a smaller one that Robbins had just noticed, who had been sitting and facing the wall.

Devon jumped up, and turned around, and shouted "Dad!"

The boy nearly stumbled over in his own new boots as he ran across the room. Robbins felt the tears rolling down his cheeks as he kneeled down, and pulled the boy in, and held him tightly. He touched Devon's thick, curly, dark hair, and ran his hands up and down his back and arms. "I'm sorry, son," he whispered.

"Sorry for what, Dad?"

"Sorry this world is so hard. Sorry I didn't take better care of you."

"But you did, Dad. You did."

Robbins leaned back, and held his son's shoulders. The boy's face was fuller than it had ever been, and his skin was richer in color. He had been eating. He was wearing the same dense, gray clothing. And he was starting to smile. "They take good care of you?"

"Yes, Dad," Devon said, nodding.

"How do you feel?"

"Better now. You're wide awake. I thought you might die, like all the other people. Like Mom. And then I'd be here all by myself."

Robbins shook his head. "No, son. Not me." He stared into the boy's eyes another moment, and gave him another hug, and looked to the woman, and then back to his son. "How long was I asleep?"

"A couple days," said Devon. "Maybe longer. I was asleep too."

"Robbins?" the woman called. She stood up from her chair.

For the first time, looking at her, Robbins noticed the helmet attached at her back. Its open end was angled toward her head, and a tense, metallic, segmented line connected it to something supportive on her back. Then he realized that Jaan had borne the same kind of mounted helmet. "Yes," he answered.

"Your son already knows me. My name is Maia. I am Lieutenant of the Watchers of the Sky, second in command to Jaan, whom you-"

"Yes," Robbins interrupted. "I'm familiar with him."

"Very well," said Maia. "He has ordered that I look after you, and we have somewhere we must go. Do you feel able to walk?"

Robbins stood up, keeping a hand on Devon's shoulder. The boots that he wore, though heavy, felt articulated in all the right places. He pushed up on his toes, and felt the boots give at the ankles. He tried to slide one foot, and felt their strong grip on the smooth, shining floor. The sides of the boots were zipped up to just below his calves, and their lining, whatever it was, seemed to be molding to his legs. He looked down at his son, and touched the top of his head. "Devon?" he asked. "Are these good people? Is this a good place?"

The boy looked over at Maia, and around the room, and out into the hall, and back over his shoulder, out the window. Then he looked into Robbins' eyes. "Yes, Dad."

Robbins looked to Maia. "Please lead the way, Lieutenant."

"Just Maia," she said with a nod, and turned and walked out through the open door.

They followed her into the bright hall. It was not very long, not compared to the corridors of the old ships they had been on. But it was wider, and clean, and the air had an artificial but pleasant smell, and seemed to be flowing lightly over Robbins' head. As they passed by open doors, he felt eyes looking out at them. There were only a handful of other patients, and they seemed curious, as did the people dressed in pale blue attending to them.

Once they had passed a woman sitting at a short desk, where before her sat a device projecting a small, glowing square of information, they came upon a solid, metal door. Maia stopped, and pressed the button labeled 'Call.' Robbins stood behind her, holding

71

his son by the shoulders, letting his eyes wander around the unfamiliar place. It was clearly too stable to be just another, more advanced ship. He looked down at his heavy sleeves, and heavy pants. Maia turned around to face them.

"I apologize for not allowing you to pick your own clothing," she said. "The nurses had to cover you, and we have limited stock here in the village."

Robbins shook his head. "No apology necessary. You saved our lives, after all, right? It's just that this place, and these things, even these clothes, are strange. And I never thought I would see...anything like this again."

The metal door opened, and the three of them stepped in. A nurse, a young woman nearly as tall as Robbins, appeared right behind them. Maia quickly waved her away. The woman nodded and stepped back, looking at Robbins as the door closed in front of her. They started to descend. Robbins turned to Maia. Before he could open his mouth, she was speaking.

"The people here are unaware of where you and Devon came from," she said. "As far as they know, you came from the city, or maybe one of the villages out west. But there are rarely children here. And sky watchers that do have children generally transfer, or leave the ranks altogether, because of how wild it can be in this part of the Middle Lands."

"So there's other kids here?" Devon asked, looking up at her, his eyes pleading.

"Kids?" Maia asked.

"Children," said Robbins.

"Oh," Maia said with a smile. She knelt down, and looked into Devon's eyes. "Yes. There are a few."

"Where are they?"

"In different places, Devon. I'm sure you'll get to meet some of them soon. But since you and your father are new here, we have to get you settled in first. Okay?"

"Okay."

"What did you mean by 'wild?'" Robbins asked.

Maia stood back up. "You'll see."

The door opened, and they stepped out into another hall of open doors. In the rooms they passed Robbins could see that most of the patients were wearing blue uniforms that were similar to Maia's and Jaan's. As they passed by, the outfitted men and women were saluting her with raised fists. She returned each gesture.

They reached a pair of clear, sturdy-looking doors. Outside of them, Robbins could see Doctor Kile, standing with her arms crossed, her ponytail gently blowing behind her long coat. As the doors slowly parted, and they stepped out, he felt a rush of air. It took his mind all the way back, how many days he did not know, to when he had opened his eyes on the deck of a strange ship, with a clear mask over his face, and men rushing him through heavy wind and rain into some sort of cabin. He suddenly appreciated his and his son's burdensome clothing. He knelt down, and pulled Devon closer to him. The boy

73

was looking all around, at the buildings.

Robbins looked to his right, to where the rushing air was coming from. A small, blue vehicle that was hovering over the rock-like surface below, constantly pushing out air to keep its minimal elevation. Maia ran up to it, and a door on its side slid back. Over the immersive, rushing sound of the engines, she yelled something to the pilot and stepped back. Its door closed, and it pulled away, gliding down the stone path, turning left, and flying out of sight. The air in the area dissipated, but a small amount still lingered, floating constantly a foot above the ground. Robbins watched as Maia jogged back to them, and stood back up slowly, keeping a firm hold of Devon's shoulder.

"It's something you'll get used to," said Maia. "All craft here operate this way. It's safe, and very efficient. You'll see."

Robbins only nodded, still in mild shock.

"Doctor Kile?" she asked. "Is it safe for them to go now?"

"It is," said the doctor, turning to face them. She looked down at Devon, and smiled. Then she turned to Robbins, and set a hand on his arm, and squeezed. "Do you feel up to it?"

He took a look around, at the buildings, and the glowing sky that was full of gray clouds. "If this is it, then yes."

"There's actually quite a bit more," said Maia. "Follow me."

Robbins watched as Kile disappeared behind the sliding doors of the bright, blue-hued hospital building, and then took Devon's hand, as they followed behind Maia. The path ahead was just wide enough for two of the blue vehicles they had just seen to fly side by

74

side. The buildings on each side were each two or three or four stories high, taller and more solidly constructed than any that Robbins could remember from his earliest years on land. Their faces were made of wide, square bricks, with very few lines of connection between the large pieces. Their grating-covered windows appeared dark from the outside, and did not shine. And their roofs were rounded. It was clear that they had been designed to endure, and not to please the eye. The only one with any form of inviting construction and color had been the hospital.

The village seemed small to Robbins. It probably housed fewer people than some of the ships that he and Devon had lived on would have, when they could have. But he could see—beyond the narrow pathways between the buildings, and straight ahead—a massive surrounding wall. It reached higher than all of the buildings. On the side they were approaching, there was a large set of bulky, metal doors, set in a frame that reached almost halfway up the wall. Maia stopped about twenty yards short of the doors, and turned, and knocked on the single, much shorter door of a building to their left. It was pulled open, gliding slowly to the side, and settling somewhere behind the wall. In the doorway stood Jaan. Maia took a step back, and raised her clenched right hand.

"Commander," said Robbins, eyeing the man, who seemed much larger than he had in the hospital. He was several inches taller than Maia, who he now realized was slightly taller than him.

"Come in, Robbins," said Jaan, stepping aside. "And young

Devon," he said to the boy.

It was warm inside. Warmer than the hospital, and much warmer than the short road they had just traversed. The main room was a large, open space. On the right was what appeared to be a galley, with a sink, and metal counters and cabinets. Next to it was a small wooden table, surrounded by four matching chairs with soft cushions in their seats. Straight ahead there was a narrow, shadowy stairway, which curved upward with each step, ascending between two walls into an unseen second floor. And on the other side of the room was a sitting area, with two long benches, and two large, soft-looking chairs. Centered between all of the seats was a rounded, metal grating that covered a pile of dark, glowing stones. Three of the seats were occupied. Robbins suddenly recognized Fits, from his rescue, but not the woman in white, or the massive man wearing black, with shining metal on his arms and legs.

Behind Robbins, Maia slid the door closed, and locked it. Jaan motioned for them to sit at the hearth with the other watchers. They did not move. Robbins held his son by the shoulders. Jaan looked to Maia, and she walked up behind them, and set a hand on Robbins' shoulder.

"This is my home," she said, quietly. "You are both safe here. I assure you."

"Maybe," said Robbins. "I suppose. But it's dark, and closed off. And we're outnumbered."

"We are not violent people," she said. "Watchers preserve life, above all else. It is how Lwo, and its people, have lasted for so long."

"And out of everyone else's sight?" He eyed the group carefully. Fits may have saved his life, but Jaan had not exactly been kind, and the other two were strangers.

"Watchers!" Jaan shouted.

Robbins shuddered, and then watched as the other three stood up, quickly and firmly, and saluted him.

"Introduce yourselves!"

Robbins kept a hold of Devon, and listened, as one-by-one they stated their names and ranks. Fits, and Shil and Brun were all commanders, heads of their respective divisions. When they were finished speaking, he nodded, and thanked Fits. Then, he felt his son start to pull at him.

"I've seen them all before, Dad," said Devon. "They're not gonna hurt us."

"We only want to help acclimate you," said Maia, leaning up to Robbins' ear. "It starts with you knowing who we are, and us knowing who you are. The commanders are all here because your arrival is something none of us anticipated. And we have to determine what steps to take next."

"Okay," said Robbins, looking at the hearth. "I'll indulge. For now."

Jaan extended his hand toward the circle of seating. "Please."

Robbins watched his son walk ahead and sit on one of the benches, next to Shil. He held his small arms out toward the heat, and started rubbing his hands. Fits and Brun, sitting on the bench across from the boy, looked at him strangely, as if they had never seen a child's wonder, but Shil briefly put her arm around his shoulders. Robbins walked up and sat next to him. Jaan sat in one of the large chairs to their right. Behind them, Maia stepped back, and stood near the door, keeping one eye out a window, and another on their gathering.

"Lwo has been here for three hundred years," said Jaan. "I was born near the end of our second century."

Robbins blinked, trying to calculate. Jaan did not look much older than he was. "You're saying that you're twice my age?"

"More than twice, actually."

Robbins shook his head.

"I can imagine, coming from where you have, that it's hard to believe. But it's true. And the other commanders here are near seventy or eighty years themselves. The first thing you need to understand about Lwoans is that we age very slowly compared to ancient humans. It's a bit of a gift, from our ancestors, and the Lords."

"And who were your ancestors?" asked Robbins. "And the lords?" He could sense the discomfort from the other three commanders, in tiny movements, and unsteady gazes. He kept his eyes on Jaan.

"Our ancestors were from all over the world, places like where you were born. The old world."

"*Old* world?"

"Outside the storm that surrounds us."

"So, you mean *the* world?"

"Fine, Robbins. The world. Or, the part of the world they escaped. They fled north near the end of what we know as the collapse. Is that what you called it?"

Robbins did not want to agree, but he answered, hesitantly. "Yes."

"Very well. As the earth's great lands were failing–battered by flames, and brought low by quakes, and covered up by the oceans–there were several thousand of our people, from many different places, who fled north. Just as you did, however many days or weeks ago, with your son here.

"Our ancestors were merely seeking survival, and the Lords granted them a way to survive, if they were willing to take a risk. Before it was settled, Lwo was only a grouping of frozen islands. The Lords developed the means to form those lands into one. They had machines, but they had very few people to do the work that would be necessary. So, those few thousand risked death to come and establish Lwo. And many of them did, in fact, die for it. It is hard to survive in near-freezing cold with little food and shelter, as I'm sure you can, unfortunately, imagine."

"I can," said Robbins, looking at his son. Devon was now sitting quietly, and leaning into him, still listening, but clearly tiring.

Jaan continued. "But most survived. And, as expected, the north slowly warmed, so that Lwo became more tolerable. Eventually, the only real risk was the near-constant storm, and the winds that came with it. Their strength and constant pressure were unprecedented at the time, so over the course of several decades, the mountains that already existed were positioned around the edge of the land, so that inside the mountains the people could thrive. But they could only thrive to a certain extent.

"They knew their numbers would never be great. Life expectancy was increasing, but childbirth was rare compared to what the rest of the world had seen for so many years. Only one or two in every one hundred women gives birth, and among them, the vast majority only give birth once, to one child. Seeing this, the Lords ensured that the majority of the population would be protected, in the city, and in fortified villages. We are part of that protection."

Robbins took a deep breath, and shook his head. "Again, who were these lords?" he asked.

"My apologies, Robbins. This is all common knowledge to us. The Lords were simply a group of men and women, many of them very wealthy, some of them not so, who saw that nature had become unstoppable. They made a way for themselves and a few others to keep living after the collapse they had predicted, even as most people doubted them. They invested in land, and technology to manipulate that land. Then, over generations, their way of life became Lwo's way of life."

Robbins stared into Jaan's eyes, looking for deception, and for delusion, but found neither. "And what way of life is that, exactly?"

Jaan shook his head. "It is nothing devious. It is simply consciousness. We preserve the nature that's left, and protect our bodies from that very nature. We cultivate healthy crops. We consume abundant minerals from the water within the land. Keep in mind that even before the collapse, life expectancy was steadily increasing. We simply optimize it. Reaching a century in life was becoming common nearly four centuries ago. At least, that is what we have always been taught. What have you been taught?"

Robbins recalled his parents. They had said they were seventy, and looked fairly young, until their bodies expired from deprivation. They had told him that before the collapse began, people had often lived beyond one hundred years, and at the same time, had begun to have fewer children. It was why they had cared for him so much, they said. But time had caught up to them. In fact, none of the many elderly he knew in his youth had aged well in their last months. "I wasn't taught much about such things," he said. "We were trying too hard just to survive."

"That is unfortunate," said Jaan.

"For us, yes. Maybe not for your lords. How long did they live?"

Jaan glanced around the hearth, and with only a look, seemed to quell the commanders' growing frustration. "Some of them lived for centuries."

"Centuries?"

"Yes. Some of them even lived just beyond two centuries.

Others, one hundred fifty years. But what's important is that life here, as in any place before it, depends on our ability to protect ourselves from the land, and the weather that dominates it. That is where our duties come into play.

"With the land being formed as it was, it is not as stable as the old continents. Brun here, and his watchers of the ground, ensure that the surface is strong. We of the watchers of the sky maintain awareness of the land from above, and the winds that push over the mountains. Fits and his division at the mountains ensure that all are aware of anything approaching from the outside, and that none venture too far out. And Shil, and her watchers in the city, protects Lwo's future. They protect most of humanity."

"Thank you, Commander," said Shil.

Jaan leaned forward in his chair, and nodded.

Shil turned toward Robbins. "Now, what can you tell us of your life?"

Robbins was still taking in all that Jaan had said. Now he wanted to see this land. He wanted to see the city, where people were somehow safer than those in this rugged village. He wondered if the city was like those he had heard tales of in his youth, full of life, teeming with potential before they had sunken into the depths. He wanted to see how large the entire land was, and how high the mountains reached. He had only seen old peaks in the ocean, and occasionally bumped against them in boats and ships. He wanted to see them from firm ground that had not been drowned. He wanted to taste food and water, so rich with minerals that they extended human life. But, more than anything, he wanted to know how these humans, these Lwoans, had managed to survive for so long, and with no one else knowing about them.

He knew that the years before his birth had been dreadful. He knew it from his own parents, and the parents of his few childhood friends, and from old folks who had already lost grown up children to the call of the sea. And he had been born into a dying landscape, seen the elders succumb to the infertile land of the East Coast. The thought that this land had been growing and thriving, as the rest of the world sank into quiet extinction, was as unsettling as anything he and his son had ever seen, or fought through.

"You must have a story," said Brun, his voice heavy and imposing as it interrupted Robbins' thoughts. "We have shared ours. What can you tell us about where you come from, and how you managed to survive?"

Robbins looked across the glowing hearth, into the large man's dark eyes. In them he finally saw something familiar–mistrust. It was the same mistrust he was feeling. But he was trying his best to subdue it, because if their story was true, then he wanted to live in this place, if not for himself, then for his son, who might come close to the century of life they all expected, even if he did not. He knew now that he had to be endearing. "Luck," he said finally.

"Luck?" Brun said, almost scoffing. "I'm sure you needed much more than luck."

"No. Luck was all anyone had. The seas were dark, and unpredictable. You have a constant storm here? It's the same out there. Not as strong, not unbearable, but always there. Large ships were the safest places." He paused, thinking back. "I met Devon's mother on one. She had been born at sea, and taught me how to survive." He paused again, recalling her eyes and her smile, and briefly, the last time he had seen them. "She didn't get to live long, but she did teach me everything she knew. And together, we used it. We could tell if a ship was liveable by how it was moving, how much steam was coming from it if it was."

"What did these ships look like?" asked Jaan.

"Tall. Tall and dark. All of them were over fifty feet high. And they were long. Inside they were like mazes. And there were never more than a few dozen people on any of them, and most of them were falling apart. There was little real food. And there was so little sun that if you managed to run into it, no one could take it for long. You'd have to turn away after a few minutes, and sometimes they would turn the ship away.

"Some old man or woman died every day. And some young man or woman became old every day. So we moved, from ship to ship, sometimes with others, if we could trust them. Sometimes just the three of us."

"Robbins," Fits said, his eyes curious. "How many ships would you say you lived on in your lifetime?"

"Maybe twenty. Maybe thirty. I left land at twenty. I'm fifty

84

now. Maybe a ship every year or two, sometimes the same ship two years later if it had somehow lasted. Time moved slowly. You could smell death everywhere. So you found a safe spot near the top deck and just floated along. Every once in a while someone would manage to catch a big fish, or venture out near a peaking hilltop and find some decent seaweed, so we could eat well for a while. But that was only far out at sea. When I first went out, most ships stayed near what was left of the land."

"And what was that?" asked Fits. "What did the last of the lands look like?"

Robbins shook his head, and stared into the hearth. "Like rotted swamps. Dark, and graying, and smelling, with soil like oil, and always breaking apart when the ships touched it or pulled away. After a while I stopped expecting to see any land. We haven't seen any in years." He looked up from the glowing stones, and turned toward Jaan. "When can we see more of this land?"

Jaan looked back at him. "We have a lot more to learn from each other," he said, stern and sure in his tone.

Robbins nodded, and sat more upright, and looked to the other three commanders. "I understand. I suppose you have done more than enough, taking us in. It's just that I haven't seen any real life like this in so long. And my son, he never has."

Devon was still leaning into him, still quiet, but still awake.

"They could come to the city," said Shil. Everyone's eyes shot to her. "It is the safest place." She looked to the other watchers, and then turned to Robbins. "You would not need as much weight on your body. And on the way there you could see a great deal of Lwo. That is, if the commander agrees."

Everyone's eyes then moved to Jaan. "Very well, Commander," said Jaan. "They may join you in the city. Tomorrow. I'm sure they could use another day to recover, and to prepare for such a trek. There is nothing in that trip that they would be used to. But understand, Robbins, you and your son are still guests here. And we are not done talking."

Robbins nodded. "I understand. I thank you, Commander." He paused, and glanced around the room. "What about tonight? Where could we stay?"

"Commander, Sir?" Maia asked, her voice carrying over from the door. "Might they stay here? They can have the second floor, and I can stay here to keep watch. If you agree, Sir."

"Agreed," said Jaan.

The commander stood, as did everyone else around the hearth, following his lead. Shil touched Devon's shoulder before stepping away. Brun extended a hand to Robbins, and met his eyes as they grasped and shook. Fits did the same, and Robbins, quietly, offered him more words of gratitude. The tall, slim watcher from the mountains seemed pleased by the gesture.

As the commanders, one-by-one, departed her home, Maia stood at the door, saluting. Jaan was the last to leave, and whispered something, to which Maia responded affirmatively. Robbins stood there, watching, holding his son by the shoulders, as Maia slowly pulled the heavy door shut behind Jaan.

"Thank you," said Robbins, catching her eyes as she turned back around.

"You're welcome, Robbins," she said.

Devon pulled away from him, and ran up to Maia, and threw his arms around her waist. She leaned over and held him, smiling.

CHAPTER 5
CIVILIZATION

Night had fallen in the city. As had been the case for months, there was no sight of the moon, nor of any stars that might be shining above the clouds, which were steadfast, allowing only dark ambience, and the sense of their heavy, looming presence. The only light was from the city, from its buildings and from the low glow of the electromagnetic shield that surrounded all of them. The high gate to the nearly-invisible wall of energy was two blocks ahead, in Nico's sights, and in the sight of the citizen racing away from him.

Nico's steps were heavy, but swift, as he pushed through the crowd. The pavement was hard beneath the soles of his boots. The red lights emanating from his helmet and his shoulders not only gave warning to the people jumping out of his way, but lit the smooth, shining pavement behind the runner's fast steps. Nico felt the sweat trickling below his visor, and down his chin, into his dense jacket. How long he had been chasing the man, he did not know, but he was far from tired.

He stretched his strides to their limit, and began to close in. He reached for the man's shoulders, giving little thought to caution, or the man's safety. He lunged forward, overpowering the citizen as he fell onto his back, and rolled, slamming him to the ground. The thud of his body shocked Nico's ears, but only for an instant.

"Don't move!" Nico yelled, pulling both of the man's arms back, and pushing one wrist down into the other behind his back. From his hip he retrieved a metal clamp, and fastened the man's wrists together. He heard his own heavy, fierce breaths as he opened a line. "This is Lieutenant Nico," he said, huffing in and out. "Do you see me?" He looked up, toward the tops of the nearby buildings, and back and forth between their windows, and down to their doorways.

"We see you, Sir," a patrolman answered. "Moving down to your position."

From above, red lights glowed, and Nico saw the large engines on the puller's underbody. A few yards away, behind him, a jumper descended, pushing out heavy, cold streams of air from its rear engine. The crowd of people–sparse, and hardly moving along the walkways–stepped further away. Nico could feel their eyes, glued to the scene the runner had created. He steadied his boots on the pavement, and stood, pulling the man up with him, keeping his bound wrists in one hand, and squeezing his neck in the other. As the puller idled on their left, and a patrolman hopped out of its port side door and approached, the perpetrator squirmed.

Nico leaned toward the man's ear. "Just where did you think you were going?" he whispered. The man was wearing dark, close-fitting pants, a matching shirt, and plain boots. He would have easily blended in with the rest of the evening crowd, had Nico not spotted his subtle, suspicious movements.

"Nowhere!" the man yelled, trying to get the crowd's attention. "That hurts! Let me go!"

"Quiet!" Nico said, whispering again, squeezing his neck tighter. "It's supposed to hurt. Talk!"

"I told you," he said, his voice lower. "Nowhere."

"From where I stood, that's not what it sounded like. It sounded like you wanted to make a break through the shield. What's wrong? Isn't your record clean? Can't you request a departure?"

"I'm clean, Sir. I am."

"Then why run?" Nico held the man steady, and spoke into his helmet, ordering his system to activate the scan function. He looked at the man from the top down. Everything he was wearing displayed in reds and blues, with his actual body only a faint outline behind the colors. Near his right hip there was a single, oblong, metallic object. Nico let go of the man's wrists, and patted the device, and felt the man's neck quiver in his hand. "Clean, eh?"

"That's just-"

"Just what?" He kept his hand on the object, clenching it over the fabric of the man's pants. It was heavy, and cold, and shaped like a long, square rod. At its center something round protruded, a switch of some kind. Nico knew immediately what it was. "Don't runners ever talk to each other? These things never work. Had you managed to get over the gate, and get to the shield, you would have hurt yourself, and alerted us in the process."

The man shook, and grunted. "Tech gets better everyday, watcher!" he shouted.

Nico tapped the button on the device gently. "Does it now?"

"Don't!"

Nico smiled, knowing that with one firm press the man would be jolted into unconsciousness. But his unrealized fear would be more useful. Nico took a look around. There were still dozens of civilians lingering, watching. There was even one child, with a hand in each of her parents', all three of them staring right at him. He let the object go, and pushed the man toward the waiting patrolman in front of him.

"Once you're out of sight, take that thing away from him," Nico ordered.

The patrolman nodded, and answered "Yes, Sir," and took the man away, holding him by his shoulder and bound wrists as he marched him toward the hovering puller. The prisoner lowered his head, trying to hide himself as beams of red light illuminated him, and he was forced in by the patrolman. As the door slid closed behind them, Nico deactivated his own lights, and removed his helmet, and took a breath. The cool air eased his mind. He took a deeper breath, and felt his heart begin to slow.

The crowd was still keeping its distance, and slowly, they were starting to disperse, picking up their paces up and down the block, as the excitement had ended. Over his shoulder, he saw the other patrolman that had responded hop down from her idling jumper, its lights still flickering red, keeping the pedestrians at bay. She ran up and saluted. Nico turned around to face her.

"Lieutenant, Sir," she said. "I'm sorry. I lost sight of you after he took off."

"It's fine, Patrolman," said Nico. "He was fast. I would have left it to you, but there was no place for you to descend. Did you hear what I heard?"

"Yes, Sir. I heard him clearly. I'm sure his friends have gone by now, but he told them he wasn't waiting anymore, that he was leaving tonight, that he'd rather be floating away than live another day here. Then he turned, and saw you, and ran."

"Good ears, Patrolman. I'll need another witness when he has his day before the council. Make sure these people keep moving. I'm going to check the shield."

"Yes, Sir."

The patrolman moved back to her jumper, and adjusted its lights to yellow, and began pacing around the area, letting her presence be known, encouraging the remaining gawkers to move along. As she did, the puller began to ascend, and entered the first stream and sped away, heading west, and then turning north, toward the city's headquarters. As the area cleared, Nico walked east, toward the gate at the end of the block, at the city's edge.

The metal bars spanned twenty feet across, between two high-rising residential buildings. There were no people anywhere near it. The last entry to each building was ten yards before the gate, and most citizens knew never to wander so far. Only watchers, or those escorted by watchers, were allowed to cross non-entry points.

As Nico reached the gate, he stopped. It was five yards high, and its long, cold black bars were spaced just inches apart. The metal plank that topped the gate was a foot wide, and being lit from behind by the shield, it cast a short shadow downward. At the center of the bars was a single, narrow door, with a covered keypad on top of the heavy box that housed the locking mechanism.

Nico put his helmet back on. He dislodged his ranking pin from his chestplate, and held it in the slot above the keypad. The door sounded with a low chirp, and its interface popped up in his helmet display. He spoke his code quietly, and put his pin back on, and waited. After he was prompted, he entered another code on the keypad. He waited again, until the gate's status was displayed in yellow letters: 'Secure. Normal.' Looking at the gate, Nico saw no signs of tampering. Through the bars, ten yards out, at the edge of the paved path that encircled the city, he saw the faint glow of the shield.

Everything appeared as it should have. There were familiar, intermittent streaks of blue light, and he could feel the magnetic energy pulsing out. He stuck his free hand between two of the bars, feeling the energy even more as it lightly enveloped his glove like someone unseen. He pulled back, and grabbed one of the cold bars, and stepped closer. He looked left, and right. For as far as he could see between the bars, down to the tall, dark sidewall of the city's east entry, and down the empty way that curved toward the north, all was

93

clear. Straight ahead, on the other side of the shield, there was only the darkness of the forest, where he could hear, faintly, the steady rustling of branches and leaves, but could barely make out the massive trunks of the trees. He pushed off of the bars, and backed away.

"How exciting," a woman said, joy filling her low voice as it carried into his ear.

Nico turned around quickly, and held out his open left palm, ready to open his gauntlet. Then he spotted her, several yards away, average sized and with her hands visible and open below her waist. She was covered in a dark, hooded cloak that fell past her knees. Her arms and hands were covered in a pasty shade of pink. Her boots were black, but adorned in sparkles of various shades. Across her eyes she wore a large, tinted visor. A lock of her dark hair ran over her forehead, past the middle of the shining frames, ending in a gold-flecked point near the top of her cheek.

"You are too close to the edge," said Nico, lowering his hand. He walked ahead, and waved Loren toward the other end of the block. "Move along."

She followed his order, but moved closer to him as she walked, nearly touching his side. "I saw what happened," she said. "The chase, from ten stories up. You were near that ring, in the pathway, where people were calm, and then parted the way. What did that man say?"

"What man?" Nico asked. He looked around. No one was paying them any attention. Loren was keeping her voice too low to draw any gazes.

"The man who ran. Was he trying to escape, through the gate?"

"Yes. How did you get down here so fast?"

"My home is near the corner, and near a lift. I left quickly, and drifted down, and halfway there, I saw you brush by the man that sold me my favorite gown. He nearly fell to the ground." She pointed ahead, at the very spot, and inched closer to Nico. "I missed your tackle, and his shackling. I left our front door to see you squeezing, and him shaking, and your patroler taking. I hid, and walked, until I could see just you. What else did you think that man would do?"

"Hurt himself. Hurt someone else."

"Hey, that's good!"

Nico kept his voice low, and leaned his head toward her. "Stop that!"

"Stop what?"

Nico shook his head. They reached the end of the block, and he turned left, and she followed. "We do not need to speak here now," he said. "I am on duty. Don't you have somewhere to be?"

"Always, Sir. Always, but never. I've been in this city forever. Perhaps I should run as the captive did, rather than sit, and wait, until you all approve my bid."

"I'll warn you, right now, to follow all the restrictions. Outside the city, the danger has not diminished. This place is all you need right now."

Nico looked ahead, trying to ignore her as they neared where he knew she was going. The walkways were bright now, lit by a few storefronts and restaurants, and gathering places. They had turned off of a quieter street with couples and families. Now they were near younger adults, and those close to becoming so. He was still able to patrol, and there was so much activity that no one was paying his and Loren's closeness any attention. It was likely, in fact, that no one knew who she was. She blended in with the crowd, as she often did.

"I follow your rules," she said, raising her voice to carry over the chatter of the dispersed crowd. She lowered her voice again after a few pedestrians glanced in her direction, and spoke toward Nico's ear. "I just need inspiration, to see more often the span of this, the last of earth's nations."

"I understand," Nico answered. "How close is your destination?" He shook his head again, at his own words, and looked around. Still, no one was paying him much attention. But he could sense eyes shooting back and forth to Loren.

"Just down the road," she answered. She pointed to a painted orange building, two blocks ahead and on the right. Her hand drifted onto the watcher's arm, and he gently pulled away. "Aren't you headed that way?" she asked, letting her hand fall back to her side.

"I am," he answered. "And then beyond it. And then elsewhere."

"You know, I'm only at your side because I feel safe. The city, at night, is sometimes not that way. A runner nearing the edge can't be the worst that's happened here today. Can it?"

"That's the worst it's been tonight, and about as bad as it gets. The shield is strong, but most people know that with the right tools, it could be compromised. That would mean certain death, especially at night."

"Why at night?"

"How old are you, exactly?"

"Past twenty. How about you? Look pretty young to be who you are, second to the woman in charge."

"Nevermind that. You ought to know better. Warnings are broadcast at least once a day. Temperature drops and darkness make night travel more dangerous. And the winds are never predictable. If a runner doesn't have a craft, they're dead. A watcher would likely be dead too."

"Yes," Loren agreed. "But word of mouth is stronger than screens and robot recordings. Real voices carry more, wouldn't you say?"

"The right voices, yes."

"Have you ever left the city at night?"

"Only on assignment. Surveyors need escorts. But it has not been safe enough for such study in quite some time. So now, with the few newly desperate people here, we have to watch even more."

"Don't you think desperation is always worth more of your attention?"

"Yes I do. So, are you desperate? Are your friends?"

"No. Not me. Never. Just eager. Same with them."

"Would any of them ever run?"

"After I tell them about tonight? No. Never."

"Really?"

"Don't trust me? Sweet little old me?"

"Not yet."

"I saw you watching me, yesterday, from the first stream, near a walkway's gleam, as I sang and swayed, and my friends played. I didn't tell. Do you trust me now?"

Nico scoffed. "There was nothing to tell. Shows have to be observed."

"And what did you observe?"

"Talent."

"Talent that's running out. I need an out, to see what's outside. Will you look for my ask, in your division's tasks?"

"When did you submit it?"

"Exactly one month ago."

"You're near the end, then. You have to wait your turn."

"Seeing clouds, all day, is fine, when they let through a little shine. But for a long time, they've stayed gray. Seeing people, from above, at the tenth story, occasionally makes things less boring, like tonight, but even such things can become trite.

"It's been years since I've seen anything growing from the soil, or seen an up close range, or sensed any invigorating change from shifting winds rumbling over a craft's wings. Not since I was a child have I heard water crash, at the ocean, or the great lake, or at a river or a stream. Even then, it was through cabin walls. Do you understand my call?"

Nico stopped in his tracks, across the street from the orange building Loren had pointed out. There was a massive man there, standing in front of its reflective pair of doors, as they swung open and closed intermittently as people entered. He was large enough to be a watcher from the ground. His dense, vertically striped shirt was sleeveless, revealing the hairy arms crossed over his chest. His face was hard, and stubbly. His hair was short. His eyes were unmoving, and focused on the two of them.

"Do you know him?" Nico asked.

Loren looked, and waved to the man, who raised two fingers from his arm, discretely acknowledging her. "You're not my only protector," she answered.

"I see. It is time for us to part then. Enjoy your evening."

"He's *only* a protector. Nothing more. I'll see you again, from a high floor, or maybe within one. Thank you for the walk, Lieutenant."

Nico watched as she pulled her hood back, and let it fall softly onto her shoulders. She raised her dark visor as she walked in front of him, and winked. Beneath his visor, he managed to keep his eyes expressionless, as he watched her turn and head for the orange wall. The other people heading for the club started to react, saying her name under their breath, and then louder. The large man put an arm out as she neared him, and kept close to her, making the other patrons hesitant as he walked her in. The door continued to swing in and out.

As dancing figures and beams of colored lights pulled Loren gradually out of sight, Nico turned, and kept walking. Above him, a jumper flew north, the pilot navigating between several civilian craft. Ahead, there was another throng of citizens, heading to their homes, or elsewhere, as the tall buildings lit their way below the dark, threatening sky.

CHAPTER 6
SIGHTINGS

Only the bottom half of the village's heavy, metal entry doors slid open. There was a powerful gust, pushing Robbins back three steps, and pushing his son back behind him. In front of him, two airmen in blue stood, their boots firmly on the ground, their arms extended, guarding the two of them. The watchers had barely moved with the wind's force. Streams of cloudy air rushed through the narrow vents on their legs and arms and waists. Ahead of them, a red aircraft floated down, and turned, and backed its tail end through the half opening, displacing the wind through its engines and up around its body. Lights flickered at four of its corners, and at its engines, and beneath its tail, where after the echoing sound of something displacing, its ramp started to lower toward the stone road.

"Now!" one of the airmen yelled back.

Robbins took his son by the hand, and together they ran, between the airmen, to the edge of the ramp, and then up the incline and into the cabin. He picked Devon up under his arms, and rushed him to a seat on the right side, near the pilot's chair, which seemed to envelop Maia. He saw her look over her shoulder at them as the ramp began to close. He strapped Devon in, with two belts across his chest and one over his waist. Then he sat down next to him, and secured himself the same way. After he saw the ramp seal, and heard it lock, he looked forward, through the windshield, at a far-reaching landscape of pale green grass and gray sky. As Maia shifted the handles at her sides, and pushed down on the wide pedal below her, the craft bounced up, and shot into the sky.

"Good job!" she yelled back.

As Robbins felt the forces below them, and around them, carrying them at a speed he had never felt before, he gripped the bottom of his seat. He looked through the short window over the bench across from them, and felt the craft angle upward more, as they ascended faster, and passed by another expanse in the distance.

"Just like you said," Robbins shouted back to Maia.

"You can take your helmets off," she said.

"Right."

Getting a hold of himself, and remembering her instructions from the morning, he took off his helmet, a snug-fitting device that was as plain and gray as their clothing was, which now included gloves and overcoats. He pulled the gloves off next, and put them into the helmet, and then helped Devon take off his own helmet and gloves. They set their protections between them on the bench, and looked out the window across from them again.

Robbins could feel every vibration. Ships at sea, floating along in muck, were too big to feel much beyond a massive wave or more massive gust of wind. This bird, as Maia had called it, allowed every windforce to vibrate through its tan-colored floor and walls and ceiling. And the bench, cushioned as it was, still had an engine right behind the seat back. Maia started to level them off. Through the windows, there was now only more gray visible, and Robbins wondered how high they had gone.

"How long have you been flying?" he asked her. He felt Devon's hand squeezing his forearm, and without looking at the boy, patted it on the top.

"Forty years," she answered, proudly. "Don't worry. You're safe with me."

Robbins briefly thought of how young she actually looked, and how old she might be. "I'm not worried."

"Good," she said.

"How high are we? I can't see much."

"We're at five thousand feet, approaching the cloud cover."

Devon tugged at his arm, and he turned to him. "What is it, son?"

"Can we stop and look at least?" the boy asked.

"Look at what?"

"Maia said there was villages, and rivers, and big mountains."

Robbins turned, and looked out through the windshield. There was now a mist covering the view. He could still make out the land far ahead and below, but barely. "Isn't this enough, son?" He pointed out the windshield, and pulled his son forward in the seat, stretching the restraints. "Look where I'm looking. Look hard."

He watched the boy lean toward the front of the cabin, and look out past their pilot, through the windshield. Then, he saw Maia shift the right control handle, and saw her right foot relax. The bird started to descend. The clouds thinned. The air became clear again. There was a single, quick drop, and his heart jumped, but they leveled off, and he looked out and saw a vast, green landscape.

"Look, Dad!" Devon yelped, pointing.

Robbins felt a sudden sense of awe. As they settled at a lower altitude, he could see fields of faded grass far below. Between the great fields there appeared to be narrow pathways, leading to unseen places over short, rolling hills, and through flatlands. There were two rivers, not much larger than the pathways, criss-crossing in directions he did not yet know. It seemed endless, on every side.

"How big is this place?" Robbins asked.

He saw Maia lean forward in her seat, looking through the windshield to some point in the distance. Then she looked back to the set of glowing screens in front of her. She tapped the one in the center, and the map that was there increased in size, but not enough for Robbins to interpret it. She looked out again, and held steadily to both handles.

"From above, Lwo is very nearly a perfect circle," she said. "About three hundred miles in diameter, seventy thousand square miles."

Robbins thought for a moment. "That's not very big."

"It's plenty, when people can hardly traverse it."

"It doesn't look constructed, if that's what happened. Everything looks solid, like it's been here forever."

"Most of it was not manipulated. The main tundras and islands were massive, and already moving toward one another. With the right amount of human intervention, you get uniformity."

"Where are the people you said live out here? I haven't seen any villages since we left."

"We passed over one before I dropped back down."

Robbins sat back, doubtful still. Then, the engines suddenly blared around them, and he felt a jolt. He and Devon were both pushed back into the back of the bench, and he swung his left arm out over the boy's chest, and held on to both their restraints, as the craft dipped and spun to the right.

"It was just a question!" he yelled. "I'm sorry!"

Maia laughed out loud. "Well, you wanted to see more people!" she shouted back. "Hold on tight. I'll show you where they are."

Devon was laughing hysterically, and started to hiccup. Robbins looked at the boy, and saw tears rolling down his cheeks. He had never seen his son in such a state, and had never expected to. He kept his arm over the boy's chest. The bird stopped spinning, and then shot forward again. He looked to Maia's controls, trying to find the readout for speed, but it must have been on the far panel, obstructed by her and her seat. He could sense the winds pushing below the floorboards. Outside, the speed made everything a blur, and for the first time he noticed the sounds of debris bouncing off the windows. Tiny bits of rock or dirt, even wood, seemed to disappear as soon as they hit the glass.

The chaotic velocity lasted for what felt like hours, but eventually Maia slowed down, and they descended even further. As they floated along, and Robbins felt his son settle enough, they leaned out from the bench and looked through the windshield. The light seemed a little brighter, and they looked out as far as they could. There, in the distance, some miles ahead and beyond more fields of grass, they saw a giant mass of white. There was a haze of what looked like powder being carried up and down high-rising peaks that were formed of dark, jagged edges and tipped with white streaks. There seemed to be water flowing from one of them, down into the brilliant, blue lake that rippled as winds blew across its surface. Robbins quickly removed his restraints.

"Wait, Dad!" Devon said. "Do mine too. Dad! Come on!"

"Wait there, son," Robbins answered, holding his hand out. The boy quieted. "Where are we now?" he asked, approaching Maia's side.

She held her right hand up at him, halting his steps. "We're in the north. Look down, before the snow. There's a village, a big one. See?"

Robbins followed Maia's hand as she pointed, and looked and saw a towering structure. It was wide at the base, and narrowed as it curved up higher and higher. Past its halfway point there were two wide discs. Above them, the center swooped up further, toward the sky, where it ended in a sharp-looking tip. He could not gauge its exact height, but as the bird slowly floated closer to it, he knew it was much taller than any of the building's back in the sky watchers' village. And he was sure it had to be made of metal, not stone. The surface was a light color, like the beach sand he had seen small patches of as a child, and it was smooth, and shined like glass from afar. "What is that?" he finally asked.

"That is the Spire," Maia answered. "It is where the watchers of the ground live, and train. See all of the buildings surrounding it?"

Robbins looked closer, and saw the rows of structures that stretched out from the base of the tall spire, and saw that they blended in with their surroundings, and that there was no protective wall surrounding them. They were all close together, but they also appeared to be free-standing, exposed to every element he and Devon had been warned about before beginning their trip. "Now I do," he said. "I was distracted. How high is the spire?"

"About three hundred feet at its peak."

"Why would they need such a building?"

"It's not a building. Not exactly. More like an antenna, with survey decks, which also serves as an apparatus for training. They're in the midst of a session now. Look."

Robbins watched Maia tap in a command on one of her screens, and then saw the view on one side of the windshield magnify.

107

At the base of the spire he saw two rows of five watchers, all outfitted as Brun had been, in black, with their shining metal tech at seven points. He saw all of the watchers in the first row raise their hands, and then spread out, and then dash forward. The five of them reached the base of the spire at the same moment, and jumped straight up. They seemed to float up its side, as white streaks of air passed through the machines on their backs and arms and legs and waists. When the five of them neared the first disc, they planted their feet just below it, and jumped straight out, and floated back down toward the ground. Then, the second row of watchers did the same, and another row lined up behind them.

"That's quite a sight," Robbins said, flatly. "Can you do that, Maia?"

Maia laughed. "Not at the moment." She deactivated the magnification of the spire, returning to a better view of the sky. "We should get going. Care to take your seat again, Robbins?"

"Wait!" Devon yelled.

Robbins turned, and walked back to him, helping him out of the barely-opened restraints. Once the boy was free, he ran past him, and looked out the windshield. He was in awe, and frowned, knowing he had missed something.

"Does Brun live there?" the boy asked.

"Yes, he does," said Maia. She turned in her seat, and looked at him, standing there, leaning against the cabin frame, his eyes bright and wide.

"Is everyone there as big as he is?"

"Actually, yes. Lwo's ground, as strong as it is, needs strong people to watch it. They have to be able to push big rocks back into a safe place, or leap and run quickly through the raw winds. But they like it. Would you sit down for me now, Devon? I don't want us to be late."

"Okay," he replied, his eyes still wide and staring.

Robbins pulled the boy away from the windshield, and turned him, and nudged him back toward the bench, but the boy stood on the seat instead of sitting. As Maia turned the bird toward the port side, and the craft eased forward, the boy looked out the short window above the bench, back toward the snowy landscape. He kept looking until the spire was completely out of sight. Then, the bird stopped. Robbins finally pulled his son down, and set him back on the bench, and strapped him in, and then strapped himself in. When they looked forward again, they saw Maia staring off into the distance, as if waiting for something. Then, from her control panels, a voice came.

"Spire to sky watcher craft," a man called.

Maia tapped a button. "This is Lieutenant Maia. Go ahead."

"Good morning, Lieutenant, Sir. This is Private Lero. I saw you hovering. Can we do anything to assist?"

"No, Private. I just noticed a lightning strike. According to the forecast there's no rain due for another three days, but I thought I'd give it a few minutes before I head to the city."

"Understood, Sir. We are also tracking some small tremors in the west."

"Only small?"

"Yes, Sir."

"Very well."

Maia tapped the center panel, and Robbins leaned forward, trying to see. The map in the screen had shifted to a view of another spot on the land. She tapped again, and a line, partially obstructed, ran from one point to another.

"I see it, Private," she said. "We'll avoid that region on the way."

"Very well, Sir. We have two men already on site, and…"

"Private?"

The line had gone silent. Robbins felt his chest tighten, and his breaths shorten. He quickly retrieved their helmets, which had somehow stayed in place after Maia's daring twists, and handed Devon his.

"Private Lero?" Maia called again. "Are you still there?"

There was no answer. She looked at the map again. Robbins saw an orange light start to twinkle, and then flicker in and out. Maia shifted the handles and tapped the pedal, and the craft quickly ascended, to what felt like another fifty yards up. There was a better view now, to whatever she was looking for in the distance. Robbins could only see green for miles and miles, until two black craft shot out in front of them, flying over the landscape. They had wide wings, and they leapt over two paths running in front of them before they disappeared.

"I'm sorry, Sir," Lero said again, his voice slightly louder than it had been. "We had to send support. There's been a crack, larger than most."

Maia tapped an icon on the right panel, and briefly touched her helmet, and continued speaking, much lower. Robbins squinted at her, agitated and confused. She had secured the line to the spire. Now he could only hear muffled words. She shouted something, and shook her head, and turned briefly in her seat, looking back at them. Then, just as she turned around again, a bright light appeared in the distance. It only lasted for a moment, and then disappeared.

It had been intense, lighting up the expanse of land ahead, casting shadows of unseen things below. Robbins had turned away, and leaned over his son. As he opened his eyes, and looked up again, he heard Maia clearly say "That was a flash. Private! Did you see that!?" Then, her words became indiscernible again.

"What's a flash?" Devon asked.

"I'm not sure, son," Robbins said.

As they continued to listen to Maia's muffled words, Robbins pulled his arms away from Devon's helmet and shoulders. He turned, and looked through the windshield, and saw that the land below looked the same as it had. Whatever had just happened, however, was undeniable. A blinding light had entered and then left the cabin. It had forced them to turn away, and hold tightly to each other, as they often had at sea, on every ship and after they had left the last. Robbins managed to make out a few of Maia's words, just before a pause in her conversation. He looked at the back of her helmet.

"What break?" he asked. She did not respond. She was busy moving her hands across the control panels, going from one task to another as the craft remained idle, floating in the sky. "Maia?" he called again.

"Robbins, please," she said. "Give me a moment."

"I only asked what-"

"I know what you asked." She raised her right hand, silencing him. Then, she sat upright, and quieted, listening again to the line from the spire.

Again Robbins heard only distorted words as Maia spoke, and listened, and spoke again. She had lowered her voice even more. He made out only a few insignificant words, words between louder words that were no more intelligible. With each passing moment, his heart sunk further down, as he waited, anticipating the worst for him and his anxious son.

Maia sat back in her seat, and lifted her helmet from her shoulders. It floated back, and settled into the curved groove of her seatback. She reached toward the cushion below, and her seat turned in place, humming as it did so, stopping when she faced the rear of the cabin. She was noticeably upset, but he could see her trying to steady her demeanor, to make them as comfortable as they had been before. "There has been a change in plans," she said. "We will have to wait here."

"Because of the flash?" Robbins asked.

She narrowed her eyes at him. "Yes. You heard me then?"

"Not everything, but you were loud in the moment. What was it?"

Maia shook her head. "We don't know, not exactly."

"But you still knew what to call it?"

"It's happened before, just not in my lifetime."

"And it was never understood?"

"No. Never." She glanced out the window over their head. "Brun and his watchers are monitoring the situation, and have things under control. But they've halted travel to and from the city for the time being."

Devon sat up in his seat, and took off his helmet. "How long before we can go again?"

"I don't know, Devon. Not long, I'm sure."

"What if we went to ground?" Robbins asked. "Down to the spire, even. Wouldn't that be safer than just floating here?" Behind his seat he felt the starboard engine's whirring, as wind continued to pass all around them.

"Did you ever fly before coming here?" Maia asked. "Before today?"

"No," he said. "I only heard about it. But this *bird* doesn't exactly feel safer than being somewhere we could run if we had to."

"Neither of you could run on the ground, Robbins. Trust me. I barely can. And at this moment, this is much safer. I guess I should have flown you by the tower, so you could see for yourself how much wind tech can do, how strong it is."

"Well, we could turn around."

She shook her head. "No. I have orders. And they're for your protection as well."

"So what can we do up here?" Devon asked, lifting his helmet in his hands, as if he were giving up.

"Good question, Devon." She smiled at him. "How about we play a game?"

"What game?"

She turned to Robbins. "Will you move to the other bench? Strap yourself in across from Devon, and pull out the compartment under the seat. There's a box there."

Robbins did as she asked. He strapped himself in on the other bench, and then reached below, and pulled on a small handle, tilting the compartment out from the bench frame. He reached in, and found the box. It was rectangular, and made of a light-colored wood, with a grain that shined beneath the polished finish. He set it in his lap, and tilted the lid open, and saw four cubes slightly larger than his palm. One was bright blue, another was red, another was yellow, and another was white with interlocking blue and red circles on each side. Each cube was smooth, and soft to the touch, and made of some kind of rubber. Squeezing one of them, he found the surface to be tense, but he could still feel that it was hollow inside. The bird rocked with a gust of wind at the forward end.

"Toss the red one to me," Maia said.

He did as she asked.

"What's that!?" Devon asked, excited.

"I'll show you," she answered with a smile.

Following Maia's direction, Robbins tossed the blue cube to Devon, and kept the yellow and multi-colored cubes. The objective of the game was simple. They had to keep the cubes from touching the ground, keep them moving, and avoid holding more than two colors at once, which meant keeping at least one cube in the air constantly. The first two rounds did not last long, and Robbins eventually decided to keep his restraints off so that he could retrieve cubes from various spots in the cabin.

"It works better with more people," Maia said at the end of another round. "But we didn't have much. Not for, uh, kids anyway. Everything else we play at in the village is task-related."

"Like what?" Devon asked, whipping a cube at her right shoulder.

She deflected it with the cube she was holding, and laughed. "Target practice. Combat practice. Body flight."

"*Body* flight?" the boy asked. "What's that?"

"We have to train for when we might be exposed to raw winds. The gym in the village has plenty of obstacles. Sometimes it's fun, when you don't leave with bruises."

"When would you be exposed to the wind though?"

"Well, if a wall in our village is compromised, or if there's an emergency outside one of the other villages, or if your craft malfunctions."

"Malfunctions?" Robbins interjected from his seat. "I thought you said we were safe up here?"

"We are," Maia said, and turned to Devon, and winked.

With the three of them getting in rhythm with the game, the next hour passed quickly. Every few minutes there would be a rush of wind from outside, nudging the bird one way or another, and each time Robbins would demand that they not toss the cubes as fast or as high. In between the rounds, when their arms would tire, and they would take a break from the game, Maia would share more with them about Lwo.

They had not seen many villages on their trip, she told them, because she had so quickly taken them to a higher altitude, where winds were strong and fast enough to provide a relatively short travel time. But, she said, there were many villages throughout the Middle Lands, the space between the city and three of the four mountain ranges. Some of the villages were occupied by farmers, who tilled the land within them to provide food for the rest of Lwo. Some of them were occupied by builders, who made tools, and assembled craft, for both watchers and civilians. Some villages specialized in ores, drawing raw materials from the few deposits that were still safe to dig. And some villages held factories, where the people made textiles, or devices, or processed whatever was brought in by salvage ships.

"So, there's more than one ship out there," Robbins said.

"Yes," Maia replied. "Two more. You were on the Southern Hammer. There's one that works in the northeast, called the Ice Maw, and another called the Roamer. They all look the same, except for some color markings to distinguish them. Their crews are quite different, however. The crew on the Hammer loves the city, and they're not above rushing an inspection to get back. You two were lucky Fits was there."

"Yes, I'd say so." Robbins tossed the red cube around in his lap. "So what about this city? How many people live there?"

"Oh, close to one hundred thousand now. And more every year."

"Dad, how many is that?" Devon asked.

"A whole lot, son," he answered, and turned back to Maia. "And how many children would you say are there?"

"There are just a few thousand," she said. "There may be a hundred or so that are Devon's age." She turned to the boy. "Devon, have you been to a school before?"

He shook his head, and looked down at the yellow cube he was holding. "There was a nice lady on the last ship," he said. "She took me and one other kid to a room with a big window sometimes, and told us the alphabet, and showed us numbers and colors. Sometimes she showed us pictures of the planets. But she died. And my friend died too."

"Oh, I'm sorry. What were their names?"

"I don't know." He took a breath, and looked up at Maia, his eyes clear. "Are the teachers here nice? I won't know as much as the other kids."

"You'll know plenty, son," said Robbins. "You'll know about the world we all came from, and what it turned into, and what to look out for. You know how to survive. You might even teach them something. And you know your words. Your mother kept reading to you after the lady had passed. Remember?"

"Yes, Dad. I remember."

A monotone ring from one of the control panels sounded, interrupting their conversation. Maia tossed her cube to Robbins, and uncrossed her legs, and turned her chair around, and set her boots down firmly. Robbins could see a blinking light, but not any indication of what it meant, no matter which way he leaned and looked. Maia reached back, and pulled her helmet back on, and began speaking. Robbins heard her say, "Yes, Sir," three times, but heard little else. She strapped herself back in, and then raised her voice again.

"Robbins, put the game away," she said loudly. "And strap back in next to Devon."

He stood quickly, and put the pieces back in the box, and put the box back in the compartment. As he sat next to Devon, and strapped back in, and as they put their helmets and gloves back on, Maia turned the bird in the opposite direction. He looked out the windshield, and then toward her.

"We can't go to the city," she said, leaning her head toward him as if she could feel his eyes. "But don't worry. We're heading to a safe place."

"Where is that?" Robbins asked, agitated by new unknowns.

"To the Isle," she answered. "It's outside the mountains, northeast of our tower. Sit tight, and hold on. We have to make a pass by the Spire."

Robbins heard the bird's engines roar as loud as they had when they first ascended, and felt their speed increase. Out the window across from them, he saw the tip of the spire again, and then saw it disappear as they descended. They passed the white mountains next, moving even faster. Then more mountains appeared in the distance, as a blur of darkness over the grassy surface.

Maia called back to them again. "We're rendezvousing with Commander Brun," she said. "Hold on. I'm going to lower the rear ramp."

"Lower the ramp!?" Robbins yelled back. "Now!?"

"Yes. Don't worry. We do this all the time."

A moment later Robbins heard the ramp, the door they had used to enter the craft from the safety of the village, disengage with a loud click. He and Devon turned to face it, and watched with anticipation as it tilted down. Cold air rushed into the cabin. As the ramp's far edge neared the ground, bits of grass flew in toward them. Devon was holding on to him, tightly.

As the bird's entry opened fully, they could see the bright spire in the distance, and the grassy ground skipping away from them, just a foot below. The wind tugged at their shoulders, and past their knees at the ends of their coats.

"Hey!" Robbins yelled to Maia. "What is this?!"

"I told you!" she yelled back. "Don't worry!"

Looking out at the wild, open land, and feeling the chaotic air reaching for them, Robbins tensed. Devon was squeezing his arm with one hand, and holding the bench frame with another. They saw nothing but the quickly retreating landscape, and the harshness that awaited them if their restraints did not hold. Then, from the left, a watcher of the ground flew into view. Covered in black, and shining copper, the man hovered prostrate just above the ground, moving at the same speed as the bird. His arms were steady at his sides. His boots were shoulder-width apart, and from them, and the tech on his forearms and on his back, streams of dense air flowed, keeping him steady and fast. Then, in one motion, he flew up the ramp, and floated into the cabin, and landed on the floor, bumping the craft toward the ground as he did so. The streams of air from his tech dissipated, and behind him, the ramp started to close again.

"Robbins," Brun said, nodding as he lifted his helmet from his shoulders. "And Devon. How has your trip gone so far?"

Robbins stared up at him, at his thick, dark beard, and his shaved head. His dark brown eyes were steady, as if nothing spectacular had happened. "Just great," he answered. "How was yours?"

Brun managed a smile. "Pretty smooth. It would have been

120

nice if your pilot could keep a straighter line."

"Sorry, Sir," Maia said over her shoulder. She angled the craft upward, and accelerated again. As they tilted, and got closer and closer to the clouds, she increased their speed even more. "We're heading over the Northern Range now, Sir."

"Very good," Brun said. He walked up behind her, his metal boot soles heavy against the cabin floor. He knelt down, and looked out through the windshield. "How long would you say?"

"Less than an hour," Maia answered.

"Excellent."

Brun stood again, and backed away from her chair, and took a seat on the bench across from Robbins and Devon. He strapped a belt across his waist, but did nothing with the belts behind his shoulders. Robbins was sure they would not have stretched enough had he tried. Brun pulled at the wide, hard-looking collar on his uniform, and breathed deeply, and seemed to relax, as he looked up, at a tiny square window in the ceiling. Robbins followed his gaze. He had not noticed the window before. He saw only more, darker clouds. Then, he looked back to Brun.

"Why are we going to this...*isle*?" he asked.

Brun slowly lowered his eyes, and focused on Robbins. "The Lieutenant didn't tell you?"

"Not yet."

"The Isle is the safest place. With the flash today, and you and your son here not being fully acclimated to Lwo, it's the best place for you. We're trying to take care of you."

"What's there? On this isle?"

Brun paused, and leaned over in his seat. "*The* Isle. The great rock in the ocean. There are caves, and remnants left from Lwo's first settlers. There's enough there for a few of us to survive, for a few days."

"Couldn't we survive somewhere else? On the mainland? Maybe in a village far from the city?"

"You might. But if things got worse, probably not."

"Are we that much weaker than you all are?"

"On Lwo? Yes. Unfortunately you are. Your muscles aren't nearly as developed. Your lungs are not as open. You have no memory from birth of how to navigate the winds should you meet them in the wild. It's why the city would have been safest for you. But that, for the time being, is off limits. And might I add, Robbins, that we could have left the two of you in the ocean. You ought to be grateful."

Robbins felt his chest tightening, his face warming, and his eyes narrowing. Brun was large, clearly near or above seven feet. And he was strong. His arms and legs stretched the dense fabric of his uniform. *He's still just a man*, he thought. Then he thought of what such thinking always led to at sea, where bones floated in murkiness. "It was Fits that saved us, Commander," he said. "And I am grateful. But I also have instincts, which at the moment tell me-"

"To hell with your instincts, Robbins!" Brun snapped. "If you want to live here, you trust us. If you don't, then when we return, I'm sure the commander would allow you to take your ragged boat back into the rot outside the storm."

"Commander, Sir," Maia said, loudly, carrying over Brun yet somehow keeping deference in her voice. "Can we avoid such talk, please? For the sake of the child at least?"

"I'm fine," said Devon.

"I'm sure you are, Devon," she said. "I know you've seen much worse than loud squabbles. But there's not much humanity left in the world. And fighting right now won't help anything."

Brun sat back against the bench. "It's your ship, Lieutenant."

Robbins kept his eyes on the man. "I am only looking out for my son and myself, Commander."

"I know that. But we're looking out for you, and not just you, but every Lwoan. So, questioning Command will do you no good. Understand?"

"Yes. I understand."

"Good."

The cabin quieted. Robbins could feel Devon fidgeting, and took his helmet off, and helped the boy do the same. As Devon set the helmet down in his lap, and started to remove his gloves, Robbins noticed the few tears that had rolled down his cheeks.

"Stop that," he said, squeezing the boy's shoulder.

"I did," Devon answered, and wiped the lone streaks from his face, and squeezed his helmet in his lap.

"Almost there," Maia said aloud.

Robbins leaned toward her chair, and looked through the windshield. The bird started descending again. It swung back and forth, and the mist ahead thinned, and parted, and he saw the ocean far below. It was a greenish, foamy looking surface with peaks of waves crashing in every direction, and it was cleaner than any water they had ever seen from the ships at sea. Then he thought of how calm, albeit corrupted, their dark ocean had seemed compared to Lwo's. He thought of the storms his family had lived through, and how much weaker their winds had seemed compared to Lwo's.

As the bird descended further, and got closer to the violence of the ocean's waves, Robbins finally saw the island in the distance. It was indeed a great rock, shaped like a single, steep mountain peak, pointing, appearing almost to touch the sky. It must have been a thousand feet high. It was dark, but streaks of bright green and brown ran up and down its sides. And on the side they were speeding towards, there was a shadowy opening.

As they approached, and Maia slowed their speed, he could see the cave's details. The entry was an oval with a flattened bottom. As they slowed more, and entered, he saw dark, glistening walls at the rear of the cave, and on its floor there was a flat, metallic surface with a bright line down the middle. Before he could make out anything else, Maia had turned the bird on its center axis, and brought it down over the landing pad.

The windshield now faced outward, toward the vast ocean. Light mists of water began to touch it, flying up from the shore far below, floating into the cave. In the distance, Robbins could see nothing but more ocean, and the drab skyline. The range of mountains over which they had departed was nowhere. They had flown much faster than the vibrations in the cabin had revealed. Now he, and his son, were even further away from the only safety they had known in weeks. Maia flipped a switch, and outside, the craft beamed its yellow lights against the cave surfaces.

"For now, we wait here," said Brun, his voice booming throughout the small cabin.

"Yes, Sir," Maia answered.

As she decreased power, and the engines quieted and settled, Robbins looked over to Brun. Then he looked to his son, whose hands were still tense against the helmet in his lap.

CHAPTER 7
ISOLATED

Fits stood behind the pilot's chair in the gull, watching as Ensign Rial guided them toward the Isle's south-facing entry. Through the thick, glass floorboard, he watched the metal fin below, watched it cut through the winds, and a hundred feet below it, watched the wild surface of the ocean speeding away.

Rial was flying steady, her hands firmly on the handle in front of her, as she kept the craft on a tight line. Gradually, she decreased their speed. As they neared the cave entry, they saw the glowing, yellow light coming from the bird that had arrived before them. It was idled on the left side, deep within.

"Land close to her," Fits ordered. "We'll need to keep tight lines if the storm picks up out here."

"Yes, Sir," Rial answered.

"Once we're down, you stay here, keep your line open, and keep watch."

"Yes, Sir."

Rial spun the gull around, and set it down as he had ordered. She looked out the starboard side, through the windshield, and saluted as she made visual contact with the bird. As she decreased power to the engines, and they dropped another two yards, Fits felt the air slow beneath the craft's floorboards. He looked down and saw the end of the fin, barely touching the cave floor. Then, he quickly opened the starboard door and jumped out, and turned to make sure it closed firmly behind him, knowing that his ensign's knowledge needed to remain limited.

He walked toward the rear of the idling bird, and saw Maia and Brun step off of its lowered ramp, followed by the new man and his son. Robbins walked up behind the commander and the lieutenant, and stopped, holding Devon by the shoulders. He was staring toward the back of the cave, at the tall, metal double doors. The winds behind them all were still strong, but also diminished due to their depth in the cave, and the shielding from the bird and the gull. As Fits walked up, and stood behind the man and his son, he felt the tech on his boots spinning and humming, keeping him steady.

"Commanders?" Maia said, turning slightly toward Fits. "Should we enter?"

Fits looked to Brun, and with no words, agreed. They motioned for Maia to lead, and he followed behind Robbins and Devon as they all moved toward the doors. The two metal faces were six yards high. There was a small, dark pad with dark buttons, set at eye level where the two doors met. Fits watched as Brun reached past Maia, and the new arrivals, and felt the pad's surface before quickly attaching his ranking pin and inputting his access code. Fits followed suit, walking up, passing between the group, removing and attaching his pin to the pad, and inputting his own code. The heavy sound of metal disengaging echoed throughout the cave. Then, a thin line of light pushed between the doors, as they slowly slid apart, dragging dust and debris along with them as they were pulled into the stone wall.

They entered the old space with caution. From the ceiling, and the corners of the floor, bright lights flickered on. The bunker was not very large, just ten yards wide and twenty yards deep. On each wall the rows of old, narrow beds—with seats and metal cabinets between them—were in the same positions as Fits had last seen them, when last he had trekked to the Isle. The rock floor, and the metal panels running along its edges and between some of the beds, were still flat, still unbothered. At the rear of the bunker, near a corner, the control station, with its trio of screens and its high-backed chair, looked unused, as always. Beyond them, the wall of dark rock loomed.

"Pretty rudimentary," Robbins said aloud. "This is where the first Lwoans settled?"

"Not necessarily settled," said Fits. Robbins turned around, and looked at him, as if he had just seen him for the first time. Fits sat down on one of the beds closest to the entry, and went on. "This was where the Lords started, and directed the formation of the mainland. As the land grew, this place became less and less used. But it is still maintained, for an occasion such as this."

Behind Fits, Brun was still at the doorway, and input his code again. The doors slid out to close again, and left an opening just wide enough to allow adequate airflow, and to allow all of them to exit when the time came. Across from Fits, Maia sat on the edge of a bed on the opposite wall, and lifted and crossed her legs, and took a deep breath. Robbins and Devon sat at the edge of a bed next to hers.

"Is there food here?" the boy asked.

"Yes, in the cabinet," Maia said, pointing over her left shoulder.

She turned and watched the boy, as he eagerly ran back, and slid the cabinet door open, revealing a shelf full of packets, four-inch squares wrapped in soft, sealed foil. Fits recalled tasting the bland, almost pasty protein cakes once before. They were, at least, filling. And they could last for years. On the shelf below them he saw the sealed metal bottles of water. The boy took three of each, and managed to get back to his father's side before the bottles fell and bounced on top of the bed. He handed one bottle and packet to Maia, which she thanked him for, and then set aside. Then the boy sat down, and started to tear at the foil, and took a bite. He did not frown as he chewed.

"Commanders!"

Fits jumped up quickly, and jogged toward the rear wall, stopping in the center of the bunker. He quickly raised his helmet, and took in the air of the bunker, and knelt down. He set one fist into the hard rock below, and the other against the pin in his chest plate. He heard Brun's heavy steps come to a stop behind him, and then heard

Maia's steps end behind his, as they came up and knelt and followed suit.

"Emissary!" Fits said, and heard the watchers behind him say the same.

He heard a bottle of water dropped to the floor, but remained unmoved, waiting. He heard the man and boy's steps as they began slowly backing away, toward the entry. Fits hoped they would not try to run, as they likely wanted to, as he would want to, were he in their position, not knowing what was happening. Then, he heard the metal doors clang shut, cutting off the cool air from the cave.

"Who have you brought to the Isle?" the Emissary asked. "They are not of Lwo, that is clear."

The Emissary's overbearing voice, a voice both distant and near, both strong and passive, both real and artificial, rang in Fits's ears. He breathed easily, and finally stood again. He turned, and saw Maia and Brun do the same, as they all looked back at Robbins and Devon standing at the door, the father guarding his son as if they were facing an enemy. Fits looked up, and spoke. "Emissary. This man and his son have come to us from outside the storm. They have been with us for days, and we have done our duty, and cared for them. Just hours ago there was a flash on the mainland. We brought them here for safety. We did not intend to call you."

"I'm sure you did not, Commander Fits," the Emissary answered. "But called I was, by one of you through your entered code. Commander Brun?"

"Yes, Emissary," Brun said, nodding. "I called to you. I thought the presence of our guests should be made known. Both I and Commander Jaan thought it best."

"Might've told me," Fits whispered toward Brun, who only raised a dismissive hand in response.

"And did Jaan *order* this?" the Emissary asked.

"No, Emissary," said Brun "He only suggested."

"Very well. Guests? What are your names?"

Fits watched as Robbins walked forward slowly, keeping the boy behind him. His eyes were wandering across the ceiling, and the walls, as if searching for the source of the voice. But he would not find one. The system was hidden, even from leading watchers, and so were most of its outputs, behind panels even Fits had never seen up close.

"My name is Robbins," he said loudly. "This is my son, Devon. We come from the outside, from the dying parts of the world."

"Address me as Emissary, outside man!"

"Alright," Robbins said, his eyes still searching. "Emissary."

"How did you find us? How did you find Lwo?"

"We did not. We were near death. Your people found us."

"Where?"

"In our boat, in the rubble of the ocean, where most people have gone, and died."

"*Most* people, you say?"

"Yes, Emissary. Outside of Lwo there is only death now. The

lands have been overcome by the oceans, which are dark, and corrupted. Bodies not sunken, or devoured by the creatures of the sea, still float near the surface."

The Emissary paused before speaking again. "You are fifty years, and your son is seven. Is that correct?"

"Yes, Emissary."

"And you have been fed, and properly clothed for Lwo, I see."

"Yes. And we are thankful for-"

"I did not ask if you were thankful, outside man!"

Robbins stood silently, but Fits saw a rage flare across his eyes. The man looked back at them, at him and Brun and Maia. Fits met his eyes, concerned, and hopeful that his own apprehension was not visible in his demeanor. The boy reached for his father's hand, and squeezed.

"We welcome you and your child to Lwo," the Emissary said, finally.

"Thank you," Robbins shouted. Then, he looked to Maia. "Did the Emissary say 'we?'"

Maia nodded, and visibly exhaled, and then they all heard the bunker's rear wall disengage. Fits turned, and watched. The stone face was lifted from the floor, slowly rumbling as it was pulled up. Artificial light poured in from below. As it continued to retract, three sets of legs were revealed. Then came their waists, and then their shoulders, and then their always-kind eyes.

In the center stood Lord Andrew, who had become an

132

elderly-looking man, appearing to be even older than Jaan. He still looked strong, and very steady, but he was holding his well-hewn, aged wooden staff. His hair was still short and white, and his bright eyes were as green as ever. Over his shoulders hung a dark, knee-length cloak, and below it, over plain pant legs, he wore heavy boots, as all Lwoans always had.

On Andrew's left stood his eldest daughter, Lord Gem, who appeared to have nearly as many years as he did. Her long, gray ponytail hung over one shoulder. She was still as tall as Fits, and slender. And she was more than sturdy, with no need for a staff. Beneath her bright gray robe she wore a white dress, which stopped just above the knee, over white pants and white boots.

On the other side of the eldest lord stood Gem's sister, Lord Coral. Her long hair had faded some, but it was still a striking shade of scarlet, similar in color to her long coat and pants. She wore sparkling, silver rings on one hand, and around her neck she wore a necklace with a jewel that hung near the center of her chest. Only her boots were plain and dark.

Behind the trio of lords was their abode, a large, open space, with ornate shelves on its walls, and distant, decorated doors that led to places that Fits had never seen, and at its center, the three green, high-backed chairs, set several yards across from a wide, green bench with a high back of its own.

Together, the three of them descended two steps down to the bunker's floor, and walked up to where Fits, and his fellow watchers, and their guests were standing. Fits dropped to one knee, and lowered his head, and waited. Behind him, he could feel Brun and Maia do the same.

"Please rise, Commander," said Andrew.

Fits stood, as the eldest lord walked past him and his fellow watchers, and up to Robbins and Devon.

"I am Andrew," he said to Robbins. "I am the eldest Lord of Lwo."

Robbins extended his hand, and answered. "I am Robbins. This is my son, Devon."

"I know," Andrew said, smiling.

"I am Gem," said his first daughter, unmoved, standing in place along with her sister. "I am second eldest. Welcome."

"And I am Coral," said the youngest, her eyes bright. "I am third eldest."

"These are my daughters," said Andrew, motioning back with one hand. "Robbins, I must say, I understand your desire to protect your child. But he is safe here, I assure you." He knelt down, slowly, holding to his staff, and looked at the boy. "Would you like to meet us, young one?"

Devon shook his head, and bit his lip, and said "Nope."

Fits closed his eyes for a moment, and quietly breathed in and out.

Andrew stood, and let out a full-bellied laugh. "Yes, I suppose I wouldn't either."

"Lord Andrew, is it?" Robbins started. "May I ask, how old are you?"

"It is just Andrew for you now, my friend." He set a hand on Robbins' shoulder, and held it there a moment, until Robbins started to shrink away. "I am over two hundred fifty years now, though I can't say I remember exactly how many years. Over centuries of life some things become muddled. My daughters, though, I can say for sure are two hundred twenty, and two hundred fifteen. And you? You are only fifty years of age?"

Robbins looked shocked, but not quite as doubtful as he had the day before. He nodded once. "Something like that," he said. "Give or take a few months."

"Yes, I understand," said Andrew. "We know something of the outside world here. I know many of your years, if not all of them, have been filled with darkness; darkness none of us here could begin to understand. My parents, who were among the first Lords, told me about leaving the old world behind as it was falling apart." He paused, looking into Robbins' eyes.

Robbins looked back at him squarely, saying nothing.

"We would like to know about what you have seen," Andrew said. "If you will share it with us. Lwo is at great risk. The storm draws closer each year, and with a flash on the mainland, I am wondering how much time we have. Whatever you can tell us of your own experience may be useful." He looked away, to nothing in particular, then tossed his staff into the other hand and turned toward

Fits, Brun and Maia, and then toward his daughters. "Come, everyone. We have much to discuss."

The eldest of the lords approached, walking between them all and then to the steps, where he quickly ascended. His daughters followed closely behind him. Brun followed them, and Fits walked after him. Over his shoulder, he heard Maia and Robbins talking quietly. He heard frustration, and confusion, as the three of them trailed behind at a slowed pace. As he reached the floor of the Lords' home, he stopped, and turned, and looked, and listened to the three of them from a distance.

"I promise," said Maia. "It'll be fine."

"You could have told us," said Robbins. "Couldn't you?"

"No. Not this. Not even if I knew it would happen today."

"Today? What do you mean 'today?'"

"You had to find out at some point. All of us do."

"All of us? You mean *every* Lwoan knows?"

"*Every one*. It helps us to maintain order."

"What does? The fear that lords still live?"

"No. The hope of long life. And the Lords' first hope, to see the world restored."

CHAPTER 8
NATURAL ORDER

Shil pushed one knee down into the soil, and reached and pressed her hand through the brittle grass near the hazy, lingering wall of bright, rising fumes. The ground was hot. Even with her gloves on, the ground almost burned as she touched it. She pushed down harder, feeling for instability. There was none. In fact, the ground felt more solid than it would have before the flash. She thought of what heat and force it would have taken to cause such compaction so quickly.

Behind her, two patrolmen–Rienne and Duuq–stood, holding body-length shields at their sides, with the idling puller at their backs, providing further protection from the winds. Ahead of her, across the long, dark scorch mark left beneath the fumes, and with their foxes tilted upward and planted into the ground, stood two watchers of the ground behind them. They had been at the site for hours now. The four wings of their foxes cast the faintest shadow over them beneath the cloudy sky.

As the hot haze continued to dissipate, carried up and away by the cold winds, Shil continued looking at the ground, at the darkened patch that extended thirty yards in each direction, but only two yards across. She stepped forward, off the unblemished soil, and tested the patch with her boot. It was hard as rock, harder than the ground from which she had been safely surveying. There was nothing left of any plant life that might have been there, small or large. She took another step forward. For a moment she was able to stand, but the rising heat quickly shot up into her boots. She jumped back to her patrolmen. As she landed, Rienne braced her at the middle of her back. She swatted the young woman's hand away.

She brushed the dirt and debris away from her uniform, from the sleeves, and the pant legs, and the notched skirt, and looked over at the ground watchers. Neither of them was the lieutenant. Her teeth clenched behind her lips. The land had not seen a flash in her lifetime. *If this is its mark*, she thought, *his second should be here*. She thought of the citizens, not far to the west, who were clamoring about travel restrictions, already sending complaints to the council, though it had only been hours.

She looked at the private on the right, and called to him through their open line. "Private," she said, waving him over.

The man signaled to his partner, and leapt through the dissipating haze, floating over the slowly cooling rock, carefully angling his limbs to gather wind and direct his body downward toward her. He landed a yard away. She felt the slight vibration in her soles.

"Commander, Sir," he said, and saluted.

"Where is your lieutenant?" Shil asked.

"At the Spire, Sir. Commander Brun's orders, given that he

had to depart."

"Understood. What were his other orders?"

"To analyze, when it's safe."

"And what do you think this is, Private, by the looks of it?"

He turned toward the mark, and looked, and then looked back at her. "It's from a flash, Sir."

She nodded. "Just making sure."

"Yes, Sir."

"Do you think that it's safe now?"

He nodded. "Yes, Sir. Will you wait for the results?"

"Yes. Go ahead."

She watched as the private jumped back across the warm surface, to his partner. They looked to each other, and disappeared behind their foxes, and quickly reemerged holding spikes. Each long, metal pole held a saucer-shaped receiver at one end, and a wide, triangular blade at the other. A line of metallic cord ran up from each blade to the receiver. Each of the receivers was now blinking red at three points around the edge.

Shil looked at her patrolmen, and then watched along with them, as the two men took careful, but steady steps out onto the darkened streak of earth. The remaining heat was apparently more bearable for them, with their heavier, more metallic soles. Their stances were firm as they raised their spikes, and then thrust them down into the hardened ground. Clouds of pebbles flew up and out, and into the sky, and toward Shil and her watchers. She raised an arm to block her unshielded neck. The readout in her helmet immediately indicated a temperature spike. The submerged, pointed ends of the spikes had stopped at even hotter points beneath the surface. She knew then that nothing below, whether a small creature, or a simple seedling, could be alive.

With some trepidation, she ordered her patrolmen to stay in place, and walked out, toward the two ground watchers. The surface was still warm, but not as unbearable as it had been just minutes before. The tech on her legs and arms and hips and back hummed, as wind was pulled through it all, keeping her steady as she took careful steps.

"What do you see?" she asked as she reached the man on the right.

"Increased temperatures, Sir," he answered, holding a hand up to his helmet as he viewed the output. "But only near the surface. Everything far below seems normal."

"How far below?"

"The maximum distance, Sir. One hundred yards."

Shil could not help her next thought. No past watcher, on the ground or otherwise, had ever found a source for flashes. Neither had any scientists. And no Lwoan had ever reported being at the site of a flash as it occurred. She asked anyway. "Can you identify what caused it?" She could hear the doubt in her own voice.

The towering men looked to each other first, and then back down at her. "No, Sir," answered the one on the right. "We've never-"

"I know," she interrupted, raising a hand, almost apologetic. She thought for a moment, about what every Lwoan knew, that the depths of the mainland had been formed in part by connecting the massive islands that had first found each other in the north, as if escaping the dying planet. The connections had been formed from heavy ores and rock, and had eventually melded into the surrounding crust. And they had never failed. "Now what, Private?" she asked.

"We make a record, Sir," he answered. "Then we report. Then we return to duty. But one of us will remain here, for every shift until Commander Brun orders otherwise."

Shil crossed her arms, and looked down at the ground, and thought. "Has your commander considered a dig?" she asked, looking back at the man.

"A dig, Sir?"

"Yes. You do know what a dig is, Private?"

He nodded. "Yes, Sir. Of course. But it's been years since it was safe to dig outside a wall, outside a village. Neither of us were even in the ranks the last time it was done."

"I know that. It's also been many more years since we've seen a flash."

"Respectfully, Sir, we traverse this ground daily. Such an undertaking would not be advisable in these conditions. The winds are not getting any weaker."

"I know that, Private." She stared back at him.

He looked to his partner, and then back to her. "But I will

bring it to both our leaders' attention, Sir."

She nodded. "Very good."

She saluted the pair, and they returned the gesture and backed away. As she turned, and approached her patrolmen, who were still steady, holding to their shields in front of the hovering puller, she considered something from her past. The day's events had cast her mind forward, and far back, over and over again. "There's nothing else we can do here," she said, passing between the two. "Let's go."

The patrolmen turned, guarding her as she stepped up into the puller, and entered behind her. As Duuq took the pilot's seat, and Rienne took a seat on the bench, Shil looked out through the closing door. One of the watchers from the ground had mounted his fox, and pointed it northward. As Duuq opened the puller's engines, and they began to ascend, she saw remnants of the smoky heat from the site of the flash, floating away like a breaking cloud, yards above the long mark of hardened, lifeless soil. Duuq slowly turned the puller westward.

"Head south," Shil ordered. "I need to see someone before we head home."

"Yes, Sir," he answered.

He turned the puller to its new heading, and it glided forward. Shil directed him toward a village on the map that was twenty miles away, and he took them up to one thousand feet, and accelerated. The engines rumbled beneath them, and it was only minutes before the village appeared in the distance. It was made up mostly of long rows of tilled soil, all surrounded by a wall made of stacked rock, some of it natural, some of it manmade. Behind the farmland there were several blocks of buildings at the southern end. As they started to descend, Shil looked out and saw the various patches of different crops, most of them either extremely bright or neutral in color. As they neared the ground, and approached the northern end, she saw the boxy, metal frame surrounding the entryway in the rock wall. The blocks of buildings disappeared behind the wall as they neared the heavy-looking doors. The watcher stationed at the entry, fifty feet ahead and ten feet below, stood on the right side of the doorway, with his fox upright on the other. He saluted as they approached.

"Open a line," Shil ordered, walking up behind Duuq. After a short beep and a click, she spoke. "This is Commander Shil. Requesting entry."

"Yes, Commander, Sir," the man answered.

Shil watched as the ground watcher walked up to the doorway, and placed his hand into a short relief, and entered an unseen code. They waited for a moment, and then, slowly, the doors slid open. The entry was just high and wide enough for the puller to float through with a yard of clearance on each side. They passed the guarding watcher, and Shil heard the heavy, clanking sound of the doors shutting and locking behind them.

As they moved ahead, Duuq kept the puller just a few feet above the ground, carefully following the path laid out by flat, blue stones between the large patches of crops, and keeping the power to the engines at a minimum. A four-foot-high, solid perimeter surrounded each crop, and a nearly-invisible netting provided another ten feet of protection from any debris. Even so, only so much force from the puller's engines would be acceptable. Too much could ruin a young crop, or even a sowing, and some of these crops, they all knew, were meant for the city.

Placed in each patch of crops were a handful of machines, treaters and harvesters consisting of long, flat ducts or sets of narrow bars, and mounted to axles attached to motorized wheels. The machines were following patterns, rolling over rows of fruits or vegetables, spraying and probing, and occasionally digging. There were only a handful of farmers visible—one stood near an idled machine, a few others were walking slowly near fences. One of those near a fence, an older-looking man in a wide hat and battered brown clothing, made brief eye contact with their puller before going back to his work.

The path between the crops held compacted soil beneath the blue stones, and was leading them to the shadowed southern end of the village. As they moved ahead, Shil saw Duuq's eyes start to wander, and then stop, as he caught sight of a patch of potatoes on the right. Then his eyes lit over to a few bushels of bright, orange carrots that had just been pulled and were sitting in an old-looking box.

"Focus," she ordered, leaning over his shoulder, watching their surroundings. "Keep straight." He listened, and looked straight ahead, following the path. Then, she spotted the landing pad, one

144

hundred yards ahead, in front of a plain, four-story building with a wide, open door on its ground level. "Right there," she said, pointing.

Duuq eased them forward, making his way past the last gated patches of crops. As they cleared the pathway, he guided the puller over the dark, metal surface of the pad, and turned it in place. As they descended, Shil felt the soft thump below the floorboards, as the pad's clamp clutched their underbody rod. She was hopping out the sliding door before the puller's engines had fully closed.

"Stay here," she ordered, just barely looking over her shoulder. "Both of you."

As the two patrolmen acknowledged, and the door closed behind her, Shil turned and headed for the main road. It started just beyond the warehouse they had touched down in front of. There were no other craft in sight. There was, however, one large one hidden away, in case of emergencies, as was required for all villages. She could not remember exactly where the hangar was.

The road ahead was just wide enough for small groups to walk through. In all there were just three blocks of buildings, and they were short blocks. None of the buildings reached higher than four stories, which was the height of the surrounding wall. The first block seemed to be all businesses–supply shops, a pair of restaurants. Between them were a few plain, numbered doors. A pedestrian, a woman who was perhaps Shil's age, greeted her with a smile as she passed by.

The second block was all homes. Some opened window

shades gave way to soft lighting, and peaceful figures moving about. She could not clearly make out any faces, but she could feel their attention. A commanding watcher, and one from the city clad in bright white, was a rare sight in any civilian village. She walked on, and greeted another pedestrian, an older-looking woman, with a wave.

As she neared the village's southern end, Shil could see the mortar lines in the surrounding wall. The wall's massive rocks seemed more jagged than she remembered. And there was barely any room between the wall and the nearest building. The space near the wall was shadowed, with no light from a shield source to push through from above. Past generations had discovered that electromagnetism had a detrimental effect on crop growth. For all the years since, the people who lived in farming villages had embraced a certain amount of risk, foregoing comfort for what they knew to be the most essential work. This simple nobility, Shil knew, was one of the reasons her old teacher had chosen to settle in such a village after leaving the city.

She stepped to her left, off of the narrow road, and turned, and tugged on the handle of the heavy, wooden door to the four-story building. As it rolled back, she stepped through, and then listened as it closed behind her. The tech around her body went from a low whisper of movement to idle silence. She walked forward, looking around the large, open room as she did so. There were short rows of round tables, each surrounded by four chairs. The walls were made of a soft-looking, processed material, and painted in bright gray. The ceiling was six yards high, with short arches forming the cross beams.

All of it drew attention to the rectangular table at the rear, where her old teacher was sitting.

She passed quietly by two older men sitting at a table on the left, each of them focused on separate projected screens bearing rows of text below boxed images. A younger woman, perhaps near Maia's age, was sitting at a table on the right, focused on her own work. Shil stopped as she reached the last desk, near the rear wall, and looked down at the man sitting there. His hair had turned fully gray since she had last seen him, but was still woven into fine braids that hung down to his shoulders. His skin was still a healthy shade of shining brown. Over his broad frame he wore a heavy, powder-colored, weather-beaten jacket that looked the same as it always had. As he looked up at her, away from the computer tablet in his hands, there was an indifference in his eyes.

"Commander," he said. "Welcome."

"Thank you, Doctor Taj," she replied.

"It's just Taj, Commander. In my office?"

"After you."

Shil extended her right hand to the side, and then removed her helmet, and held it under her left arm as she followed him. They passed the clear door to the lift, and the narrow, open stairwell, and went through the swinging wooden door that was hidden beneath a short overhang. Taj's office was small and inviting, with eight-foot ceilings and minimal but warm lighting. There was a single, wide desk, with a soft chair behind it, and a large computer station on one

147

side near the wall. In front of the desk there were two contoured, rigid-looking chairs. The wall several yards to the left of the desk was made of shelves, and held ornate metal boxes. The plain floor was decorated with a woven rug, which sat between the wall and the desk, where it was weighed down by two legs. Shil sat in one of the hard chairs, and watched the old man as he moved around the desk and sat down across from her.

"Doctor," she said. "It is good to see you."

"And you, Commander," he answered.

"Please, just call me by my name."

"Very well, Shil. If you'll address me as you always did."

She nodded, and watched his eyes, pressing into hers.

"Why did you come this time?" he asked.

Shil hesitated. The trip had not been an order, not something about which she had consulted any of the other commanders. She had come to this village, to the most learned man on the mainland, because of the doubt she could not shake. "It's the ground, Teacher," she said. "I fear it may be giving way, after all this time."

Taj took a deep breath, and leaned forward, joining his hands and resting his elbows on the desk. "And why do you fear that?"

"There was a crack in the surface earlier today. And from it, a flash."

"A flash?" he asked plainly, lowering his voice.

"Yes. Did no one in the village see it?"

He shook his head. "Not that I know of, and I've been up

since dawn. I would have heard."

"That may be good, but it may not."

"We haven't had a flash since before you were born," he said. "Are you sure?"

She nodded. "Yes. It was confirmed by watchers from the ground who witnessed it, along with a handful of others."

"Others?"

"Not everyone was sleeping, Teacher."

Taj laughed under his breath, and looked at her, and sat back in his chair. "So why did you come here?"

"I was hoping that you would study it for us."

"For whom?"

"For the watchers."

He hesitated. "There are scientists in your ranks. Did you not ask them?"

"I just left two of them. Their tools are limited."

"So are mine."

She felt her whole face pursing with doubt, and did not try to hide it. "Teacher, please."

"Right. I told you too much, you and the few others that could bear it."

"They are all watchers now."

"So I've heard. Go on."

"The readings from the flash site are insufficient, only one hundred yards deep, and revealing no anomalies. But flashes *are* anomalies. I imagine you can do much more."

"Maybe, Shil. The tools are old. And I've only examined them, never actually used them." He sighed, and stroked the stubble near his chin. "What does Commander Brun say about all this?"

"He's on another assignment. This one falls to me, for now."

"That's a bit strange, if there really was a flash."

"There was, Teacher. And yes, it is strange, but that is where we are."

"And what about Commander Jaan?"

"He passed the ground on to me, with Brun's approval."

"As if he could say otherwise."

She smiled at him. "You know the ranks well."

"I suppose, for someone who's only taught watchers before they left the classroom."

"Those were the first, most important lessons."

"You know, there are others you could consult. Three others, actually."

Shil paused, and thought, about how the Lords might have already known, from the Isle's visitors or from their own data, and could either be planning or not planning to assist. "Watchers are the first responders, Teacher. The Lords are our guides, keepers of our history, history that they have already passed down to all of us. They have aged far, and we have learned so much without them. With your help, we may be able to solve this on our own."

Taj stared back at her. "Some time ago, Shil, I told you and several other watchers that this could happen. But none of you listened. Do you remember?"

"I do," she answered. "We were young, back then."

"You, maybe. Your predecessor was not. Nor was Jaan."

"I'm here now, Teacher. And with Jaan's approval, even if it was not explicit."

"Would he make it explicit?"

She leaned in, and pressed her hands into the desk, and looked into her old teacher's eyes. "Whether or not he would is something that he does not need to know. You can work in secret, can you not?"

Taj leaned back into his seat. "Yes, I suppose I could."

"You suppose. Teacher?" She stood, slowly, and set her helmet on the desk, and looked down at him. "I could make this an order. I do not want to."

He nodded. "I know. You will not have to."

Shil nodded, and folded her arms, and watched as Taj stood, scratched his chin, grumbled to himself, and walked over to the wall of shelves. He set a hand on the lid of one of the boxes, one made of smooth, gray metal, with blue gems that formed four sparkling squares on the front side. He raised the lid, and retrieved a small, black data drive. This was the fourth time Shil had visited Taj's office since she had become the city's commander, the second time since he had moved it out of the city, but it was the first time she had seen him retrieve anything from one of his old boxes.

"I've lived well over one hundred years now," he said, closing the lid, and turning back around. He walked back to the desk, and sat. "I do not fear dying. None of us should. After what humanity did to this world for so long, it should be expected. I do, however, fear the quality of our lives deteriorating over time, and Lwoans dying the way the old world did."

"I fear the same," said Shil. "And if the people think their time is short, they will become unmanageable."

"They still could." He tapped a button, activating his computer's screen. "The storm picks up every year, does it not?"

"It does."

"What do you think will happen if the city runs out of space?"

"Another reason to examine the flash, Teacher. The city's already near its limit. We'll need another for sure if we can't manage to keep the ground stable. And I'm not sure we could build another."

"Neither am I. The city took decades to finish."

"But, Teacher, I am sure we can manage this, if we know more."

She watched as Taj slid the open end of the small drive into the computer's front port. After a lengthy series of keystrokes, his face suddenly glowed with the light of something new in the display. He tapped the screen, and an image projected out from the small lense in the side of the screen's housing. The expanding beam of light revealed a multi-dimensional map of the mainland. Shil looked down at the wide, multi-colored picture of Lwo's landscape, as it touched the edges of the desk.

"Here," she said, pointing at the spot of the flash site. "That's where it was. Twenty miles north of us."

Taj stood, and looked at the location. He ran his hand through the warm light of the projection, and then entered a command on the keyboard, placing blue arrows around the spot, and magnifying it. "That's closer than I expected," he said. "I wonder how we missed it?"

"Farming is tiring," said Shil.

"I'm no farmer."

She watched him, as he eyed the spot on the map. "What are you thinking, Teacher?" she asked.

"The phenomenon of flashing has always confused us," he said. "They seem to be the result of some unseen instability, but the Middle Lands put the least strain on the ground. The people are spread out here, in villages with leagues and leagues of space between them. And there are no mountains weighing on the surface."

Shil looked to his eyes, but he would not meet her gaze. "No mountains," she said. "And no heavy buildings either."

He looked up at her. "The city is far away. I did not say that had anything to do with it."

"I know, Teacher. I'm saying it."

"I never taught you to jump to conclusions. Flashes have been few and far between, and they were always unpredictable. They could be the result of anything; something deep below the surface, something carried in by the storm. Anything." He looked back at the glowing projection. "I'll need to do some up close work, to try to find anything at all."

"I can get you anything you need, Teacher."

"I just need time. And a craft."

Shil stared at the highlighted spot on the warm, luminescent map. "You'll have one by tonight."

CHAPTER 9
UNREST

The crowd at the city's south entry was on edge. Dozens of citizens had formed lines across the whole width of the road, some of them standing even against the walls of the buildings on either side of the entry's wide, high-reaching metal gates. There were only inches of space between any of them, and all but a few of them were shouting, in unison, at the top of their lungs, 'Let us go!' Let us go!' Some of them shook their fists in rhythm, at the watchers stationed on the platforms on either side of the gates. Through the narrow, crossed bars, and over a shorter solid door, and through the thin haze of the shield, they could see the distant peaks of the Southern Range. The mountains were getting darker and darker, as the gray light of day continued to fade, teasing the citizens with the freedom of the land.

The watchers' platforms were two stories high. Mounted high above each of them, and framed with thin speakers, was a wide display. Repeatedly scrolling across each screen, in bright letters, was their most recent report: 'Due to a weather anomaly, all outside travel is prohibited until further notice.' It was the 'further notice' that had brought out the first few protesters, one of whom knew Loren, and had called her down, hoping that she might compel the crowd. But she had only watched, from the back end of the formed lines, hooded to cover herself, and guarded by her most dependable employee. The two of them had stood there for over an hour, as craft approaching the gate were turned away one after the other. Some of their pilots, as Loren overheard, had returned on foot, increasing the crowd's numbers.

"Citizens!" the watcher on the left belted out through the platform's speaker. "You are welcome to stay and protest, but the gates will not be opened until it is safe. It will be daylight at the earliest."

"Let us go!" the crowd yelled back. "Let us go!"

Loren remained quiet, but did shake her fist.

"It has only been twelve hours!" the watcher continued.

They chanted louder.

The two watchers looked across the wide gap between them, to each other, and shrugged. They had been making the same announcement every twenty minutes. And the protesting had continued on. Loren recognized some of the others in the crowd, from their storefronts, and from her occasional public transport rides, and even one from her building, an older woman who never made a fuss over who she was, or her latest performance. The woman owned a market. Loren was sure the travel restrictions must have interrupted a delivery for her to walk so far.

High above the crowd, another two stories above the platforms, there were two pullers idling in the first stream, their lights intermittently radiating orange to indicate caution. They had been there the whole time, turning away civilian craft. Loren found it hard not to hear their engines, even though they were not fully open, even though the protesters had only grown louder. She looked back down. Over her head, a few inches in front of her, she saw Chad reach up and tap the plain, black receiver that was wrapped behind his left ear. She reached into her hood, and tapped her own receiver, and increased the volume.

"I don't think you can make it," Chad said in his heavy voice. "How about you try tomorrow?"

"No," Loren replied. "Tonight." She looked to her sides, wary of any attention. The women on either side of her were looking between the stage and Chad. "It's the perfect time, when there's no light, and no one, no onlookers, to expect such a flight."

"No onlookers?" he said. "Are you and I still in the same place?"

"We are indeed, and your deed is being done, drawing attention from admirers, while upon me looks not one."

"I don't think they're admirers. More likely they're afraid."

"As well they should be, once you start to earn your fee."

"This isn't the right moment. Where's your man?"

"He'll be here soon. Do not doubt, or assume, any unthought thing, from me, or my drummer boy."

"The man's barely finished growing."

"To you, none are. He went to points in the city near and far, and found out what once could not be."

"We'll see."

"Keep in mind, your payments are not for your thoughts, but to guard, and to mind me."

"Fine."

Loren looked up again, and turned around, and around again. The buildings that towered above were aglow, with dim lights from safe homes. The first stream held very few craft, even for the later hour. The entire city, she was sure, was now aware of the restrictions. They had been broadcast from headquarters intermittently from midday on. But there was one craft, a mile out, that was on approach, and closing in fast on the entry. It was small and narrow, a jumper. She tried not to smile as it passed over, and Nico's rank markings on its white underside were revealed.

"Look who's here," Chad said, into her ear.

Loren moved up, and stood closer to him, and held his arm, and pulled her hood forward another inch. She watched as the jumper descended from the stream, and settled on the left platform. As it idled, the lieutenant sat up, and hopped off, landing near the patrolman, who turned to face him, saluted, and stepped aside. Nico approached the platform's computer station, and motioned toward the pullers above. In an instant their lights changed from orange to red, and one of them started to slowly descend.

"You're up," she said to Chad, and rubbed her hand gently up and down the back of his heavy shirt.

"I know," he answered. "Let me work."

Nico held one arm up, and spoke through the speakers above. "Citizens!" he called. "The anomaly outside the city has passed, and is being studied. All gates will reopen tomorrow afternoon. You are ordered to disperse until then."

The crowd groaned, loudly. Loren looked around, and saw no one moving. Then a few of them started to shout back their objections.

"Disperse!" Nico ordered, loudly. "Or, be apprehended, and held for two days. We have plenty of open cells."

Still reluctant, and still noisy, the people started to separate. Loren stood closer to Chad, almost hiding behind him. Then, as he moved forward, she walked with him, gradually letting him get more distance from her. A few of the protesters noticed them, moving toward the entry as they slowly moved away.

"Now's your chance," Chad said.

They came face to face with the puller as it reached the street level. Its sirens began to sound in intermittent blasts, almost pushing them back. A female patrolman, one much bigger than Loren, but still a head shorter than Chad, jumped out the starboard side door, and began approaching him with one glowing gauntlet extended. Loren moved to the left, distancing herself from her protector. She walked with ease, toward a group of protesters near a building, who were watching the scene unfold as they hesitantly followed the order to leave. She lowered her eyes, and darted past the four of them, to an overhang along the side of the building closest to the entry. Then she waited, and watched.

As Chad argued with the patrolman, inching closer and closer to being hit with a ring of electricity, Loren heard something whisper above. She looked up, confused. It was another set of engines. The air streams seemed even more dense as she looked out from the shadows, but she could make out the cold, white lines of all three. Then, as her ears attached to the faint sounds of a minimal speed, she saw it. The craft was dark in color, reflecting almost no light from the buildings around it. Its shape was nearly indiscernible, but long with flat ends and curved sides. She leaned out carefully from the overhang, and watched it more closely. Then, from the left, she heard a patrolman land, and saw him approaching. He had been on the platform, next to Nico. Before the man could say anything, she pointed up.

"What's that?" she asked. "It's pretty and black."

"None of your concern, citizen," the man answered. He looked at her oddly, for an instant, before grasping her arm.

"And what would the council say?" she went on. "Were I to ask, were I to find it to be my task?"

The man narrowed his eyes at her. "What does it matter what they say? The city isn't theirs to protect."

"And is this dark mystery for our safety?"

"I'm going!" Chad yelled out, his voice booming through the space.

Loren turned and looked, and saw him getting up from the street. The patrolman was still standing near the puller, still aiming her gauntlet at him. *Was he hit?* she thought. She yanked herself away from the patrolman holding her, and as she did, looked back, and saw Nico jump down from the platform. The tech on his boots blasted short bursts of air as he landed heavily on one knee.

"Citizen," he called to her, standing up straight, looking into her shadowed eyes as he approached. "Why are you still here?"

"Sir, I was just getting rid of her," said the patrolman, grabbing at her again.

"Stand down," Nico said, calm, but forceful. "Back to your post. I will deal with her."

"Yes, Sir," he said, and jogged back, and began climbing the rungs on the platform's outer side.

"What are you all up to?" Loren asked.

Nico got closer to her, and set his hand gently on her shoulder. "Why do you ask that?"

"I saw the dark craft, up above, trying not to be seen, about to leave, when not another has left the city for whatever is at the distant scene. Is it so dangerous outside?"

"It is," he answered. "So go."

"The council will hear, unless I get to bear witness."

His eyes and lips tightened behind his visor. "You're just trying to negotiate, trying to escape, when all you have to do is wait one day."

She smirked at him, and hoped he saw it.

"You can go tomorrow," he said. "Your request is in the

system."

"Took long enough, given how simple it was. But another day, I cannot take, not in this place, when I could see mountains and farms and lakes."

"There's even more to see, if you wait."

"And since you so rarely leave, how is it that you know such things?"

"You do not know as much as you think. My movements are my own, and your drummer is easy to spot, and easy to distract, with a woman's attention, and a drink."

She stared back at him, silent.

"So, wait until tomorrow."

"No," she said, shaking her head. "Tonight."

Nico looked around. Loren did the same. Chad had disappeared. The patrolman on the ground was re-entering the puller. The crowd had fully dispersed. The last of them were turning corners two blocks away.

"Everyone else got away pretty easily," Nico said. "How about I take you in, and throw you into a cage?"

"You wouldn't throw me," she answered. "Besides, that would mean that I get to speak, much sooner, to the old folks on the row, maybe this week. What would it mean, if the people see, broadcast, their beloved songbird deemed an outcast, and hear from the same, the sneaky ways of the watchers, with a sneaky unlit craft?"

"That's enough!" Nico quietly exclaimed. His eyes went over

her head, and he stepped closer. "We have work to do, and I can't waste any more time. You stay close, and listen to me, and do it quietly. Let's go."

Loren nodded, and followed him to the platform ladder, where he moved up swiftly. She had to take her time. Her new boots, boots she had acquired solely for the trek outside the city, were much heavier than any others she had. She got into a rhythm slowly, finding the grooves on each of the metal bars, and managed to finally lift herself up onto the platform. As she stood, and looked out, she could not see another civilian citizen anywhere nearby. There was, however, much more to see. From twenty feet up, with no windows to distort the view, the city was vast and open, ascending and expanding from the edge in a way she had never seen. The walls of each building, even under a darkening sky, seemed to glow. The road surfaces glistened. And as close as they were to the first stream, the air felt more invigorating.

"Get in," Nico said, interrupting her observations.

The dark craft had come down from the third stream, without her even noticing, and was now hovering between the platforms. She looked to Nico, and then leapt out two feet, to the open side door. The craft jostled as she landed and pulled herself in. The cabin was a light shade of gray, with a wide bench at the rear, a shorter bench on the starboard side, and a large storage console on the other. Around the top half, surrounding the cabin, there were clear, polished windows. At the forward end they flowed out in curving lines, forming a wider view in front of the pilot's chair, where a patrolman was seated. The man looked back at Loren, peering at her through his visor. Then he spun the chair around, stood, and moved toward the open door. She quickly took a seat on the side bench, and turned herself away, careful not to lose sight of anything around her.

She felt the pilot glance at her once more before he jumped out. Then, Nico leapt in, nudging the craft downward as he landed, and quickly sat in the pilot's chair. He spun around to the control panel, and she heard him tapping, and then manipulating the short handles in front of him.

"Strap in, citizen," he ordered. "And keep your head covered."

Loren did as he said. She heard both cabin doors lock, and looked out through the windows, as they backed away from the platform and slowly ascended into the first stream. The cabin went dark. The only light was from four corners at the rear, and from the controls at the front end. Beneath her, she heard air begin to rush faster through the engines. She looked back at the lively light of the city, and then toward the south entry. The gate in front of the first stream opened, and Nico guided them outward.

They passed over the first stream's massive wind-tech engine, and she heard the roar of its turbines, spinning, and filtering and focusing the wind, even as they generated power. Then they passed through the metal frame of the opening in the city's shield, and she sensed energy all around her. Nico turned the craft left, heading west.

Off to the right she saw the lights of a puller, the one that had remained watchful of the protest, but not descended to disrupt it. Its yellow glow shrank away, as it fell back and settled a short distance behind them.

They sped up, and began to ascend just as fast. Loren looked out the port side window, and saw darkness, and within it, the hints of the high-reaching branches in the forest. They disappeared quickly. She turned around, and looked out the window behind her seat, and in the distance, saw the last of the gray light of day, disappearing behind the dark line that was the mountains. Before she could marvel at any more of the evening landscape, Nico angled the craft higher, and the city became nothing more than a big dot of light below and behind them. Around them, gusting winds pushed against the cabin, and the mist of the lowest clouds became thicker and thicker, enveloping them as their engines opened further, and hummed loudly as they leveled off.

"I can't see a thing," she said to herself. She looked through the rear window. The trailing puller's lights were still there, somewhere within the clouds, but there was nothing else. "How unkind a thing."

"Well, you couldn't wait," Nico said.

She could almost hear his smile, but all she could see was his white uniform, and the top of his helmet, and his hands on the controls. "Can't fly any lower, or slower?" she asked.

"No. This is a short trip."

"To where, exactly."

"Exactly none of your business."

"I wonder what the council would say, about the dark mysteries of today?"

"What could they do? And what would they know, if we return, and your mouth is tied in a perfect little bow?"

"You're terrible."

"You know that's not true."

She leaned back against the soft back of the bench and crossed her arms. Then she pulled her hood back, just enough to breathe a little more, to let out the rising heat in her densely-knit cloak, the other item she had purchased for the trek, which was shaping up into nothing. Except for the sounds of flight, the cabin was quiet for another ten minutes.

"I'm going to tell you something," Nico said. "But you can tell no one else unless the watchers decide to share it widely. Do you understand?"

"Yes," she answered.

"There was a flash today."

"A flash?"

"I know you're young, but-"

"I know what a flash is."

He paused. "Good."

"I'm just confused, surprised, that the ground, at its age, would allow such a rise. Are you sure it was a flash?"

"We are."

"How can you be?"

"By touch, and by history."

Loren shifted in her seat, and unbuttoned the top of her cloak, keeping her hood up. She rubbed her hands on her knees, over the soft fabric, and squeezed her thighs, and breathed heavily, once, through her nose. "Where did it happen?" she asked.

"Between the Spire and the city," he answered. "Not far from here."

"In the past, they were a mystery. Are they still?"

"They are," Nico answered. "But that may not last. Research will be done, using this craft, which is why we had to leave as we did."

"Why not tell all of Lwo? Don't many already know?"

"Consider your own reaction, just now. And consider the protest over a small thing. We can't tell the masses immediately about something that is not fully understood."

"Well, they've never been fully understood, which could be good."

"Not if history records flashes as wild and dangerous, and untraceable. Everyone knows, if our world is under threat, existence itself is under threat. We have to tread lightly."

Loren nodded, to herself. "I understand."

"Nothing else?"

"No, nothing else."

"Now, how can I be sure that you'll be quiet?"

She smiled to herself. "I will. But, if you don't trust me, you can watch me, more closely."

"I have little time for that."

Loren heard some lightness in his voice, but quieted again, as she suddenly felt weighed down. The silence did not last long, as moments later she heard him enter a distinct-sounding pattern in the control panel. She looked forward, through the windshield, and then back to him. He shifted the handles, and tapped an unseen pedal, and the craft began to slow. Then, the trailing puller passed behind her, and pulled ahead, settling in front of them at the same decreased speed. The cabin lights came up just enough to give some light to the floor.

"The other divisions don't know about this trip, do they?" she asked.

"Very few do, which makes you a confidant."

"I did not want to know that watchers can operate this way."

"And what way is that?"

"With deception, covered with supposed discretion."

"We do what we do, always, to protect you."

"So you say. I could have traveled before this day, before there were unseen dangers in the way."

"There is always danger, Loren. The only citizens that travel enough to know it are us and the salvagers, who barely spend any time in any place. Hey, that gives me an idea. How about the next time you want to take a trip, you go out on one of their runs?"

"Ha!" Loren laughed, and scoffed. "I'm too small. And I know enough to know that oceaners tempt fate, that through the Middle Lands and the forest is where it's safe."

"Tonight, let us hope so."

Nico continued guiding the craft behind the puller. Then, slowly, they began to descend, and Loren saw that they were on approach to a village. The puller slowed, and stopped, and they stopped behind it, a thousand feet above the southern end of the village's surrounding stone wall.

"There's a helmet under your seat," Nico said. "Put it on."

Loren looked down, and found a handle, and tilted the cabinet open. She pulled out the plain, black helmet, and quickly pulled back her hood and slid it down over her head. It felt light, and the front panel was wide enough to cover her entire face. It was also tinted.

The cabin lights lowered again, and Nico lowered the craft, descending away from the puller. The winds outside pushed harder at them. The engines seemed to be struggling, but not quite faltering. Streaks of white air rushed up and over the windows as Nico guided the craft into a steady angle.

Loren remained quiet. She gripped the seat beneath her legs, and leaned over, stretching the belts over her shoulders, weighed down with anticipation, until the dim lights from the top of the village hit the cabin window, and lit her gloved hands. She looked up, and saw the outlines of several blocks of buildings, and beyond them, far-reaching rows of crops. She felt a tinge of joy, imagining the people there, moving about freely within the stone walls. *There are probably families of farmers*, she thought. *Probably children. Probably teachers. Probably talented food artists.* She imagined her and her bandmates, performing in the village for the first time, singing for new, young ears. Then, she was jolted back to reality. Nico was now leaning forward as he piloted, cutting a hard line toward the flat roof of a building near the barrier wall.

"Hey!" she yelled, as she was pushed back into her seat. The belts around her waist and shoulders tightened. "How about a warning!?"

"No time," Nico answered, calmly. "We were moving too slow given the wind forces."

A moment later, their speed slowed again. They curved over the high wall, and swooped down, and leveled off a yard above the building's flat roof. Then they idled, and hovered. Loren could see her breaths inside the helmet, and tried to calm herself down. She breathed deeply, and it was not long before she looked out, and saw a hatch in the roof slide back, and then saw a man emerge. He had broad shoulders, and a bundle of braids tied under the back of his dark helmet. The winds on the roof were still steady and strong, and the man was taking careful, heavy steps as he approached them.

The craft's port door opened, and Nico spun around in his chair. As the mysterious man grabbed the door frame and hopped up into the cabin, Loren saw the ranking pin on Nico's chestplate sparkle.

He stood, and extended his hand, and as the man gripped his arm, he pulled him all the way in.

"Doctor Taj?" he greeted him. "I am Lieutenant Nico."

The man shook Nico's arm firmly. "It's just Taj," he said.

Taj turned, and looked around the cabin, as if taking stock of its potential. Then he looked down at Loren. She smiled at him, and waved, and spread her hood out more, away from the helmet, nearer to her shoulders.

"And this young lady is?" Taj asked.

"Just a trainee," said Nico. "Are you comfortable taking the helm? We need a ride back up."

"Certainly."

Nico stepped aside as Taj took the pilot's chair, strapped in, and spun around to the controls. He took a few seconds to survey the glowing panel, and the control handles, and the pedals below, and then hit the button to close the door. He leaned forward, and looked up and out.

"I suppose that's your ride back," he said, sitting back in the chair, pointing at something blinking on the panel.

"Yes," Nico answered. He knelt down beside the chair. "Take her up easy. She's bare bones, and brand new."

"I can see that. How did you acquire it so quickly."

"Classified."

"Understood. Will you strap in?"

"Not necessary. This won't take long. Keep her dark, and

follow the line here." He pointed down at the panel.

They ascended from the roof slowly, and Loren felt the winds pick up behind her and beneath her. Taj spun them around, to the south, and then pulled them forward. They flew out over the wall, and angled upward. Nico remained kneeling, and steady, holding on to the back of the chair, evaluating the old teacher's skill. Then he reached past him, and opened a line to the puller.

"Patrolman Kine," he called. "This is your Lieutenant. We are on approach. Open your port door halfway." After Kine had confirmed, Nico turned to Taj. "Approach the puller from the front, and line up your port side with his. Get as close as you can."

Taj nodded, and leaned forward slightly, focused on the faint yellow glow in the sky, which Loren could now see through the windshield. The puller had descended, at least a few hundred feet, and lowered its lights. The winds roared louder as they got closer. Then Taj leveled them off, and Loren saw the puller's pale front end appear in the darkness.

As Taj positioned the craft, Nico tapped the panel, and the port door opened once more. Loren could see the narrow opening to the puller's cabin through the windows. Their door stopped, leaving only a yard of space, and Nico turned toward her. She looked back at him, confused, and angry, but said nothing. She unstrapped herself, stood, walked back toward their starboard side, and then turned, and ran for the opening. She leapt, and stretched her body, and pointed her fists, as she had been taught as a child. The wind blowing through the narrow gap between the two craft hit her legs, chilling them, but she carried her weight forward, and rolled to a safe landing on her side, on the puller's cabin floor.

She looked back through the door, and saw Nico say something to Taj before jumping out himself, extending his arms and legs, tucking and rolling, and landing on one knee right in front of her. He was standing upright before she could even sit up. She watched as both crafts' doors closed, and Taj pulled away from them, into the darkness.

The puller turned about, toward the east, and Nico turned to Loren, and extended his hand. She stared up at him, still agitated, but took his hand, and let him help her up. He guided her to a seat near the holding cell at the rear. She strapped in as he walked back up to the pilot.

"Sir, he's already back in the village," said Kine.

"Very good," said Nico. "Take us home."

"We have a small problem, Sir. There's a fox en route."

Nico stared down, past the pilot, at the control panels. "Can they see us?"

"Not yet. I think the wall is blocking our signal, but he knows there was someone moving over it."

"Alright. Take us out."

"What about our contact?"

"He just deactivated the craft's tracking. He should be safe. Take us out, as fast as you can, but not too high."

"Yes, Sir."

As they pulled ahead, Nico turned and walked, past Loren, to the cell. She watched as he looked through the gaps in its bars, and out the small window at the rear. Loren followed his gaze, but saw nothing. Beneath her boots, she felt the puller's engines humming as their speed steadily increased, and felt the push from below as they began ascending. Her stomach started to sink.

"Fox to city watcher craft," a booming voice called through the puller's control panels.

Nico walked back up to Kine. "Keep going," he said, and leaned over, and tapped a button to answer. "This is Lieutenant Nico. Go ahead."

Loren heard nothing else from the watcher of the ground, but heard Nico's voice get louder as he responded to the man.

"I know that, Private," he said. "We had some business in the village. It could not wait." He paused, listening. "Well, when your commander returns, have him contact Commander Shil." Another pause. "What was that, Private?"

"He's gone silent, Sir," said Kine. He tapped at the panels.

Then, through the windshield, Loren saw something flicker. There was a distant click in her ear. She could not tell how high or how far they had flown away from the village, or whether or not the sound had come from the ground or the sky, but faint as it was, it was like nothing she had ever heard.

There was hardly time to react, as bright, hot light shot

through the windshield into the cabin. They banked right, and rolled. Loren held tightly to her belts, and closed her eyes, and buried her chin in her chest. She tried to sense where they were, where she was, as her head rattled, and they spun. Then something hit them, hard, from below. She heard the engines open, heard Kine shifting the handles and pedals to try to get them away, but they had lost control.

"We're going down!" he yelled. "Hold on!"

Loren felt pushed and pulled around as they bounced up from the ground, and floated, helpless. It felt like Nico was nearby, but she was not sure. When she finally felt the puller steadying itself, she opened her eyes, and saw his white boots in front of hers. He was kneeling there, hovering over her, pushing his arms down onto her shoulders, steadying her helmet with his own. As she gripped him at the hips, they crashed.

She heard the hard dirt fly up all around them, and heard rocks crack against the puller's body, as they slid forward, roughly, to a short stop. They waited, for minutes. Her breaths felt uncontrollable, but slowly steadied. Then, she leaned back up. Nico stood, patting her on the shoulders before turning, and walking up to Kine, who was frantically tapping at the panels, in patterns, going through some sort of protocol.

"We're stable," Nico said, leaning over his chair. "Settle down. Let her rest."

"The engines won't open, Sir," Kine said back, panting.

"It's okay. I'll take a look."

175

Nico walked to the starboard door, and looked out through the window. All Loren saw was streaks of dirt against the translucent surface, and beyond them, the darkness of night. He got hold of the handle on the door, and spread his stance, and pulled it back by force.

"Stay here!" he yelled back at her.

She felt the raw winds hit her, hard, even pushing through her heavy cloak as they flew into the cabin. But her helmet was strong, and she had a clear view. Nico's tech produced angled white streaks as it steadied him outside the craft. She saw him standing in place, as if feeling nature's raw energy, as if embracing it. Then, he moved toward their front end. She heard him yell something, something she could not make out.

"Yes, Sir!" Kine yelled back.

Loren started to move, but Nico pointed right back through the door at her, and held his hand out. She stopped, and sat back in her seat. Then, he walked forward again, and disappeared.

The puller was jolted back, toward its port side. It settled, and then was jolted again. Loren realized it was Nico, ramming into the craft, trying to dislodge them. There was one more hard push, and they bounced up. She heard the winds start to stutter through the engines below, and then start to flow in a steady roar. As the puller floated up, and back, she looked out, and saw Nico jump for the door. She quickly unbuckled herself, and jumped to the starboard wall, and kneeled, and moved slowly toward him. She got to within an arm's reach of his hands.

"No!" he yelled. "Get back! I'm fine!"

"I'm almost there!" she yelled back.

"Stop!"

Then, her heart sank. It was as if a giant hand had reached in, reached for her as she crouched near the door, and pulled her out. Her cloak was yanked off of her shoulders. Crackling, ice cold air hit her chest, and then her legs. She grabbed one sleeve of the cloak, hoping. Nico had grabbed the other end. She looked through her helmet, to his, to his obscured eyes. Another ghostly grasp pulled at her boots. She held on, shivering all over as the fabric stretched between them.

Nico had a firm grip on the puller's door frame. She pulled herself along the cloak once, and then again. She grabbed for the flailing hood. Then came another gust, and another. Through her helmet she could hear the wildness. This storm was not what it had been when she had last left the city, in a mass transit craft, as a child, to learn, long before the watchers had come up with so many restrictions. This storm had a heartless, freezing grasp. It would not let her go.

Something hit her side, and then her helmet. She blinked, and felt tears in her eyes, and as the cloak's sleeve ripped apart, was finally yanked away. *She worked so hard on that cloak*, she thought, sad inside. She heard Nico cry out for her, and as she was flipped about, over and over again, saw him become a spec in the distance.

The wind force was unbearable. Loren's gloves and dense bodysuit felt useless, as debris scratched at her, and she was pulled, up, and back, and away. *Where am I going!?* she thought, frantic. She realized she was panting. She coughed into her helmet. Blood splattered against the tinted panel. Her arms and legs were becoming numb. Her feet in her boots, her head in the helmet, had not yet frozen. *This is… I've been…! This is…!*

She could not form a thought. She wanted to sing, once more, to the void, but her throat was cramping, and closing. She coughed out more blood. She was barely feeling the wind blasts and debris strikes anymore. She could only accept their constancy. She glanced at the nothingness of the wild sky. *It's end…*, she tried to think. Her helmet fogged up, inside and out. *I can't…! What is…!* Her eyes opened and closed. Tears froze against her cheeks, and then chilled within her eyes. Through the fog she thought she saw a single star, hovering in the blackness of space. Then, there was only darkness.

CHAPTER 10
THE CALL

Maia knew that night had fallen, though not from any observance of the outside. There were no windows in the Lords' cavern. She knew from the wide display behind their great chairs, which relayed the same information as the small display in her bedroom in the village: the position of the sun, the velocity of the storm, and the distance between the storm's edge and the mainland. The latter two had not changed in weeks.

She was sitting on the bench across from the Lords, relieved to have the weight of her helmet off her back and shoulders, and instead on the shelf against the wall behind them. She wanted to lean back, and relax against the high, cushioned back of the bench, but it would not have been proper. Fits and Brun had also disconnected their helmets, and were sitting upright near the other end of the bench, listening attentively. Between her and her commanders sat Robbins and Devon. The boy was next to her, almost leaning on her arm.

Except for the soft sound of his drinking, Devon had been quiet. He had been tilting the metal bottle up repeatedly, as if he could not get enough. It was just water, but Maia understood. The water on the Isle was crisper, and sweeter than what they had on the mainland. The difference was subtle, but discernible. And the boy, she gathered, was likely not interested in anything else happening around him. The Lords had been engaged in discussion with them for hours.

Andrew had explained, to all of them, his family's journey. His father, as a young man, had seen the collapse first-hand, seen the earth's lands begin falling, to fires and storms, and sinking beneath ocean forces and earthquakes. Andrew himself had seen old video recordings, before they were lost during Lwo's formation, of the seemingly unending catastrophes. Even before his father's time the planet's population had been forewarned, for decades, about what destruction was likely. After years of hard work studying the warnings, his father had taken a trip, and sought out the scientists and engineers that had most loudly parroted the warnings, and found that they were secretly building land forming machines. He had provided the last of the funds they needed, which had been almost all he had. Then, as his own resources neared their end, he found others who believed as he did, and though they had been few, they contributed what they could, whether it was time, or materials, or more funds.

Those who had first committed to the establishment of Lwo came to see great hardships. Many abandoned the cause, and not long after the last of them had fled, the storm, which had already been battering the land for years, finally encircled it. It had been tolerable at first, but eventually, not long after Andrew had been born, it became too much to bear. The first Lwoans then began constructing higher, stronger walls around their villages, walls that could withstand the storm's forces. And they developed vehicles that could more easily navigate the winds.

Andrew's wife, the mother of Gem and Coral, had been a builder of craft, and had been lost in one of the final tests of wind tech. She had also been eighty years old, and still full of vigor. It was not long after her death that they had discovered that Lwo's freshwater had a higher concentration of minerals than the water that had sustained the old, fallen lands. It had aided in keeping the first Lwoans alive for so long.

"The Mother wants us to live long," Andrew had told them. "She even sent her heat to our new ground, to help sustain us. When the earth finally heals, Lwo will make humanity flourish again."

In return for all of Andrew's knowledge, Robbins had shared what must have been all he could remember. Some things, Maia gathered, even Devon had never heard. He spoke of how the boy's mother had saved his life, keeping him from falling overboard two days after he had embarked on his tenth ship. And he told them of how, many years later, he had thrown two men overboard himself, to keep them away from his sleeping family. Robbins' eyes had begun to water by the time he finished the story, and seeing it, Coral had asked Fits to stand, and sat down next to Robbins, and rubbed her hand gently up and down his back, and whispered something to him. After this, they had all taken time to rest, and move about the Lords' home, as much as they would allow.

Maia had lingered near the sealed, wooden doors, at the rear of the cavern. There were three of them. The one in the center was between the kitchen and dining spaces, the other two were on the far, rear sides of the cavern. They were all carved with artful designs, with swooping, recessed lines and forms, and trimmed in multi-colored, shining stones. She had never passed through any of them, but she had always been curious. Before they sat to speak again, she turned around and saw Devon, quietly standing a yard behind her, looking curious himself. She rubbed his head, and took his hand as they walked back to the bench.

"Did you ever expect to die, Robbins?" asked Coral, sitting across from him again, in the chair to the right of her father's, closest to the bunker.

"I thought we could," Robbins answered. "But I was still hopeful, somehow. There was not much beyond death, and warnings of more death in the north. I could only try to make sure we lived another day. But after my son and I embarked in our small boat, after we had met the heavy rains and been threatened by so many unseen things, I only tried to make sure that we were comfortable, that we could slip into it peacefully if we passed on. As far as I knew, before Fits rescued us, we were fast asleep and on our way."

Maia watched Robbins as he sat back into the bench, and took a deep breath. She could see that he was breathing easier, but heavier, as if he had not truly breathed in years. He tipped his bottle up and drank more water. Devon did the same.

"And on the last ship…" Coral went on, pressing for more.

"It was dreadful," said Robbins. "It was sinking. I was sure of it. There had always been cracks in the hull, and they were spreading. People started disappearing. Healthy people. At least, healthy for a ship at sea. We were stumbling across their abandoned belongings every week." He paused, and looked up. "But on the last day, I knew my son and I had enough health left to make it off, and get away, so we did."

"Well," said Andrew. "It's a good thing our watchers are so capable."

"Thank you," Fits answered, modestly, almost bowing.

"That is something I would like to know, Andrew," said Robbins.

Maia felt everyone's attention shift to him, and felt the mood tense. Robbins' voice was too relaxed for speaking to a lord.

"And what is that, Robbins?" Andrew replied.

"How did the watchers become so capable?"

Maia reached over Devon, and set her left hand on Robbins' shoulder. She was about to speak, but Andrew raised his hand, and looked over, stopping her.

"It is fine, Lieutenant," he said. "Robbins and his son are with us now. There is no need to keep any secrets. And we are not offended." He leaned out, and braced himself on his wooden staff, pointing the brilliant, green jewel near his hands toward the man and his son. "The watchers of Lwo are its greatest asset. You can see, I am sure, how strong they are, how much stature they have, how much control they maintain. They are–even were–meant to be this way."

Robbins' eyes were focused on the man, and revealed his confusion. "*Meant* to be? You mean, the way the earth meant for Lwo to be?"

"Not exactly, my friend. When we realized what we were facing here, early on, all those years ago, we knew that we would need strong, capable people for humanity to go on. So, as much as we were able, we made sure that the youngest, healthiest, biggest, strongest people were settled in close proximity to one another, whether they were in the north, or south, or east or west." He paused, and looked to Devon, and then back to Robbins. "Tell me, Robbins. Does your son know about how people come to be?"

Robbins nodded. "He does. Big ships have echoes. You couldn't hide much out there."

"Good. Well, not to be too detailed, but people can fall in love with any number of potential mates. Human history proves it. When my girls were just Devon's age, the men and women of my generation began more strategic settlements. We directed people to certain villages, and to certain regions, before the storm became too strong. And eventually we provided guidance to those who would enter the city, for what sectors they should live in when they did. But, as I am sure you and your son well know, people can easily come to despise each other, for reasons even they cannot determine. So, the outcomes were still somewhat up to chance."

Robbins began to look around, and Maia finally sat back against the bench, and crossed her arms. Fits looked over at her and smirked. Brun raised an eyebrow at Robbins, as if to say 'I dare you to judge us.' Maia lowered her head slightly. And felt Robbins' eyes on her.

"At least they weren't arranged marriages," she said, almost to no one. "That was something that used to happen." She looked up, and saw Robbins shrug.

"I heard the same," he said. "But where I was born, it did not. And with my wife, definitely not. She could have chosen…"

"Anyone?" Maia asked.

"Almost. Being one of the last born on land, and being healthy, and decently strong, I guess I had some appeal." He turned back to Andrew. "So, how does one become a watcher, then?"

"The people choose them," said Andrew. "It starts among the youth. Classes of students choose *class watchers*, for their age groups, each year. And teachers help them along. It is based on attitude, and physical ability, and fairness with others. The criteria grow as the students do, and by the time they reach nineteen years, a final set of potential watchers has been established. Then the chosen may decide on whether or not to enlist for training. And all training starts on the ground, so the few chosen from the city have to learn very fast, to catch up to those who have grown up in villages. The ground has a way of pushing them to the brink, of determining whether or not they are cut out for life as a watcher."

"And what if they don't cut it?" asked Robbins.

"Well, then they are welcome to pursue whatever life they choose. But if they can endure, and go beyond training with Brun and his watchers, then they officially enter the ranks. After that, each commander can choose from those who are ready who they would like to join their division. This process, however, is only completed every five years or so. I'm sure you know by now that our numbers are small. We do not have children at a high rate."

Robbins looked to his son, and patted him on his shoulder, and rubbed at his curly hair. "We know. My son hasn't seen any others his age. Not yet. We were hoping he would, before we were brought here." He looked back to Andrew again. "So, what about the commanders, and the lieutenants? How are they chosen?"

"Sounds like you're interested in the job, Robbins."

Robbins leaned back, shaking his head. "Oh no. Just curious."

"Ah ha. Well, to ascend the ranks, watchers are evaluated here, by the three of us." He glanced at his daughters, and then looked at Robbins again. "By then it is not a matter of physicality or durability. It is a matter of mindset when those attributes are pushed. Each commander may determine if a watcher is ready to come to us and ascend rank. However, that is also a rare occurrence. It happens only when needed, when one leader passes on, or another chooses to stop serving, or when one proves themselves so much that promotion must be considered."

Robbins looked to Maia. "May I ask, which were you?"

Maia pinched her lips together, and tried not to let any tears form. "I had to be considered, but there was also an unfortunate loss."

She looked away, at the thought of her old lieutenant, who had not been much older than her when he passed on. Then she looked to the wide entry of the cavern, which was still open. She looked at the bottom of the massive, stone wall that was still settled high above, stable between its unseen, mechanized supports. She looked out at the bunker, at the rows of beds and chairs still in their proper places. Then came a noise, a crackling electronic blip, followed by the Emissary's voice. She looked to the Lords as the security system spoke in its distant, nearly-human voice.

"A watcher calls!" it said. "A watcher calls!"

Fits stood quickly, half-bowed to the three Lords, and turned and ran to the wall behind the bench. Maia stood right after him, and went to the shelves with him, and grabbed her helmet. Brun was not far behind her. She stood there, re-attaching her helmet brace at her back, listening to the mumbling behind her from the Lords and their guests. Fits and Brun were already stepping down to the bunker as she turned around, and glanced at Robbins and Devon, and then jogged to catch up to her commanders.

"I left her out there," Fits mumbled, walking toward the door to the cave.

"I'm sure she's fine," Maia said as she reached them.

Fits stopped, and looked up. "Emissary," he called. "Please, broadcast the watcher's call."

After a distant click Rial's youthful voice came through clearly. "Commander Fits, Sir," she said. "Can you hear me?"

"Yes, Ensign," he replied. "Go ahead."

"There's been another flash. I only saw a little bit of light from here, but Lieutenant Orve just sent a message to us from the north station. The report is flying through the ranks. What should I tell him, Sir?"

"Hold, Ensign." He turned, and faced Maia and Brun. "That's two in one day. It's unprecedented."

"I'm afraid it is not, Commander," Andrew said, loudly, as he stepped down into the bunker. "It has happened before, just once, and not since I was your ensign's age."

"My Lord," Fits said. "I have never seen a record of it."

"I know." Andrew walked slowly toward them, his staff in hand but not quite touching the ground, followed by his daughters. "When you're building a new world, so much happens that some details are easier to forget. The records are here, in our home, somewhere. We thought the ties beneath the ground had stabilized, had been fully absorbed. Your predecessors were sure of it. We were sure of it. I suppose we may have been wrong."

"What shall we do, my Lord?"

"You shall do what you are trained to do, as always. Preserve the land. Protect the people. However, in this instance, I believe one of us should go with you."

Maia considered his words, and then looked to his daughters, who were standing in front of Robbins and Devon, as if guarding them. There was a hint of surprise in the womens' eyes, as their father took a step back and turned toward them.

"Coral," said Andrew, and extended his staff toward her. "Go back with Maia, to the tower in the sky, and offer our wisdom to Commander Jaan."

Coral hesitated, but only for an instant before nodding, and answering, "Yes, Father."

Maia watched her step quickly out of the bunker, and back into the cavern, and walk off behind their three seats, toward the ornate door on the right. Then her eyes went back to Andrew, who was approaching her. She stood more firmly, and set her hands behind her back, as he set a hand on her shoulder.

"I trust you, Lieutenant," he said. "To look after my daughter. Although, she won't need much of it." He almost laughed.

Maia nodded. "Yes, My Lord. Of course."

"Ensign," Fits called loudly, looking up and turning toward the bunker entry. "Are you still there?"

"Yes, Sir," Rial answered.

"We're going back. Let the lieutenant know."

"Yes, Sir."

Fits turned his head slightly. "Emissary?" he called to the system.

"Yes, yes," it answered, somehow conveying agitation. "I heard everything. Doors opening."

The muffled sound of metal disengaging echoed throughout the space, and the doors began to slide apart, revealing the cave, and the two waiting craft. Maia could see Rial, looking toward the bunker as she climbed into the gull, and then quickly looking away, as if afraid.

"It is good to see so much life from the mainland," said Andrew.

Maia turned to face him again, but he was already walking away. She walked toward Robbins and Devon, and Gem stepped aside. She knelt down, and hugged Devon, and held him for a moment. Then she stood, and set a gentle hand on Robbins' arm.

"Should we come back with you?" Devon asked.

Maia looked to Gem, who nodded to her, and then looked back down to the boy, and shook her head. "No. You and your father are still safest here. Don't worry. The Lords are excellent hosts. And we will return soon."

"Are you sure?" Robbins asked.

She looked into the man's eyes, and said nothing. Then, behind Gem, Coral re-emerged. She was covered in a dense, dark suit that bore layers of contoured armor at the shoulders and legs. Her gauntlets and boots looked older, but not battered. And the thick, split skirt over her pants was stitched with flowing patterns, matching the heavy, unraised hood that spread out over her shoulders, and flowed to a pointed end just above her waist. In her arms, she carried a dark helmet that reflected the light in the bunker. She looked right at Maia as she passed by her sister.

"Let's go, Lieutenant," she said.

"Yes, my Lord," said Maia.

She nodded to Gem, and calmly waved her open hand at Robbins and Devon, who raised their hands, and waved back at her. When she turned around, Brun had already walked out into the cave, and was moving up the lowered ramp of her bird. Coral walked closely next to her as they approached the ramp, and Maia stepped aside to let her enter first. She looked back once more, and saw the doors to the bunker closing, and no one behind them. Then, she went up the ramp.

Brun was leaning over the control panels, entering codes, searching for something. Maia walked by Coral, who had finished strapping in on the port side bench, and had started tying her red hair behind her head. She walked up to the empty pilot's chair, and sat, and spun it around to face the controls. She tapped the ramp control, and listened as it raised up behind her. As it locked, she looked out to her left, and saw the green gull float up from the cave floor. Its forward lights beamed bright white out into the darkness over the ocean, and she followed suit, activating the bird's high beams. Brun was still leaning over her.

"Commander, Sir?" she asked as she reached for the chair's belts.

"Nothing," Brun muttered. "Nothing from my own people."

"It was from the ground. I'm sure they're preoccupied."

191

"Tighten your tongue, Lieutenant."

"Yes, Sir." She secured her belts, and reached beneath his lingering presence, for the glowing right panel. "How should we depart?"

He stepped back, and knelt behind the chair. "Take us up," he said. "As high and fast as you can."

"Yes, Sir."

Maia watched as the gull shot out of the cave ahead of them, and then lowered her helmet, opened her front engine, and flew out behind it. She kept a tight line behind the mountain watchers for five miles, building up the bird's speed as much as she could without overworking its engines. Then, she broke upward, ascending at a steady angle as air rumbled faster through the rear and side engines. The pressure on her chest increased, and the waters below became darker and darker. As the bird approached two hundred miles per hour, she felt Brun's massive hands squeezing the seat.

"Keep pushing," he ordered, his voice now distorted by his helmet. "And see if you can open a line."

"Yes, Sir."

Outside it was dark, and within the darkness, there was only the unyielding winds, and the wet mist of the lowest clouds. The bird's lights let them see only a few hundred feet ahead, but the center panel showed that they were still on course, headed southwest toward the mountains. As Maia banked slightly right, avoiding an array of ice crystals ahead, Jaan's voice came through.

"Sky Tower to bird," he called. "This is Commander Jaan."

"Do not tell your commander I am with you," Coral said, her voice carrying well past Maia's seat.

"Yes, my Lord," Maia replied.

"And do not address me as Lord until we are back on the Isle."

"Understood." She reached for the right panel, and answered. "Commander, Sir. This is Lieutenant Maia."

"Good to hear from you, Lieutenant," said Jaan. "Looks like you're already on your way back."

"Yes, Sir. The Lords' orders. Fits's ensign heard from their north station about the flash, and she saw it as well."

"All the way from the Isle?"

"Only partially, but yes."

Jaan was quiet for a moment. "Very well. How long before you reach us?"

"I estimate fifty minutes, Sir."

"Thirty," said Brun. "If we take her over the clouds."

"Sounds good to me. I'll see you in half an hour. Jaan out."

The line was closed before Maia could interject. "Sir," she said, glancing at Brun. "I've never taken my bird that high."

Brun leaned forward, past her shoulder, looking further through the windshield. "Isn't she built for it, Lieutenant?"

"Yes, Sir. But, we rarely-"

"Listen to your commander, Maia," Coral said, interrupting

their argument.

Maia quieted.

"There is no time to second-guess, or be extra cautious. The mainland is strong, but as my father said, we have been wrong before. I do not want to remember I failed if the land begins to break. Take her up."

"Yes," said Maia. "Very well."

She pulled up the engine display above the map on her center panel. With her access code and a single tap she deactivated the elevation limits of every engine, and then, gently, pointed the bird upward and accelerated. Once again the pressure hit her, and she was pushed back into her seat. She heard Brun's boots shrieking away against the cabin floor. She looked over her shoulder to see him holding on to the empty bench. He gave her a thumbs up.

As she turned back around, the rumbling through the engines flooded her ears. All of the panel displays were blinking with constant, orange warning lights. Looking out at the vents on either side of the craft, she saw streaks of air being breathed out in unfamiliar patterns. Then, after another minute, the pressure eased, and they floated out, above the cloud cover. Maia held tightly to both handles, and kept one foot steady on the pedal below. Then she looked down to the center panel. They were above the storm. She looked out and up, and for the first time in months, she saw the night sky. It was full of stars. And for the first time in years, she saw the moon, glowing brilliantly, thousands and thousands of miles away.

The bird drifted, and then floated down gently into a hazy, puffy wind stream, where the engines could still pull from the storm's forces. Maia watched the wild air being pulled in through the front engine, and the bird's speed picked back up. The panels stopped blinking orange, downgrading to a constant yellow. The center panel showed a speed of three hundred miles per hour. She kept holding tightly to both handles.

"How long has it been?" Coral asked aloud. "How long since you two have seen the moon?"

Quietly, and still somewhat in awe, Maia answered. "I am sure that it's been five, or six years." She paused. "It doesn't feel right."

"How so, Lieutenant?"

"We have this moment of peace. We get to see this brilliant night sky. The people do not. And it seems that they may never again, that the storm will never let up."

"It will," said Brun, now sitting on the bench opposite Coral. "Eventually."

"And if it does not?" Coral pressed. "Then what? Do we give up?"

"No, my…" Brun stopped himself. "No. Never."

"And you, Maia?"

"No, we do not. That was not what I was suggesting."

"Then clarify yourself."

A sudden gust of wind pushed them to the right, and Maia

quickly compensated, shifting and stomping, changing their speed and direction until the bird moved back into a stable vector. The center panel showed their adjustment over the map. The cabin walls rattled around them. She took a breath, and exhaled. "I meant that we, that humanity, may never thrive again; not as it has in the past."

"Oh, but it will," said Coral. "We may not live to see it, but it will. People have never stopped thriving. It sounds as if you may want things to be easy. Is that it?"

"No. I am not looking for ease, just more safety, more predictability. We fight now for every breath, every step. I wonder how long Lwo can go on like that."

"As long as it takes." Coral paused, and shifted in her seat. "Are you not a bit young to be so tired, Maia? You have yet to reach sixty years."

"I am not tired."

"Maybe your concern is for the boy, then, and his father."

Maia thought about Robbins, and Devon, back on the Isle, in another strange place. "The boy is very hopeful. Especially given what he has lived through. I have never encountered a child like him before."

"Oh, sure you have."

"Not that I am aware. When we are born here, we are immediately confronted by the reality of our instability. Our infants are barely crawling before they have to get used to wearing boots, and then think about being or not being a watcher, just so they can live.

Devon is very free. I suppose I do not want to see him burdened as we are."

"He is already quite burdened, Maia. It is just that, to him, Lwo is easy."

Maia heard Brun stand, and felt his boots against the floor as he walked up behind her seat, and knelt. He held the chair tightly again, bracing himself. "We can not see what is coming, Lieutenant," he said. "But as Lord Andrew has always said, Mother Earth has let us live for a reason. We could have been wiped out like the rest of the world, but we were not."

"I know, Sir," she answered.

"Maybe the boy and his father are a sign that a better existence is on the horizon. Maybe you will get to share it with them."

"Sir, I do not want-"

"Don't try to hide it, Maia," said Coral. "Not when an old woman like me is nearby."

Maia quieted, and checked their position. They had flown over fifty miles, and were less than ten minutes from the Sky Tower. "Commander, would you care to strap in?" she asked over her shoulder.

"No," he answered heavily. "Just take me to the ground before you get to the tower."

"Yes, Sir."

Maia accessed the engine controls, and reactivated the elevation limits. The bird swayed from side to side, as she guided

197

them down through the clouds. The winds pushed them off their vector every few seconds, and each time Maia found a steady line and angled them downward, quickly taking them out of the wet mist, and down toward ground, until the mainland finally came into view.

From a distance they saw the lights of the Sky Tower, blinking in a familiar pattern that beckoned any approaching watcher craft to land. She activated her underbody lights, sent a coded message, and then accelerated as she began her descent. As they sped toward the surface, she looked over her short, starboard wing, to the north. The Northern Range was somewhere in the distant darkness, and she wondered if Fits and Rial had already made it to the station there.

The bird neared the ground, and Maia leveled off at one hundred feet. Brun was standing over her, looking, and as she saw the signals for two nearby foxes, she tapped the button to lower the ramp. She heard him step back, and walk toward the rear.

"Say nothing of my presence, Commander," Coral ordered.

"Understood," he said.

Cool air rushed into the cabin. Maia turned, and Brun saluted her, and then leapt out, and landed on a fox wing, and sped away, heading north. She closed the ramp, and took them back up, to five hundred feet, and then to one thousand feet, and spun around toward her port side, and aimed for the tower. Behind her, she heard Coral unstrapping her belts. The youngest lord walked up behind her, and set her hand on the back of the chair.

"When you get to your hangar, call your Commander down,"

she said. "I do not want to explain to your whole division why I am here."

"Understood," said Maia. The tower's large vents came into view, and she adjusted their speed and direction. "You are well-outfitted, if I may say so. And with a helmet on, I am not sure most would recognize you."

"That was my intention. Still, I do not want to take any chances. Not yet."

"Yes, of course. They do adore you, though. All watchers do. All of you."

"Thank you, dear."

CHAPTER 11
THE DAWN

Usually, generally, rain helped Nico to sleep. When it poured over the city, through the open roof in the shield, and more citizens stayed inside to avoid soaked pants, or decreased power to the wind tech on their craft, he would sleep easier until his shift began. But he had not slept since returning the night before, when the clouds had finally had enough, and began to let loose their heavy downpour.

After returning, he had gone through the motions without thinking–undressing, bathing, lying down–but he had only been able to close his eyes. He had not drifted off, not even for a single minute. His breathing was still unsteady, as he stared up at the warm-colored ceiling, replaying the image of Loren being snatched away over and over again in his mind. Her bright, fear-filled, shocked eyes had penetrated him before the winds had taken her up and into the darkness, and they would not leave.

He had no idea how many hours had passed, but the light coming from outside was brighter than it had been after the last rain. It was daytime, and as he realized it, he heard the subtle tone of the alarm chime over his head, sung out from the display on the wall behind him. He sat up on the right side of the bed, and turned and looked at the screen. It was nearly afternoon, nearly time for him to begin his shift. The storm's status, as always, remained the same, unwavering in speed and direction.

He reached back, and tapped the screen, stopping the alarm. Normally he would have tapped the button to play instrumental music, from the station that owned the oldest recordings, but today he knew that hearing any music so early would be an unbearable reminder. She was gone. Her raw, heavy melodies would never be sung again. And for the moment, but not for long, only he and Kine knew.

The apartment's window faced east, and faced another building, and allowed little light to enter when its digital blinds were shut. Only a haze of daylight was peaking in. He stood, and walked down the three short steps beneath his bed, and walked around the couch, past the tall, aromatic plant. Its smell served to invigorate him on most days, but not today. He walked up to the left side of the wide window, tapped the control panel near the entry door, and ran his finger from the bottom to the top of the small, glowing square. A bright line of blue followed his motion, and the darkness in the window was drawn upward, toward the ceiling, until the city was revealed through a thinly tinted view.

Nico stood there, staring up at the traffic in the second stream. It was sparse. The stream below was the same. Straight across from him, a building not unlike his own reflected gray daylight off its metal walls, just enough to brighten the block, but not enough to distract. He could see its tiered walkways, and a few people moving along behind the re-formed plastic barriers protecting them. Just outside his own window, a familiar neighbor passed by, a woman in a long, dark coat. She owned a restaurant, and always bought from the farm villages farthest east. On most days he would have been out the door by the time she reached his unit, and would have conversed with her about the monotony of her regular customers, and how the watchers might help her in this way or that. And he would have kindly listened, and took note, in case any of it might lead to useful information. But not today. Today he could barely move, and her long, dark coat reminded him again of the young woman he had lost to the storm.

He sank, slowly, down to one knee, and pressed both his hands into the window pane, and felt the sweat begin to rise there, and tried not to scream. Instead, through his teeth, he seethed, and growled. Minutes passed, but his mourning would not last long enough for tears to form. A light, familiar tone rang out through his home's array of speakers, signaling a call from headquarters. He stared down at the wooden floor, and then stood, and answered.

"This is Lieutenant Nico," he said aloud, feeling exhausted.

"This is your commander," said Shil.

He straightened up, and shook out the start of a full-body quiver. "Commander, Sir. Please go ahead."

"Lieutenant, what time did you return last night?"

He turned and walked, back up the short steps, and past the bed. As he entered the closet he tried to think. "It must have been after midnight, Sir. I left you a message. We completed the task."

"Yes, I heard from the recipient. But then, I heard from Commander Brun. You left something out of your report."

Nico quieted, and felt his whole body tense. He had known it would come up, but he had expected to have more time, more time to at least speak with Kine. "I did as you ordered, Sir."

"Don't you think another flash was important to report?"

He whispered out his exhale, masking his relief. "Yes, Sir. I apologize. It was late, and I expected the watchers of the ground to report it."

"They did. Travel is restricted again, but the wet paths must be keeping the people from complaining, for now."

"Probably so."

"We'll have to tell them, soon."

"Agreed, Sir."

"And is there anything else you would like to tell me, Lieutenant?"

He paused. "No, Sir."

"Fine. Get to headquarters. You're running late as it is, but before you do anything, come to my office. Shil out."

The line closed. Nico pulled on his boots, and zipped up his jacket. He walked past the open bathroom door, back down the steps, and past the kitchen. At the entry, as he always did, he donned his helmet, and then his gauntlets, and his hip tech, and his shoulder tech, and his heavier back tech. He ran a quick check of each of the compact engines, and when it was finished, removed the helmet, slid the large entry door aside, and stepped out onto the short deck. The thin, cool breeze passing through the walkway rose up, surrounding him, and carrying with it the scent of the fallen rain, which gave him none of the comfort it usually did. As the door slid shut and locked behind him, he took one step down to the walkway, and headed left, toward the northeast lift.

He could feel his heart pounding in his chest. He could not be sure that Shil was unaware of Loren. He could not be sure that she had not already met with Kine, or the other patrolmen involved in the operation. Her tone had been strong, even for her. And having already left out the detail of the flash in his report, he expected he would endure much more of it.

The door to the lift opened, and he took it up to the tenth floor. When it opened again, he looked across the wide hallway, and through the access gate, to the transit platform. He recognized the two residents standing near the large, grated door, a man and a woman close to him in age, who were conversing, as they often did. He stepped out of the lift, and walked through the sliding doors, and stood two yards behind them. The man turned toward him, and offered a nod. He returned the gesture, and put his helmet back on. A moment later, the public transport arrived.

Through the platform's clear walls Nico could see the long, shining body of the craft, as it came to a stop in front of them. With a chime its rectangular door frame extended, and met the frame on the platform. Then, both sets of doors opened, revealing a short, metal plank tilting down from the transport and connecting with the platform. Nico waited as three riders disembarked, and then followed behind his neighbors as they entered. After the door closed behind them, and the walkway and frame retracted, another chime sounded. The transport hopped away from the building and floated back into the second stream, heading south.

The craft's forty-six seats were nearly full, revealing only hints of their red coloring. The rest of the cabin was a dull blue, with metallic bars to hold, and matching window frames. Checkered light panels, some with arrows and directions and warnings printed on them, formed the flat ceiling. Nico's neighbors took two seats to his left. He walked toward the front, where the pilot was stationed, holding on to one of the long bars overhead.

Despite his regular presence on the transport, at almost the same time almost every day, he could feel the attention of the other riders. As the pilot carried them through the assigned sectors, turning every few blocks, but never ascending or descending, Nico tried not to look back at them. When light passed through the cabin, he looked out at the buildings nearby. When they made a scheduled stop at a platform, he tried not to watch those getting on and getting off. But always, after they were in motion, some number of eyes turned toward him. One gaze came from a child, the only one he had seen since boarding. The boy was only a toddler, too young to be in a classroom, and his mother was holding his hand tightly, and looking out the window. Nico smiled, and raised his fist, saluting the boy, who smiled back.

They were only two stops from the headquarters sector when Nico noticed a man sitting at the rear of the cabin. The man only glanced up at him briefly, and then looked back down, paying him little attention. He seemed to be focused on the glowing screen of the phone in his hand. His head was covered by a hood, and though he was sitting, and was slightly hunched over, he was visibly large. He also seemed familiar, and uneasy.

As the transport turned right, heading east, Nico turned toward the front end again. They were coming up on the north side of headquarters. Two other transports were already there, idling at the north platform, with their lights glowing in a subdued shade of blue. As they came to a stop behind them, Nico looked out the windows, at the building's wide, blunt walls, and at its corners, at its massive, shining pillars. He felt his body tense up again.

As he disembarked behind the other riders, he tried not to move too quickly. He kept their pace as they moved along the gated, covered platform. He passed by those waiting to board transports, and entered the building through the dark, covered doorway. Once he was inside, he slowed to a near stop, watching as several other citizens made their way straight ahead to the security gates. Beyond the gates was the wide, spacious atrium, constructed of a sandy color of polished stone. He spotted the desk at the rear, and the two familiar women, in golden-hued uniforms, who were currently staffing it.

Above them, painted upon the thirty-foot-high ceiling, and lit by lines of soft lighting, was the city's largest work of art.

The mural was a vibrant approximation of how the city had been envisioned, had the visionary been able to see it from outside and above the forest. The headquarters, with bright pillars below the swooping levels of the watchers' station, was at the mural's center. The building appeared to be much larger than it had actually turned out to be, and though it was the focal point, the rest of the image, with the massive mountains and the wild ocean both in closer proximity than reality, was a vibrant reminder of the rest of land. There were no depictions of people, but there were depictions of craft. The image's darkest shades were those that depicted the green trees of the forest. And at the bottom of the painting, nearest to the far wall of the atrium, the image transitioned into smooth, shadowy clouds, which immediately reminded Nico of the night that had just passed. His heart started to beat faster.

The small crowd of citizens was still slowly making its way through the security gates. Nico walked up to the back of one of the lines, and waited, watching as others provided their identification cards, and answered required questions from the golden-clad building officers. When he reached the gate, the officer there asked nothing of him, instead saluting sharply, and standing more firmly as he waved him through. As was always the case, the sensor that was silent for most citizens rang out as Nico passed through, activated by all of the equipment he bore. He paused a moment, and looked over his shoulder, and hearing no inquiry, walked on. He passed the atrium's desk, and the saluting women there, and walked down the long, wide hall of doors, up to the building's central lifts.

He entered his code at the lift on the far left, the only one with access to the watchers' station. The door opened almost immediately, and he took the lift up three levels, exiting on the building's thirteenth floor. The short hall outside the lift led to the clear door to the hangar. As he walked up, he could see a short row of idling pullers, and two jumpers. He passed through the door, and saluted three patrolmen as he made his way to the station's lift, and entered. He took the lift up to the twentieth floor, and as he exited, made a sharp right, and then a left, passing by the square equipment room and heading straight down the hall to the set of solid metal doors. They slid open, revealing the command office.

From the office, one could look out and see most of the city, and on some days the southern horizon. The curved window panes beyond the monitors and control panels rose up three yards to the ceiling. The city's tallest buildings shined, even under the dull light of the cloudy sky. The pathways throughout the city were steep drop-offs, running between each block, defining each sector. At the far, southeast end, curving around the city's edge, the high, dark line of green revealed the high trees of the forest.

Shil was sitting at the center of the expansive view, in her high-backed chair, the only chair in the office. Behind her was the large, square command table, with its bright, white schematic map of the city's sectors. She spun around slowly in the chair, and faced Nico as the doors shut behind him.

He straightened up, and saluted. "Commander, Sir."

"Lieutenant," she said, plainly.

She stood, and pushed her chair aside, revealing the active screen. Nico looked and saw the blinking, black symbol of the watchers of the ground. Then, Brun's image appeared. Nico walked around the table, and stood next to Shil. Brun was unmasked, and clearly angry.

"Commander, Sir," said Nico.

"Lieutenant," Brun said, nodding. "It appears we have a situation. The flash last night, did it hit your puller?"

"Yes, Sir," said Nico. "The damages will be examined today."

"That's nice. Would you care to tell me why you were even outside the city at that hour?"

Nico turned to Shil, who was staring out the window, her arms crossed in agitation. He looked back to the screen. "We had already planned an operation before the travel restrictions took effect. Sir."

"What kind of operation?"

"I'm not at liberty to say."

"Ah ha. The same response as your commander. Well, was the order straight from our Lords?"

"I'm not at liberty to say, Sir."

"Since when do we keep these kinds of secrets? This is life and death."

Nico quieted, and turned again to Shil.

She uncrossed her arms, and got closer to the screen, but kept her eyes on the city as she said "I have a man in the Middle Lands, Commander."

"A man?" he replied. His eyes narrowed at her. "Who? And why?"

She looked down, facing his image. "Are you going to question my judgment?"

"At this point? Yes?"

"Fine. I could not trust that your men would find enough information just with spikes, and simple observation and analysis. I found an old, wise teacher to assist."

Brun laughed, loudly. "Assist how?"

"The old instruments aren't all lost, or broken. I believe he can use them to get a better read on what's happening below the surface."

Brun's smile disappeared, and he stared through the screen, full of anger once again. "Commander, I cannot agree with your actions. You're circumventing my own command."

"No. I've only authorized an expedition. You guard the ground. I guard the city. We do not *own* any of Lwo."

"You should have told me first."

"You were off land."

"For good reason. Following orders."

"I know that."

"And yet you couldn't think to at least contact my lieutenant first?"

"I did. Then I remembered, I don't need his approval. And there's hardly any time to go through every channel, Commander. You said it yourself, this is life and death. Dual flashes are unprecedented. We have to act quickly, and use every resource. If you have a real problem, take it up with Commander Jaan."

"Perhaps I will."

"That's fine with me. In the meantime, tell your men not to interfere with Doctor Taj, if they see him."

"I will." Brun paused, and turned toward Nico. "Now, I have another question for your lieutenant."

"Go ahead," she said, backing away from the screen.

Nico got closer to the screen, and focused on Brun. "Yes, Sir?"

"Lieutenant, you saw the flash up close, did you not?" he asked.

"In a way, Sir."

"What does that mean?"

Nico looked out at the city, and then past the buildings, and the line of the forest, in the direction of Taj's village. "It was too fast to notice much of anything. It was bright. There was a moment of increased heat. And we were blinded."

"We? So there were three of you, correct?"

Nico looked back at the screen. "Three?"

"My watcher told me there were three heat signatures in your craft."

"Well, he was far behind us, Sir. And far below. And we were moving fast. I only had one patrolman with me."

"Are you saying our sensors are faulty, Lieutenant?"

"Wait," Shil said, stepping in before Nico could respond. "Commander, this is not the time for such a minor argument."

"My men were exposed," said Brun. "And your man left fast. Why is that?"

"Because we knew they were capable," said Nico. "And we had to get back. Our work was done, and our craft was functional, but we could not know how long it would stay that way."

Brun hesitated, and almost hissed as he spoke again. "I have to say, I don't like anything I'm hearing. Could I speak with the patrolman who was with you?"

Nico stood up firmly, with his hands behind him, and looked away from the screen. As Shil walked up, he stepped aside.

"Come to the city, Commander," she said. "We will discuss this in person."

"Very well. Sir."

"How soon can you come?"

"I do have work to do out here. I will come tomorrow morning."

"Very well. Shil out." The line closed, and she turned to Nico. "I can hear it in your voice, Lieutenant."

Nico was quiet, fearful of saying any more as Shil continued to look at him.

"Something happened last night," she went on. "Tell me what it was."

Nico looked into her eyes, but stayed silent, unmoving, unable to move. He was stuck in a memory, of his last formal teachings, trying to remember the last unnatural deaths. *Has it been decades?* He thought. *It was before I was born, wasn't it?*

"Lieutenant!"

He focused again. He looked back and forth, from his commander to the city, and then back to her again. "Sir, I'm afraid we've lost someone," he said. "I'm afraid *I* have."

"Lost?" Her eyes narrowed at him, and she took two steps closer. "What do you mean 'lost?'"

"A citizen, who came with us last night."

"What!? Came *with* you?!" Her eyes widened, her lips tensed. "Where? Where did you lose them? In the village?"

"No." He hesitated. "To the storm. I'm sorry, Sir."

Shock flooded her eyes. *"To the...How could you..."* Her words were barely whispers. She stopped herself from shouting. She looked over to the closed doors, and then back to him. She grabbed him, and turned him, forcing his eyes into hers. "Tell me what happened."

"She was at the protest, at the south entry, last night," he said. "We had dispersed the crowd, but she lingered. She saw the craft we were taking to Taj. She threatened to report it to the council, and more widely if she got the chance, if we took her into custody. In exchange for her silence, she wanted to see the land outside."

He felt himself almost shaking as he recalled the series of events, but went on. "Everything was fine. No one saw her leave with us. We got to the village, and made the drop off, then, as we were leaving…" He saw Loren's panicked eyes again, and remembered the chilling, wild winds that had surrounded the puller. "It was after the flash hit us, after we were down. I had to dislodge the puller. After I did I leapt for the door, but she hadn't listened to me. She'd removed her restraints, and-"

"No!" Shil yelled, raising her hand, stopping him. "It could *not* have been her fault. Our duty is to protect the city, but we always protect the people first. You should have sent her to the station, had her held here until morning."

Nico shook his head. "There was no time, Sir. It was getting dark. We had to get out to the village and back as fast as possible. We couldn't let the people find out. Your orders-"

"Don't put this on me!"

Nico looked away, silenced again.

Shil turned, and walked up to the window, and looked out at the city. Nico looked with her, at the traffic flowing below, at the growing number of craft now carrying civilians about. The air and ground were no doubt much drier by now. Shil turned again, and walked away from him, to the far wall. She stood there, silent, thinking. He looked away from her, dreading what she might be contemplating, for him, or for Kine. It was minutes before she moved, and walked back to him. She leaned back against the command table, and stared out the window again.

"It's been sixty years," she said. "Sixty years since a civilian citizen was lost. Did you know that, Lieutenant?"

He nodded, finally recalling. "Yes, Sir." He turned to face her, and stood firmly, keeping his arms behind his back, in full deference.

"We've gone so long. I cannot fathom how the people will react, but we have protocols to follow." She sighed. "I will notify the council that we need to meet. And we will have to tell the people. Who was she?"

Nico hesitated, shaking his head, as another wave of disbelief passed through him. "It was Loren, Sir."

Shil stared back at him, searching his eyes. "*The* Loren? The Songbird?"

He nodded. "Yes, Sir."

She closed her eyes for a moment, holding her emotions in. "Does she have family? Friends? Besides you, that is."

"Sir, it was an acci-"

"Just tell me, Lieutenant!"

"Yes, Sir. There is her band. I'm sure I can find them."

Shil sighed again, and pushed her hands into the table surface behind her. "It hasn't been a full day yet. Wait until tonight, then inform them. Go about your day. Go on your patrol. And make sure you monitor all four entries. We don't need anyone else trying to sneak out."

"Yes, Sir."

"But before you do anything, tell me, which patrolman went with you last night?"

"It was Kine, Sir."

She nodded. "Tell him to come see me."

"Yes, Sir."

"You're dismissed."

Nico saluted, and backed away, as Shil took her seat again in the high-backed chair. He exited through the metal doors, and immediately sent a secure message to Kine. The message was simple, nothing that would rouse suspicion if any others happened to read it. Kine would know why Shil needed to see him. He ignored the temptation to open even a secured line. He dared not speak to him before Shil did.

He made his way to the lift, and down to the fifteenth floor. As he exited the lift into the hangar, he saw a row of three idling pullers, and across from them, his jumper, parked next to another. Four patrolmen were in the hangar. Three of them were at the farthest puller, which was facing the wide, airy entry to the outside. They were inspecting the craft before two of them would enter to go on patrol. One of them was examining the rear vents. Another was standing with one foot in the open starboard door, resting her hand on her knee as she spoke to the man inspecting the front engine.

Nico walked up to his jumper, just as the other patrolman in the hangar jumped on the one next to it. She saluted him before leaning down, grasping the handlebar, and floating away. He watched as she approached the hangar entry, and checked for traffic, and then bolted out, her engines humming as she flew straight out, heading north.

Through his helmet display, Nico accessed the station's system, and checked-in for his shift. He ran a check of his tech once more, and double checked his gauntlets. For some reason they felt heavier. In fact, his whole body felt heavier. He ignored it. He knew what it was, and that he would have to bear it, for however long.

He activated his jumper's engines, and walked around it, feeling its light exhaust around his legs. He checked the control panel, and the seat, and the vents. The body was still clean from the day before. The white paint still shined. His rank marks were still there, on the underbody, and beneath the bold station designations on the side panels. He turned the lights on to yellow, and then purple, and then red, and then orange, and then back to yellow. He left them on as he hopped up onto the seat, and leaned forward, and took hold of the handlebar. As he pulled out, and turned toward the entry, he saw the other three patrolmen. They each stood more firmly, and saluted. He nodded back, and then slowly entered the airstream, and turned right, and curved wide around the station, and sped up as he headed west.

CHAPTER 12
AWAKENED

Haluna's was not the only bar open early in the day, but it was the only one that offered a full view of the city's park. Its tall windows faced the greenery and pathways that led to the north side of the stage, which, save for a few small children playing in front of it, was unbothered. The parents, three couples, were sitting on smoothed stone seats nearby, watching as the two boys and one girl moved about freely, running and screaming and making up games. Their small shrieks carried through the wide open space. By the time the playful sounds reached Chad, sitting at his booth behind the window, they were actually pleasant, to his surprise.

He had been sitting in the same spot for half an hour, barely sipping a cup of bland tea, looking back and forth to the small screen on his phone. He watched the scrolling, glowing lines of text. The headlines were repetitive. Travel outside the city was still restricted, for the third day in a row, but every other piece of information seemed unimportant, as was often the case. However, today he was expecting more. He was sure something had happened to Loren outside the city, and if it had, the watchers would have to report it, publicly. He took another sip of tea.

"It's been a while, big guy," Haluna said happily.

Chad looked up at her, at her bright, green eyes, and her graying bangs of hair, and her wide smile, and at the annoyingly imperfect red hat that she had been wearing for the past year. The thing was too big for her, and the top half always came down loosely over both her ears. It looked as old as she was. He could not guess her age, but he was sure that if she had a son or daughter, they would be older than he was.

She was holding a small, empty tray on her hip. He looked around the room. The dozen other tables and booths were nowhere near full. And there was only one other server working.

"How about you charge me for another hour?" he asked. He took the etched, metal card from the pocket near the top of his jacket, and held it out to her.

"Oh, it's no charge, dear," she said, gently guiding his hand back down. "I just wanted to check on you. Are you hungry? You must be."

"No, I'm not hungry, Hala. I'm waiting."

"For a *who*, or a *what*?"

He took up the cup again, and finished the tea, and set it back in the saucer before sliding it to the edge of the table. "I'll have another. Please." He set his card down near the saucer.

"Okay, big guy," she said, taking the saucer and cup up onto the tray, and taking the card into her hand.

He watched as she turned and walked away, stopping at another table to take a young couple's order before going back to the counter. Before he could finish reading another redundant report on his phone's screen, she was back with his card and his tea. It was steaming, the cup hot to the touch. She had whisked herself away, halfway to the other side of the room before he could thank her. She had known him for years. She had served him in the daylight, and at night, when he had been alone, and when he had not. He knew she would not ask him anything else. And he knew not to stay much longer.

As the lines of text on his phone continued scrolling, Chad finally saw what he had been waiting for. In a more pronounced font that stood out from the other headlines were the words 'Watcher Report - 10:00 AM.' It was two minutes away.

He tapped the text, and set the phone down, and watched as a rectangular image beamed up from the lens below the small screen. It was black for a moment, and then the council's chambers slowly came into view. The room was massive, with polished, wooden walls and floors, and a large set of double doors on the far side, where two gold-clad officers stood. On the near side, just below the camera, there were five equally-spaced seats behind a long, curving desk. The row, as most people in the city called it, was currently empty. In front of it, however, at the middle of the three desks used by any who were called to, or were seeking to speak, sat three watchers.

Chad peered at the image as he took a sip of tea. The heat

moving down his throat and through his body was almost calming. What he wanted to do was throw the cup across the room. The watchers looked too calm, too at ease. The city's commander, a lean, strong woman with dark hair, was in the middle. The man to her right, wearing black with metal, armored tech, was clearly from the ground. His beard was thick, and his ranking pin indicated that he was the commander, though Chad was not familiar with him. To the woman's left, sitting further back, upright and present, but with a face full of concern, was the city's lieutenant. The rest of the chamber was empty.

At the sound of a soft, echoing bell the three watchers stood, and from both sides of the image, the council's row of seats began to fill. The profiles of the councilors' faces were varied, but recognizable. Each of them, as was required by the Lords, was over eighty years of age, and they each appeared to be so. All of them had at least a strand or two of gray running through their hair, and the two men on the row had gray in their beards. They all wore long coats made mostly of fabric that was plain and brown, but included flowing, distinctive, elaborate stitch patterns in a golden thread that ran along their sleeves, and up and around their high collars. The effect was that all of the councilors, once sitting and facing away from the camera, were made nearly static by their coverings, appeared to be nearly identical, and had the same warm glow. Chad had never been to the chamber to see if they had the same presence in person. He reached to his left ear, turned the volume up on his receiver, and watched closely as the proceedings began.

Councilor Bethe, a woman who, according to the text on the screen, had been on the council for ten years and had led it for two, began by pressing her palm into the short, square microphone in front of her. Its perimeter beamed a low white light, and it chimed softly to life.

"We are honored," Bethe began. "To have a trio of watchers, chosen as leaders by our Lords, to speak before the council. Commander Shil, please begin."

The watchers sat back down, and Shil pressed the lone microphone on the desk, leaned forward, and set her arms down. As another camera panned to her, the glow of the microphone lit the strong lines of her face. "We thank the council," she started, her voice strong, and raspy. "For making time for us to speak this morning. We have a report of great importance to share with the population at large. It concerns the state of the land, and more specifically, the state of the ground." She paused, and looked to a computer tablet next to the microphone, glancing over its screen before continuing. "In recent days we have seen flashing from the surface. In fact, there were two flashes within twenty-four hours. This is the specific reason for increased restrictions on travel."

Bethe leaned forward intently. "The closure of the city's entries for a third straight day was unexpected," she said. "However, hearing that it was due to flashing, I think I can safely speak for the city when I say thank you for your precautions."

"It is our duty," Shil replied.

Bethe leaned back, and she and the other councilors began to speak amongst themselves, in whispers too quiet for any of the words to be discerned. As Chad watched, he thought about the broad, misleading reason the watchers had given for closing the city's entries, a supposed anomaly in the weather. Then he thought about the only flash he had ever heard of. Over a decade prior, not long before he had come to the city, one of the village elders had spoken of a flash from his childhood. The story had excited Chad, and a friend of his, for a day or two.

In the projection, Bethe leaned back over her microphone. "Commander, what are the watchers of the ground doing in response?" she asked.

Shil turned to the watcher covered in heavy black. He whispered something to her, and nodded before she turned back to the council. "Commander Brun here has instructed his examiners to take data from the sites of each flash and perform a more in-depth analysis."

"*More* in-depth, Commander?"

Chad saw Shil's eyes shift, and saw her hesitation. Bethe was pressing, but the council had to adhere to the watchers, just like every other citizen. Her question was necessary, but her tone was a posture, to appease any observers that might feel watchers, in general, needed to be more accountable. Chad was such an observer, but he still sensed Shil's stronger position.

"Yes, Councilor," Shil answered. "The initial readings at the

223

sites provided only typical information. The ground's surface was partially altered, and there were temperature shifts. Brun's division will look for more."

A man on the end of the row, resting his elbow on the table as he stroked his chin, tapped his microphone and leaned forward. His eyes were bright, and his neatly-trimmed beard was the same reddish color as his short, crisp hair. A line of text identified him as Councilor Pett. "Where exactly have these flashes taken place, Commander?" he asked. "Are there any villages in danger?"

Shil paused, and took a breath. "The second flash was not very far from a village, but the people are in no immediate danger, as far as we know. Historically, no flash has ever broken through a settlement. In fact, because so many villages are on the most fertile land, we believe there may be a correlation between lack of plant life and susceptibility to flashing. There is also no historical evidence of a flash in the forest, where the oldest trees grow."

Another councilor, a woman with a slightly rounder shape than the others on the row, and with a slightly more youthful face, tapped her microphone. She was identified as Councilor Senna. "What about *near* the forest?" she asked.

Shil hesitantly nodded. "Yes. There was one flash, two centuries ago, that tracked just miles from the forest. That is another reason we thought it necessary to inform the citizenry."

The councilors spoke amongst themselves again, whispering for minutes as the cameras moved between them and the watchers.

Chad could feel his heart pumping. The news, news that was already affecting the city at large, was necessary, but it was not what he had been anticipating. It was not what he still feared.

Bethe leaned over her microphone again. "Commander Shil. How soon can you report to us again?"

"We believe we will have more information in two days," Shil answered.

"Very well. As is customary with all watcher reports, we will re-broadcast this throughout the day. To the citizenry, we ask, and we believe the watchers to be in agreement, that you do not react in panic. And please continue to follow the guidance of the watchers of our city."

"We are in agreement," said Shil.

Bethe nodded, and leaned back in her chair. A bell rang, signaling the end of the proceedings. The councilors began to speak amongst themselves again. Rows of text on the screen repeated what Shil had reported, and the agreement between the watchers and the councilors. The watchers, however, were not leaving. They had not even stood. Shil tapped her microphone twice, deactivating it and then activating it, sounding the chime. The sound got the attention of the councilors, and they turned toward her again.

"If the council will allow..." Shil started. "There is one more thing to report."

The councilors quieted, and Bethe leaned over her microphone again. "Please, Commander," she said. "Go ahead."

Shil intertwined her gloved hands, and took a deep breath. "We, regrettably, must also inform the citizenry of a death."

The councilors became even quieter. The camera panned to their stoic faces, and then back to Shil. Chad felt his heart starting to burn. Shil went on.

"Two nights ago, while on a special assignment with the watchers, a citizen was lost to the storm. It is the first such loss in sixty years."

Bethe's eyes, and the eyes of the other councilors, remained steady. Then she lowered her head, and stood. The other councilors stood with her. Then the watchers stood. The gold-clad officers at the back of the room lowered their heads. Then Bethe spoke, in a more pronounced tone.

"At the unfortunate loss of a fellow Lwoan–and one of the last of a struggling humanity–to the winds, we the council, and those in attendance, will now observe with three minutes of silence. At the end, if the teller of the loss will do so, please speak the Lwoan's name and age."

The cameras moved slowly, in and out and around, showing all who were in the chamber with their heads bowed, and their hands behind their backs. As it moved to and from each of the watchers, Chad watched intently. He could see the tiniest changes in the lieutenant's posture. The man was nervous. Chad felt his heart beating faster, felt a rage forming. Finally, Bethe tapped her microphone twice more, ending the silence with another chime.

Shil leaned over her microphone and spoke. "Loren. Twenty-two."

After a short pause, and an almost inaudible gasp from someone unseen, all in the room spoke the name again, and in unison. "Loren."

The camera panned back out, to the view behind all of the councilors, who took their seats again. The room was not loud, but there was a murmur, as the watchers stood there, waiting. The two uniformed men at the door were clearly waiting for Shil, who was not moving. Deep down, Chad hoped she was waiting for chastisement, but that would not come. The row of five was there to handle disagreements between citizens, and prosecutions brought by the watchers. And they were chosen by citizens, not the Lords. Only on rare occasions had any row ever even reached out to the Isle, or so Chad had heard, and even then it was to assist with relations with the watchers. A single death was not a good enough reason. Bethe leaned forward again.

"Commander Shil?" she asked, as if speaking to a friend, as if offering sympathy. "Has the citizen's family been informed?"

"She had no known family," Shil answered. "However, her friends have been informed."

"Very well. We thank you, Commander, for sharing this difficult news."

Shil nodded, and then turned, and headed for the door, followed closely by Brun, and then by her lieutenant. After the trio had exited the chambers, through doors held by the officers, Chad deactivated the projection. Exasperated, and without thinking, he let his hands hit the table. The impact was not loud, not to him, but he still felt Haluna's eyes shoot over to him from behind the counter. He took a few more sips of the now-lukewarm tea, and looked out again at the expanse of the park, thinking. He could not help imagining what Loren's last moments must have been like, yanked up helplessly, into chilling air, with no tech to aid her, swiftly crushed by the unseen forces of the winds.

Finally he stood, and took his phone and slid it into the pocket on his left pant leg. He stepped away from the booth, and walked to the pair of heavy, glass doors. He gently slid one open, and closed it behind him as he stepped outside. He did not turn around to look, but he could still feel Haluna's eyes on him as he departed.

The night before, having heard nothing from Loren for a day, Chad had gleaned information from a number of other citizens in his sector. He had learned that the lieutenant was most often stationed in the south, so he had ventured today to the park sector, and queried any who looked comfortable and knowledgeable, and happened to pass by the alcove he had staked out for himself. Most had been taken aback by his size, but none had sought to run. In his growing grief, he had even been polite to some.

He had learned that the lieutenant generally started his shift at 11:00 AM, and that he started in the west, and made his way around the city by noon, which was when he would usually settle in or near the park sector for a regular patrol. Haluna's bar had been the perfect place to start, with its view of the park, and the buildings that surrounded it.

As time crept forward, Chad moved slowly around the area. He stopped in a boot shop, and browsed as if he was interested. He was already wearing heavy, durable boots he had acquired a year before, on the city's north side. He stopped in the small office of a teller, and checked his available credit. Afterwards he finally made his way into the park, and sat on a rock bench near the stage. He could almost see Loren dancing again, and her bandmates playing.

On the days they performed he had served as a de facto guard for all of them, with one other man for support. Only when called, and paid well, had he ever accompanied Loren alone. But now, it seemed, he had failed. Or, perhaps, she had failed. But certainly, the lieutenant had failed. She had been lost. He looked up at the sky, and saw the light gray, unending clouds. He heard the distant forces of the storm high above, and imagined the dread she had surely felt in her last moments.

Chad had seen a near-loss as a child, back in his village near the Spire. A woman had been yanked up a dozen yards, and wailed a terrifying sound that everyone within a mile had heard. She had been rescued by a watcher of the ground, who had shot up from his speeding fox just in time to swipe her away from the sky, and fly her back down to solid earth. The village had spoken of it for a week. The woman, barely forty years of age, had died not long after. Fortunately her son had just reached adulthood, and was able to take care of himself. He had eventually been chosen for the ranks of the ground watchers, or so Chad had heard.

When he pulled out his phone to check the time again it was 12:05 PM. He had timed things just right, he hoped. He stood up from the bench, and began walking again. More people were in the park now, spread about. The families with children had gone. Now there were couples who appeared to be well over sixty years, and some on their own that appeared to be no older than forty. He heard engines roaring above, and looked up at the traffic in the first stream. Four lanes surrounded the open space above the park. He was directly beneath one, heading west, moving at a steady pace. Then, he spotted a jumper, fifty feet up, its lights pulsing yellow as it flew south. He narrowed his gaze. It was not the lieutenant. As he reached the north-south path below it, he looked north, to where the jumper had come from. Another jumper was approaching.

Chad looked up again, and as it passed over, saw the familiar, dark insignia on its underbody–three encircled crosses with a stripe alongside one of them. He lifted his hood from his shoulders, and cinched it around the sides of his face, and started to jog. The path was not crowded, but he kept his pace slow, not wanting to draw any attention. Every few seconds there was someone to maneuver around, but he kept his eyes on the narrow, compact craft flying above. After three blocks, the lieutenant curved left around a building. Chad jogged around the same corner, keeping him in sight.

After heading east for one block and one building, the lieutenant came to a stop at the corner, facing a north-south stream, and idled there. Chad slowed to a walk, and looked up, and saw the man sitting upright, resting his hands on his legs, with his head on a swivel as he watched the steady flow of traffic.

Chad stopped at a shopfront, and slid open the short door, and stepped inside. It was cool, and small, no more than fifteen feet on each side. Three of the bright, painted walls were lined with large canisters, each of them labeled with the name of one drink or another, and affixed with a mechanized spout at the bottom. Chad pulled the small, metal bottle from his right hip, unscrewed the top, and walked up to the canister labeled 'Tea.' After he had filled his canister, and replaced the top, he walked up to the counter. He nodded at the clerk, checked the cost on the mounted display, and slid his card into its reader. As it beeped, he set his bottle down on the counter, and stepped away. The clerk called to him, but he ignored it, and walked back out to the street, and stood.

He pulled out his phone, and pressed down firmly on the center button beneath the screen. Three options popped into view. The first read 'Emergency' in red letters. The second read 'File a Report' in black letters. He selected the third option, which was in green letters and read 'Non-Emergency Assistance.' The words disappeared, and the city watchers' icon, an outline of their high-reaching station, flashed. A tiny green dot rotated around the screen, as the city's system identified him, and his location. He looked up, and east, at the still-idling jumper, and watched. The lieutenant backed the craft away from the north-south stream, and turned around, and began descending.

Half a dozen pedestrians moved aside as the jumper's engines blew downward and it slowly neared the street. Its lights glowed a continuous yellow, as the lieutenant idled it two feet off the ground, and then took his hands away from the controls, pressed down on the seat, and hopped off. Chad watched as the man approached, and then held his phone's screen out at him. The lieutenant acknowledged it, and stopped in front of him, and removed his helmet. *He's too young*, Chad thought. *Too young to be the lieutenant.* The man's skin was clear and firm. His green eyes seemed unburdened. And his short, brown hair shined with rich color. He looked well short of fifty years.

"Citizen," he said, looking up at Chad. "I am Lieutenant Nico. How may I be of assistance?"

Chad slid his phone back into his pocket, and loosened and lowered his hood, and answered quietly. "I just watched the commander's report, in front of the row. You can start by telling me if it was Loren's fault, or yours."

Nico's face tensed. "Who are y-"

"Please, Lieutenant. Don't waste our time. Loren left with you. I helped her get to you. So just tell me what happened."

Nico put his helmet back on, and crossed his arms over his chest, and looked up into Chad's eyes. "I see," he said. "You must be the guard dog. The one the patrolman put on his back at the protest."

Chad felt both his fists clinch. "I am a friend. *Was* a friend."

"Take it easy," said Nico, holding his hands out. "*Chad*, is it? According to her mates, you were more of an employee, and one she did not always treat well."

"Maybe I liked it. And she paid well, so what did it matter?"

"Is that why you're upset? The money? I'm sure a man of your size would be of service to any number of other citizens."

"No. That's not it. I have no problem surviving. I have a problem with your lies. The supposed weather anomaly you reported was actually flashing. And your commander said Loren was on a special assignment, but Loren left for adventure, not to work with you. And she left with *your* help."

"And yours. Right?"

Chad quieted, fighting off the sudden, burning sense of guilt. He could have taken Loren back to her home that night, in one arm, with no trouble. Of course, she probably would have called out for help in some melodic rhyme. And she had already paid him. He felt sadness, and anger. As he looked away, he felt the lieutenant take a step toward him.

"It's nobody's fault," Nico said quietly. "I will tell you exactly what happened. We ran into trouble. She did not listen. The door to our puller was open. She was..." he hesitated. "She was trying to help me, and she took off her restraints, and leaned out near the door. Her boots and her helmet were good, but she had no tech, and no armor, just that cloak. And, as is always the case at night, the winds were hard to gauge. I tried to save her. I held on for as long as I could, but I am not as strong as Mother Nature. None of us are. Not even you."

Chad looked down at Nico. He could still make out his eyes through the visor. There was regret there now, regret he had been hiding. "She wasn't always careful," said Chad. "And she was hard to manage. But all she wanted was to see the land. All she wanted was inspiration. She shouldn't have been lost for it."

"I do not disagree with you, Chad. I am bearing this burden. But like I said, we ran into trouble."

"What kind of trouble?"

"You watched the report to the council. Put two and two together."

"You saying the flash was the trouble?"

Nico nodded, and looked around, at the pedestrians.

Chad stared back at him, silent. He could feel the eyes all around them. People were watching them, as was always the case when a watcher approached anyone. And the clerk in the store, where no one else was entering or departing, was eyeing him even harder. But Chad needed the man's eyes, to bear witness, if necessary. "Didn't you have a decent pilot?" he asked.

Nico closed his eyes for a moment, and took a breath. "I have nothing else to tell you, Chad," he said. "More will be known soon enough. All you can do now is continue to watch our reports." He crossed his arms again. "I assume there is nothing else?"

Chad shook his head. "No. But if the next report isn't

complete, Lieutenant, I promise, I'll tell this whole city. Everyone will know that it was you who took her, when you didn't have to. And they'll know it was in an unmarked craft, after the entries had been locked down."

Nico's eyes came alight behind his visor. "You know more than you let on."

"You really think you can hide everything you want to? From everyone?"

Nico raised his right hand up, and then, let the cold end of his gauntlet touch Chad's jacket, and gently squeezed his shoulder. "One more threat like that," he said. "Just one more, and you won't be free, or able enough to tell anyone anything."

Chad stared back at him, silent. He wanted to move, but could not, not yet. Nico backed away, keeping his eyes on him as he mounted his jumper again. Its engines hummed slightly louder, and its lights continued to shine down, as he ascended, and turned eastward again, and re-entered the first stream. Chad watched from the street, as the watcher stopped at the corner where he had first been idling. Two civilian craft passed in front of him before he pulled out into the north-south stream, and then flew out of sight.

CHAPTER 13
PROOFS

Taj had spent half the night making it to and from the sites of both flashes. Flying near the clouds had saved time, but dropping the old probes had taken hours. It had been tedious–maneuvering to just the right position, setting the craft's engines to hover properly at one hundred feet, and then holding each heavy device just right, waiting minutes for a target confirmation before dropping it. The raw winds, even pressing through doors less than one yard open, had been vicious. A handful of his braids had been frayed, and he had been knocked back more times than he could remember. He was sure the boot locks he had installed near the door had saved his life at least three times.

He had made six drops, three at each site, with two at the ends of each charred strip of earth, and one at each center. And between each drop, it seemed, the craft's system had warned him with soft tones, forcing him to ascend, and avoid the paths of the patrolling ground watchers. He would have preferred to work with their division. Their data, however incomplete Shil thought it to be, would have been useful. Their spikes had always been accurate. But his old student, now in a position that demanded deference, had insisted that the work had to be his own. She had also told him, in their last call before his trek, that the men on the ground knew of it, and would not interfere. They had done even less, refusing to acknowledge him as they sped by, never lingering in case he needed assistance.

Now it was midday, and Taj had hardly slept. In his mind, repeating over and over again, were the illuminated views of the dead land the flashes had left behind. They had only been glimpses, but their lack of color, and their size, had been jarring. The first scans to arrive from the probes, just minutes after they had been dropped, had only deepened his concerns. The strips of land left behind by the flashes were like the deepest scars from a blade run into flesh, stopping just short of anything vital. The compactions of soil extended beneath the surface for at least two hundred feet. And the low mounds that had formed on top of them were like rock.

Taj raised his head from the desk in his office. He stared at the wooden box, off to the right, sitting on the floor in the corner. It was empty, except for the decorative throw on top of it, hanging folded over the front side. A woman in the village had made it for him, from purple and blue yarn. Only a day before the box had housed the receiver that was now affixed to the library's roof, pulling in signals from the distant probes. In front of him his computer, warm with a glowing screen, intermittently blipped and beeped as more data arrived.

There were two bright wave lines on the screen. One was

white, and represented the steady motion of the earth below, with nearly-indiscernible peaks indicating unseen tremors that no one would ever notice, even if they were standing right above them. The other curving line, which was red, indicated severe disruptions. It was moving, and rhythmic, mirroring the sounds that the probes were pushing out beneath the surface. The pointed ends of the devices ensured that the sounds went deeper with each broadcast sent. The red wave had been steady for hours. But as Taj started to set his head back down, it spiked.

The sharp jump in frequency meant that at least one probe's soundwaves had bounced off of something, something with a higher density than the masses left behind after the flashes. Taj's hands leapt to the keyboard, and he opened a rendering on the screen. The condition of the land on the surface had not changed, but the image now extended to one thousand feet below. As more data arrived, and the image refreshed, the rendering went down another one hundred feet, and the shape of a long, flat rock was revealed.

Taj shook his head. The old machines were not perfect. They provided data that still needed to be confirmed on site. They had also never, in all the years that they had been used, been incorrect. At Lwo's founding, centuries before, the probes had identified the most fertile land for farming, and the most stable land for homes. They had found underground water tables and springs, and they had found caved-in lairs of long-extinct creatures. Now, it seemed, a quarter-mile beneath the surface, they had identified a previously undiscovered rock. As Taj continued to examine the image, he saw that the rock appeared to have an extensive line running through it.

Taj sent the image out through a projection. As it materialized over his desk, he looked out at his door. It was still closed, and no one ever knocked. He looked back at the projection. The multi-colored light hit his eyes, and wiped away his fatigue. He stared at the three-dimensional box, lit with grays indicating soil, and light green indicating the limited vegetation above it. The scars left by the flash, extending all the way down to the miles-wide slab, were white, and spaced only inches apart in the projection. The shape of the massive rock was colored with deep orange. The dark line running through it, seemingly a wide crack, extended out of the probes' range, and west.

Taj thought back to his earliest years, and then to his last years of formal education. The rock's location had never been documented, not by his teachers, and certainly not by the Lords. He considered all of the data that he held in his office. He turned, and looked at the ornate boxes on the wall of shelves. At some point he had used every data drive, examined all of their contents, whether it was for others or himself. The drives had been made by the Lords, copies of the land's geological and meteorological and biological history. Only a handful of the great rocks beneath the surface had ever been identified. Others were suspected, but never found. The orange one in the projection had to be one of them.

Taj deactivated the projection, and minimized all of the windows of data on the screen. He sat down, and brought up a call window, and input the private signal Shil had given him. The black, rectangular box filled with lines of sequential code, and chirped repeatedly. He set his arms up on the desk, and leaned forward as Shil's image arose. In her eyes, without a word from her, he saw a heaviness that had not been there before.

"Commander," he greeted her. "Are you alright?"

"Hello, Teacher," she replied. "Yes, I'm fine. Just burdened by a report to the council this morning. Please look for the broadcast when you have time."

He nodded. "I will. I have some information for you. However, I think you'll want to see it in person."

"A call is fine. Just tell me what you've found."

"I hesitate to burden you any further, but especially over a call."

"Please, Teacher. The line is secure, I assure you. What is it?"

"Very well. Do you remember, Shil, your lessons in science, in the studies of the earth, and the materials deep beneath our surface?"

"I do."

"Very good. We knew of a number of great rocks beneath Lwo's surface after it was fully formed, but not all of them. I have all of the records here. I placed a number of probes last night, and it appears that they have found another. It seems that it runs from the west, all the way out to the Middle Lands."

"Which means what exactly?"

"It wouldn't mean anything, really, except that it is cracked, and that the crack is a likely contributor to the flashing."

Shil's eyes narrowed at him. "And why would it be cracked?"

"Pressure. From somewhere."

She stared back through the screen. "Like the city?"

Taj nodded. "Possibly. Likely."

"So, I was right."

"I cannot say for sure, but the probes have never failed before. This great rock is there, and it is compromised."

"How far down is it?"

"Over one thousand feet."

"The city's foundation only extends a few hundred feet. And there were no great rocks beneath the site, just strong soil, and various gems and stones. Maybe it's not us."

"I do hope that it's not."

Shil exhaled, and looked away, and then back through the screen. "But if it is," she said. "Then the city could be in great danger. Teacher, what else can you tell me?"

"Nothing yet. We have to determine where the crack started, and then what kinds of forces may be coming up through it. So, I would request that you meet me, out in the field."

She nodded. "Good idea."

"And I think you'll want to tell your commander, and if I may suggest, the commander of the ground as well."

She paused. "Alright. I will let them both know. Where should we meet?"

"At the second site. It is closest to the city."

"Very well. And when would you suggest?"

"Tonight."

"Understood. Will you send me the data first?"

"I do not think that is a good idea, no matter how secure-"

"Please, Teacher," she stopped him, raising one gloved hand. "Just send it. I'll connect through the Spire, if it'll make you feel better. Here's a file space for it."

As Shil tapped unseen keys on her end, Taj saw a blue circle pop up on his screen. It blinked with a green line around its edge, and her ranking symbol popped up below the symbol of the city's watchers, followed by the symbol of the Spire.

"Alright," he said. He found the updated graph and rendering files on his screen, and moved copies of each into the blinking circle. "Do you have the files?"

Shil's eyes moved around the screen, and she nodded. "I have them. Thank you. I will be in touch with a time to meet. It may be late. Try to get some rest. Shil out."

Rest did not come. It was seven more hours before the library's last patron, an aging farmer who delighted in studying the insects of the soil, finally departed. Taj locked the doors behind him, and then made his way around the hall, deactivating lights, pushing chairs back into place, looking for any items left behind. There were none.

Above, on the roof, he heard the ambience of winds picking up. Every evening, it seemed, they would push harder over the high walls of the village, enough to make their presence known, but rarely enough to cause any damage. Taj shut off the last lights, walked past his desk at the back wall, and headed up the open stairwell.

He moved slowly up the first flight, listening to the creaks in the wooden steps, thinking about those with whom he would soon meet. He turned and headed up the second flight just as slowly, and reached the door to the loft. He entered his code, and it slid open.

The building's public hall was expansive, and high reaching, but there was still a need for storage, especially for the few things more valuable than data drives. To the right of the doorway were boxes made of polished wood. They were sealed, and held artifacts that the village's very first farmers had left behind. There were also small, metal boxes, which held printed books, some of the last known to exist. To the left was a couch and a small hearth, for the rare occasions when the building's staffer needed to stay the night to avoid stronger winds. In the center of the room was a wide, heavy ladder, which led up to a locked hatch, which led to a short attic, which opened to the roof.

Taj took his heavy jacket up from the couch, and put it on. He took his backpack and helmet from the same spot, and moved to the ladder, stepped up its rungs, turned the knob on the first hatch, and slid it back. He stayed kneeling as he entered the attic, and slid the hatch back into place. The space was shadowy, and dusty, with only small, covered lights in the far corners that lit the edges of supply boxes. He slowly raised his hand, and wandered toward the center, until his palm found the surface of the hatch that led to the roof. He found the heavy lever, turned it to disengage the lock, and slowly slid the hatch backward.

The winds immediately pushed down, and hit him hard. His tied braids were pushed from his shoulder to his back. He quickly knelt lower, shoved his helmet down over his head, and strapped his backpack on. As he slowly stepped up onto the roof, he saw that the black craft was still where he had left it, idling, but shaking in place as the winds pushed through its barely-open engines and down to the roof surface. He turned, and pulled the hatch shut behind him, and then stayed low, and made his way over to the craft.

The receiver was still there. Its shallow, circular dish was still spinning, just below the short wing at the rear of the craft's starboard side. The device's rectangular base was still tied down to a bolt in the roof, and still anchored to the craft with a heavy cord, but it was starting to shuffle back and forth. Taj kept low as he walked up, and kept one hand on the starboard wing as he worked to free the device. Then, suddenly, the wind around him began to die down. He looked up, and saw another craft descending from the sky.

The bottom of the bird was mostly black, but Taj could still make out a few brilliant streaks of red. The lights on the underbody were at a low intensity, and came to a stop just a few feet over him, illuminating the space near his idled black craft. He finished freeing the receiver, took it up into his arms, stepped back, and faced the bird's front end. The lights in its cabin grew brighter, and the pilot, a helmeted woman in blue, looked out and waved.

As the bird's engines quieted, and it hovered in place, Taj heard the faint sounds of the rear ramp lowering, and then touching the roof. He stood there, holding the heavy receiver, with its still-spinning dish, in both arms. Then, the commander of the sky watchers emerged, stepping down the ramp, and around the bird's starboard side to face him. Taj heard a click in his helmet, and then heard Jaan's voice.

"Come on!" the commander called, waving to him.

Taj took careful steps toward the rear of the bird, and watched Jaan move back up the ramp, and felt relieved as he ascended it himself, and escaped the winds. The ramp started to close behind him as he stepped toward the starboard side bench. He set the receiver down, and its heavy base thumped against the floorboards. As the ramp sealed and locked, the device started to beep in a pattern, and its dish began to spin faster. He sat down next to it, took off his pack, and strapped in. Across from him, Jaan strapped in on the other bench, and tilted his helmet up and back.

"Airman," he said. "Take us up."

"Yes, Sir," the woman replied.

The bird ascended slowly, jostling back and forth as the pilot angled it toward the village's south wall. Taj looked over his shoulder, through the short window, and watched as his home became smaller and smaller. "I was not expecting an escort," he said, turning back around.

Jaan smiled at him, and set his hands down on his heavy-looking pant legs as he leaned back into the bench. "Good to see you too, Doctor."

"I didn't mean to sound ungrateful, Commander," Taj said. "I'm just surprised."

Jaan waved the suggestion away. "I thought Shil would have told you. But it's fine. I just want to make sure that the man who might save us has a safe trip. And the winds are picking up. And your village was on the way."

"Right. Well, thank you."

"Not a problem." Jaan looked down at the receiver, and raised his chin. "That's a noisy thing, isn't it? What has it brought in?"

"Nothing good, I'm afraid. Did Shil not tell you?"

"She told me something, something quite upsetting. I'd like to hear it from you."

"It's better if I show you."

Taj opened his pack, and pulled out the lap-sized tablet. Its body was made of metal, and the dark, rectangular screen was made of hardened glass. He ran his hand over it, and as it came to life with blue light, found the signal for the receiver, and connected. Then he tapped the icons for the graph and the rendering, set the tablet down next to him with its lens facing out, and activated the projection.

The bird rocked twice, bumped by the winds as it ascended

another two hundred feet. Taj leaned over, and set his left hand down on the receiver, and kept his right hand on the tablet, holding them in place.

Jaan leaned over in his seat, eyeing the bright, projected image, his face alight as he examined all of the dimensions and detail. Taj looked at the flash sites, and their depth beneath the surface, and felt the same flood of concern he had hours before. He looked at the great slab beneath them, and searched his memory again, and again recalled no previous documentation of its existence. In the rendering, more of its size was now visible. The probes' readings were still expanding. Past the projection, Jaan sat back in his seat, and looked up, and took a deep breath.

Taj leaned back in his own seat, more assured of the gravity of the situation. Most watchers rarely reacted to anything from nature. "May I ask, Commander," he started. "What are you thinking?"

Jaan clasped his hands together, and turned toward the front of the craft, eyeing the pilot's actions. "We're only a few minutes out," he said. "I need to hear what the others have to say first."

"I understand," said Taj, nodding in agreement.

The bird picked up speed, as it zipped just beneath the clouds, cutting through the turbulent forces. Taj felt somewhat uneasy, having rarely flown so fast, but it was not long before the pilot eased up on the pedals, and began to descend. The bird was jostled back and forth as they entered the dense lower winds. Taj leaned out and looked through the windshield, and saw six glowing craft already on the ground. As they descended further, he could see that all of the watcher craft were situated around the center of the second flash site.

"Let's close the circle, Airman," Jaan ordered.

"Yes, Sir," she answered.

The pilot turned their aft end toward the gathering, and stopped just above the surface. Jaan stood, and walked up to the ramp, and hit the button to lower it. As it slowly opened, Taj looked out and saw that they had settled between two foxes. Both of them were upright, with their sharp tails dug into soil that had not been burned. Their underbody lights shined outward, illuminating the hardened ground, and the other watcher craft. There were two other foxes upright and directly across from them. In front of one of them stood a watcher of the ground, with one arm behind his back, and the other holding on to one of their technology-laden spikes. In front the other set of dark wings was the man that had to be their commander, Brun. Next to the fox that was on the bird's right, hovering over the site, was a glowing puller. Standing in front of it, and holding a tall, white shield at her side, was Shil. Far across from her, kneeling in front of a hovering, flickering gull, was the commander from the mountains, Fits.

The winds were howling, and pushing in and out of the cabin. Jaan pulled his helmet back down onto his shoulders, and started down the ramp. Taj unstrapped himself, took his tablet up into one arm, slung his pack onto his shoulder, and held on to the wall as he followed behind the commander. He was stopped, however, as Jaan

248

turned around and held up his hand.

"Stay here, Doctor," he said. He moved one hand to his helmet, and muttered something inaudible. "I've connected your line to ours. You'll be able to hear everything we say."

Taj saw the watchers' four command rankings begin glowing in red on the right side of his helmet's panel. Then, a gust hit his heavy boots. He lunged forward, stabilizing himself, but still fell into Jaan's outstretched arm.

"It's dangerous," Jaan said, lifting him back upright. "I cannot imagine that you placed the probes while standing on the ground. Am I wrong?"

Taj stood, and took a step back, and leaned against the cabin wall, and shook his head. "No, Commander."

"So, let us not tempt fate. The land does not need another loss."

Taj nodded, thinking about the report he had seen from the watchers of the city, which he had only been able to watch once. "I won't argue with you," he said.

"Good," Jaan said, and pointed at his helmet. "They'll blink according to who is speaking."

"I know that."

Jaan laughed. "Right," he said, and held out one hand. "And if you would, I'll take the tablet."

Taj handed the device over, and as Jaan took it, and continued down the ramp, he turned, walked back, sat on the end of the bench, and looked out. The winds howled, and he strapped in again. He watched as Jaan stepped down to the dark, lifeless swath of earth, holding the tablet at his side. He looked down for a moment, at the ground, as if in shock, and then walked out another yard, and stopped at the center of the flash site.

The other commanders slowly approached him, and Taj saw white exhaust push out through all of their tech as they formed a circle. They were flanked, at a distance, by the other three watchers of the ground. All seven of them saluted, as wind passed evenly through each of the commanders' tech, even going from one to the other, as if forming a shield of concentrated air behind them. Brun's symbol blinked in Taj's helmet as he spoke first.

"Commander, Sir," he started. "I would like to state something. I would have appreciated being informed of the old teacher's expedition ahead of time."

Taj could hear the agitation in Brun's heavy voice, and thought he saw the massive man look past Jaan and into the bird.

"I understand," said Jaan, his symbol blinking above the other three. "But Shil was within her rights as second. And she only did what she thought was best, and had I known her intention, I would have approved."

"Yes, Sir," said Brun.

"I thought that was settled," said Shil.

"It is now," said Jaan, stopping any further argument. "And no matter, because here we are. Commander Brun? Have one of your privates send their data from this site to this tablet."

"Yes, Sir," Brun answered, and then waved toward the private directly behind Jaan.

Taj watched as the man took a step back, held up his spike, and then thrust it down into the hardened ground. The dish on top of the tool flickered with red lights. A few moments later a light, the light of the projection from the tablet, emerged between the commanders. The four of them each took one step back, allowing more room for the multi-dimensional rendering.

"It's so far down," said Brun, his voice noticeably softer. "And there is the crack. It must have been the earth's heat that pushed up through it."

"Looks that way," said Jaan.

"Where does the crack lead to?"

"The city," said Shil. "I've had hours to look at the data that Doctor Taj sent. The trajectory of that line suggests the crack started right below us." She took in a breath, and sighed.

"Where are the ties?" asked Fits. "The ties beneath the ground."

"Not in that cross-section," Taj said aloud. To his surprise, the watchers turned toward the bird, and looked at him. "Sorry. I didn't know you could hear me."

"It's fine, Doctor," said Jaan, and turned back to the other commanders. "He's right. There are no ties nearby. They are not the problem."

"That is not what the Lords thought," said Fits.

"They are not here to see," said Jaan.

Taj heard the pilot shift in her seat, and turned to look at her. She was silent, but inputting codes into one of the control panels. He wondered for a moment if Jaan had also patched her in to their meeting, if she was reacting to commentary about the land's eldest, most revered people. As he turned back around, he had another thought.

"Does the data from the spike show anything new?" he asked. Out among the commanders, he saw the light of the projection shifting, and Jaan working on the tablet.

"It's only three hundred feet down, Teacher," said Shil. "But it mirrors the shape of the scar from the flash. Temperatures remain higher here on the surface. There is not much else."

"Then I would suggest a deeper examination," said Taj.

"I would agree," said Brun. "But our diggers won't go beyond a spike's deepest scan. And the old machines are long gone. We'd have to build one from scratch."

"Everyone, go to your secondary channel," said Jaan.

Taj watched, as above Jaan's blinking ranking, a code appeared. Then, he heard the click of another line opening. "Am I still on?" he asked.

"You are," said Jaan. "Just you and us commanders. What do you say about the old machines, Doctor?"

"They are not gone," he answered. "They're here. They've

been repurposed, even broken down in some cases, but they're here, spread across the mainland."

"How do you know so much, old man?" Brun asked.

"Commander, I have lived several decades longer than you. I am even older than *your* commander, believe it or not. And most of my years have been spent in study."

"I've never seen one of the old machines. Isn't it possible that your studies led you astray?"

"No, it is not," said Jaan. "Taj is right. I've seen the files, and even seen one of the original surveyors up close."

"And how is it that I, the commander on the ground, did not know any of this?"

"Did you ever ask?"

Even from a distance, Taj could feel the tension among the commanders. Looking out at the whole gathering, he could see that the three privates from the ground were also focused on their leaders, as if knowing what was happening, despite being closed off from the conversation.

"I am not judging you, Commander Brun," Jaan continued. "You are more than capable, as the Lords confirmed with your promotion years ago. You just had this one blindspot. Until now."

"Then, I apologize, Sir," said Brun.

"That is not necessary."

"I should apologize," said Shil. "The problem is beneath the city. We're too heavy. We've become a burden."

"You are not to blame," said Jaan. He paused, and knelt down to the ground. "The Lords, even the first Lords, understood that most people would not be able to bear the burdens that we do, and would need to lead more protected, stable lives if humanity was to go on. They allotted that one space for the city, and they knew that it was not ideal."

"What do you mean, Sir?" asked Shil.

"All of Lwo sits on rock that is much weaker than what the old continents sat upon, before the collapse. So, the Lords built pillars beneath the city, built them almost the same way they built the ties." He paused, and looked down. "They trusted that forming the pillars as they did would be enough. They only had two choices. It was either stabilize and establish a city, or suffer the same fate as the rest of the world had, and be extinct. Looking at the data here, I'd say it is likely that one of the pillars has pressed into this great rock."

There was silence. Taj was stunned, and quiet. He glanced at the pilot, but she was still focused on her controls, and the movements of the winds outside the windshield. When he turned back around, Jaan was standing again, and facing Shil.

"Sir, I have never heard of these pillars," said Shil. "As the city's commander, should I not have been told?"

"Did you ask them about the city, when you were promoted?"

"Of course, Sir. But not..."

"Not what?"

"Not about this, not anything close to it."

"Well, I asked many questions, about the city, and much more. And eventually, they told me much more than I expected."

"Then could you not have told me yourself?"

"It was long ago, Commander. And it was not my place, just as it is not my place to inquire of what you asked at your ceremony. But now, that history can no longer be hidden."

Through the midst of the wild air and the gathering, Taj could almost see Shil's body tensing. He had seen the same frustrated, but focused energy in her from the time she was a young child.

"That the Lords built the city on weaker ground is upsetting," she said. "That they may have made things worse with these pillars is…" she stopped, as if afraid of her own line of thinking. "Could we not have built smaller cities? Or, larger villages?"

"At that time it was not optimal. The people may not have lived long enough."

"But look at us now. Aren't we stronger than that? And weren't we then?"

"Not most of us," said Brun. "Not the people who were placed in the city."

"Like my family?" said Shil, turning her head to the towering man. "Is that what you're saying?"

Brun paused. "Please don't jump to conclusions. Sir. That is not what I meant. It's just easier there. Those who can't live at the Spire, or even near it, often go there."

"And they don't exactly thrive when they do."

"Enough!" Jaan shouted, and then waited for their attention to turn back to him. "I wish this could have been revealed under different circumstances, but none of us could have predicted any of this. It has taken generations just to get to this point, of the last of us crawling through existence, but here we are." He breathed deeply, and strongly. "It's all so sudden, that I wonder if Mother Earth has finally grown tired of us. But no matter the case, we have work to do. Now, what actions do you all suggest we take?"

"The old teacher is right," said Brun, his voice lower, and humbled. "We need a deeper examination."

"Then, I'm sure he will help us," said Jaan. "I suggest you and your men work closely with him."

"Yes, Sir."

Taj kept quiet, staring out at the meeting, at the light of the projection between the commanders. He watched as Shil knelt down, and set a hand on the ground, pressing. The exhaust from her tech shifted. She rubbed the top of her helmet with her other hand.

"The ground beneath the city also needs to be examined," she said. "Especially if the instability does in fact reach as far as that rock. But before that, the city will need to prepare for an evacuation."

"The whole city?" asked Fits.

"Yes. The next flash could come from anywhere along this line. We have to be ready. But, it won't be easy. The people will resist, as they did when we cut off transportation, maybe even more."

"That makes sense," said Fits.

There was a pause, and Taj felt uneasy, struggling to process all that he had been entrusted to hear, concerned by the secrets and infighting among the land's protectors.

"Well, the storm is hardly bearable," Fits continued, sounding defensive. "We all know that. And where exactly can the people hope to go if they have to leave the city?"

"To the villages," said Jaan. "With their combined space, and their emergency craft, I'm sure they could house most of the citizenry, at least for a time. And that would give us time to find a way to fortify the ground without putting them in danger. We will find a way to protect the people."

"Yes, Sir," said Fits.

"They'll have to be ready for the worst," said Shil. "Commander Fits, what is the latest status outside the mountains?"

"The storm has not changed direction, or decreased in speed. And there is no break in the encircling. It is as unruly as ever. And it still slowly creeps closer."

"Then I will have my patrolmen work with you to prepare."

"Agreed."

"Very well," said Jaan.

Taj blinked as the line suddenly went dead, and he watched as the commanders all saluted, and firmed up their stances before turning away from each other, and returning to their respective craft. As the four watchers of the ground returned to their foxes, and pulled them up from the ground, Jaan approached the bird's ramp. As he entered the cabin, and the ramp began to close, the sounds of the roaring engines of the other departing watchers filled Taj's ears. Jaan brushed the dirt off of the tablet, and set it down next to him on the bench.

"Airman," he called. "Back to the doctor's village."

"Yes, Sir," the woman replied.

As they bounced up from the ground, and Taj felt the air rush beneath the floor and behind his seat, he removed his helmet. Across from him, Jaan sat down again, and retracted his own helmet, and leaned back and strapped back in. Then he looked into Taj's eyes.

"All of this is sensitive information, Doctor," Jaan said, his voice stern. "Do you understand?"

Taj nodded. "Yes, of course."

"We can not have worry spreading throughout the land."

"I am no gossip. Nor do I want to worry anyone."

"Good. Now, about these old machines. I have seen one. Where are the rest?"

"In different places, different villages."

"Very well. I will have Commander Brun contact you. He can escort you wherever you need to go. You'll need to get back to the flash sites and get to work quickly. I doubt we have much time to prepare for another."

"I agree."

The bird shook around them as they ascended toward the clouds, and Taj looked over his shoulder, and out the window. The horizon to the south was all shadows, of the dark line of the mountains, and the heavy sky above.

CHAPTER 14
THE IMPARTING

Gem looked up from the screen, and looked over her right shoulder, toward the stairwell to the cavern. She heard steps, coming from the west hall, and then rustling, near the sitting area. She removed her thin gloves, and set them down. She walked to the steps, and then, quietly and carefully, began ascending. As she reached the top, the door slid open, and she looked out past the dining area, and saw Robbins. He was lying on the bench, beneath a blanket from their guest room, resting his head on a pillow from the same.

She turned and closed the door behind her, and locked it. Then she moved past the kitchen, and approached her seat, set just before her father's. As she sat down, and looked at the man, his eyes popped open. He sat up quickly.

"I'm sorry," she said, quietly, smiling. "I heard you. Is everything alright? It is rather late."

Robbins held his hand up graciously. "Yes, I'm fine," he said. "It's my son. He has nightmares, from time to time. And he thrashes in his sleep." He rubbed at his left arm. "He's strong to be so young."

Gem leaned back in her seat, and smiled again. "Yes, it would seem so. I thought I heard him earlier."

Robbins looked into her eyes. "I'm sorry. I hope he didn't wake you. He's still dealing with all of this newness. So am I."

Gem shook her head. "No, no. I was already awake. And it's alright. Our home was built to carry sounds well. It helps keep us aware of each other, and of what's happening on the outside, which keeps us safe."

"Thank you. And thank you for taking care of us. I have not felt this well since I was young myself, maybe not even then."

"You are our guests. And as you know, across creation, humanity is very rare now. It would do us no good to be unkind."

"Yes."

"Tell me, though. What does your son dream about?"

Robbins took a deep breath, and took a moment to roll up the blanket, and set it at his side. Then he leaned away, into the high back of the soft bench, and looked down. "He dreams about his mother," he said. "About my wife. So do I."

"Well, they should be happy dreams, shouldn't they?" asked Gem.

"They would be, but she was young when she died. And...well...it hasn't been long."

"How long has it been?"

Robbins shook his head, and did not look up. "I'm not sure, exactly. Maybe three weeks now."

Gem held in her gasp, and quietly breathed out. "I'm so sorry,

Robbins. That is so...so recent. How did you go on?"

He looked back up at her. "There was no choice. I had to protect him. There was no one else to look after him."

Gem nodded. "Of course." She paused, and thought back, nearly two centuries. The time was hazy, but still painful. "You know, I still remember when my mother died. It was the hardest time for all of us. But, we pushed on. We had a land to build, a people to sustain. You have a child to protect."

Robbins nodded. "Yes."

"May I ask, how did she die?"

Robbins glanced at her, and then looked away, and stood from the bench. He walked toward the closed door to the bunker, and crossed his arms, and looked up, at nothing in particular. "It was our last night," he said, stopping near the door. "On the last ship. I didn't know it would be. There were only a few people left on board. Our navigator was an old, tired woman, and she had passed out at the helm. I had been helping her, but I knew then that she wouldn't last more than a day or two, so I let her be.

"As I headed back to our room below deck, I heard yelling. When I got to the door, my son was there, banging on it, screaming for Tamra, his mother. I pulled him aside, and managed to break through. It had been barricaded with an old desk. I found two men there, old but strong men, trying to..." he trailed off, and exhaled. "Trying to hurt her."

"Her face was bloody. So was her shirt, but she was standing, holding them off. I got past the desk, and grabbed the one closest to me. His name was Carl. I broke his neck, and dropped him to the floor. He landed hard and heavy. The other one, Paul, heard it, and when he turned, Tamra gouged out one of his eyes. He spun around, screaming, and ran at me. I had already pulled my knife, and I ran him through. He started to fall, and stared up at me, gasping, his lone open eye filled with tears. He whimpered the words 'I'm sorry,' and then he fell on top of the other one. Then, I heard Tamra breathe out hard, and saw her fall back.

"The blood on her shirt was hers. They had...They had slashed just deep enough to reach her organs. Devon and I, we tried to patch her up, but over the next few hours, she only got weaker and weaker, and paler and paler. She couldn't recover."

Gem wiped a tear from her cheek, as Robbins turned around, and wiped his own face. "I'm so sorry," she said. "How did you...How did you..."

"She died the next day. We wrapped her in some old, floral blankets we had, and had words, and took her up near the bridge, and laid her there, out of sight. A few hours after that, Devon and I left in our small boat. We had all three of us been building it, working in secret, for months."

Gem stared up into Robbins' eyes, hoping the shock that she was feeling was not visible below the sadness. She watched him as he walked back to the bench, and slowly took his seat again, exhausted from recounting his story. He looked over the back of the bench for a

263

moment, toward the door to the west hall, which was still partially open.

"I am sorry, Robbins," said Gem. "So very sorry."

He looked back at her. "We're fine, now," he said, waving his hand dismissively. "That was life out there. We were lucky to make it as long as we did. We were lucky to have a son. She was..." he hesitated, thinking again. "She was just too strong for that world."

"And so are the two of you," said Gem. "You made it all the way to us, after such a tragedy. You belong here, on Lwo."

Robbins stared at the floor. "I suppose so. There's nowhere else."

"There will be, one day. We are the foundation for the next world."

Robbins rubbed his head and face, and took a deep breath. "I'm so tired. I never got so tired out there. It's been days here, days of food, and water, and quiet. I shouldn't feel tired."

"You're still mourning," said Gem. She stood, and walked over to him, and sat down, and put an arm around his shoulders. He was not as slim as she had thought. "And your body went through decades of strain. It will take time to get used to comfort, if you could call Lwo comfortable. Go ahead and lie back down. I'll lower the lights, and leave you to rest."

"Thank you," he said.

She stood, and as he lay back down, setting his head on the pillow, and unfurling the blanket over his body again, she slowly stepped away. She walked to the door to the east hall, and touched the panel there, and as the light controls came into view, dimmed the lamps in the ceiling. Once the room was dark, she slid the door open, and stepped into the hall.

The panel on the left illuminated, and she looked and saw the status of the weather outside the Isle. Everything was as expected, wild and unchanged. And the rock that formed the Isle was still cold. Then, from the end of the hall, she heard her father's steps. She turned to him, as he walked up to her, carrying his staff. He leaned against the wall. Gem reached back, and pulled the hall door closed.

"Did you hear?" she asked.

"Yes, I did," he nodded, his eyes heavy, but not tired. "No wonder the boy makes so much noise in his sleep."

"I wonder what he sees in his dreams," she said.

"I would rather not know." He took a deep breath, and glanced at the control panel, at the Isle's status. "It is time."

"Now?" Gem asked. "It seems a bit soon, Father. They have only been here a few days."

"Now is as good a time as any. There is no need to prolong it. They will become too comfortable. And they would bring their broken ideals into our society, if we allowed it."

"But, they are still innocent."

"The boy, perhaps. Not Robbins. He is proof that the old world is still savage. The new one cannot be."

"Father, think of the position he was in. Would you not have

265

done the same for us? For Mother?"

"Certainly, dear. But, I did not have to. Our founders saw what was, and what was coming, and what could be, and they set things in order so that we *would* not have to."

Gem paused, thinking, hesitant. "The people in the city, they are not much better. Robbins could adapt, I'm sure. And the boy *certainly* will."

"Gem, my dear. Our citizens are well beyond those old ways. A little wound up, yes. And still carrying that spark that keeps humanity going. But none of them could ever do as much harm as a man who has seen, and done, what Robbins has." He ran his hand gently up and down her arm. "And you know this, Daughter. You understand."

Gem looked away, and then back into her father's eyes, and nodded.

"Emissary," Andrew called, quietly.

A soft chirp came from the panel on the wall. "Yes, my Lord," the system answered.

"It is time. Subdue Robbins. And make sure the boy continues to sleep."

"Yes, my Lord. However, the boy is not asleep."

"Then subdue him as well."

"Yes, my Lord."

Gem took a step back, and stood against the wall, watching the panel, as the image of the cavern materialized. A single, glowing drone emerged. Robbins only grunted for an instant, as the round device hit his chest, and the unseen needle pierced his skin. His body fell limp. From the edges of the drone, the electromagnetic shield poured out, surrounding his body in a haze of green light, tossing the blanket to the floor and elevating him from the bench. His arms reflexively crossed over his chest, and his legs stiffened, and his frightened eyes slowly shut.

"Dad!" yelled Devon.

Gem shuddered as she heard the boy's scream spread throughout the cavern and through the door, pushing into their hallway, echoing what came through the panel. She watched as the boy ran out through the west hall door, toward his father.

"Gently, Emissary," said Andrew.

Gem closed her eyes, and leaned more into the wall, exhausted as she heard Devon run, and yelp, and then fall silent. As she opened her eyes again, she saw the boy lying on the floor, in the same state as his father–stiff, unconscious, and surrounded by the energy flowing from the drone that had settled over his chest. The device seemed too big for his small body.

"He'll remember," said Gem. "The boy will remember this."

"And his father will tell him why it was done," said Andrew. "And that all is well. Emissary?"

"Yes, my Lord," the system answered.

"Take them both to the chamber. Set the boy in the lounge. Place his father on the bed next to the young woman."

"Yes, my Lord."

Gem continued to watch, as the engines on top of the two small drones spun with bright green energy, and the cavern's unseen, magnetized rails raised them up, pulling Robbins from the couch, and Devon from the floor. Their stiff bodies were guided slowly away from the sitting area, and past the kitchen and dining spaces, and through the wide, newly-opened door to the chamber.

"Gem, you stay here," said Andrew. "I will handle the preparations."

"Yes, Father," she replied.

Andrew gently rubbed her shoulder, and then turned away, and walked back to his room at the end of the hall. She watched the door close behind him, and then turned back to the screen.

"Emissary?" she called.

"Yes, Lord Gem," it answered.

"Show me the chamber."

The image on the panel shifted, to an angled view from above the chamber, where she had been working before Robbins' somber confession. The large, open space, just below where she stood, filled the center of the Isle. She could see the vented walls, and the glass doors that fronted the cooled storage cabinets spread around the room. At the far end was the large, rear access door. At the other end the mobile treatment station, with its single computer and closed supply drawers, sat idle. Her gloves were still there.

Four beds sat on either side of the aisle that ran between the rear access door and the stairwell to the cavern. Behind the beds across from Gem's view was the metal door to the lounge, where she, her sister, and their father had often rested when needed. The beds outside it were empty, and remained neatly made. Directly below Gem's view were four more beds. Only the second bed from the right was occupied. The woman lying there, covered in thick cloth from the neck down, and adorned with various flowers, had now lost all of her color, and clearly passed on.

Gem recalled the woman being brought to them two nights before, tracked by their system in the sky, and carried all the way from the Middle Lands by one of its unmanned craft. Her body, beneath the colorful, fitting suit, had been severely battered. Her dark, gold-flecked hair had been stained with dried blood and saliva. Her fingers had been frayed, as beaten as her body, likely by debris and ice that she had tried to defend against. She had succeeded, to a point. Her helmet had not been broken at the front. Her face was still lovely, mostly.

Gem had been first to the chamber, and had heard the woman's voice, somehow melodic as she weakly pleaded for help before slipping out of consciousness. For two days she had laid there, under the Emissary's watch, as her body collapsed into itself from the unhealing breaks and bruises, both visible and internal. Not long before Gem had heard Robbins leave the west hall and lie down, she had heard the woman's last, nearly-inaudible cry, and then her final, sharp breath.

Behind the woman's head, connected by tubes flowing to and from her shoulders and other unseen places, sat the tall, metallic preservation device. It had worked countless times, to both extend life, and to take care of those who expired. And it had extracted billions of the most precious human cells, after so many losses to the storm. A few glass tubes of the cells were resting in one of the cooled cabinets on the other side of the room, near the door to the lounge.

The preserver was humming quietly and constantly, as it had been when Gem had last attended to the woman, who had yet to be identified. She had looked very young, and had been the first loss to the storm in years. If a ceremony had taken place on the mainland, or had been planned, word had not yet come from the watchers.

Gem folded her arms, and slid her hands up into her wide sleeves, warming herself as she continued to watch the screen. As the drone set Robbins down on the bed next to the woman, her father entered the chamber through the rear door, now covered in his own hooded, bright white coat, with tight sleeves beneath it that ran down to his wrists. He set his staff near the door, and approached the woman's bed. The shield around Robbins' body finally disappeared, and as the drone ascended from his chest he seemed to relax. Beyond him, in the background, and still rigid and unconscious, Devon was carried through the lounge door.

"Emissary," Gem called. "Show me the lounge."

"Yes, Lord Gem," the system answered.

The image changed again, to a view of the narrow room, with

its long couch, and two beds on the far wall. The boy was carried in, with the drone holding him over the space between the small hearth and the couch.

"Lay him there," she said. "Gently."

The system obeyed, and the drone set the boy down onto the couch cushions. The shield retracted away from his body, and he settled, gently.

"How much sedative did you give him?" Gem asked.

"Very little, Lord Gem," said the Emissary. "He will be fine."

"I'm sure he will be."

As Gem watched the boy, resting, almost peaceful now, the system chirped. A code on the panel revealed a sudden influx of information, and a view of the Isle's south cave appeared. Within the glowing image, one of the unmanned craft from their system in the sky appeared. Its long, dark body passed through the cave opening. Its rounded, clamping arms remained retracted. At its front end, a single red light glowed, and it stopped in front of the bunker door's control panel. Its light flickered twice.

"A message from Lord Coral," said the Emissary.

"Retrieve it, and send it here," said Gem.

"Yes, Lord Gem."

Rows of text filled in over the view to the cave, and Gem read to herself:

The watchers attend to the land with great diligence. The four commanders have met to determine a course of action to address the two flashes, which have occurred twenty miles due north, and five miles due west of a farming village that lies southwest of the Spire. The second flash led to the loss of a very young civilian named Loren.

The old teacher, Taj, has used the ancient probes to penetrate the sites of the flashes, and discovered a crack in a previously-undiscovered expanse of founding rock. The great rock extends west, passing under the city. With this knowledge, Commander Jaan decided to reveal the existence of the city's pillars to the other commanders, and suggested that their pressure is what has likely caused the crack, and contributed to the recent flashes, rather than any weakness in the ties beneath. Commander Shil has determined that the city should plan for evacuation.

Is there any suggestion from my Lords?

Gem stepped back from the screen. "Father?" she called.

The system chirped. "Yes, my dear?" Andrew answered, his voice carrying both down from above and through the panel.

"Coral has sent a message. Would you like to read it?"

"Yes, send it to me here."

"Emissary," she said. "Do as he says, and show me the chamber again."

"Yes, Lord Gem," it answered.

It chirped again. She stepped back up to the panel, and watched as the feed from the cave faded away, and the view to the chamber returned. Her father had moved the treatment station to the space between Robbin's bed and the bed of the woman, and stood there, reading intently.

"So, we have a name for this young lady," said Andrew.

"Yes," Gem said, speaking toward the panel.

"That is good. And Taj is still as sharp as ever. That is also good."

"What about what Commander Jaan has done?"

He paused, and folded his arms. "I suppose he had no other choice. It will not hurt for the commanders to know."

"Would you agree that it is not the ties?"

"I trust the commander, and the old teacher. Yes, it must be the pillars."

"Is there anything we can do?"

He shook his head. "The mainland has endured centuries of compaction and shifting. The watchers are best suited to handle this now. All we could offer them is old data, but it is likely that Taj has already held on to it."

"Shall we tell my sister anything?"

He nodded. "Simply that the message was received, and we offer no further guidance. She is more than capable."

"Yes, Father."

"I will handle things here, my dear. You rest, and do not worry."

"Yes, Father." She looked up from the panel. "Emissary, show me the cave again."

"Yes, Lord Gem," it answered.

The view to the cave appeared in the screen again, and Gem saw the red light of the drone craft, still glowing and hovering. She brought up the keyboard within the screen, entered the simple response to her sister, and transmitted it to the craft. Then she watched, as its light flickered from red to green, and it backed out of the cave, turned, and shot back up into the sky. As it disappeared, the screen went back to displaying the climate's status.

She exhaled, and turned, and walked toward the end of the hall, and turned just before her father's door, and entered her room. The bed was still made. The lamp's light was low. She sat down on top of the blanket, and then laid back, against a large pillow, and looked up at the smooth rock ceiling, and let her eyes shut.

CHAPTER 15
THE DECLARATION

Maia stepped out of the lift and into the tower's observation level. The viewing walls sat unmagnified. Outside, the early morning sky was its usual shade of gray, with the distant light of the sun barely pushing against the clouds. A thousand feet below, the land appeared unbothered.

The seats in front of each viewing wall were all occupied, and straight ahead, at the wall that faced south, Jaan was standing between two observant airmen. He was speaking, quietly, to one of them.

Behind Maia, the lift door closed, and she could feel Lord Coral lingering in front of it. The woman's gentle hand settled at the middle of her back, and she felt the nudge urging her forward.

"Go on, Lieutenant," Coral whispered. "It will be fine."

Maia nodded, and took one step forward. "Commander, Sir?"

"You're late, Lieutenant," Jaan answered without turning around. "Do you have an explanation?"

"Yes, Sir. Our new enlistee wanted to accompany me."

After a short pause Jaan turned around, and looked past her. "I see," he said.

His eyes did not waiver, but Maia could feel the eyes of the airmen in the room as they focused on Coral.

"Airmen," Jaan said, loudly, his voice carrying through the entire level. "Leave us."

It was quiet. Jaan looked around at the unmoving watchers, who all seemed transfixed, and confused.

"Airmen!?" he shouted.

"Yes, Sir!" they all finally replied, in unison.

One by one they rose from their seats, and marched quickly to the lift, trying not to look, but failing. Maia only listened as their boots passed her, and hit the floor of the lift, and then turned to see the door close in front of them. As they dropped out of sight, she turned back around to see Jaan kneeling, one fist to his chest, and the other touching the floor.

"My Lord," he said. "Welcome, once again, to the tower."

"Stand up, Commander," Coral said, and walked past Maia. She pushed her blue helmet up and back, off her shoulders, letting it rest behind her as comfortably as any watcher of the sky would. She breathed in the level's filtered air. "I asked you not to do that while I am here. Your lieutenant was late because of me. I do apologize."

Jaan stood, and shook his head. "It is a habit that is hard to break. My apologies. Would you like to sit?" He motioned to the now empty seats facing the south viewing wall.

Coral raised a hand. "No. Not yet. I am eager to listen this morning."

Relieved, Maia smiled—a thin, reserved smile—and looked to Jaan.

He raised one hand. "At ease, Lieutenant."

"How soon before Commander Shil speaks?" Coral asked.

"Any minute now," said Jaan.

"Would you bring it up on the wall, please?"

"Of course."

Jaan stepped to the station on the left, and entered a code on the right panel, and then stepped back behind the chair. The view to the south, of pale green grass, and a river in the distance, faded away. The wall of glass then filled with black, and bright white letters at its center emerged, and read 'Upcoming: Watcher Declaration on Repeated Flashing.' Coral walked up, and stood behind the chair on the right.

"Our suit fits you well," said Jaan.

"Thank you, Commander," Coral replied. "It feels better than anything I've worn in quite a while. We do not venture here enough."

"The trek has not grown any safer."

"That is true."

"Did you have the opportunity to look more closely at the data?"

"I did. But let us look again."

"Very well. Maia?" he said over his shoulder. "Bring it up at that station."

"Yes, Sir," Maia answered.

She walked carefully behind Coral, to the other side of the station, and input her code on the right panel. Outside the division of the ground the data had been made accessible only to commanders and lieutenants, and even then it was hidden. She dove through the system's pathways and folders for a full minute to get to the files, and then brought up the graph and the rendering on both of the station's screens. She stepped back as Coral moved closer.

Coral moved her right hand across the panels smoothly, taking note. Maia did the same, from a yard back. The data had been updated one hour before. The wave graph's pattern was mostly the same. The rendering, however, was more expansive, reaching almost to the forest, where the crack in the great rock a quarter-mile below continued on.

"Is there anything new?" Jaan asked.

"Not that I can see," said Coral. "The old probes are still impressive, to reach so deep. It is clear that the crack in the rock originated beneath the city." She sighed. "I remember seeing the pillars being formed, finished, as a small child."

"They've done their job," said Jaan. "The city, all this time, has remained strong."

"But at what cost?" she asked aloud. "That is the question." She paused, and ran her hand along the screens more slowly. "The old teacher is impressive. Is he doing what he agreed to?"

"Yes," said Jaan. "One of the old machines has already been retrieved, and he is en route back to one of the flash sites now.

Commander Brun and his watchers are escorting him."

"Really? Can the old man stand on a fox?"

"I do not believe so. They're using a civilian craft."

Coral laughed quietly. "Good."

A low tone interrupted their conversation, arising from the viewing wall. The darkness and plain text in the feed gave way to a slowly-arising, bright image, and there, from her command office at the city's headquarters, Shil came into view. Her eyes were steady. Her dark hair was perfectly trimmed just below her ears. Her high, white collar sat just beneath her jawline. And her shoulders and chest plate seemed to shine in the light hitting her from the city. Behind her, at the wall, stood two of the city's councilors, identified by short lines of text on the screen as Bethe and Pett. Maia remembered meeting them, once.

"People of the city," Shil started. "And people of Lwo. I am Commander Shil, of the Watchers of the City, and Second Lead Watcher of Lwo. I come before you today due to a great trouble that has come upon the land.

"As many of you know, our land is full of great dangers, both seen and unseen. The wisdom and guidance of our Lords has kept us safe, and strong. The ties that bind the land have only grown stronger, becoming one with the earth, making the mainland whole, and helping to sustain us under harsh circumstances like the world has never seen before.

"Many of you also know that, in times past, the heat from the beating heart of Mother Earth has been too much for our land to contain, resulting in flashes not unlike the eruptions of old volcanoes centuries ago.

"For all our lifetimes, these flashes have been unpredictable, but also non-threatening, too sparse and mysterious and fleeting for worry. This is no longer the case. If you saw the recent broadcast of our report to the council, you know that there have been two flashes in the past week, and within twenty-four hours of each other. And you also know that one of these flashes led to the loss of a beloved citizen.

"Though neither of these flashes has endangered a single village, we have discovered that they may follow a path that flows beneath the forest, and beneath the city."

Shil paused, looking into the camera, her eyes still steady. "I do not report this to alarm any of you, but to make you aware, and to prepare you for what may come. The potential for more flashing poses a growing threat to the people of the city. I have been to both flash sites, and I assure you that no human could ever endure the amount of damage that one can cause. With this in mind, all watcher commanders have come to the same conclusion: The city must prepare to evacuate.

"I want to reassure every Lwoan, whether you are watching this now, or will watch it in the hours and days to come, that you should not be afraid. Preparing for an evacuation is a precaution. Our watchers of the ground are now being aided by Doctor Taj, whose brilliance and insightfulness many of you have experienced first-hand.

And as data is provided from study of the ground, it will be provided to you here, on this broadcast frequency.

"In the coming hours, citizens will receive alerts through their phones, and in their homes, with details on how to prepare, and what paths can be taken out of the city, and where watchers and shelter craft will be stationed to assist. Also in the coming hours, village leaders will be preparing to provide aid, if needed, to those who may leave the city.

Shil paused again, raising a hand to push strands of hair back from the sides of her face, making her eyes that much more insistent. "Before I sign off, I want to remind each of you of who we Lwoans are descended from. The last great men and women of the old world migrated here three centuries ago, and established a land that could withstand the constant storm that was to come. Our bodies, with proper attire, have managed to endure the raw winds of the storm for all this time. And our buildings, and aircraft, and villages, and city, have all withstood the winds, even using it to generate nearly-limitless energy to aid humanity as we go on.

"Now, as we are faced with another test from our mother, please be encouraged, that we have endured all this time so that we may keep enduring, and reestablish a world better than the last. Thank you for your attention. And as always, if and when you must brave the storm, take great care. Shil out."

The viewing wall darkened again, as Shil's fading image gave way to a black screen, and a line of bright yellow text that read

'Upcoming: Evacuation Preparations.' Jaan was quiet, standing with his arms crossed, his chest visibly moving in and out with each breath. Maia felt a pride begin to well up in her, and a waft of fear lingering just beneath it. She looked to Coral, who was looking back down at the right station's screens, examining the data again.

"She's gained something," Coral said. "Something not quite tangible, since her promotion. Wouldn't you agree, Commander?"

Jaan nodded, and uncrossed his arms. "Yes," he said. "She has."

"We were right about her. So were you."

"And I am glad that I was."

"It does not sound like it." She stepped away from the station, and turned to face Jaan. "I hope that you are not worried, Commander. Your position is not in danger. The city needs Shil. And all of Lwo needs you."

Jaan nodded. "Yes. Of course. I am not concerned for myself, but for what steps we must take next."

"You should not worry about that either. Mother Earth will keep us here for as long as she needs, as she always has, until we can care for the rest of her again."

"Agreed." He looked into her eyes. "Do you have any suggestions?"

"I do. Shil is well-suited, and so is her sister here." She turned toward Maia. "I suggest we send your lieutenant to aid the city's efforts."

Jaan turned toward Maia and nodded. "Agreed. Lieutenant?"

"Yes, Sir?" Maia answered.

"I want you to take a squadron to the city to support Commander Shil."

"Yes, Sir."

"Good luck, Lieutenant," said Coral.

"Thank you," she replied.

Maia moved quickly back to the lift. As she entered, she turned and took one last look at her superiors. They had turned their attention away from her, and back to each other, conversing about things she had no time to consider. As the doors closed, and the lift descended, she pulled her helmet back over her head, secured it, and opened a line to four airmen. Her display showed that each of them was stationed at a different point in the sky, and miles away from the tower. Each of them answered, and their names came up in bright blue letters.

"Airmen Dilah, Sedi, Malo and Yuden," she called. "I trust that you are all aware of Commander Shil's declaration. Our division will now offer support to the watchers of the city. Inform your wingmen, and meet me en route."

One after the other the four of them acknowledged the order. In front of her, the lift opened to the mezzanine. The airmen who had been stationed on the observation level saluted, and firmed up their stances as she stepped out.

"Stay here until you are called back," she ordered with a

salute of her own.

"Yes, Sir," they all said in unison.

She passed between them, and descended the steps to the hangar floor, and saw her bird, hovering where she had left it, with its aft engine facing the west entry. As diminished waves of early morning winds carried in from the entry, and rushed through her tech, she cautiously approached the craft. The wing that housed the starboard engine reflected soft light into her helmet. She walked up, and eyed it carefully, and seeing and hearing no issues, walked to the forward end. She checked the front vents, making sure they were clear. She walked around the port side, between her craft and another, and examined the other wing, raising a hand near its exhaust, feeling the slight push of air stabilize as it passed through her gauntlet. She reached the aft end, and after a whispered command, watched as its ramp lowered. She hopped up, and was in the cabin before the ramp had touched the floor. Then she pressed the button to close it, and moved quickly to the pilot's chair.

In the center control panel she brought up her map. Her position in the tower blinked in red. She expanded the map, and in the left panel brought up the signals of the airmen she had just called. They were all nearing the tower. She sent each of them an updated path to the city, redirecting them, and watched the panel as each of their trajectories shifted by a few hundred feet.

On the right control panel she brought up a communication window, entered her code, and opened a secure channel to the city's headquarters. She sent a coded message directly to Shil, informing of the approaching squadron, and that their support of the city had been ordered. The screen chirped three times before the small box of text read 'Delivered.' Then she took a deep breath, strapped in, and set her covered palms down on both cold, hard control handles.

She eased the bird backward, and then turned it about, and guided it steadily through the hangar door. As she hit the raw winds, and felt their force push through the engines, she stomped down onto the pedal below. The engines opened fully, and roared around her, and she held tightly to both handles as the bird shot forward. She felt the familiar pressure in her chest, and felt the heaviness in her boots, as she flew southwest, and began to ascend.

As she neared the lowest clouds, she looked out to her left. Far above the faded, grassy surface, she saw two blue birds approaching her. She rolled toward them, continuing to ascend, and then leveled off as they met her altitude. The left panel beeped twice, and she looked off to the right to see the other two in their squadron reach her position. She opened a line to all of them.

"Airmen, this is Lieutenant Maia," she called. "Do you copy?"

"Copy, Lieutenant Sir," they all answered in unison, their signals flashing in her helmet.

"Very good. Commander Jaan has ordered that we provide support in the city, and each of you are natives of the city. Your knowledge will be vital. When we arrive, we are to follow the lead of

Commander Shil. Whatever she orders, we do. Understood?"

"Yes, Sir," they answered again.

"Very good. Keep your lines open, and keep a tight formation. Maia out."

The steady sounds from the other birds carried through Maia's windows, rumbling as they sped alongside her, forming the sides of a triangle for which she remained the point. The clouds surrounding all of them were a typical, pale mist that their engines were swiftly pulling in and forcing out. Tiny droplets were blowing off of Maia's windshield as soon as they touched. Barely visible dust, and grass, and tree debris bounced off or disintegrated on impact, adding to the chaotic ambient sounds. It was like any other flight to the city, and it reminded Maia that just days before, when last she was en route, she had been ordered to turn away, and take Robbins and Devon to the safety of the Isle.

"Commander Shil to Lieutenant Maia," her sister called through the right panel.

Shil's strong voice was enough to distract Maia from her growing anticipation. She opened a secured line through her helmet, and saw Shil's signal pop into view. "This is Lieutenant Maia," she said. "Go ahead, Commander, Sir."

"I received your message," said Shil. "The city appreciates your offer of support, but we did not ask for your assistance."

"I do not believe it is an option, Sir."

"So I gathered."

There was a pause, and Maia was assured of Shil's annoyance.

"I see you have four airmen with you," Shil continued. "I do not want the people of the city to be unnecessarily frightened. Do not pass through any of our gates. Enter from above, and head straight for headquarters. You may dock on our roof. I will alert our patrols."

"Understood, Sir," Maia replied.

"Very good. Shil out."

Maia called again to the squadron. "Airmen, I have received word from Commander Shil. I am sending you a new approach vector. We will go over the forest, *and* over their shield."

"Yes, Sir," they all answered.

As she finished sending the new vector, she decreased her speed, easing up on the pedal as she slowly began to descend. The other birds drifted down with her. As they left the clouds, and the air began to clear, the forest started to come into view. It was a dark line along the horizon. On her center panel, signals from the watchers of the ground began to blink in their deep-colored hues. There were three of them nearby, and idled. One of them belonged to Brun.

The squadron was approaching the second flash site, where Brun and his watchers, no doubt, were supporting Taj as he continued his examinations. They had already passed over them before Maia could think to call down, to ask what else, if anything, had been discovered. But that was outside the scope of her orders. There was little time left to explore every possibility before acting.

She guided the squadron further down, and watched as their

signals on the center panel fell in line directly behind hers. They cleared another three miles of plain, grassy, empty land, and finally reached the forest. She kept her eyes wide open, watching all sides, as they gradually descended to two hundred feet and began to slow down again. Ahead of her, the city sparkled into view. Its surrounding shield was a barely-visible haze of energy, but the sides of the buildings that faced the perimeter were bright, reflecting the shield's light, and the minimal light of the sky. Maia found the city on her center panel, and zoomed in for a better view.

The forest surrounded three-fourths of the city, and there were still four miles of it directly ahead. Maia rolled a few degrees to her left, getting a better look at the trees. They were as tall as they ever were, and still grew closely together. Most of them had thick, dark leaves, and dark trunks that often made the forest appear to be opaque from afar. But she had walked between the trees before. They were among the few species that still thrived on the mainland, with trunks full of thick bark of varying shades of brown. Nearest to the city, the ground that held their long roots was littered with petals of countless flowers that, with the protection of the many trees, managed to grow in bunches at least once every year.

As Maia leveled the bird off again, she saw a spark just ahead, disappearing just beyond a tree's crown. She squinted, wondering just for an instant what it might have been. *Lightning*, she thought, and at first, let it pass. Then, without another thought, she jumped back in her seat.

"Bank right!" she yelled out.

She gripped both handles tightly as the flash burst out in front of her. As she rolled to her right, she pulled back on both handles, moving the bird upward as much as she could. Light filled her vision, but she would not close her eyes. She looked, and saw the raw, rising heat. The temperature reading in her helmet spiked. The bird shook all around her. She tried to hold on.

Somewhere behind her she heard the engines of the other four birds bellowing out. Her bird was tossed, and spun, and bounced around, and as she was shaken in her seat, she closed her eyes. When she opened them again, a moment later, she was floating. Her seat was upright and steady, but in front of her, the control panels had been burned. They steamed, and sparked, and were collapsing down to the floor. The control handles, still in her hands, now felt loose, and useless. As she looked down at them, a blast of air hit her in the chest, and she looked and saw that the front left corner of the bird had been burned away.

There was barely enough time for her to remove her harness before another blast of raw wind rushed into the cabin, sending her flying over the back of the chair. She cried out as she hit the hard floor.

"Sir!" Malo yelled through the line. "Are you still there!?"

"I'm here!" Maia yelled back, rolling to a stop near the bird's ramp. Her helmet bounced off of the floor. She could feel the bird's engines trying to compensate, trying to stabilize, but as she looked up, and out, she saw the front engine, whatever was left of it, smoking in front of the shattered glass that had been the windshield.

The cabin shook, barely level as winds pushed around and through the other engines without any guidance from the likely-destroyed system. She got to her feet, and felt dizzy, and immediately felt another gust of wind, and braced herself as she was slammed against the starboard wall. She cried out again, as her shoulder hit, and pain ran down her right side. She turned away from the front end, away from the winds pushing at her, and slammed her hand into the ramp control.

"Someone get under me!" she yelled out.

She heard the ramp's mechanism, but it barely moved. Another gust, carrying smoke and heat with it, hit her from behind. She looked back and saw lines of fiery energy burning through the floor, and the hull. The pilot's seat had fallen to rubble. She turned back toward the bird's aft end, and knelt down, stabilizing as much as she could. She felt the tech on her boots and shoulders and back and arms working to keep her in place. She jumped up, and ran forward, and leapt feet first into the unmoving ramp, and it fell back.

She landed near the ramp's base, and held on to the bird's frame, as the long, wide door broke off, falling first toward the ground, and narrowly missing the front end of the bird trailing her, and then floating off to nowhere. She saw the shine of Malo's helmet through the windshield.

"I see you, Sir!" he yelled. "Jump!"

She got to her feet, and leapt with all the strength she could manage, as the floorboards continued to break apart. She entered the winds, and straightened her body. She kept her eyes on the top of Malo's bird, on the grasping bar affixed to its roof. She angled her body downward, keeping her arms at her sides, and uttered quiet commands, ensuring the tech would keep her on a line. Malo guided the bird up, meeting her position. Her gloved hands hit the roof first, then her knees. She was pushed down, and spun on her chest as she slid toward the bird's rear, until she got a hold of the crossbar with one bent arm.

"Are you there, Sir!?" Malo called again.

Maia coughed out an exhausted breath, and clasped her hands, as the bar pressed between her right forearm and bicep. "I'm here," she said.

She worked to slow her heavy breaths. Her helmet panel had fogged up, but quickly cleared. She felt her eyes watering, but shook the tears away, ignoring whatever had prompted them, whether it had been pain or terror. She felt the rumble of the bird's engines pushing around its body and up to the roof beneath her. Her tech was still working, keeping her stabilized atop the bird. Finally, she looked up, and saw the city, shining brilliantly in the distance. A few yards above her, and to the left, another airman was flying steady and straight. The other two were on her right.

"Is everyone safe?" she called.

"Yes, Sir," the airmen answered.

"Well then, that will be a story to tell."

"Are you all right, Sir?" Dilah called. "You look steady from here."

Maia looked to her left, and nodded, her helmet rubbing against the roof. "I'm fine, Airman. Everyone, form a new line to the city's headquarters."

"Yes, Sir," they all answered.

Maia kept her arm wrapped tightly around the crossbar, and kept her hands clasped near her chest. She kept the toes of her boots bent, and pressing firmly into the bird's roof. As they all passed over the city's shield, she exhaled once. With steady wind flowing over the bird's front end, keeping her pressed down, she felt just safe enough to look back over her shoulder. She magnified her view through her helmet panel. In the distance, now far beyond the roofs of the buildings on the city's edge, smoke was rising from a single point in the forest, and fading into the winds as it did. Not far from that spot she could just make out her bird, splitting into pieces. Some of it was taken up by the storm, and some of it fell into the green darkness. For an instant, she remembered the game that she and Devon and Robbins had played in the cabin. The soft, colorful cubes, which had been so hard to come by, were now lost, or burned to ash.

CHAPTER 16
THE RESPONSE

Brun's signal beamed into Shil's visor, as she stood on the roof of the city's headquarters, watching as the line of four blue craft from the sky approached. Maia's red bird was missing, but Shil could see her sister, clinging to the roof of the second bird in the squadron. The pounding in her heart began to slow. She opened the line. "This is Commander Shil," she answered. "Go ahead."

"Commander, Sir," said Brun. "We were at the second flash site when we saw another burst, less than five minutes ago. It was in the path of the squadron from the sky. Did they reach you?"

"They did," said Shil. "But they're battered. And the lieutenant's bird is gone, but she is here."

"Very good. It erupted close to your perimeter."

"I know. What has Doctor Taj found so far?"

"The deep scans from this old machine have revealed traces of an unknown gas. We have much more to learn about Lwo than our parents or their parents could have anticipated."

"So it seems." She listened as Brun exchanged indiscernible words on the other end.

"I think you should evacuate as soon as possible," he said. "I can have emergency craft from the Spire there in less than two hours, and from a few villages in three."

"Hold that thought, Commander. Let me speak to Maia. She is landing."

"Very well, Sir. I will wait for your call. Brun out."

Shil slowly stepped back, away from the two hovering pullers that were angled at her sides, and toward the door to the observation level. She looked up, and waved to the first pilot from the squadron. The four birds broke their line and spread around in front of her. The first bird descended on the other side of the puller on her right. The last two settled past the puller on her left. The second bird approached her position, and hovered ten feet over her head. Its exhaust pushed all around her as it rolled over, inverting. Shil reached back, and braced herself on the wall, and looked up as Maia first swung her boots down, and then let go of the grasping bar and dropped down to the roof.

As Maia rose to her feet, their eyes met for a moment. The second bird floated away from them, and rolled back over, and descended in front of the pullers. Then, Maia approached, and held up her right fist.

"Commander, Sir," she said, loudly.

"Lieutenant," Shil replied, returning the salute. "Come in."

Shil turned, and pulled the door to the observation level aside, and held it as Maia passed through. She stepped in behind her, and closed the door, and walked with Maia to the center of the long workstation. She ordered the lone patrolman to leave, and waited for him to disappear down the ladder before speaking again.

"What happened?" she asked. "Are you okay? Are your wingmen?"

Maia nodded. "Yes, Sir. We're fine. Only my bird was hit, and hard, but I managed to escape before it was destroyed. Did you see it from here?"

"Not only did we see it," said Shil. "The citizens in the east saw it. Dozens of them. They called us, terrified."

"They should be." Maia paused, and shook her head, and firmed up her stance. "I would recommend, Sir, that you evacuate the city as soon as possible."

"Commander Brun agrees with you," said Shil. She turned her attention to the workstation, and stepped up toward the south-facing windows. She looked back and forth, between the view to the city and two glowing screens below it. "The people are still moving along as usual. We'll have to send out an emergency order."

"We will help you enforce it," said Maia.

Shil quieted, and stared down, and then looked back into Maia's eyes. They were steady, and waiting, but not at all at ease. She reached up, and set a hand on her sister's shoulder, and felt her shrink away, and saw her eye twitch. "You're injured. Are you sure you're up to it?"

Maia took Shil's wrist, and guided her hand back down. "Yes,

Sir. I'm sure."

Shil hesitated. "I am not doubting you, Lieutenant. But before I send you out, I want you to tell me how close you were."

"How close I was to what, Sir?"

"To being taken up." She paused. "To being lost."

Maia closed her eyes, but only for a moment, and then steadied herself again. "As close as I have ever been, Sir, which is why I am urging you to evacuate. If a flash, for some reason, pushes up through the city's foundation, many could be taken. And taken not just by the sky, but by fire, and by the ground. We need to move quickly. I am ready. And so are my airmen."

"Very well, Lieutenant. Follow me."

Shil moved down the ladder first, and waited for Maia to step down into the twentieth floor after her. They entered the lift, and descended one level, exiting in front of the equipment room, where a dozen patrolmen were examining and equipping their tech. All of them saluted as the two of them passed by. Shil turned down the hall, and passed through the metal doors to her command office, and listened as Maia entered behind her and the doors closed.

Shil walked up to her station, and took in the wide scene of speeding craft and high drop-offs and dim gray light from the cloudy sky. Distant, ambient sounds of rushing air, and engines, pressed through the glass. She removed her helmet, and took her seat. She opened a secure line through her computing station, calling to Brun, Fits and Jaan. Fits came into view first, in the bottom half of the screen. Behind him, rain from the coast was beating down against a small window. Brun answered next, but only with his signal blinking in a black square above Fits. After another minute, Jaan came into view, with the Sky Tower's observation level in the background.

"Commanders, we are in a dire situation now," Shil said. "As Brun, and perhaps all of us by now know, another flash has occurred, this time in the forest."

"That's news to me," said Fits, plainly, softly. He clasped his hands beneath his bearded chin. "That's the closest it's come to the city. So what now?"

"Immediate evacuation," said Jaan.

"Yes, Sir," said Shil. "I will address the city again shortly. Commander Brun has said that he can mobilize the emergency craft from the Spire and some villages within hours."

"We've already started," said Brun. "I've sent watchers to every village within an hour of the city. We'll get the first craft to your perimeter as soon as possible."

"Thank you, Commander. I know we just spoke, but has Taj found anything else that can help us? Anything at all?"

"No. Not yet."

"There was lightning," Maia interjected.

Shil looked over her shoulder, and saw Maia standing firm, her helmet now retracted. "Lieutenant?" she inquired.

Maia walked up, and saluted the screen, and spoke again. "I saw it. Before the first flash, days ago, there was a lightning strike.

And before this flash hit me, there was another, fleeting, barely visible, but definitely there. I imagine there was one after the second flash as well. I think Doctor Taj should consider it."

"Are you well, Lieutenant?" Jaan asked.

"Yes, Sir."

"Good."

"I'll let Taj know," said Brun. "Thank you, Lieutenant."

"Yes, Sir," said Maia.

"Commander Shil," said Jaan. "You should send the people out through the city's north and west entries."

Shil narrowed her gaze, surprised by the assurance in Jaan's voice. "Why do you say that, Sir?"

"It's logical. If the flashes are following a path, then those two entries would be furthest from it."

"But do we know that they're following a path?"

"We do not. I only suspect it."

"It will slow things down if we don't use every entry. I'd like more evidence before closing any of them off."

"Enough, Commander," a woman's voice rang out through the screen.

Shil's brow furrowed in confusion, but it was fleeting. She quickly straightened up in her seat, and the youngest of the Lords, outfitted in the blue of the division in the sky, stepped into view behind Jaan. Shil turned to her sister, and saw no reaction, and then turned back to the screen. She lowered her head, and set a fist on her chest. As she looked back up she saw Commander Fits do the same, and then glance over his shoulder, making sure he was alone. Brun's line was silent.

"My L-"

"Don't speak it," Coral stopped her. "Not like this, at a distance. And not if you happen to see me either. Commander Shil, this is not a time for argument. Trust your commander, as you are trained to."

"Yes," said Shil. "I apologize, Commander, Sir. Only the north and west entries will be used during the evacuation. Brun, do you copy?"

Brun's signal blinked as he hesitated. "Yes, I copy," he said finally. "I'll direct the transports there. Do you need my watchers in the city?"

"No. Not yet. It will be tight as it is. Maia's squad will be enough for now."

"And what can the mountains offer?" asked Fits. "We can spare people and craft."

"No," said Shil. "Stay in your positions. We cannot leave the rest of the mainland vulnerable just for the city."

"Well said, Commander," Jaan added. "However, I will be sending four more birds to you. Maia will direct our airmen, as you see fit."

"Very well. If everyone would, please watch for my next address. I will deliver it very shortly. Shil out."

The screen went black, and Shil pushed herself in her chair, away from the station, and lowered her head.

"I'm sorry," said Maia.

"No apology necessary, Lieutenant," Shil replied. "It would have been nice to know, but it was not your place. How long has she been here?"

"Three days. She came back from the Isle with Commander Brun and myself."

Shil stood, and pushed her chair back up to her station, and turned to Maia, and set a hand on her uninjured shoulder. Then she set both her hands down onto the wide command table, and leaned over it. The map's background was bright and white. Blue lines of varying thickness detailed each building and pathway, and green dashes outlined each sector. She looked first at the sectors closest to where she was leaning, in the city's southeast quarter. She saw the red line of the electromagnetic shield, and the footprints of buildings on the perimeter that backed up against the outer pathway inside the shield. The central path that ran up from the south to the north was on her left. On the other side of it, the sectors of the southwest quarter, except for the park, mirrored those in the southeast. All of the buildings along the southern perimeter were fully residential.

"We'll have to evacuate from the outside first," she said, running her eyes back and forth across the map. "You and your airmen can block off the south and east entries."

"Two of us at each one should be enough," Maia said.

"Agreed. After we're in motion, the other four birds can patrol the paths in the perimeter sectors." She ran her right hand around the edge of the map, pointing. "Sectors eleven, twelve, and thirteen in each quarter. Seeing craft from the sky with pulsing red lights ought to get people moving."

"Any reason they wouldn't be moving?"

"You haven't lived here in a long time, Lieutenant. The mindset of the city is much different now. Watchers are respected, but we do get pushback. There's a sense of independence that the storm does not allow for in the villages, and it's been building up for years. Already this morning patrolmen have reported doubts among the citizens about the dangers from the flashing."

"Well, people in the east just saw the last one."

"True." She paused, and sighed. "However, there is also the fact that this is also a day of mourning."

Maia hesitated. "For the Songbird?"

She paused again. "Yes. I don't want to worry you, Lieutenant. I'm only warning you that we will face some resistance."

"I understand. This is the safest place in the world. Who would want to leave if they didn't have to? Not counting watchers, of course."

"Of course." Shil ran her hand along the map again, touching the central east-west pathway. "The plans I've sent to the patrolmen will still work. The hardest part will be the movement from the south to the north. It's just a matter of timing. We have to move fast, but we have to keep the people calm as well. The streets may fill quickly, even with the doubters."

"That's why *we're* here."

"Right." Shil turned to her sister. Maia's eyes had steadied, as if death had not just touched her. "Lower your helmet," she said. "And stand right there." She pointed to a spot just left of the map's center line.

As Maia obeyed, shifting and firming up her stance, and facing out from the table, Shil took her seat again. She opened a line to her lieutenant first, who had already reported seeing the flash from his assigned sector.

"Lieutenant Nico, this is your commander," she called.

"Go ahead, Commander, Sir," he answered.

"We will now begin evacuation within two hours. We will have eight birds from the sky in support. Four of them will block off the south and east entries, and we will direct the people only to the north and west entries. The other four birds will monitor the movements of the citizens. The rest of our arrangements remain unchanged. Adjust your patrols accordingly."

"Understood, Sir. Nico out."

As the line closed, Shil heard the faint chatter of several patrolmen down the hall outside her office. A moment later, it faded away. Looking out through the wide window, she saw eight pullers fly out, one by one from the hangar directly below them. Each one moved quickly, and in a different direction, descending to the third stream

302

before disappearing below the highest rooftops, their lights blinking red in the pathways. She looked over her shoulder to see that Maia was unmoving, and then activated her camera. Four more pullers flew out in front of her, from three levels down. She quickly enabled the broadcast. After a sequence of chirps, her signal was live.

"Citizens," she started. "Once again I must call upon you. I regret to inform you that less than one hour ago, another flash broke through our land, and this time, it erupted through the forest floor. Some of you in the east saw this flash. Its heat and force nearly resulted in the loss of the Lieutenant of the Watchers of the Sky, who stands behind me now. With a threat like this, strong enough to threaten the life of a watcher who has excelled for decades, we must now act with haste.

"The south and east entries of the city will be blocked off, as we have learned that the areas on the outside that are nearest to them are most at risk of being impacted by another flash. Additionally, the evacuation of the city will now begin in less than two hours. Patrolmen will be stationed throughout the city, to guide you north and west, and to allow you a departure through the shield if you have a craft and so choose. We will also have the support of multiple birds from the division in the sky. Upon exiting the city, emergency shelter craft will be available for those not traveling otherwise, which will be most of us.

"Please remember, you will be leaving the city for much harsher conditions. Please be safe. Please be patient. Please bring only what you cherish most. Please be kind to one another as you depart. And please trust that when we return, in due time, and after we have studied this phenomenon, and made the city safe again, that Lwo will be stronger than it has ever been. Thank you. Shil out."

As the screen went black, Shil saw Maia walk up near her, and push her helmet back, and look out at the city with heavy eyes. "You've become quite the diplomat," she said.

"I hope that you do not feel used," said Shil. "They need to know how real this is."

"I do not, Sir."

"Good. Then, I need you to get that arm straightened out, and then get going."

Maia stepped back from the window, and turned to face her. "It's fine," she said. "I'll get aid from one of my wingmen."

"Very well." Shil stood, and saluted. "Good luck, Lieutenant."

Maia saluted back. "Thank you, Sir."

Shil watched as Maia turned away, and marched out through the office doors, and lowered her helmet once again. Then she turned, and faced the city once more, and looked out at the unending traffic, and the expanse of their endangered society.

CHAPTER 17
FLIGHT

It seemed that every unit in every building in Nico's assigned sector, whether it was small, or family-sized, was projecting the same image of Loren into at least one of its windows. The image was a bright still of her on the park's stage, with her four bandmates in the distant background, smiling at her as she closed her eyes and belted out a heavy note into her microphone. Her free hand was perfectly posed and dynamic, and her clothes and hair and skin sparkled under the city lights. As Nico turned and headed south, and descended from the second stream to the first, and passed into another sector, he saw more of the same. It was the worst possible day for the city to evacuate.

He had heard more than enough whispers in recent days to remind him of the moment when he had watched, helplessly, as the storm pulled her away. He needed no more reminders from Shil of the dangers of the outside. And now he had seen, from a distance, the red bird from the sky watchers torn apart by the heat of another flash, the same heat that had only singed their puller three nights before. There was no doubt in his mind that evacuation was necessary. The citizens might need more time to mourn–to feel closure, to know that life would have joy again–but more than that, they would need to live another day.

As Nico tried to shake Loren's last moments from his mind again, he saw another window, just as he was approaching the south entry. It projected the same effervescent photo of the young, gifted, life-filled singer.

He slowed to a stop, and descended, and idled his jumper over the edge of the entry's left platform, where only patrolman Kine was standing, watching groups of people as they slowly departed their homes and businesses for the street below. The crowd was sparse, for the moment. The buildings shone above them. And the light from the clouds seemed somewhat brighter as it drifted down.

Nico hopped off of the jumper, and landed behind Kine, and looked past him to the computer station. In a window on one side of the screen, the redundant text of evacuation instructions was running on a loop. In another window, a green circle blinked and vanished repeatedly, washing over the map of the nearest blocks, indicating no calls, and no craft on approach.

"Lieutenant, Sir," Kine said, turning and saluting, and stepping aside.

"Patrolman," Nico answered, and walked up closer to him. "Anything from our friends from the sky?"

"Not yet, Sir."

"Any disruptions among the citizens?"

"No, Sir. It's been smooth so far."

"For most it should stay that way. For others, it will be difficult. The streams should be filling up soon. By nightfall, we should know how many doors we'll have to knock on."

Kine nodded. "Understood, Sir."

On the screen, Nico adjusted the map to get a full view of the city, and highlighted each housing structure. Using his code, he accessed an emergency line to each building's security system, and sent out a message to each of their listed managers, asking them to ensure that each unit was empty before departing. He hoped that none of the managers had fled yet.

He moved to the next task, overlaying the map with the glowing lines of traffic flow. As he watched the dozens of signals from craft moving through the city's pathways, his mind wandered. "Patrolman?" he asked without looking at Kine. "Can you share what the commander spoke with you about, regarding the loss of the citizen?"

Kine hesitated, and then spoke, quiety. "No, Sir. I'm sorry."

Nico ran his hand up the map, toward the northern sectors. "Not a problem. Do not apologize." Suddenly, the signal of the lieutenant from the sky blinked into his visor, and he heard a line open. "This is Lieutenant Nico," he answered. "Go ahead."

"This is Lieutenant Maia," she replied. "I'm on approach to you."

"I see you," he said, checking the map. Please idle in the first stream when you reach us."

"Will do. Maia out."

It was only one more uncomfortable minute with Kine before Nico looked up to see the shining, blue bird. Below the platform, a few groups of citizens, carrying little and walking quickly, gazed up, distracted by the craft. Its underbody was dark, but had streaks of shining blue lines. And its engines were much louder than even a puller or a public transport. Nico watched as its aft end turned toward the platform, and the ramp lowered halfway, just enough for Maia to run and jump out. She guided herself down through the first stream, and then landed heavily on the platform. Kine stepped back, and saluted as she arose, and then leapt over to the other platform.

Nico extended his right hand, and gripped Maia's right gauntlet on the inside, as she did the same to his. "I could have come up to you," he said, looking through her helmet panel, and finding her dark, familiar eyes.

"I'm quite used to body flight today," she answered, and smiled.

"I'm sure. I saw your bird from where I was stationed." He set his hand just above her elbow, and squeezed. "I'm so glad you're safe."

"So am I." She rubbed at the side of her helmet. "So, we've got four birds here, and the other four will be here soon enough. I'll leave my pilot here, then another will approach shortly."

"Two here and two at the east entry?"

"Right."

"Perfect. All patrolmen are on duty, and all have been notified."

"Then I only need to know where you want the rest of us."

"I'll show you."

As Nico turned to the computer station, dozens of responses from the residential building managers came into view. Their confirmations ran in a steady row of text near the bottom of the screen. For a moment, some of the weight in his heart was lifted. He pushed the window of evacuation instructions off the screen, enlarged the map, and turned off the pulsing status blip over their position. The signals indicating moving craft remained. He saw among them another bird on approach, and two more turning down the path to the east entry.

He ran a pointing finger around the city's perimeter as he spoke to Maia, and explained exactly where and how the birds should patrol. "As you know, there are three outer sectors in each of the city's four quarters," he said. "There are multiple pathways in each sector. Your airmen should fly in sequential patterns, checking the windows and covered walkways of each floor of each building. Every twenty minutes they should move inward one block, until they reach the next row of sectors and start the next flight pattern."

Maia agreed, with no questions, and as they saw the second squadron approaching the city's shield from the east, she contacted each pilot and relayed the instructions. After the airmen acknowledged, she used the computer to send each of them the flight patterns for their assigned sectors.

Another half hour passed, and Nico continued to watch from the platform with Maia at his side. The traffic in the streams steadily increased, as more and more craft departed from each building, heading north and west. Along with them, the public transports began to run more frequently, stopping as far as the sectors just north of the south entry. The paths on the ground became more and more crowded.

"The open entries are miles from here," Maia said, keeping her eyes on the people walking below. "I thought more people had craft."

"There are still fewer than one thousand," said Nico. "And there are not many owners near here. The sectors near the edges are mostly commercial now. But don't worry. Most of them are just walking to get to transports. And look here," he said, pointing at the map again. "We have patrolmen stationed near every pickup point."

"I see," she answered.

"They are all monitoring and aiding where needed."

As the wind streams above and the paths below became busier, Nico looked back and forth to the sky. Midday had passed, and the clouds were plain and pillowy, still letting only the most necessary light through. He hoped the winds would bring no more trouble than usual.

As he looked down again, he saw steadier movement. The crowd was no longer growing, only shifting, and moving ahead, as those who had first left had already departed on transports, and those behind them moved north and west on foot. He looked as far out as he could, and then magnified the view through his visor to see beyond the park sector, to the city's center. The activity was the same. It appeared that every citizen was following Shil's orders, but he could not be sure.

"I'll need to patrol," he said to Maia. "Will you continue to watch from here?"

"Of course," she answered, nodding. "Where will you go first?"

Nico stepped back, and leapt onto his jumper. "All over," he said. "I need to check on my patrolmen, and get a better look at the city. By the time I get back, one bird should be able to depart from here."

"Very well," she said. "I will see you soon."

Nico nodded, and motioned toward the computer station. "Feel free to track me."

The engines beneath him huffed, and he boosted the jumper up and away from the platform, and into the first stream. He was pulled forward with little effort, and he opened the engines further, and flew past the aft end of the hovering bird. He looked up, and caught a glimpse of the bird idling in the second stream, and then steadied himself and bolted forward. As he looked out, the only craft he saw were public transports, all of them quickly moving in and out of their assigned sectors. He kept near the center of the streams, steering clear of their routes.

As he approached the park, he saw a crowd near its edge, where the city's widest, most central pathways crossed. The people were leaving the park space steadily, and he turned off to the right, heading east. After two blocks he saw a puller idling near the street, and descended to see what help, if any, may be needed.

The pilot was still in the cabin, but the other patrolman was aiding an older couple. The man and his wife looked healthy, and strong, but had to be past a century in age. And they were carrying too much. As they bickered with the patrolman about what they could and could not take, Nico approached, and as was often the case, the sight of him made the people more agreeable. He ordered them to take only one case each, and offered encouragement.

"You'll be back home soon enough," he said.

As they took haste to follow his orders, with help from the patrolman, he boarded his jumper again, and continued east.

At the east entry he remained on his jumper, but opened a line to the two patrolmen stationed there, and the two airmen stationed above. All four of them confirmed that the entry had seen no activity, other than one citizen asking which public transport pickup points were least crowded. Seeing that all was as it should be, Nico turned away from the entry, and ascended to the second stream, and flew two blocks back toward the west before turning north.

As he sped through the stream, one civilian craft caught his eye, as it pulled out from the tenth floor of a building in the twelfth sector of the northeast quarter. The craft was small, and pale in color, and its windows were crystal clear. Within it, a woman that may have been slightly older than him was piloting. He slowed down, and waved her out. She only glanced at him, and then turned, and headed west between two other buildings.

Looking off to his right, beyond the wide paths of wind and the few short alleyways outside of them, Nico was able to see the haze of the shield, and beyond it, the high, swaying trees of the forest. They were as dark as ever, with barely enough light pushing between them to distinguish one from another. He sped up again, and before reaching the north end of the path, turned left, and headed west, into the quarter's eleventh sector.

As he moved along he saw one of the blue birds from the sky. His radiating red lights flickered off of the bird's gleaming, blue side panels. There were two airmen inside. The pilot saluted. The other was obscured by angles and reflections, except for their blue helmet. Nico kept his head down, and nodded back, and approached another intersection, one that was usually busy, but now was unexpectedly quiet. A lone transport was hovering across the intersecting stream in front of him, near the corner of a building. Its cabin was well-lit, and it appeared to be nearly empty. The pilot waved. Nico nodded back, and flew two more blocks, and then turned right, entering the central north-south path.

He descended to the first stream, and made his way up to the north entry. He had expected near chaos, but when he finally saw the crowd they seemed relatively calm. There was minimal noise, and the patrolmen there had followed their orders perfectly. Two of them were on the platform, watching, and making intermittent announcements to keep the citizens at ease as they moved toward the entry. On the street, four patrolmen were stationed outside the high-reaching gates that surrounded the lowest point of entry. Nico looked past the entry, and ran a scan, and saw that eight massive craft were already idling there. They were rudimentary, but long and sleek, and each one could safely move five hundred people. He was sure that each of them would exceed their capacity as they departed the city.

As he hovered there, watching, the first groups of citizens began to pass through the entry, walking between the outward-opening, protective gates, and ascending the steps to the waiting craft without trouble. Seeing things in motion, Nico did not linger. He turned away, passing over the crowd and entering the northwest quarter's thirteenth sector.

For another two hours he made his way around most of the city. When he passed near headquarters he saw the long, golden-trimmed craft of the council as it pulled away from the building. Its windows were dark, but he had been inside the craft before. There was enough room for all five councilors, and the spouses of the two that were wed, and several others if necessary.

At the west entry he saw another well-managed crowd, though it was smaller than the one at the north. This time he was not surprised. The west entry had always been the slowest. There was no tree cover beyond it, just a clear view of the Western Range, the peaks of which were the least distinctive on the mainland. Before pulling away from the entry, he ordered the redirection of two of the eight shelter craft that were there to the north entry, where they would be more useful.

As he made his way south again, a signal from the Spire came up in his visor, blinking rapidly. The line was secured, limited to only commanders and lieutenants. He watched as the signals of Shil, Maia, Fits and Jaan appeared below Brun's. Nico answered last, and listened.

"This is Commander Brun. We have seen another flash, less intense, but this time near the southeast edge of the forest. We were, with Taj's help, and following Maia's advice, able to track it fairly quickly, and observe it as it erupted. We are all safe, and Taj was able to get a full reading. I am now giving the call over to him."

"This is Taj," said the old teacher. "With the commander's help I was able to modify the sensors on my helmet, and as a result, obtained some excellent data. The flashes are, indeed, made up of magma from deep beneath the surface. The storm cools them quickly once they break through, which is why their damage is not widespread. As this last flash dissipated in the sky, I was able to get a scan below the surface. Combining it with the growing data from the probes that are still in the ground, I expect that there will, in all likelihood, be at least a small disruption beneath the city."

"What do you suggest we do?" asked Shil, her voice calm.

"We cannot move any faster."

"You do not need to, Commander," Taj replied. "The city's foundation is so fortified that any cracks forming far below are not likely to reach the surface, and therefore not likely to absorb any lightning to break through and release any of the gases and rock. However, we cannot rule out some destabilization."

"Meaning what?" Nico asked.

"Meaning a possible earthquake, or a sinking of some kind."

Nico hesitated. "Big, or small?"

"There is no way to tell, Lieutenant. Following the readings, the area most at risk would be the southeast quarter, as Commander Jaan suggested. How is it looking there?"

"It is nearly clear, Doctor," Maia said. "The airmen sweeping the area have reported no citizens staying in place. The park, however, could be an issue."

"I see it," said Nico. He slowed his jumper, and idled in the first stream, watching from above, just outside the edge of the park. "There's a crowd near the stage."

"For what purpose?" Jaan asked.

"For Loren's memorial, Commander Sir," he answered. "I will take care of it. I am on approach now."

"I'm sending a bird to meet you, Lieutenant," said Maia.

"Very well."

After a short silence, Shil's signal blinked, and she spoke again. "Is there anything else, Teacher?" she asked.

"No," said Taj. "Just my prayers, for all our safety."

CHAPTER 18
SHAKEN

From the base of the park stage Chad could see Nico descending on his jumper. He landed fifty feet behind the remaining mourners, blocking the view to Haluna's unlit windows. After the lieutenant disembarked, he lingered, and watched. There were only ten or so people left in the park, remnants of the earlier crowd. As Loren's gentlest, kindest lyrics played out through the stage speakers, her former guitarist was delivering a final eulogy. The rest of her band was standing behind him, each of them resting a gentle hand on his back.

"Today there is not enough time," the young man said through tears. "It is a day when she would be happy; not because of the threat from Mother Earth, but because of the promised sight of the natural world. Loren adored the city, but she dreamed of a life outside of it, of a life surrounded by everything and everyone that supports us. And on this day she would ask us to remember that we are not the last of old humanity, but the first of new humanity, and that the world will, someday, be full again." He looked up, and raised an open hand, as if waiting for the sun to land on his palm. "To my sister in spirit, Loren."

"To Loren," all of the mourners echoed softly.

As Chad finished speaking her name, he saw Nico begin to approach, and seeing that the band was in no danger, he walked out, past the last in the sullen and somber gathering. As he got further and further from them, there was only open space between him and the watcher. He walked straight, passing by stones, walking over pathways and grass, and looked into Nico's eyes. He took slow, shallow breaths, easing the tension in his chest. The air around him seemed cooler. There was little life left in the area now. The surrounding streams and streets had all but emptied.

Nico looked past him, and called out. "Citizens. I too grieve Loren's loss, but you have been ordered to depart. You must finish mourning another time."

Chad looked down at him. "You see we've all brought our bags," he said, motioning back with one arm. "We'll leave soon enough."

Nico shook his head. "There is no time." He walked by Chad, and spoke louder, with his voice amplified by his helmet. "Citizens! I understand why you linger here, but the ground below us is now at even greater risk. The entries are clearing quickly. Your trek will be easy. You are ordered to depart the city immediately."

Chad turned, and watched as the band moved toward the steps on the right side of the stage, all of their eyes focused squarely on Nico. Those on the ground finally began to disperse, and take up their belongings, heading in the same direction of the band, toward the north-south path west of the park. As the stage and the space in front of it emptied, and the group quietly murmured and departed, Chad saw only his bag still on the ground.

Nico turned around to face him. "Still here?"

"You have some nerve," Chad grumbled. "Coming to her memorial to order us to leave."

"I told you, Chad. It was her own doing. I did everything I could that night, to keep her safe. I'm trying to do the same for you now. Your friends here are smart enough to see what's happening. What exactly are you missing?"

"What are you trying to say?"

Off to the left, a blue bird from the sky appeared, its red lights radiating. It hovered in place, five yards over the park ground.

"How about this, Chad?" Nico said, motioning toward the bird. "I'll give you a ride."

"Is that pilot any better than yours?"

Nico scowled under his visor. "Probably."

Chad shook his head. "No, thanks. I'll make it on my own."

"Fine with me, as long as you leave now."

"I'll leave when I'm ready."

"You're ready *right now*."

Nico stepped back with one foot, and held one open palm up, and reached the other behind his back. He said something into his helmet, and Chad looked over as he heard the bird humming, and then saw its ramp lowering. He knew they wanted to subdue him, in one way or another.

"Let me get my bag," he said.

"Fine," said Nico, and turned toward the bird.

Chad took one step toward the stage, and then lunged forward with his shoulder, hitting the watcher square in his chestplate, knocking him back.

"Chad!" someone yelled from the street. "Look out!"

Chad looked to his right, and saw the mourners running up the road. To his left, the bird was still hovering, but no airmen had approached. Then, beneath the soles of his heavy boots, he felt rumbling. He looked past the downed watcher, and saw a break in the park's ground. A crackling line was running from the now buckling stage, and shooting at him fast. In front of him, Nico leapt back up to his feet.

The watcher swung both arms out, and made swift motions with his hands, and Chad saw the weapons on his forearms disengage. As the watcher closed his hands into fists, and aimed them at him, bright rings of blue energy emerged, and hazy lines of air formed around his elbows. Chad felt frozen, by shock, by the light projecting into his eyes. Beneath their feet, the ground shifted again.

The park began to crumble around them. Chad could hear the grinding of rock shaking loose beneath them. Looking around, he could see that the ground had sunken a yard below street level. Then he looked and saw Nico kneeling down, and in desperation, lunged forward again, knocking the watcher back with one heavy fist. Broken rock fell over the man, but he got up quickly. Shocked, Chad rushed him again, and as he did, saw the watcher's arms swing up, and his hands open. The blue light from his arms jumped out in a concentrated blast, hitting him, and launching him backward. He floated, for how long he did not know, and then crashed into the ground. Energy surrounded him, stinging his body all around.

"Aaaarrgh!" he cried out.

The energy both burned and chilled, and he felt the hair all over his body standing on end. He tried to open his eyes, but felt fire across his eyelids, and quickly closed them again. He rolled over, and buried his face in the ground, clenching his fists. Then, someone was on top of him, and his wrists were pulled behind him and clasped in metal, and he realized it was Nico. He tried to resist again, but the lieutenant had full control of both his arms. The burning around his body remained unceasing.

"Up!" Nico ordered.

The ground shook again, and Chad felt them sink another foot.

"Hurry!" Nico yelled. "Get up!"

Chad found the strength to get to one knee, and then to both feet. "Cheap shot!" he managed to yell out. Another shock pierced him all around, and he dropped to one knee again.

"That was just the beginning!" Nico yelled back. "Get up! Hurry!"

As he struggled to his feet again, Chad looked up and saw the blue bird. It was in front of them, and its rear ramp was tilted down, beckoning them. The watcher standing on the ramp, a woman outfitted in sleek blue, was leaning against the frame, keeping herself steady. She pulled a rolled cord up from behind her, and tossed it out. Behind him, the metal clasps were pulled off his wrists.

"Grab it!" Nico yelled.

Chad jumped as hard as he could, and with a boost from Nico, grabbed hold of the bright-colored handle at the end of the rope. A moment later, it started to retract. He jumped off of another section of broken ground, and the cord pulled him higher. As he reached the base of the ramp, the woman reached out, grabbed him by the arm, and pulled him in. He felt the bird's engines boost the rear end back upward, and crawled toward the center of the cabin. He heard the ramp close, and then, no longer surrounded by chaos, he felt a fuller shock from the energy surrounding his body.

"Aaargh!" he yelled.

"Toughen up!" the woman said, and marched past him.

Chad collapsed within himself, bringing his knees in, and lowering his head as he squirmed against the hard cabin floor. He tightened his eyes, and felt them watering, and tried and failed to open them again. The woman returned, and turned him onto his belly, and pushed through the haze of energy over his back to bind his wrists again. Then she sat him up, and reached under his right shoulder, and his legs seemed to move on their own as she guided him back toward a bench and up into the seat. He leaned back against it, and tried to take a breath. He winced, as the shocking energy pushed over his teeth, but the pain around him was starting to subside. He managed to open his eyes, and looked up to see the helmeted woman pulling harnesses out from behind him.

"Don't try to escape," she said, as she pulled the belts down over his still-glowing shoulders.

She seemed small to Chad, for a watcher, but she had been strong enough to pull him into the craft. "Where would I go?" he replied.

"Just sit there and keep quiet," she snapped back.

As she secured the belts near his waist, he felt the clasps on his wrists pushing into the seat, and stinging his wrists. But around his body the torturous light was steadily fading. The lingering sting slowly became only a tingle, and the light in the cabin became clearer. The woman left him, and stood near the pilot. He saw her rubbing at her arms, and realized that his weight had, in fact, been a struggle for her.

*   *   *   *   *

Nico was watching as he ran. The bird's ramp closed, and it cleared the park, as he had ordered. He shook his head, and retracted his gauntlets, and continued running. He jumped from one piece of broken ground to the next, keeping his strides long, and landing softly each time, until finally he reached one of the pathways that had not been broken.

The stone beneath his boot soles dropped another few inches, and he turned around to look for his jumper. Its lights were still radiating twenty yards away, as it hovered in the midst of flying rocks and dust. He leapt to a piece of broken ground, near the street, and ran again. After five long, swift steps he leapt out, and passed through dusty air, and felt his tech hum as he adjusted his body and landed on the jumper's seat. It bounced backward with his weight, and broken soil and rock continued to fly up around him as he opened the engines and boosted the small craft up and out, toward the path that led north.

He entered the first stream, and got to a safe distance, and then idled. As he hovered in place he looked back, and watched the park get darker and darker as it was pulled further and further down. The stage had fully collapsed, and the elegant, crafted speakers had disappeared into the rubble. A loud rumble through the space seemed to pull down more bright grass, and shatter another winding stone path. Behind the park, toward the south, the buildings were shaking, and their highest floors were starting to tumble. Their lights flickered on and off, and sparks flew, and dust clouds seemed to be pushing out from every street. Turning, and looking east, he saw more of the same.

Maia's signal popped up in his visor. "This is Lieutenant Nico," he answered, and coughed. "Go ahead."

"Lieutenant," said Maia. "My airman there says that the park is clear."

Nico looked ahead, to where the bird that had rescued Chad

remained hovering. Then he looked past it, and down to the street, where he had last seen the last of the mourners fleeing. It was cracked, but not sinking, not yet. He leaned forward, and guided the jumper up, past the bird, and into the north-south stream. He looked north, and magnified his view, and saw the last of the group in the distance, boarding another bird. As its ramp closed, and it flew off toward the west entry, he exhaled.

"Yes," he answered. "The park is clear."

"Very well," said Maia. "Kine and I are leaving the south entry. The platforms have, unfortunately, been compromised. And the buildings here may be on their last legs. My other airmen are leaving the east entry, and we are ending our support patrols."

"Thank you. I'll see you on the outside."

"See you there. Maia out."

Nico turned his attention to the bird that had aided him. It had moved up, and was hovering right behind him. Another rumble filled the air, and he saw the crack in the street below them growing, and continuing north. He opened a line to the pilot. "Nico to bird," he called. The pilot saluted him through the window.

"This is Airman Noor," the man answered. "Go ahead, Lieutenant, Sir."

"Airman, that citizen needs to be restrained."

"Already done, Sir. We saw him attack you from here. He's not going anywhere. But his breathing is labored, and he is still shaking some from the shot you gave him."

"Good. Let him suffer. Let him think."

"Yes, Sir. Shall we go?"

"Lead the way."

Nico wiped his chin, and brushed the dirt and debris from his sleeves. The bird pulled past him, and as it did, he looked to the cabin and noticed the other airman standing behind the pilot, leaning down over his seat. As they sped forward, he leaned down onto the jumper, and accelerated, following closely behind them.

As he flew, Nico sensed how much lighter the winds of the stream felt. He brought up the city's status in his visor. All of the buildings had been reported clear. The breaks in the ground were visible as warnings in red. The wind engines in the south and the east were functional, but unsurprisingly, were all down to half power. Shil's blinking signal interrupted his reading.

"This is Nico," he answered, as gusts from the stream pressed upon him. "Go ahead, Commander, Sir."

"The city is nearly clear," said Shil. "But we have to make one last sweep. Meet me in the third stream at headquarters."

"On my way. Nico out."

He watched as Noor's bird turned left, and continued toward the west entry. He continued north, and made his way up to the second stream, and then the third, passing by no other craft as he ascended. With each jump he felt less and less secure in the streams. Their air seemed to thicken as he moved into the northwest quarter, but it still was not what it had been. As he turned toward headquarters, he checked the status of all four of the city's wind engine arrays. Those at the north and west entries had not yet compensated for the others. He looked out, and saw Shil's hovering puller, and opened a line to her as he slowed to a stop.

"The arrays are compromised," he said, saluting through the puller's windshield. She was alone in the craft.

"I'm aware," she answered. "The last of the public transports have emptied, and the last of the shelter craft are boarding now. I'm not letting *anyone* stay behind to work those engines. We'll just have to move fast."

"Agreed. The perimeter might be safest to pass through, then. Shall I lead, Sir?"

"Go ahead," she said, and motioned with her right hand.

Nico leaned down again, lowered his head to fully engage the engine on his back, and shot forward. Through his visor, at such speed, his view was not as wide. He focused on the streams, and the air movers, and what he could see of the buildings. Behind him, he heard the constant, heavy rushing of the puller's engines. He made his way into the northeast quarter, and quickly covered the first four blocks.

"Anything, Sir?" he called to Shil. "Anyone?"

"Scans show all clear," she said. "No one's in sight. Keep moving."

He slowed as he reached the end of the last block, where he caught a glimpse of the empty apartments and walkways of the last building, and then turned right, and swung his end around just short of the shield.

The air in the perimeter was always thinner, but it still held firmly to his jumper. He ascended ten feet, getting a closer look at the raw force of the storm as it passed over the forest. He felt the jumper's engines hum as they pulled in more wind, and followed the perimeter's curve as it moved south. He passed over the east entry, over its engines, which were visibly shaking. Further south, and yards below, there was a haze of dust, and to his right, buildings were toppling, and sinking, and enveloping and extinguishing lights as they fell. He looked forward again, and shook off the growing sadness.

"We still have the shield," said Shil. "I'm closing the frames at the east entry. Don't fret, Lieutenant. We'll rebuild."

"Yes, Sir," he said. "I know we will."

He continued along the curve, and passed over the south entry. As Shil closed its frames behind him, he saw the confirmation in his visor. He curved again, heading west. Looking out, he could see that many buildings in the southwest quarter were still standing, but they were surrounded by a cloud of brown and gray. Their lit windows were obscured, but Shil confirmed that every unit was clear.

As he approached the west entry, he looked and saw that the last shelter craft had landed, and as he scanned, he saw that it had been boarded, and that its doors had been closed. He slowed to a stop, and waited there, just over the entry, and watched as the massive, green ship ascended, over their head, and turned north. Beyond it, in the distance, he saw the mountains of the Western Range. They were towering, even from miles away, and he felt a hint of assurance that the land and the people would endure. Behind him, Shil closed the west entry's frames. He leaned forward, and continued north.

In the northwest quarter everything, except for the empty buildings, looked the same. A few blocks to the east Nico saw the city watchers' station, with its lights still glowing red up and down its edges. He took what felt like his final look at it, before picking up speed, and curving around to the north entry. There he saw one shelter craft hovering near the ground, as two others floated up into the sky with pullers behind them.

"That's the last one," said Shil.

"Can it carry my jumper?" Nico asked.

"Ha. I doubt it. Just leave it with the others, Lieutenant."

Nico slowed his speed, and looked down to the road, and saw the two lines of jumpers, with twelve on either side of the street, all of them pointed toward the north entry and flickering with yellow lights. The patrolmen had all followed their orders perfectly. He sped forward again, over the north entry, and made the last turn through the perimeter. He curved around, and descended three yards, and dropped back down into the third stream, and turned down the same path they had started from.

He sped over the movers at each intersection, and approached the central north-south pathway. He turned onto the path, and descended to the second stream, and then to the first, and slowed his speed. As he dropped out of the first stream, and floated down toward the street, he guided his jumper up behind another. He turned its lights from red to yellow, and hopped off. Shil's puller slowly descended to his left, and stopped in front of him.

He walked carefully along the pavement, and up to the puller's starboard side. As the door opened, he turned, and looked back once more, to the distant, dusty haze in the south, below the darkening sky. He stepped up into the puller, and as the door slid closed, he sat quietly near the rear holding cell and strapped in. Ahead of them, the last of the citizens passed through the north entry and into the shelter craft, and Shil guided the puller back up to the first stream. They hovered there, waiting, until they saw the massive ship ascend, and then saw the last patrolmen follow in two puller's behind it.

Shil took the puller up, into the second stream, and then the third, and guided them out carefully. They passed through the metal frame in the shield, and she closed it behind them, and flew out easily toward the roof of the dark forest. As they cleared the treeline, she shot up, and followed closely behind the pullers, and the shelter craft ahead of them.

CHAPTER 19
SANCTUARY

The holding area at the Spire was underground, beneath the wide, circular base of the high-reaching, central structure. There were small vents in the corners of the ceiling on the south wall, and the storm's winds had whistled through them all night, but Nico had still managed to sleep. One of the privates that maintained the space had set up a small bed for him against the wall, across from the two small cells. As Nico opened his eyes, and saw the tiny amount of natural light peaking through the vents, he remembered no nightmares. It was the first time in days. He sat up straight, and breathed in deep, and swung his heavy boot soles down to the smooth, rock floor.

To his left was the door to the hall, which led out to the village. To his right were closed metal cabinets, and a single control panel. Three yards straight ahead, behind heavy, closely-set metal bars, was Chad. The large man was lying on his back, but wide awake, and rubbing his neck and wincing as if he were still in pain.

"It's been half a day," said Nico, as he touched each piece of his tech. He picked his helmet up from beneath the bed frame. "The shock has worn off by now."

"Have you ever felt one?" Chad asked, his voice heavy, and carrying out through the bars.

"Of course. We all have. That's why I gave you so much time to do the right thing."

Chad sat up, first onto his elbows, and then upright. He turned, and set his boots down on the floor, and leaned over, resting his arms on his knees. "You shouldn't have access to such punishment."

Nico smirked. "Then what would we do with people like you?"

"People like me?"

"Yes. The unsettled. Those who cannot find their way in a world that is as simple as it's ever been, where the only thing they need to do is embrace a role for the sake of all of us avoiding extinction." Nico stood up from the bed, and stepped forward, and looked down at the man through the bars. "What would you say we should do, besides subdue people like you when they cause disruptions?"

Chad looked up, and into Nico's eyes. "You should answer to all the people, let them decide."

"Wrong. Try again."

Chad scoffed, and stood up from the bed. He rubbed his forehead, and reached for the metal cup on the sink next to the bed. As he touched it, Nico raised his right gauntlet, and absorbed and released a small burst of air, knocking the cup away. It fell to the floor, and clanged as the water spilled out of it, and bounced to a stop.

"You can get more water," said Nico. "You only get one life. I saw your file. You've lived far too long now to not understand."

Chad swiped the cup up from the ground, and took it to the sink, and rinsed it and filled it again. He turned, and stared back at Nico as he took a long chug from the cup, and then splashed the rest against his face. He wiped his eyes on his sleeves. "What's my punishment?" he asked.

Nico lifted his helmet, and set it down carefully over his head, and pressed it down, and felt its snugness against his temples. There was a notification from Shil, blinking on the right side of the visor. He acknowledged it, and as it stopped, turned his attention back to Chad. "You attacked a watcher of the city," he said. "Without cause, and in the midst of catastrophe. You potentially impeded the protection of other citizens. You may get to speak before the council, if they can find a way to establish themselves while everyone else from the city is trying to determine how and where they are going to live. But you may not. If it were up to me, you'd be dead. But typical punishment is simple expulsion, to a village focused solely on heavy labor. Some Lwoans enjoy it, some don't. Which do you think you are?"

Chad sighed, and sat back down on the bed, and looked through the cell bars again. "It wasn't without cause."

Nico's eyes narrowed. "What?"

"You got off too easy, watcher. *You* should be doing hard labor, if your average strength can handle it." He slammed his heavy hands into the bed. "It was *you* that lost her! How can you wish anyone dead!?"

Nico felt his fists clench. "Do you actually *want* to live?"

Chad lowered his eyes. "Of course."

"With all the life she had, do you think she would want you to live, after what you did yesterday?"

Chad sighed. "I don't know."

"She most definitely would. You didn't know her as well as you think. It seems to me you've wasted a lot of time in your life, Chad. How many years do you think you have left?"

Chad laid back down on the bed, and stared up at the ceiling. "You're not going to guilt trip me, watcher. Go on to your work."

Nico huffed to himself. "I guess not many."

He turned away from the cell, and made his way over to the door. He input his code to exit, and stepped through as it slid open, and waited and listened as it closed and locked behind him.

The hall was long, with low light coming from the ceiling, and dark walls. At the other end, a single private was standing at a workstation with his helmet retracted. Nico walked forward, slowly, over the hard floor, thinking about the raw wind he was about to take on. He passed by two closed, barely noticeable doors on the right, and heard the winds through thin vents on the left. It felt like a hundred steps before he reached the tall, armored man at the station. The private saluted him with no words. Nico nodded, and walked past him, entering the narrow, shadowy stairwell.

The stone steps led upward, and he walked up each one carefully. As he neared the top, he hit the large, yellow square on the left. He heard the metal shutter disengage, and watched as it tilted upward in front of him. As his boots hit the last step, he clenched his fists, and looked out at the brightness around the ground watchers' village. He felt his tech awaken, humming all around his body as the winds began passing through each engine. He moved carefully as he left the last step, and set his soles on the village's main road. Behind him, he heard the shutter begin to close again, helped along by the gusts pushing over it.

He turned, and looked around, and looked up. It was the snow—looming at the top of the mountain to the north—that made the village so bright. The sky was still its constant gray, not letting the lingering sun peak through, but the snow from the peak in the north was still bright white. It was the only consistent snowpack in the entire land. It diminished as it moved down the mountain face, where the snowmelt led to a stream near the ground, which sparkled. The stream led toward the village, and then around the eastern side, where it settled in the lake. Just before the stream's turnoff, the village's main road began, running in from the north, surrounding the Spire, and leading back south into the Middle Lands.

As Nico turned and looked off to the south, a chilling gust knocked him backward. He leapt just in time to not fall, and descended back to the ground, and nearly stumbled as his boot soles hit the closed shutter and he bumped into the Spire's hard wall. He gathered himself, and shook his head, and pushed himself off the wall. Off to his right there was a two-yard-wide street, which ran between two rows of boxy, tough-looking buildings. He saw two privates there, and saw them stop staring and salute as their eyes caught his. He turned back toward the south, and walked.

He kept his steps heavy, and his arms just a few inches from his waist, as he had done in training so many years before. He kept his fists clenched, and his chin low, so that his unattached helmet would not be pulled off. He felt every force as the wind passed through the tech on his arms and boots and back. He picked up his pace as he made his way around the curved wall of the Spire, to its south side, where he stopped, and looked up at the wide, circular observation levels. Shil was on the first, and wanted him to join her. Behind him, he heard engines approaching, and turned around to see a manned fox stop two yards away. The wide engines in its wings pulled the winds away from him. The black-clad pilot looked down at him, saluted, and called to him through an open line.

"Lieutenant, Sir," the man said. "I was ordered to take you up."

Nico nodded, and leapt up and out to the fox's wide port wing, and moved behind the pilot. He knelt down, and with both hands, grabbed one of the low bars behind the pilot. "Go ahead," he said through the line.

A moment later the wings roared, and they shot upward at a speed that was almost shocking. Nico steadied his breathing, and focused on the status of the engine on his back. A few seconds later, they were hovering over the wide, metal disc that was the base of the Spire's first observation level. He hopped off, and landed heavily, and moved along the hard, textured surface toward the inner wall. Behind him, the pilot took the fox back out, and flew back down.

Nico felt no more secure on the platform than he had on the ground, but he stood there anyway, and let himself feel the wind forces, and looked out at the rows of buildings that formed the village. On either side of the main road below there were at least ten rows of fifteen to twenty buildings. They formed lines running from east to west, and none of them were more than three stories high. Most of the flat roofs were billowing out steam or smoke that was being whisked away as fast as it was expelled.

Furthest south, at the undefined edge of the village, there were two manned foxes stationed on either side of the road. Past them, there was a single, idling shelter craft. Its green color stood out in the shadowy landscape, where even the discernible blades of grass had a subdued shade. The large craft's engines were pushing out massive streams of dense air. He wondered if there was truly enough space inside it, and if the citizens were being managed well by the watchers who had been assigned.

"I see you, Lieutenant," Shil called through an open line. "Let your thoughts pass, and join us inside."

"On my way, Commander, Sir," he answered.

He turned, and walked up to the high, thick wall of curved

glass. He could see the operations space on the other side. As the door slid open, and he entered, he immediately felt warmer, as was always the case at any watcher station. Ten yards in, past the spread-out workstations and empty seats, and behind a short, solid divider made of a polished wood, he saw that four other ranking watchers had gathered. He could see Jaan's stern face, and his dark red chestplate. To his right was Maia, and to her right was Shil. Across from her, near the foot of the bed, Nico could see Brun standing with his massive arms crossed. Nico saluted as he reached them, and stood next to Shil. Then, he looked down.

The woman lying in the bed was unconscious. She was wearing the blue uniform of an airman. Her right arm was in a sling, and the sleeve had been removed. There was a glowing, metal sensor strip affixed to her bare shoulder, curving over it from her front to her back. She looked too old to be an airman, but not quite elderly. Then Nico noticed her hair, and its scarlet shade, and the uniquely-knit braids that started at the front of her head, and ended in an unfurling bun over her healthy shoulder. His heart jumped, and he knelt down, and set his fist into his chest, and whispered "My Lord."

As he stood back up, he removed his helmet. "It was Lord Coral in the city?" he asked. "In the bird?"

"It was," said Jaan, his voice steady, and heavy.

"She pulled Chad in," said Nico. "I didn't know it was her. I would've…"

"It's alright," said Shil. "We know. She told us everything,

339

before she lost consciousness."

"I don't understand. Why was she even there? Why is she even on the mainland?"

"Lord Andrew sent her here to assist us," said Jaan. "And when the city was put in more danger, she gave me no choice in the matter. I tried to dissuade her, but she insisted on helping, so I ordered an airmen to take her with him."

Nico turned around, and looked back out the windows, past the village below and toward the city, though it was miles away. He had no idea what he had expected to see. He had only felt a sudden sense of doubt. He turned back around, and looked down again, at the youngest Lord. He had not seen her in years, not since his promotion. He was surprised, as he was then, at how little she seemed to age. But she was not breathing as if she were young. With her short inhales and exhales her chest was barely rising. He looked past her head, to the monitors, and then looked around the room.

"Where's your doctor?" he asked.

"Come and gone," said Brun. "There's nothing more he can do. And it is not worth the risk to call another."

"Not worth the risk?"

"It's her biology, Lieutenant," Jaan said. "It's different. And it's compromised. We do not know how. The doctor could only add this stabilizer to keep her muscle from falling apart. We will have to take her back to the Isle, and soon."

Nico looked down at her again, and shook his head. "It's just her arm. I don't understand. Why is she unconscious?"

"It was just too much for her," said Jaan. "For whatever reason. Maybe it was the citizen's weight. Maybe it was the stress of seeing, and feeling, the city's distress. Maybe it's her age, even though she looks the way she does. Her body is just different than ours are. To have lived so long, all of the Lords' bodies are probably much different."

"Commander, Sir..." Nico hesitated, struggling. "Had I known it was her..."

Jaan raised a hand at him, but stopped himself from speaking as Shil did the same. She turned to Nico, and set her hand on his shoulder.

"Lieutenant, this was not your fault," she said. "This was no one's fault. Lord Coral even said as much. She told us how well you performed, under attack from all sides. Take comfort in that, and worry no more. We have work to do." She turned away from him, as he nodded, and looked to the others in the group. "Who will take her?"

Jaan looked at the status monitors over Coral's head. They still showed her as stable. Then he looked to Brun, and to Shil, and to Maia, and finally to Nico. "I will take her," he said. "Maia will come with me."

"Sir, I would like to go," said Shil. "This happened in the city, because of the city. It should be me, if any of us, that answers for this."

Jaan shook his head at her. "No, Commander. You will stay here. You will serve as lead until we return. I give you full command of the sky, and the rest of the mainland. If anyone should bring her home, to the other lords, it should be the leading watcher." He paused, and looked to Maia. "And my lieutenant would like to check in on the boy, and his father."

"They're the least of our worries," said Brun.

"That may be true," said Jaan. "But they are still innocent lives. They may live as long as we do, now that they are here. No matter what the Lords may do with me, Maia can at least look after them."

"What could they do?" Brun asked.

"If Lord Coral recovers, she of course will tell all, and all will be well. If not, I may be discharged from our ranks."

"Have they done so before?"

"No, not that I'm aware, but it is what I would anticipate. In any case, Commander, I have instructions for you as well."

"Yes, Sir?"

"I want you to continue to oversee Doctor Taj's work on the ground, and the resettling of the citizens. Understood?"

"Yes, Sir."

"Commander Shil, you will need to continue communicating with the people. Their tensions must be kept to a minimum. They have very little space now, as do the villages that are providing aid. If ever they needed to be reminded of the need to be patient, and care for their fellow man, it is now."

"Yes, Sir," said Shil. "How long do you expect to be on the Isle?"

"Lord Coral has been here for four days. I do not know how long it will take for her to recover, but I want to stay until she is well. Lieutenant Maia?"

"Yes, Sir?" Maia answered.

"Bring my bird about, to the mountain side. Lieutenant Nico, you help me with Lord Coral."

As Maia departed, moving past Nico and quickly out to the open platform, Brun began moving the dividers away from the bed. Nico donned his helmet once more, and followed Jaan's direction, moving to the head of the bed. The frame was made of hollow metal, with the mattress holder supported by angled, interlocking rods attached to mechanized wheels on the floor. They rolled Coral over the smooth surface slowly, and Nico was surprised by the amount of resistance. Coral was not small, but was also not very muscular. And all of the tech on her watcher's uniform had been removed. As they reached the center aisle, he slowed down, and held tightly to the bed's frame. Jaan swung his end toward the wide, clear doorway that faced the mountain behind the Spire, and Nico pushed as he pulled.

They reached the rear doors, and four of them stood there, in the shadows of the observation space, surrounding Coral's bed, waiting. It was minutes before they heard the bird swoop around the glass walls. As they approached the doors, Brun activated them, and stood aside as Nico pushed the bed, and followed Jaan. The curved doors slowly rotated outward, protecting them from the winds pushing in from the east and west. The bird's ramp had already been lowered, and was touching the platform.

Jaan stood in place, and Nico moved the head of the bed around, toward the bird, and then moved quickly up the ramp with Coral's weight in tow. As Jaan gave the bed one final push, Nico moved aside, and then walked back toward the ramp.

"Good luck, Sir," he said, as he stepped out of the cabin.

As he reached the platform, and turned back around, he saw Jaan lower the bed to the cabin's floor, and lock its wheels. He walked around to Coral's side, and saluted the three of them, as they stood on the platform, watching. As the ramp started to close, Nico saw the commander sit down on the starboard bench and strap in. Then he saw the light near Coral's face, as the sensor over her shoulder continued to glow.

The ramp finally closed, and Nico heard its faint lock. He watched as the bird began to rise, and heard its engines grow louder, and saw it float away from the platform. Then it rose higher, past the tip of the Spire, and hovered for a split second before racing off to the east. Its brilliant red shape got smaller and smaller, as it increased in speed, and ascended toward the clouds. In his visor Nico tracked the bird's trajectory, and saw it shift, as its signal headed over the Northern Range, toward the ocean, before he let it fade away.

CHAPTER 20
ADORNED

From the highest point in their cavern–above the living space, and just outside the Emissary's warm, humming core–Gem, sitting on the wide window sill with her legs up, looked out into the southern sky. The sun, somewhere above the clouds, was starting to set. And somewhere in the distance, where the clouds rolled into darker shades, the mainland seemed almost visible.

Gem pulled her long, gray hair back from the sides of her face, and sipped from the mug of hot tea. It did little to help with the cold coming in, floating through the thick glass and the rock that framed it. She set the mug down on the small table behind her, and folded her arms up into her soft, roomy sleeves, and looked down toward the other end of the sill, at her boots. They were plain, and heavy, and mostly hidden beneath her skirt. And they bore no tech. There was no need for it, not in their cold cavern, not even when they opened the Isle's entries, when either their systems or the watchers were always there to guard against the winds. Tech was only needed when leaving the safety of their island, as Coral had done four days before. Gem thought about her sister, and the evidence of continued flashing that she and her father had seen, and hoped that the mainland's dangers had not touched her.

"My Lord?" the Emissary called.

Gem looked over her shoulder, past the railing around the stairwell, to the vented doorway. "Yes, Emissary?" she answered.

"The extension process is complete."

"Very well. I will be there shortly."

She took a deep breath, and took another sip of tea, and looked at the sky once more, and then swung her boots down to the floor. She stood, and walked five steps to the top of the stairs, and grabbed the inner railing, and held onto it as she descended. She followed the winding turn with each step down until she reached the bottom, and faced the door to the west hall. The door slid aside, and she stepped out. She passed by the door to the guest quarters, where Robbins and his son had last slept before being subdued. She ran her hand gently across it, and then along the wall, until she reached the end of the hall, and stepped out into the living space.

As she passed by the dining table, and reached the open stairwell to the chamber, she could hear the preserver humming. As she moved down the steps, and reached the chamber's floor, she looked to the right side of the room, to Robbins' bed. The device's glowing, green light filled her with pride, and she smiled. She approached, and looked at the two long tubes running from the preserver and down behind Robbins' neck. They had been cleared of all fluids, both his and those containing the origin cells.

346

The small screen over the machine's control panel displayed the man's vitals, with blinking curves showing steady improvement. Gem leaned back, and reached behind the machine, and found the glass tube that had been inserted into its rear port. The tube was no longer cool, and looking at it, she saw that it was completely empty. As she looked back to Robbins, she saw the earliest sign of successful extension. The roots of his hair had thickened, and darkened.

She reached down, and set her hand on his forehead. The screen showed his temperature as slightly above normal, and she could feel it, but he was breathing easily. And despite the circumstances of his sedation–the stress, and his resistance–his face looked relaxed, and peaceful. She looked back, over her left shoulder, to the closed door of the lounge.

"Emissary?" she called. "How is the child?"

"Resting peacefully, my Lord," the system answered.

"No side-effects of him being subdued and sedated?"

"No, my Lord. He is well, and well-nourished, and in perfect health."

"Very good. Robbins will awake soon, I am sure. I am adding a saline tube. Adjust your sensors accordingly."

"Yes, my Lord."

Gem turned round, and made her way to one of the cooled cabinets near the stairwell, and retrieved a tube of the clear liquid. As she turned back, she saw the rear access door begin to slide open. It moved slowly, until her father was revealed. She went to Robbins' bed, and quickly inserted the tube into the rear of the preserver, and activated the machine's stabilizing mode. After taking one last look at the man, touching his arm, feeling his warmth once more, she stepped away, and moved along the chamber's center aisle toward her father. As she reached him, he opened his arms, and gently embraced her.

"How is our patient?" Andrew asked.

"He is well, Father," she replied. "How is she?" she asked, looking past him, and down the short, dark hall, through another open door, where the coffin had been set.

"She is beautiful," he replied. "Come with me."

Andrew extended his arm, and Gem walked with him, through the hall, traversing the cold, stone floor, and passing the doors to the stairwells to their private rooms. As they reached the open door to the small ceremony room, she saw that it was fully aglow. The colorful, sparkling lights that floated in the ceiling shined down onto the red carpet. At the center of the room, the long, metal, gray coffin sat mounted on polished, wooden supports, and various flowers were affixed to its metal edges.

At the nearest end of the coffin there was a small, thick window, and walking up and looking through it, Gem saw the woman's lovely face, looking healthier than it had at her death, and outlined with more flowers. She could almost smell the perfume she had treated the body with. Beneath the viewing window's frame, in elegant, etched, gold-colored lettering, was the woman's name, 'Loren.'

"Would you like to say anything, Daughter?" Andrew asked.

Gem ran her hand softly along the coffin, and shook her head. "No," she said. "That is Coral's gift, not mine."

"I will say something then. Something simple." He paused, and looked down through the window. "We are thankful that this Lwoan's life, though it was short, will give life to others."

Gem nodded. "We are thankful."

"Emissary?" Andrew called, and looked up. "It is time for this Lwoan's rest."

The system remained silent, as it always did after burial commands, but four of its circular drones emerged, passing through the door behind them. Each one hovered over one of the coffin's rounded corners, and then descended, and activated its magnets. The doors to the north cave disengaged, and began to slide open. The carved stone grumbled as it was pulled aside, and stopped as an opening just wide enough for two people to pass through was created.

The air from the outside pushed into the ceremony room, and Gem, and her father, walked up to the sides of the opening, guarding themselves, and breathing the fresh air in deeply. As the drones lifted the coffin up from its supports, and carried it past them and through the open doorway, an unmanned craft descended from its place in the top of the cave. Gem leaned against the heavy stone, and watched as the drones rose, and the black craft's clamps opened to receive the coffin.

The drones detached, and the craft's engines pulled in and

expelled dense white air, as it flew straight out from the cave, over the wild ocean, and into the sky. Then it flew east, and disappeared. The drones returned through the doors, humming over Gem and her father's heads, and quickly passed through the ceremony room and entered the short hall, where they floated up into their unseen holding places. She turned away from them, and stared out at the waters, and took in more of the natural air. A moment later she heard her father at the control panel behind her, and then leaned away, as the heavy stone began to slide shut.

She turned, and walked up behind her father, and watched the panel, as the dual signals of the unmanned craft and the coffin flew together. Then, five miles out, they stopped moving, and the signals separated, and the coffin's signal disappeared. As the craft began its trip back to the Isle, Gem turned away from the screen. She watched as her father went to the coffin mounts, and collapsed them, and returned them to their small cabinet in the wall.

"Do you think she's well?" Gem asked.

Andrew turned and looked at her, surprised. "Your sister?" he asked.

"Yes."

"Of course. Why do you ask?"

"Because of all the light that's entered the sky over the mainland, and the darkness that remains in the clouds."

"You mean the clouds that you can not keep your eyes off of? I told you to sleep, Daughter. There is no need to worry."

Gem rubbed her arms, and lifted them into her sleeves again, and followed her father out of the room. Behind them, the Emissary deactivated the twinkling lights in the ceiling. "This Lwoan was young," she said, nodding back toward the cave. "And she was healthy. And she was within the care of the watchers. We are aged. Our bodies would not fare even as well as hers did."

"I imagine the young woman was also careless. Your sister is not."

"But we have not heard from her since the last flash, which was just hours ago."

Andrew stopped in front of her, just short of the light shining in from the chamber, and turned around. He set his hand on her arm, and squeezed. "It may be risky for her to do it now," he said. "It would have been difficult for her to send the last message as she did. It came to us late, remember? Life is hard enough with all of Lwo knowing nearly all there is to know. Your sister is capable. And we may be aged, but we are strong. Trust me. She is fine. Now, why don't you go to your room and rest? I will keep an eye on our guests."

"I'm fine, Father," she said. "I won't miss Robbins' new beginnings."

"Very well."

Gem followed her father into the chamber, and listened as the door to the hall closed behind them. She looked to Robbins, still lying there, motionless except for his breathing. She walked around the end of his bed, and approached the preserver. His improved vitals had

351

stabilized. His heart was steady, and beating slower than it had before, and pumping more blood with each cycle. His temperature had come down. She reached toward his shoulders, and pulled the sheet down slightly, and pressed upon his skin. The tension had increased, both on the surface and in his muscles. Looking at his closed eyes, she saw fewer lines around them.

"He may have reached seventy," Andrew said from the other side of the bed. "Now, he will easily pass one hundred years, if he listens. How is his mental state?"

Gem tapped the third button on the machine's control panel. The status lines faded away, and a brain scan was revealed. "He's relaxed," she said. "But his mind is still very active. He must be dreaming quite a bit. The cells have increased firing more than they usually do. I just hope it's in the right places."

"If not, then we have our methods, if we need them."

"Right."

"My Lords," the Emissary called down to them, its voice low, but insistent. "A watcher calls, from the south cave. Lord Coral has been injured."

Gem's eyes shot to her father's, and then to the stairs. She reached them in four long, quick steps, and ascended ahead of him. She ran between their high-backed seats and the wide guest bench, and carefully descended to the bunker. She stopped for an instant, and looked back, and saw her father moving steadily behind her, carrying his staff with him. Then she raced up to the entry.

"Open, Emissary!" she ordered.

The tall, heavy, stone doors disengaged, and parted, and slowly slid aside. She saw Jaan there, standing firmly. He looked at her, and immediately knelt down, and looked at the ground, and set his fist into his chest. Behind him there was a wheeled bed, where Coral was lying face up with her head at the far end. Behind the bed, Maia was kneeling as Jaan was. Behind her, their red bird hovered, and glowed with yellow light.

"Rise watchers," Andrew said as he reached them. "Tell me what happened."

Jaan stood, and spoke. "My Lord, there were multiple flashes, and the city had to be evacuated. Lord Coral insisted on helping us, and I had her escorted to the city. The disruptions beneath the surface caused an earthquake that collapsed the park and the surrounding areas. Lord Coral aided in the evacuation, and in the rescue of one particular citizen, one who was very large, very heavy. Her heroic efforts led to her injury."

Gem looked into Jaan's concerned, but steady eyes, and looked to her father, who was doing the same.

"Lieutenant?" Andrew called, his eyes still on Jaan. "What do you say?"

"It is all correct, my Lord," Maia answered. "I was there, but I did not know that Lord Coral had entered the city. I am so sorry."

Andrew shook his head, and sighed. "Do not apologize. We make our own choices." He turned to Gem. "Daughter? How is your sister?"

Gem walked up to the bed, and looked Coral up and down. Then, she focused on the blinking sensor attached over her shoulder. "She looks well, Father," she said, touching and pinching around the sensor. "It appears some of her tendons are damaged, and I'd say she's exhausted. The watchers did well in stabilizing her. I think she will be just fine." She looked back through the wide entry. "Emissary! Move Lord Coral into the cavern, and down to the chamber."

"Yes, my Lord," the system replied, its voice carrying out to them.

Jaan and Maia stood aside, and Gem looked, and saw two of their drones descend, and heard their engines hum as they flew out into the cave. Each machine settled near one end of the bed, and disengaged it from the wheeled frame before lifting it up. Coral was carried quickly through the bunker, and into the cavern, and Gem followed behind her. She walked swiftly up the short steps, and through their living space. As the drones angled the bed, and carried it carefully down the stairwell, Gem got closer, and walked down behind it, keeping one hand hovering near her sister's head.

*   *   *   *   *

As Gem disappeared into the cavern, Maia took up her end of the bed frame, and in front of her, Jaan did the same. They carried the frame into the bunker, following closely behind Andrew, and then set

354

it down near one of the made beds. Behind them, the door to the cave closed and locked. Andrew had stopped walking, and Jaan had stopped behind him. Maia followed suit, walking up and standing firmly behind her commander. Andrew was stoic, with his staff firmly in his right hand as he looked into the cavern.

"My Lord?" Maia called. "May I ask, what is the chamber?"

"You may, Lieutenant," said Andrew, turning his head slightly toward her. "It is our treatment facility. As old as we are, we have to have a safe place to monitor and maintain our health. The two of you may come in now, and sit."

Maia followed Andrew and Jaan, out of the bunker and up the short steps. Ahead of them, between the kitchen and dining areas, the ornate wooden door closed. Andrew sat down first, in his center chair. Jaan sat on the far end of the high-backed bench across from him, and retracted his helmet. Maia sat on the near end, and did the same.

Andrew held to his staff, and leaned forward upon it, bracing himself, and looking at nothing in particular, and at neither of them. His eyes moved steadily, all around the cavern, toward the kitchen, and the bunker, and the closed doors. Then he set his staff down, lengthwise on the small table in front of him, and leaned back into the chair, and set his hands in his lap. Maia could see now how solid the staff was, how strong the polished wood looked, and how the minimal carvings made it look more stable. The green stone that balanced it near the center appeared to be a perfect circle. Usually Andrew's hand at least partially obstructed the stone. Maia had never paid it much attention before, but now she felt anxious, and had to focus on something.

"Please relax, Lieutenant," Andrew said, smiling at her.

She looked into his eyes, and could only manage a nod.

"We can only wait. We are more than capable of treating our own injuries, even though we are rarely at risk of any. No trouble will come to you. You've been forthright, both of you. And you've cared for my daughter."

"Thank you," said Jaan.

"My Lord," said Maia. "How are Devon and Robbins?" She looked around the cavern, and then back to Andrew. "With all the excitement, I'm surprised they have not come out to see us."

"Well, Lieutenant, they are resting."

She quieted again, as did the two men. Andrew's hands moved back and forth over his knees. They were all avoiding each other's gaze. Maia looked to the ceiling, to the vents and recessed shafts within all of the stone, and then out to the bunker again, where she and Devon and Robbins had entered together days before. *It's not late*, she thought. *They should be awake.*

Before any more worry could set in, a loud commotion broke the silence. It was followed by an even louder scream, from Gem. Maia's eyes shot to Jaan, and then to Andrew, who had already jumped up, and was jogging toward the closed door near the kitchen. Maia got to her feet, and followed Jaan as they ran behind him. For a fleeting moment, Andrew's agility surprised her.

The wooden door opened, and Andrew began stepping down. Jaan followed him, and Maia followed closely behind. The smell of chemicals, and clean, processed air, rushed into her nostrils. She breathed deep, and stepped off the last step, down to a solid, white floor. She looked past the two men, and saw Robbins, wide awake, and holding Gem tightly around her neck.

Fear shot through Maia's whole body, and Robbins looked just as terrified. He had his bare, left forearm pulled beneath her chin, and his left hand was clenching his right bicep. Maia, as all other watchers, had been trained to avoid using such techniques unless absolutely necessary. Humanity had been on its last legs from the time she was born, and even centuries before. Clearly, in the old world, there had been no such qualms.

"What did you do to me!?" Robbins yelled out. "And where is my son!?"

Maia stepped to her right, toward a disheveled bed, and a buzzing, fallen machine that had spilled clear fluids. Two beds beyond it, Coral was lying down, unmoving and still unconscious. Maia set her right foot a yard behind the other, held her arms down to her sides, and pressed her two center fingers into her right palm, activating her right gauntlet. To her left, she caught a glimpse of Jaan as he did the same, and sensed the faint glow of energy near his wrist.

"Let her go, Robbins," Jaan said calmly.

"After they answer me!" he snapped back.

Gem was larger than Robbins, and she was not weak, but he

was not struggling to keep her in place. Her knees were bent, and her boots were unsteady, and slipping as she tried to get her footing. Maia could see the uncertainty and fear in her eyes. She had never seen fear in a lord before, nor had she ever heard of it.

Andrew held one hand out toward Robbins, and with the other, motioned for them to stand down. Maia deactivated her gauntlet, and heard the low whirring from Jaan's begin to recede. Then, Andrew approached slowly, and held both empty palms up toward Robbins.

"I promise you," he started. "No damage has been done, and your son is safe. You have been extended, Robbins. Your life has been extended."

Confusion shot through Maia, and she looked to Jaan. His fists were firmly clenched.

"What do you mean!?" Robbins shouted. "What am I feeling!? Why can't I...Why can't I remember..."

"You are feeling power," Andrew replied. "And health. And life itself."

"I feel pain!"

"It is not pain, it is just new. Look at what you are doing. Pain would hardly allow it. Just days ago, my daughters were both stronger than you, even with all their years. Now, you are easily holding one in your grasp. You no longer have any weaknesses."

Maia saw the shift in Robbins' eyes as he took in Andrew's words. Then, his arms relaxed, and Gem swiftly stood upright, lifting him off the ground. As she dropped back down, Robbins was tossed helplessly toward Andrew, who jumped back. Maia jumped in front of the eldest lord, and Jaan leapt forward, but he was not fast enough. Beneath thin, white pants, Robbins' muscular legs twitched, and he jumped to his feet, and spread his stance, and held out both his visibly tense hands, toward Jaan and Gem.

"My son!" he yelled. "Tell me where he is! And then, we're leaving!"

"Where will you go?" Andrew asked, stepping out from Maia's cover. "This is the last habitable place on earth. I know that you are in shock, but please get a hold of yourself. You will waste the life that you've been given."

"What life!?" he yelled back, keeping his arms out. "I had life!"

Suddenly, Robbins coughed, and fell to one knee. A clear liquid sprayed from his mouth, and splashed against the hard floor. He looked disoriented, and he panted, and coughed again. Jaan took two steps toward him, but before he could take another Robbins had looked up, and thrust a forearm into his chestplate, sending him flying back past Andrew. Maia looked out at Robbins, into his eyes, keeping her arms spread as she guarded Andrew, trying to convey her worry, and fear, and the likelihood of death all at once.

"Please settle down, Robbins," she pleaded. "No life is worth more than a lord's."

He panted out. "And are their lives worth more than any

others?" he asked.

Maia was silent.

Robbins looked past her, to Andrew again, and stood. "Where...is my son?"

"Daughter," Andrew called. "Retrieve the boy."

Maia watched, as Gem moved cautiously, away from Robbins, and then between two neatly-made beds across from her still-unconscious sister. She reached the vented wall behind the beds, and then moved along it, to a wide door, which slid open. She entered, and after a few tense moments, emerged with Devon in her arms. The boy was not awake, and his face looked pained. Gem carried him between the beds, and past Jaan, and slowly approached Robbins.

"He is fine," Gem said, as she held the boy out. "He will awake soon."

Robbins took the boy, and looked down at him. The anger in his eyes started to fade. Gem stepped away from him, and then behind him, and moved over to Coral's bedside, and stood. Robbins looked to Andrew again.

"Let us go," he said.

Maia saw Robbins' bare feet tensing on the floor, and saw his muscular arms flex as he held the boy's weight, and saw the determination in his eyes. Behind her, Andrew took a deep breath, and then stepped further away from her outstretched arms.

"I must ask again," said Andrew. "Where will you go?"

"He can come with us," said Jaan, getting back to his feet.

"He can come back to the mainland."

"He is not ready, Commander," said Andrew. "He still behaves as if he is in the old world. And as you can see, he barely has a hold of his strength, let alone his thoughts. It will take another week."

"My Lord. It did not take me so long."

Maia looked back at her commander, and felt her eyes narrow. He only glanced at her, and then took a step toward Robbins again.

"They did this to you too?" Robbins asked.

"How do you think I look so young, and stay so strong, at my age?" Jaan replied.

There was an uneasy gaze between Andrew and Jaan, and it lasted for what felt like minutes. Maia's mind was racing. She was still focused, somehow, on protecting the Lords, but she could not shake what she was hearing, and she could not ignore the two unconscious, helpless people in the room. Jaan got closer to Robbins, and held out a hand that almost reached his right arm.

"Now you know part of the secret," said Jaan. "Why not give us an opportunity to explain?"

"Why should I?" said Robbins.

"So that you do not, as Lord Andrew has said, waste it. You could live another hundred years, maybe more, if you will listen. And you must understand why it must be kept secret."

Robbins looked down at his son, and then to Andrew. "Fine," he said. "Let's talk." He raised his chin toward the open stairwell.

"Out there."

CHAPTER 21
THE INQUIRY

Robbins watched as Andrew and the two watchers stepped aside, and walked between them, and looked to Maia, whose eyes were filled with shock, and what might have been shame. He moved up the stairs carefully, holding his son tightly in his arms. The memory of the cavern's layout rushed to the front of his mind, and as he reached the top of the stairs, and stepped into the living space, he stopped. The sets of steps he heard coming up behind him were heavy.

He walked straight out, between the kitchen and the dining area. He looked up at the ceiling, at the lines and recesses, and remembered the painful needle, and the strong light that had lifted him up from the bench. He moved to the bunker door, and walked through, and passed the control station on the right, and stepped down to the cold floor. The space was still as dry and plain as it had been. He carried Devon over to the closest bed on the right, and laid him down, and looked at him.

His anger was waning with each moment, as he slowly accepted that his son had been kept safe. The boy was breathing easy, but his face was still tense, as if he were still having nightmares.

Robbins wondered if his son's dreams were of his mother, as they had been, or of the new threat they were facing. As Robbins stood, he touched his own arms, and his face, and his chest. He was stronger. He touched the top of his head. His hair was thicker. He looked out, and around the bunker. The light in the space was the same, but he could make out more detail–on the rock walls, and in the corners, and on the beds and chairs. He wondered, finally, how exactly his life had been reinvigorated.

He looked down at his son again. It had not been long since they had left the last ship, in the dark parts of the world outside of Lwo, outside of the storm that surrounded this amazing and terrifying place. He was sure, now, that it did indeed hold the last of humanity, and the last hope of any possible future for his son. He had no choice but to listen to the lords and the watchers. As he tried to ready himself, he felt someone approach behind him, and turned and started to raise his arm.

Maia looked at him, her eyes steady. She held up one arm to defend, and with the other, held out a shirt. He relaxed, and took the shirt from her. It was the one he had last worn, when he had attempted to sleep again. It was plain, and beige colored, and soft. As he put it on, Maia slung a pair of boots off of her shoulder, and he took them, and sat next to his son. As he pulled the boots onto his feet, and over his shins, and fastened them behind his calves, he looked at the weapons on Maia's arms.

"It was only a precaution," she said. "We would not have used them unless you had attacked the Lords."

He stood, and stretched, and anxiously squeezed at his own forearms. "Sure you wouldn't have," he said, and looked back at his son again.

"I've been ordered to keep watch over Devon," she said. "Until you and Lord Andrew and the commander finish talking. Will you let me?"

Robbins looked into her eyes. They were still honest, and still kind. "They did not ask me," he said. He looked down at his legs, and his arms, and then back at her. "Did you know that? Did you know it was against my will?"

She shook her head. "I still do not know what's happened, and I gather they did not want me to know. *Extended?* I have never heard of it before, and I certainly didn't know that Jaan had undergone anything here, other than promotion and enlightenment, like any of us."

"I almost believe you," said Robbins.

"Have I lied to you, even once, since we've met?"

He shook his head, and then looked past her, through the bunker door. "But I still don't trust them." He looked up, and around. "And I don't trust this Emissary. It's followed me around this whole place since you left. It took me when I rested, for...for whatever they did to me. I'm sure it took my son, too, and kept him asleep."

Maia looked up, and around, and then back to him. "I will not let the Emissary, or anyone else, hurt Devon." She tapped one of her armored forearms. "I promise."

Robbins nodded, and took one more look at his son, and then turned and stepped past her. He walked to the wide doorway, and up the short steps, and clenched his teeth in anger, as he saw Andrew and Jaan, standing nearly eye-to-eye at the far end of the bench, bickering under their breath. He tried to soften his steps and reach them quietly, but they turned and saw him just as he reached the bench.

"Please sit, Robbins," Andrew said, motioning with his long, wooden staff.

Robbins sat at the center of the bench, and tried to push his last memory from the cushioned surface to the back of his mind. Jaan moved around the high back of the bench, and sat on the far end, nearest to the bunker door. As he did, Robbins slid toward the other end. In front of them, Andrew sat in his center chair, and set his staff down in his lap, and looked over at Robbins.

"You came from a broken place," the aged man said. "And your mind and body were broken."

"No," Robbins said, shaking his head. "They were not."

Andrew held up one hand. "Please. Let me explain. Lwo, since my own parents helped found it, has become more and more united. Each generation, through the shared effort to preserve our species, has become less and less aggressive. There has not been a single war here, not even a skirmish. Very rarely do our watchers have to restrain—or worse, hurt—a civilian. If there is one thing the great storm does for humanity, it keeps us focused on shared survival, and progress. Now, the last thing shared with us, if you will recall, was how you killed two men, out there, in the darkness. Do you remember?"

Robbins peered back at the old man. Then he turned to Jaan, who was sitting up straight and firm, showing no emotion. "I told Gem of how I defended my wife, Devon's mother," he said, turning back to Andrew. "Yes, I remember. I also remember her trying to comfort me, offering understanding, which I now know was disingenuous."

Andrew shook his head. "No, Robbins. We genuinely feel for you, feel for your suffering. But we simply could not let such a memory, such potential for violence against mankind, go unchecked."

"Unchecked?"

"I want you to *really* think about what it is you are feeling right now, Robbins. Consider your thoughts. Do you feel any fear, as you did before? Do you feel any lingering unease? Or, do you feel controlled, and strong?"

Agitated, and confused, Robbins set his hands upon his knees, and squeezed. The old man was right. His heart was beating stronger than it ever had, but it was also steadier. His mind was not racing at the thought of impending death. He felt anger, at whatever had been done, but even that felt controlled. Before, on his last ship, Andrew might have been dead already. "So you're right," he said. "So my body is better. So what? Does that justify doing...whatever it was you did to me? And without a thought for what I would want?"

"Had we asked, would you have agreed?"

Robbins hesitated. "Maybe."

"Really?"

"Had you explained it? Maybe...but probably not. I was fine as I was."

"Were you?"

Robbins stared back at him. "Why don't you tell me what it is you did to me? Tell me exactly."

Andrew shook his head. "You are not ready for that."

"For what? The truth?"

"Yes. The truth."

"Then, my Lord," Jaan interjected. "Please, tell me."

Andrew turned toward the watcher, and offered him a stern look. "In private, Commander. I will gladly tell you, but not in front of this new man."

Jaan sat up straighter. "My Lord. Years ago you told me, after I was extended, that it would only be used on watchers and lords; that it was to ensure our strength and endurance in this brutal environment, so that we could carry forth our knowledge and wisdom, for the world that is to come. But now, you have extended a..." He paused, and glanced at Robbins. "A brand new Lwoan."

Andrew leaned forward in his chair. "Are you calling me a liar, Commander?"

Jaan shook his head. "No, my Lord. Of course not. I would simply like an explanation. I am curious now, knowing that you, and

Lord Gem, changed your minds for Robbins. Whatever was done to him, it was done to me first. I never asked then, because I quickly realized the strength that you had promised. But now, my Lord, I wish to know. And I believe this man, after all that he has endured, *deserves* to know."

"I will tell you," Andrew said with a nod. "But I will not tell a man who is so new to us, and who still lacks control." He stood, and took his staff up in his right hand. "Robbins, will you leave us?"

Robbins stood, and stared back. "I will not. Not yet."

"It is a simple request. Please reconsider."

Robbins shook his head. "I'm not beholden to any of you. I come from a place just as wild as Lwo, but there was still freedom. You...You changed me without my say so. And for all I know, you may have hurt my son. I have a right to know what has happened."

Andrew's eyes were steady, but he swiftly slammed the bottom of his staff into the hard floor, and as the sound echoed, held it out at Robbins. "You still fail to understand. You need time. You need time to adapt to the procedure. And I *know* that you are not beholden to us. No one is."

"That's not what it looks like."

Andrew looked up, and called, "Emissary!"

Robbins followed the old man's eyes, and heard smooth, distant movement in the ceiling. He quickly leapt at Andrew, and as he did, dodged a blast of heat and light from the green stone in the staff. As it hit somewhere behind him, Andrew's hard palm slammed into his abdomen, sending him upward. He rolled over, and held tightly to Andrew's shoulders, keeping him from getting away. Together, they fell over the back of his toppling chair.

Robbins got to his feet quickly, and grabbed Andrew as he stood, pulling him close to his body. The old man swung the staff down at his legs, but Robbins kicked it away, and lifted his left arm up beneath Andrew's neck, and held it there. The old man felt as strong as Gem had, but Robbins could feel that his new strength, from the extension, was taking hold.

Over his head, Robbins looked up and saw that four round, glowing machines had appeared. The hovering drones were the same as the one that had taken him from the bench, however many days before. But now, he had an advantage. He had their master in his hands. Andrew squeezed at Robbins' gripping arm, and swung his staff at his head, but Robbins used his free arm to block it again, and with another swift kick, knocked the old weapon down to the floor. It shot out a wide, weak blast of energy as it landed. The wave of light hit Robbins' boots, but did not move him, and quickly faded away.

"Now..." Andrew started, struggling to speak through the choke hold. "Now you have wasted...what you have been given. You cannot...be allowed to live."

Robbins whispered into the old man's ear. "I thought you were beyond violence."

"Death...does not have to be violent. Do you...Do you want your son to live?"

Robbins squeezed the old man's neck tighter, and felt him wince. "Careful, Andrew. All I want is the truth. You try to hurt my child, there'll be more than enough death to go around. So start talking."

He loosened his hold on Andrew's neck, but kept him in place, and kept his right hand firmly on the man's right arm. When he looked out, at Jaan, he saw that the watcher had lowered his helmet, and had activated the glowing weapons on his arms. "I thought you wanted the truth too," he said out to the watcher. "How about you take a seat?"

Jaan shook his head. "I will not. As strong as you think you are, I am stronger. As fast as you think you may be, I am faster. I have a duty to the people, and to our Lords, no matter how much I may disagree with them."

Robbins backed away, slowly, pulling Andrew with him until he felt the cold wall at his back. He looked around, and from between the kitchen and dining areas, saw Gem and Coral emerge. Together, they shrieked in shock, and took quick steps toward them, but stopped as Andrew held one of his hands out. On the other side of the room, Jaan was starting to inch closer and closer. Robbins squeezed the old man's arm, and pulled him back, and held his neck tighter again. As Andrew gasped, his daughters did the same, as if mirroring him. They stepped forward again. Above them all, Robbins saw that the four drones were still hovering, and glowing, holding back punishments he could only imagine.

He whispered to Andrew again. "I've been ready to die for a long time. Are you?"

Andrew let out a short breath. "Back away," he said, his words barely audible. "Emissary. Amplify my voice." He waited, and then spoke again. "Back away." His voice spread throughout the space. "Commander, lower your defenses. Daughters, stand back."

As he saw Jaan's weapons stop glowing, and saw Gem and Coral backing away, Robbins loosened his grip. He leaned back harder into the cold wall, keeping Andrew in his grasp. "Order them not to hurt me," he said. "Or my son."

Andrew nodded, and spoke again, his voice still amplified. "Do not harm Robbins, or the boy. Do you all understand?"

"Yes, my Lord," said Jaan, setting his arms behind his back.

Gem and Coral relaxed their stances, and in unison, answered "Yes, Father."

"Good," said Andrew. "Emissary. End amplification." He turned his head slightly toward Robbins. "Now, please let me go."

"Not yet," Robbins said. "You talk first."

Andrew swallowed, and coughed. After a pause, he took a deep breath. "Very well, Robbins. Ask your questions."

"I already did. What did you do to me? What does it mean to be extended?"

"Extension is a simple process." He paused, looking at Jaan, and then took another deep breath. "After you were put under, made unconscious, your body was sterilized, and flushed of all potential

372

toxins. Then, slowly, steadily, you were inoculated with origin cells, the cells that are the foundation of life itself. After that, it was only a matter of waiting, waiting for your cells to absorb the new cells."

Robbins squinted, and stared down at the thick, white hair on the old man's head. He could smell him sweating. "Origin cells?"

"Yes," Andrew said, sounding exhausted. "We all have them, deep within, in small amounts. Once they are retrieved, they are treated with a simple chemical solution, so that they can be absorbed, by anyone, without trouble."

"So, you took my own cells, and reinserted them?"

"No. Someone else's cells."

Robbins squinted down at him. "What?"

"Every Lwoan that passes on still has origin cells, though only for a short time. Those we introduced into your body came from…"

Agitated again, Robbins squeezed the old man's neck tighter. "Came from where!? Came from who!?"

Andrew reached for his arm, and squeezed back, and managed to pull it away just enough to breathe easy again. "I do not remember. They had been stored for quite some time."

Robbins looked out at Gem and Coral, still standing there with their arms at their sides, their eyes full of worry. They turned their gaze to Jaan, whose eyes, even behind the helmet panel, were staring straight at the old man. Robbins looked down at Andrew again. "How long have you been killing your own people?" he asked.

"Not killing!" Andrew snapped back. "We never kill!"

"You three are all the way out here, on this island. And only watchers come here, right? So how do you get cells from the dead?"

Andrew sighed. "I've said too much. And you, Robbins, are reaching *too* far."

Robbins started to tighten his arm around the old man's neck again, but instead, immediately felt two hard elbows shoot into his ribs. As he hunched over, Andrew pushed off of him, and rolled forward. Robbins started to get back to his feet, and saw Gem and Coral rush to their father's side. Then he looked up, and saw the drones. They descended swiftly, and lined up, hovering in front of him. He leapt out to his right, lunging for Andrew's fallen staff. As he got hold of it, he rolled over, and got to one knee, and looked up again. The old man looked at the drones, and then looked at him.

Robbins could feel his heart pounding, and his breath getting heavier. "Gonna go back on your word?" he asked.

Andrew stood, and for a moment, let his weight rest on his daughters. Then, he smiled. "I told the humans not to hurt you," he said. "Not the Emissary."

Four bright, blue, piercing blasts of energy flew up from behind the lords, and hit each drone one after the other. Robbins knelt down, holding firmly to the staff with both hands, and watched. The machines were bounced toward the ceiling, and then stabilized, and turned their single, glowing eyes toward the point of fire, where Jaan stood, with his gauntlets encircled in brilliant energy.

The drones circled the watcher, and as they did, he tapped the

374

long edges of his forearms together, and was immediately surrounded by a translucent blue light. His boots, arms, and waist glowed brightest, and he leapt toward the wall. He used his arms to knock two of the drones down to the ground, where their frames broke into pieces before he had even landed. Another drone flew toward his head, and with one strike from his glowing, gloved fist, exploded. The last drone began flying around him, seemingly moving in a pattern, before shooting out two burning, green circles of energy. The blasts bounced off of the shield around his body, and scorched the floor and the wall. Then, with one shot of blue from his right arm, the machine was frozen, and shook in place, and shot out sparks as it fell to the cold, hard floor.

With his back to the wall, and his breathing visibly heavy, Jaan stood up straight. The energy around him retreated to unseen places. Robbins stood, and looked to Andrew, and to his daughters, who were all staring at the watcher in anger. He gripped the staff tightly, and then saw Jaan's outstretched finger pointing at him. The three lords turned their attention away from the watcher.

Robbins held the staff out at the three of them, and tilted the end forward. He felt an unusual heat arising near the stone, and an unexpected shot was released. Gem jumped forward, protecting her father and sister. In front of her, a shot of blue energy met the green blast from the staff. There was a clap, and an exploding cloud of smoky color and heat. Then, flying through the cloud, Jaan emerged.

Robbins saw the watcher contort in the air, and he tried to

react, but he was hit squarely in the chest with the soles of Jaan's boots. As he fell back, the staff flew out of his hands, and as he hit the ground, he held his arms over his face. He felt his head bounce off of the hard floor. He knew that he was dazed, but he could still see clearly. As he looked up, he saw Jaan's extended arm, and the glowing ring around his fist. Then, it filled his eyes with light. He felt the blast of heat hit his chest, and a moment later, saw only darkness.

CHAPTER 22
UNBOUND

As he stood over Robbins, keeping his right gauntlet activated, Jaan heard the Lords moving behind him. Seeing that the man was no longer conscious, he looked back, and saw Andrew set both of his arms around his daughter's shoulders, and pull them in close.

"Are you well?" he asked Coral.

She leaned back, and nodded. "Yes, I'm fine, Father. Thanks to Gem."

Gem wrapped her long arms around both of them, and then looked to Jaan. "Commander," she said. "What on earth were you thinking?"

Jaan stepped away from Robbins, sensing that he had taken little damage, if any, and walked toward the Lords. "I was thinking–as my Lords have always taught us–that whenever possible, life should be preserved."

"Really?" Gem pressed.

"Yes. And I was thinking that I would like to know where the origin cells have come from. Or, more importantly, who they have come from."

Andrew stood up straighter, and let his daughters go. "That really is not your concern, Commander. Especially after all this."

Hesitant, but no longer afraid, Jaan held up one still-glowing gauntlet at the three lords. As their condemning eyes met his he tried to ignore the sinking feeling in his heart, tried to disregard their superiority. *The truth matters more*, he thought to himself. *More than my rank, more than my life.* He felt his own strength–strength that had been renewed, extended, decades prior–and wondered, *What have they done!?*

"Very well, Commander," said Andrew.

The eldest Lord let go of his daughters, and walked toward Jaan. He stared into his eyes, and as he neared the glowing end of the gauntlet, knelt down, and retrieved his staff. He took it up in his right hand, and examined its carvings, and touched the stone near its center. Then he turned away, and walked past his daughters, to his fallen chair. He lifted it back up onto its feet, and walked around to its front, and sat.

Jaan watched Andrew carefully, and kept his readied weapon pointed out, at Gem and Coral. The two sisters moved to the backs of their own chairs, but did not sit. Instead they held out their hands, beckoning him to sit. "My Lords," he said. "Please tell the Emissary to stand down."

Andrew sighed in his chair, and looked up at the ceiling, and called. "Emissary. You heard the commander. Lower all cavern defenses."

The system sounded a heavy tone, one Jaan had not heard before, and answered. "Please provide confirmation from a second Lord."

Gem looked upward. "Confirmed."

"Acknowledged," said the system. "Cavern defenses lowered. Isle perimeter remains guarded."

"Now, Commander," Andrew said, holding his arm out, and pointing one long finger at the bench. "Let us converse."

Jaan deactivated his gauntlet, and felt it retract back against his arm, and knelt down to Robbins. The man's breathing was steady and easy. He took him up by his arms, and then lifted him onto one shoulder, and stood. He carried him, slowly, toward the long bench, and as he neared it, looked to the open bunker door, where he saw Maia. She was at the bottom of the steps, kneeling, with her helmet on and her gauntlets activated. He opened a line to her. "Lower your weapons, Lieutenant," he ordered. "And continue to watch over the boy."

She nodded, and walked out of sight. He knelt down, and laid Robbins on the bench, and seeing that he was stable, turned to face the Lords again. He remained kneeling in front of them, almost involuntarily. His mind was still on his gauntlets, and his deactivated body shield. His heart was on a possible resolution. He set his hands down on his knee, and looked into Andrew's eyes. His system identified him, and his daughters, only as human, and not in distress.

"Let us start with extension," Jaan said.

"Very well," said Andrew. "Then let us go back to our foundation. Human reproduction slowing down meant that science *could not* slow. We could not halt the progress of our most forward-thinking founders, especially not in the face of extinction. One hundred good years was not enough with just a few thousand in our populace. So, over time, the process of extension developed. A simple process. A harmless process."

"If it relies on death, my Lord, how is it harmless?"

"Death is natural, Commander. The lives that have provided the cells that have extended you, and other watchers before you, and even us, were lives that…"

Jaan peered into Andrew's tired, hesitant eyes. "Were lives that what, my Lord?"

"Lives that had been resolved, in one way or another."

Jaan felt the lingering heat of his gauntlets floating through his suit, and breathed deeply. "And how did these lives come to be resolved here, on this Isle, miles away from the rest of Lwo?"

Gem squeezed Andrew's right shoulder, and Coral leaned down between his chair and hers, and touched her father's hand. He gently guided their hands away, and looked into Jaan's eyes. "Men and women lost to the storm are not lost to us."

Jaan was shocked into silence. He tried to search for what the eldest lord could have meant, but was sure he already knew the answer. A burning anger was creeping up into his heart.

"You will not judge us, Commander," said Andrew. "I will not allow it."

Jaan could feel his chest moving in and out, but was too distraught to slow his breathing. "How could I not?" he said. "It has been so many years, many more than I could have expected." He looked around the room, and then back at them. "Do you know how many lives I have seen lost, with my own eyes?"

Andrew stared back at him.

"In all my years, from my youth to today? Lost to a storm that does not let up? Do you know, my Lord?"

Andrew continued staring, still silent.

"Dozens! I have seen men, women, even children. I have looked into their eyes in their last moments, as cold and heartless winds broke their bodies and yanked them away, from the ground, from the ones they loved. And you would tell me, now, only when threatened yourself, that you have retrieved each of those souls?"

Andrew hesitated, but finally spoke. "No, Commander. Not each of them. Only the ones that our system could retrieve."

Jaan held up his right hand, trying uselessly to stop what was happening. He looked at the cooling weapon on his forearm, and tried not to point it at them again. "What system?"

"For the commander of the sky, with all your years, it surprises me that you have not seen it. I would have expected you to know, to have deciphered the signals."

Jaan stared back. "What system, my Lord?"

Andrew set the end of his staff into the floor, and leaned out, resting upon it. He glanced briefly over his shoulders, to his daughters, and then looked back at Jaan. "We are committed to humanity, Commander. Do not forget that. It is also your commitment. Long ago, a system was placed in the sky. It is not complex, not in comparison to what we all have now, but it endures, above the storm. It tracks signs of life through the cold. If it identifies a human, then one of its unmanned craft, which are as fast as any of yours, retrieves the body that is giving off heat. Then, it brings it here, to the Isle."

Jaan could still feel his chest moving, heavily, in and out. He could feel the heat of his breath, circling in his helmet. He clenched his still-raised hand, and motioned with his center fingers, and flinched as the gauntlet twitched and hissed in activation once again. He focused on the eldest lord. "For all my time as a watcher, we have reported every loss to you. I suppose that was not necessary."

Andrew shook his head, and held his staff to his side, and leaned forward. "No, Commander. Each Lwoan lost to the storm and brought here receives a proper, honorable burial. And each casket is engraved with their names. Their bodies, their very lives, are honored more so because of watchers' reports."

"Is that *really* so, my Lord?"

"We have recorded each one–those brought here, and those lost to the sky forever. I can show you." He held his right arm out to his side, toward the chamber, toward the other end of the Isle.

Jaan turned his eyes to the open stairwell, toward the chamber, and the ceremony room, where he had been promoted, decades before. Then he looked back to Andrew. "My Lord," he said. "In this moment, I do not trust you to show me anything. I need time to think about all of this. I need to get away from this place."

"Commander, would you rather their lives had been wasted?" Andrew asked. "Would you rather they had been chilled, and fallen to pieces in the ozone, or worse yet, devoured by an unseen beast of the sea?"

"No, my Lord. But, what *say* did they have, or did their families have, in what happened to them here? Why have you kept this from us?"

Andrew looked through Jaan's helmet. "Commander, not knowing–for their families, their friends–surely served as both a mercy and a lesson. You say you have seen dozens lost? How many thousands tread more carefully, thinking that those few suffered a terrifying, painful death?"

Jaan lowered his weapon, and stood, and took a step back toward the bench. He looked down at Robbins, who was still unconscious, and opened a line to Maia once more. "Are you there, Lieutenant?"

Andrew stood, and looked at him. "Why leave now, Commander?"

Jaan looked at Andrew, and then saw Coral behind him, holding his arm, as if she wanted to pull him away. Gem was stepping away, toward the east wall. "Respond, Lieutenant," he whispered.

"Yes, Sir," Maia answered. "Go ahead."

"It is time for us to go."

"Yes, Sir."

Jaan looked down at Robbins again, and knelt, and set his left hand on his arm. He found a strong pulse, and knew that the man might awake soon, that his body was, indeed, much stronger. Most civilians would have been near-dead for a whole day from such a blast at close range. He had seen it before. He stood back up, and looked at Andrew again.

"Please wait, Commander," Andrew said. He motioned again toward the ceremony room. "Let me show you what I can, while I can. You know almost everything now. And my daughters and I, we will not live forever."

Jaan breathed deeply. "But I gather, my Lord, that you will not stop trying. How many lost Lwoans' cells run through all of your bodies?"

Andrew quieted. Behind him, his daughters' demeanors became anguished, as if their hearts had broken. "Perhaps that, Commander, was the last straw."

Seeing the eldest lord's eyes shift, Jaan aligned his gauntlets, tapped them together, and widened his stance as the energetic shield emerged from his tech. The hazy feeling passed quickly, and he looked through the blue light at the three lords in front of him. He stepped right, blocking Robbins' body, and resigned himself to an intense clash, and a likely death. *They're strong*, he thought. *At least it will be quick.*

*   *   *   *   *

"Wait!" Maia yelled, as she saw the frightening scene.

She ran up to the bunker door, and Devon's weight suddenly became heavy in her arms. She jogged up the steps, and ran up to the long bench, and knelt down and laid him there, with his head near his father's. As she stood up, she saw it again, what she had hoped was a trick of the eye, a mental manifestation of what she had feared. Jaan was facing off with the Lords. He had brought up his shield. Andrew was holding his staff as if he were a seasoned warrior of old. Behind him, Coral's stance was just as strong, as if she were the watcher that she still dressed as. Gem was near the wall, hunched over one of the downed drones.

Maia moved up behind Jaan, and held both her hands up in front of her, trying to get the Lords' attention. "Please, my Lords!" she cried out. "What's happened!?"

"Can't you see, Lieutenant?" Andrew replied. "Your commander has turned on us. We told him everything, but he cannot process the truth through his own righteousness."

"What truth, my Lord?" she asked.

Andrew shook his head. "It is too heavy for your young heart. Maybe in another decade. But if you want to live that long, and if you want to return with the new Lwoans to the mainland, you side with us,

385

and you do it now."

Maia shook her head. "Please, my Lord. Let us talk. What truth?"

"Enough!" Gem yelled from the wall, and tossed the drone up over their heads.

Maia jumped up and over the bench, landing in front of Robbins and Devon, and barely had her body shield up when a shot from the spinning, humming machine hit her in the chest. She was sent backward, into the high back of the bench, knocking it over. The boy and his father rolled to the ground, but did not awake. She got to one knee, and looked up, and found the drone in her helmet panel's bright, floating crosshairs. She got off one shot with her left gauntlet, and saw the drone pushed back.

As the machine recovered, she lifted the heavy bench back to its feet. Then another blast hit her, in the back, knocking her down. She stood quickly, and found the drone again, floating and humming near the wide open bunker door. She aimed, and hit it once more. Sparks flew as it was knocked backward. Then she stood, and breathed out, and turned to see chaos.

Gem was running, through the door beyond the kitchen, down a hall. Jaan was evading grasps by Coral, and deflecting swooping attacks from Andrew's staff. As Maia felt her heart jumping through her chest, she was hit again, and knocked far back into the hard, stone wall.

She fell, and landed on her side, and looked up to see the

drone flying at her again. She crossed her gauntlets over her face, strengthening the front of her shield as the machine dove at her. Then she swung her arms out, sending it away with a wave of energetic light, and got to her feet again. The machine retreated toward the other wall, and shot at her again, but she was ready, and the hot, green blast bounced off of her shoulder.

She jogged toward it, and ducked and dodged two blasts, but another shot somehow found a spot behind her knee. She buckled, and heard the machine buzz angrily as it dived for her again. It was near her head when she looked up and swung her left arm out, knocking it off its path, sending it toward the bunker door. It hit the stone frame harder than she expected, and as it floated down, she ran up, and fired a heavy shot from her right arm. The machine's metal body cracked, and split, and then fell to the ground. She kicked the shrapnel off of her boots, and turned around.

She saw Jaan swing the sole of his left boot up, and hit Coral square in the chest. The youngest lord yelled, and held herself as she flew back, past the kitchen, and hit the floor. Maia ran around the three tall chairs, and stood over her, and aimed her right gauntlet down. But she could not look at Coral. There was too much confusion, and shame. As she sensed Coral's arms raising in surrender, she continued to watch Jaan. He caught Andrew's whipping staff in his hand as it swung down on him from behind, but he still had to kneel from the old man's force. *All these years*, she thought. *They were always strong.*

With Andrew's staff in his grasp, Jaan stepped forward, and then lunged back with one leg out, hitting the elder in the gut. He pulled the staff away as Andrew was sent back and down to the ground. Jaan moved up quickly, holding on to the staff as he looked down at the old man. Andrew reached behind his back with his right hand. Maia saw nothing there, but Jaan aimed with his free hand, clenched his fist, and fired.

There was a bright explosion of light. Maia shielded her eyes, and Coral's scream pierced her ears. As the light quickly disappeared, she looked again, and saw that Andrew's long, gray sleeve was gone, and that his exposed arm no longer had any skin. The muscle and bone that was there was smoking, and sparking, and sitting in a pool of dark red liquid that clearly contained more than blood. Coral leapt up, pushing Maia's arm aside with her bare hands, and yelped as she ran toward her father.

"Stay back!" Andrew yelled. He looked at his arm, and laid his head back on the hard floor. He reached, with his undamaged left arm, over his chest, and grasped what was left of his right arm. He looked at his damage, and then closed his eyes, and breathed heavily.

"My Lord!" Jaan shouted. He jogged to Andrew's side, and knelt down, but would not touch him. "My Lord, it was barely a stun." He gently laid the old man's staff down, and then lowered his shield, and deactivated his gauntlets. "Please forgive me. I did not intend-"

"I know, Commander," the old man said weakly, stopping him. "After...After such a battle, that was all it took." He took a long, labored breath, and coughed. "These bodies can no longer endure such forces. They can only maintain us."

"Father, stop!" Coral yelled, kneeling behind her father's head. "Stop talking!"

Andrew shook his head. Then his whole body shook, gently, just once. "We cannot live forever, Daughter."

As he quieted, Coral yelped, and fell over him. His eyes fell shut, but Maia could still see, just barely, Andrew's chest moving up and down. Coral laid her head into his chest, and opened her eyes, listening. As tears started to roll over her cheeks, she sat up. She removed her watcher's jacket, and set it over her father's torso.

"Gem!" she yelled back, over her shoulder. "Sister!"

Maia knelt down, taking in the scene, as adrenaline continued pumping through her. Jaan retracted his helmet, and slammed his fist into his chest, and lowered his head. She could see his anger and sadness and frustration, all at once. Then, from her right, she felt a powerful force knock her over.

She hit the ground, and looked up to see Gem jumping on top of her. The tall, slender lord had donned ancient-looking, gray gauntlets, which seemed to fit her arms perfectly. They glowed with a subdued energy, and as Maia began to wrestle with her, she felt their heat, pressing through her uniform.

"Please, my Lord!" Maia pleaded. "Please!"

A moment later she was face down with her shoulders pinned, helpless.

"Sister, no!" Coral yelled toward them.

At the sound of Coral's voice, Gem seemed to relax. Maia felt her arms pulled tightly behind her back, and her wrists pressed down, one over the other. She grimaced, and grunted, but could not move. As her helmet was dislodged, and pulled back over her right shoulder, she felt the heat of one of Gem's gauntlets, inching toward her face. She closed her eyes as its warm light got closer.

"No, Sister!" Coral yelled. "Father is hurt!"

"I know," Gem answered, calmly. "I saw, and there has to be retribution. They cannot get away with this. A life for a life, and then, perhaps, the commander may leave."

"No!" Coral shouted. "There's been enough pain," she said more gently. "Father is not gone yet."

Gem pulled her gauntlet back, and leaned toward Maia's ear, and whispered "Stay."

As Gem's weight left her, Maia hesitantly rolled over, and reached back and pulled her helmet back onto her head, and looked up to see Gem walking away. She got to one knee, and watched as the middle lord approached her injured father. Gem looked at Jaan once, and then knelt down, lifted up the jacket, and shuddered. Maia had already seen the damage, but shuddered herself, at the full realization that Lord Andrew, and his daughters along with him, had pushed their bodies beyond their natural humanity. She stood slowly, and looked over to Jaan, who was now standing, and still.

Gem looked up at him, and loudly said "Take them." She

pointed toward the opposite wall, where Robbins and Devon were still laying behind the bench. "Take them, and leave us."

Maia took three long steps away, toward the bunker door, and stopped near Coral's chair, and waited.

"My Lord," Jaan said. "What shall-"

"No more words!" Gem snapped back at him. She nodded toward Coral, and together they lifted their father up by his waist, and tried to steady him as his consciousness started to return. She looked to Jaan again. "Leave us peacefully, while you still can."

"You have a land to look after," said Coral. "Were that not the case, all of you would be dead. But Lwo needs you, Commander."

Maia moved across the room, closer to the bench, and watched Jaan, still stuck in place. He started to speak again, but Coral stopped him with one look.

"For that reason, Father gave you leeway," she said. "More than he should have. And he gave you more knowledge than you need, or deserve."

Jaan swallowed, but was still not moving. "My Lords, I-"

"Leave us!" Coral yelled. She looked to Maia, and then back to Jaan. "And speak nothing of any of this." She glanced at her sister, and her father. "And neither shall we."

Maia watched, as the two sisters slowly began walking, with their father in tow. They moved to the open stairwell, and Gem turned around once more, and with a piercing look, set Jaan in motion. He finally turned away, and she did the same.

Maia took Devon up into her arms, and waited as Jaan knelt down, and took Robbins up onto one shoulder, and approached her. Their eyes met only for an instant, and they said nothing as they turned toward the bunker. The burning smell of Andrew's damaged limb lingered in Maia's nostrils as she descended the short steps from the cavern. As they walked toward the cave doors, Devon started to move in her arms.

The heavy doors parted, and opened in front of them. Maia exited first, into the cold darkness, and moved toward the hovering bird. She stopped, and waited as Jaan labored behind her. She thought she heard him cry out under his breath, but said nothing. Behind him, the doors to the bunker shut, and locked with a heavy, echoing sound.

With a whispered command the bird's ramp lowered. Maia walked up first, and laid Devon down on the port side bench, and secured him with two belts. As Jaan did the same with Robbins, she hit the button to close the ramp, and then turned, and moved toward the pilot's chair.

"Let me," Jaan said, and walked past her.

"Yes, Sir," she said with a nod.

She sat down near Devon's head, not far from the pilot's chair, and strapped in. She looked out, through the windshield, at the wild ocean. The storm was still strong, as always. As they rose from the cave floor, and flew out over the water, she looked to the sky. It was not late, not yet. Somewhere, above the unending, billowy grayness, the sun had not yet set. She grabbed the base of her helmet, and lifted, and pushed it back. Then she breathed in, and let the tears fill her eyes, and cried.

CHAPTER 23
AWAKE

Devon could not sleep. He had sat up in the bed, with the covers slunk over his fidgety legs, for hours, just thinking. Through the bedroom window, beyond the hazy shield of energy over the village, and far above the floating, blinking building in the sky, he had watched the clouds turn from gray to almost black.

Below him, out on the road in front of Maia's house, there were two airmen. The blue of their uniforms reflected in the windows across from hers. The two of them were unmoving, closely guarding her front door, as if they were under threat. But from what Devon had managed to hear through the floorboards, there was no threat.

He looked over to the bed on the other side of the room, where his father was sleeping, breathing easily under a heavy blanket. His hair looked darker now, and there was less worry in his eyes. He had not awoken since they had returned to the mainland.

Devon carefully scooted off of the soft mattress, and stepped as quietly as he could to the door. It was already cracked open. He sat down near it, and nudged it open another inch, and listened more closely for the voices of the watchers he already knew were there. He heard Shil's strong voice first, humbly imploring Jaan.

"We must make a record," said Shil. "They tried to kill you, and...your lieutenant."

"I'm not sure that's the case," said Jaan. "Lord Andrew wanted our compliance more than anything. I saw the regret in his eyes, as he was lying there, broken."

"That doesn't mean that his daughters will ultimately be forgiving. And the people need to be aware of what they've done, and what they *could* do, and what they are."

"And what are they, Commander?"

"Not like us, certainly. Not anymore."

"They are still people. The oldest, wisest people in the world."

"Maybe. But what do they think of us?"

"They let us go, Sister," Maia said kindly. "They let us come back, so that we could take care of each other, and take care of the land. They still trust us, and I trust that they know we had no other choice. We did what we are trained to do."

"Oh? Did you submit to them?" Shil pressed.

"That was not the best option," said Jaan. "We needed to know as much as they would allow."

"So you agree, then? If you needed to know, then after all that has happened, and all that may yet happen, the people also need to know."

"No, Commander. Some things are best left unsaid, and unknown."

"It seems that is how *they* think, not us."

"Perhaps. It was their last order."

After a short pause, Shil spoke again. "Is it your order, Commander, Sir?"

Jaan hesitated. "No," he said. "But I hope that you will consider it."

Shil breathed out quietly, sounding exhausted. "I will tell Doctor Taj first. He is our greatest keeper of history, besides them. If he agrees with you, then I will agree."

"If he instead agrees with you, contact me before you tell any others."

"Yes, Sir."

Confused, Devon slid away from the door, and leaned his head back against the wall. He did not remember much from their last day on the Isle. He mostly remembered being tired. And he remembered strange dreams, some with his mother singing, and she had never sung to him when she was alive. And there was another dream where he saw bright lights, and felt unable to move. By the time he had awoken on the bird, whatever had actually happened was already leaving him. But he did remember a few long days of exploring—moving around the cool, rocky space with his father by his side, as Gem watched them closely. He looked at his father on the bed again, and wondered what would happen when he awoke. He was different, somehow. And the watchers' words made him wonder if his father would let them stay on Lwo.

Out the door, and down the short hall, Devon heard the watchers' conversation end, and heard a door close, and then heard footsteps. He got up quickly, and went back to his bed, but by the time he had pulled the cover back and tried to jump underneath it, Maia had lifted him up from behind. He yelped quietly, and she lifted him higher, and the smell of whatever soap or perfume she had used wafted into his nose. She turned him around, and smiled, and set him back down on the bed. He pulled the covers up over his head, and felt her push down through them, and onto his belly, and squeeze as she held him in place.

"You're supposed to be asleep," she said quietly.

He tugged the covers back down, and looked up at her. "I can't," he said. "I feel like I slept for a whole month."

Maia hesitated, and looked at him, and touched the top of his head. "Okay. Well, what did you hear?"

"What do you mean?" he asked, hoping she believed his eyes. "Nothing."

She squeezed his leg beneath the blanket, and pinched. "Nothing, huh?"

"Ow," he grumbled, and turned to his father, who did not move. He looked back at Maia. "He looks different. I think they did something to him. But he doesn't look sick. Do you know what they did?" He paused, and thought. "Was he screaming? Did I...Did I scream?"

Maia stared back into his eyes, strangely, and shook her head.

397

"I don't think so, Devon. But whatever happened, I can promise neither of you is sick, or hurt."

"Why did we come back? Is it okay here now? Is it safe again?"

She nodded. "Almost. While you two were gone, we took care of a lot. And the Lords even said you two definitely can stay. And soon, you'll be able to find a place to live."

"Can't we just live here?"

"Here in the village?"

"Yeah. With you."

She smiled, and looked over to his father, and then back to him. "Maybe for a little while. Why don't we ask your father when he wakes up?"

Devon nodded. "Okay."

Maia pulled the covers up over him, and gently rubbed his shoulders, and ran her warm hands over the sides of his face, and then over his eyes, closing them.

By the time Devon awoke again, the sky was lighter. He sat up straight, and saw light floating through the thin curtains over the windows. When he looked to his left, he saw that his father's bed was empty, and neatly made. He threw back his blanket and sheets, and found his clothes and boots, and quickly dressed. Then he raced out into the hall.

As he reached the stairs, he slowed down. He held his arms out to balance, and moved down the winding steps one at a time, carefully setting his sturdy boot soles against each one. As he reached the last step he looked out past the galley, at the table, and saw his father. He was sitting across from Maia, with a cup of something steaming in front of him. He looked up, and smiled at him, and Devon smiled back.

"Good morning, son!" his father said.

"Hi, Dad!" Devon replied. He jogged quickly to the table, and sat between the two of them, in a chair near the window. He looked at Maia, and noticed that her braids of hair had been let down, past her shoulders. "Hi, Maia!"

"Hi, Devon," she said, smiling. She slid a plate of peeled fruit and warm bread over to him, and as he began eating, looked out over his head. Then she looked to his father. "There's my airman," she said. "Will you let him stay here, in the house? Just this once?"

His father shook his head at her, and lifted his cup to take another sip, and breathed out in satisfaction. "No. I won't leave him anywhere. Not for a long time."

"Very well," said Maia. She stood, and zipped up her jacket, and looked down at Devon. "Don't eat too quickly now, okay?"

He nodded back, keeping his full mouth closed.

She left the table, and slid the front door open, and told the airman to give them another thirty minutes before closing it again. Then she turned, and walked toward the hearth, and sat down on the nearest bench, and began checking each piece of her tech. Devon watched as she used a small tool to tighten connections on her boots, and on her gauntlets, which appeared to have dark burns streaking through their red paint. Then she began tying her long braids behind her, blindly knitting them into a near-perfect circle at the back of her head.

As Devon finished eating, and his father did the same, they stood from the table, and went back up the steps, and washed up. They put on their coats, and grabbed their helmets and gloves, and descended the stairs again. As they approached the front door, Maia, with her helmet and equipment now all in place, held it open.

They stepped out to the road, and Devon stayed close to his father as they followed Maia and the airman. They walked around corners, and passed by a dozen buildings he had not seen before. They walked down two more roads, and turned, and turned again, until they reached a tall, wide set of doors, which opened to a long walkway. The airman stopped there, and saluted Maia, and they followed her out of the village.

Devon looked up as they walked, through the clear roof over the path. The light coming down was brighter than what had come through the bedroom window, and he could hear things outside, blowing around them, and hitting and bouncing away. He felt his father grab his hand, and looked up at him, but he did not look back. His eyes were on Maia, who lowered her helmet as they approached another door. They followed her lead, and put on their gloves first, and then their helmets.

As the door opened, and Maia walked through, Devon heard

her boots clank against the metal floor. It reminded him of the last ship they had lived on, and he shook his head, trying not to remember. She sat down in a seat in the middle of the space, and strapped herself in.

"Let him sit on your lap," she said to his father.

His father nodded, and said "Come on," gently pulling his hand as they walked to the seat next to her.

His father sat down first, and then lifted him up. He leaned his head over just enough to keep their helmets from bumping each other, and his father pulled two belts down and across his chest. In front of them, the doors slid shut, and locked. They were the only ones there, and no one else had entered after them.

"The lift won't take long," Maia said loudly, pushing her voice out through her helmet. "Just hold on."

A bell chimed, and something heavy released beneath them, and they were jolted up. Devon felt pressed down into his father's lap, and felt him squeeze him tightly around the chest. Behind them, a whirring sound gave way to intermittent clanks, and he felt the lift being pushed slightly from side to side. Then, after a few moments, they slowed, and came to a stop. Something heavy sounded behind their seat, and the bell chimed again, and the doors opened.

His father unstrapped them, and they followed Maia out, and Devon looked out and saw rows of blue birds, shining, and hovering over a wide floor. In a corner he saw a single, red one, like the one Maia had carried them on before. He smiled wide beneath his helmet. His father walked in front of him, but kept hold of his hand, and as they walked, Devon felt the air rushing around his feet. He looked out, and saw an opening, to the sky. It was blank, but airy, and he could see heavy, white streams being pulled inward and below them. As they made their way to the right, three watchers in blue ran past them, back to the lift.

They turned away from the craft and the door to the sky, and continued following Maia, moving up a set of metal steps to a grated metal floor. Yards ahead, and at the center, a nearly-clear door to a much smaller lift was open. They entered, and Maia pressed a button, and the door closed, and they were pulled upward. Devon stood in front of his father, and felt him grab both of his shoulders.

The lift stopped, and the door slid back open, revealing a great, wide room. Devon stepped out, and looked left, and right, and all around. He saw workstations with large screens, and in front of them, giant windows with bright, clear views of the land. It was as if all of Lwo was visible at once, and the grass, and the pathways, and the villages were all at their fingertips. He tried to shake free of his father, but could not. His large hands felt even stronger than before.

Straight ahead, the only other person in the room was standing between two stations. It was Jaan. He turned around, and saluted, and Maia saluted back. As she approached, Devon took a step forward, and felt his father's grip loosen before he walked past him. Devon followed closely behind.

"Welcome, Robbins," said Jaan. "My lieutenant tells me that you remember everything that happened."

"Yes," his father answered. "Except for when I was unconscious, I remember."

"So then, what do you say?"

His father looked down at his arms, and legs, and then at him, and said "I feel well, better than I ever have."

"Do you care to share more?" Jaan asked.

"Like what?"

Jaan hesitated, and looked down at Devon, and then back to his father. "Perhaps you would feel more at ease if your son was not here."

"No. He's gone through nearly as much as I have."

Jaan knelt down, and set a hand on Devon's arm. "Devon?" he started. "Whatever we speak of here, you have to keep to yourself. Alright? You may meet other children soon, but none of them are strong enough to hear what you hear, or see what you have seen. Do you understand?"

Devond nodded. "Yes, Sir."

"Good." Jaan stood again, and looked back at his father. "Would you like to sit?"

"No, thank you," his father said.

"Very well." Jaan turned, and walked between the stations, and motioned out toward the landscape in the windows. "Everything you endured, all the strength you now have, Robbins, will help you as you settle here. And I am giving you the choice, to pick a region to live in, when there is room."

403

"Can I not stay here?" his father replied. "In your village?"

"Every Lwoan has to contribute to our survival. What skills could you offer us in the village?"

"I don't fear death. And I can build."

"We don't need builders here. Our structures have stood for centuries, and rarely need repair. Our wall is made of the oldest, strongest stone from the mainland. What else could you offer?"

"Knowledge."

"Knowledge of what?"

"Of what your lords really are, or perhaps *were*."

Jaan paused, and turned, and stared into his eyes. "Our people already-"

"No, they don't," his father stopped him. "They do not know the whole truth. You didn't even know yourself. Otherwise, you might not have done what you did to save me. You need me, to understand yourself, and to offer perspective to those that will come after you."

"*After* me?"

"Well, you can't get another extension, can you?"

Jaan was silent. Devon was confused again, but kept quiet.

"And neither can I," his father added. "And based on what I feel so far, with new strength every moment, making me almost dizzy by the hour, I might even outlive you. So, let me stay in your village, and I will work by your side, doing whatever best serves you and your watchers of the sky. Otherwise, the whole land may be disrupted, and sooner than you feared."

Jaan stared at him, with the wide view to the land still at his back. "You speak as if you're invulnerable, as if you are in no danger. That feeling of invigoration will not last long. I can assure you of that."

"Can you? I come from a different place, a different climate. My body endured much worse before we landed here. What if I can make better use of...of the procedure?"

"And what if you cannot? What if your son here is soon left to fend for himself?"

His father shook his head at Jaan. "I know your character, Commander. I know your lieutenant's character. The two of you fought to save me. You'll do anything and everything to look after anyone, even a boy you just met, because you know humanity depends more than ever on preserving itself. I can see it in your eyes, even now, with your agitation. I may be new, but I already know your hearts."

Jaan smirked back. "Do you? What if I were to send you away right now? What would you do then?"

"I thought I might seek out a life in the city, once it's up and running again. If I have to, I will go there, and work with Shil, and help her and her old teacher friend make a record of everything that happened on the Isle."

Devon looked up at his father, and peered at him, wondering. "I thought you were asleep," he said.

He looked back down at him. "No, son," he said. "Only my

muscles were tired. I heard everything, very clearly."

Jaan walked away from the window, and slowly approached them. "Maybe your body was, in fact, more suited to extension than any of ours," he said. "Maybe you would do well out here, with us."

"I think so," his father said, nodding. "For now."

"Then you will need to learn much more."

Jaan held out his left arm, motioning to the windows on their right, and Devon walked. He followed Maia until she sat down at a pair of screens. Then he walked past her. He felt his father close behind as he reached the high, glass wall. Suddenly, the view to the land shifted, into a closer view, and they saw an open field, and in the distance, a line of darkness. Then a village came into view. Beyond its far wall a massive, green craft hovered in place. Steam was flowing out of its roof, and being carried off with every wild gust of wind.

"What's that?" Devon asked.

"I think that is a shelter craft, son," his father answered. "The city had to be evacuated. Right, Commander?"

"Right," Jaan said.

"It's almost as big as that village!" Devon said, excited.

"It almost is a village, Devon," Jaan said. "And there are dozens spread around the land. It will take some time for us to examine the city. And while we do, I'm sure you'll be able to visit one of the nearby villages, and meet a few other children your age. That is, if your father will allow it."

"I will," his father said. "When it's safe."